ECHOES
AND
EMPIRES

ALSO BY MORGAN RHODES

ECHOES
AND
EMPIRES

MORGAN RHODES

RAZORBILL

RAZORBILL

An imprint of Penguin Random House LLC, New York

First published in the United States of America by Razorbill,
an imprint of Penguin Random House LLC, 2022

Visit us online at penguinrandomhouse.com.

LIBRARY OF CONGRESS CATALOGING-IN-PUBLICATION DATA
Names: Rhodes, Morgan, author.
Title: Echoes and empires / Morgan Rhodes.
Description: New York : Razorbill, 2022. | Series: Echoes and empires ; book 1
Audience: Ages 12 and up | Summary: Snarky seventeen-year-old Josslyn Drake
gets infected by a dangerous piece of forbidden magic and teams up with
wanted criminal Jericho Nox to remove the spell corrupting her soul.
Identifiers: LCCN 2021034710 | ISBN 9780593351659 (hardcover)
ISBN 9780593351703 (trade paperback) | ISBN 9780593351680 (ebook)
Subjects: CYAC: Fantasy. | Magic—Fiction. | LCGFT: Fantasy fiction.
Classification: LCC PZ7.R347637 Ec 2022 | DDC [Fic]—dc23
LC record available at https://lccn.loc.gov/2021034710

Book manufactured in Canada

ISBN 9780593351659 (HARDCOVER)
1 3 5 7 9 10 8 6 4 2

ISBN 9780593524138 (INTERNATIONAL EDITION)
1 3 5 7 9 10 8 6 4 2

FRI

Design by Rebecca Aidlin
Text set in Fournier MT Pro

To my friends, near and far . . .
and those I've yet to meet.

ECHOES
AND
EMPIRES

ONE

I wore red on the night I slammed headfirst into my destiny.

It was the Queen's Gala, the biggest social event of the year. Held at the Ironport Royal Gallery, it was the chance to wear the latest fashions, adorn oneself with glittering jewels, and rub elbows with the rich, the famous, and anyone else lucky enough to be personally invited by Queen Isadora herself.

You didn't say no to an invitation to the Gala. Even if you really, really wanted to.

"First lesson of the night," I said. "Pretend you're thrilled to be here."

My best friend, Celina Ambrose, had been staring fearfully out the window of our limousine for a small eternity. A succession of beautiful, immaculately dressed people were making their way up the gallery's thirty stone steps while being photographed by a gauntlet of reporters—pictures that would immediately hit the newsfeed for the millions of people who could only dream of being here in person.

"I don't know how you've done this all these years, Joss," Celina whispered, clutching her tiny beaded handbag like a life preserver. Her normally pale skin had gone nearly translucent with nerves. "All these people judging you, every moment. Every move. Every flaw."

"Judging? Or admiring?" I said with a shrug. "Here's what you do. Chin up, big smile. Pretend everybody's your best friend."

"But they're not."

"That's why you're *pretending*," I reminded her.

"You mean I should lie."

"Sure—lie, pretend, whatever. Use any word you like. The funny thing is, nobody knows the difference. If you look confident, everyone believes you *are* confident. Trust me on that."

"It's all so easy for you." Her brows drew together. "You seem so calm and at ease. Does none of this faze you? Or are you pretending, too?"

Constantly, I thought. *And especially tonight.*

Deep down, I knew I shouldn't have come, but I couldn't let Celina face this Gala without support. And here I was.

"Practice makes perfect," I said lightly, holding on to my encouraging smile. "Come on, let's go. We're already late. If we're any later, your father is seriously going to kill me. Are you ready?"

Celina nodded stiffly. "I think so."

"Excellent." I motioned to the chauffeur standing patiently outside the limo, and he opened the back door. I stepped out of the car with my best friend right behind me and hooked my arm through hers. "Let's do this."

At first sight of Celina, Prime Minister Regis Ambrose's gorgeous, redheaded eighteen-year-old daughter, and the equally stunning, blond seventeen-year-old *yours truly*—a hundred flashes went off, and we began making our way up the stairs.

A big shiny smile for the cameras came easily for me thanks to my lifetime of practice, and seven Queen's Galas behind me. For Celina, though, this was the first major event where she'd been a huge focus of attention.

"You okay?" I asked her under my breath.

"Okay enough," she replied through a pained smile. Then her gaze moved to the top of the stairs. "My father doesn't look happy."

I followed her line of sight to see the father in question, who was currently glaring down at us.

Or, rather, glaring down at *me*.

The prime minister had wanted the three of us to arrive together, but the black dress I'd already bought was just not right. The delivery of the scarlet-red satin perfection currently wrapped, zipped, and snapped snugly around my body had been unfortunately delayed, and we'd arrived late. *Fashionably* late.

Still, it wouldn't have mattered if I'd been ten minutes early. Celina's father had never been my biggest admirer. He'd always considered me a bad influence on his perfect daughter, so he would have been delighted if I'd chosen to stay home tonight. But that wasn't going to happen. Something was bothering Celina, well beyond her understandably high level of social anxiety. And I was bound and determined to get to the bottom of it so I could help her deal with whatever it was.

We didn't have secrets between us. Zero. Zilch. My whole life I'd always wanted a sibling, and Celina was the closest I'd ever had to one, so if she thought she could hide anything from me, then she'd better think again.

The prime minister beckoned to Celina with a curl of his index finger.

"Go," I told her. "I'm going to let him have you all to himself for a minute while he cools off. I'm not really in the mood to be scolded about my time-management skills."

She turned her worried gaze to me, but I held up my freshly manicured hand to stop her from saying anything.

"It's fine," I assured her. "Let your father introduce you around like he wants to. Smile and nod and look deeply interested in whatever is said to you, and you'll have them eating out of your hand. You'll get used to it."

"Do I really want to get used to it?" she asked. "Shoulder to shoulder with all of these snobs?"

"Hey, you're talking about some of my very best friends." I gave her a wicked grin. "And me, of course. I'm literally the biggest snob here. And proud of it."

I'd coaxed a weak laugh out of her, which I took as a victory.

"Go," I urged again.

Celina opened her mouth as if to say something, then bit her bottom lip, nodded, and scurried up the rest of the stairs to join the prime minister.

Yes, something was definitely bothering her. Something big. And I swore I'd figure it out by the end of the night.

I leaned into the flashing lights, hand on hip, posing for pictures and trying to look like there was nowhere else I wanted to be. The last year had been stuffed full of too much sadness and regret, and I was ready to start being the old Joss again, some-one who didn't obsess about the past. Tonight, I would focus on being present and open to the wonderful possibilities of the future. Nothing else mattered.

And, for a moment, it was the truth. After all, I loved having my picture taken, especially in this to-die-for dress that would look absolutely amazing on the newsfeed—a splash of vibrant red in a sea of beautiful but drab black and gray designer gowns. Worth every penny.

I shifted position and draped my hair over my left shoulder, which was my preferred way to pose, since my long blond waves covered the birthmark on my neck. I'd disliked the small heart-shaped mark growing up and had seriously considered having it removed, but never got around to it. Since then, I'd decided to appreciate this unique part of me.

Until I was in the spotlight, that was. Then my old habits always kicked in.

"Miss Drake! Josslyn Drake!" A reporter a few feet away from me yelled my name loud enough for me to notice him. I swiveled on my sky-high heels and gave him a dazzling smile.

"Hi there," I said.

"You look beautiful, Miss Drake."

"Thank you."

He thrust a microphone toward me. His associate pointed a camera in my direction. "Exactly one year ago tonight, your father, Prime Minister Louis Drake, was assassinated on these very steps leading into the Queen's Gala. The entire Empire of

Regara wants to know: How is Josslyn Drake, the former First Daughter of Ironport, feeling?"

My smile fell. The din of the crowd faded into background static. My heart pounded, loud and fast in my ears.

"I . . . I'm doing well, thank you." I managed to force out the words.

These steps. This night. Exactly one year ago.

My gaze fell to the white marble stairs, scrubbed clean of my father's blood immediately after the tragedy. No trace of what had happened here, but the memory remained as piercingly vivid as if it had been only moments ago.

The microphone drew closer to my face, and I fought the urge to shove it away from me. My throat tightened, making it nearly impossible to speak.

"It's incredible that you're even in attendance tonight. What gave you the strength to attend this year's Gala?" the reporter asked.

Pretend, I'd told Celina. I had to pretend—to *lie*—that this was all right, that every cell in my body wasn't screaming at me to run away and hide.

I'd expected this. Of course I had. And I could handle it. I could handle one pushy reporter with grace, even if his questions felt like arrows launched right at my heart.

"Queen Isadora's strength gives me all the strength I need," I said as smoothly as I could. "I support Her Majesty in everything she does and every decision she makes, and I greatly look forward to hearing her speech tonight."

The reporter nodded. "Her Majesty's latest decision was to

raid Lord Banyon's compound, but the legendary warlock ultimately evaded capture yet again. Do you believe the Queensguard will find him and bring him to justice for your father's death, and the deaths of thousands of Regarians in his unrelenting drive to destroy the Empire?"

No one usually dared ask questions like this on the steps of the gallery. The Gala was about lightness, about glamour and prestige. Not about warlock terrorists, death, and magic.

I couldn't even fake a smile anymore. My eyes stung with tears, but I fought not to let any fall.

The reporter's microphone didn't waver. It remained only inches from my lips, waiting for my reply. Cameras trained on my face, ready for any sign of emotion or weakness.

I'd been First Daughter my entire life, until my father's death. I'd grown up in the public eye—glowingly admired or harshly criticized, depending on the day. I'd always given reporters what they needed, never hiding from attention when someone wanted to take my picture or ask me questions.

But in the last year, I'd kept to myself, spending time mostly with Celina. I hadn't given any interviews or attended any big, flashy events. I'd shied away from publicity or media attention. I'd gone to a few private parties with a small cluster of friends, but that didn't really count.

I'd stayed away from anywhere reporters or photographers could get this close to me. I didn't want to show them that I could be weak, or that I could cry. Because I wasn't weak. And if I cried, it sure as hell wasn't going to be broadcast across the Empire for everyone to see.

So, yes, I would lie my butt off that Josslyn Drake, the former First Daughter of Ironport, was just fine and dandy, thank you very much.

And they would believe it.

"I have absolute faith in Queen Isadora and her incredibly skilled and loyal army of Queensguards to finally bring an end to the threat of Lord Banyon," I said evenly, my words clipped. "And peace will reign in the Empire once again."

I was shaking by the time I finished speaking. The reporter asked me a follow-up question, but I'd had more than enough by then.

I gave him a pinched smile. "Thank you so much," I said, and I turned away from him and navigated the rest of the steps without seeking another photo opportunity, swiping with annoyance at the one tear that managed to escape and splash down my cheek.

Hopefully no one had seen it.

Once inside the gallery's entrance, I pressed up against a stone pillar, closed my eyes, and took several deep and—hopefully—calming breaths.

"You can do this," I told myself under my breath. "You're fine. Everything is fine."

After a minute, I opened my eyes and glanced around the busy entrance. A memory immediately rose in my mind of my father next to me, my hand in his as we entered the gallery seven years ago at my first Gala. For all his years as the queen's personally chosen prime minister here in Ironport, the capital of the Regarian Empire, Louis Drake despised high-profile parties every bit as much as Celina did.

My father and I had been different in too many ways to count.

Only ten years old at the time, I had been the one to help him navigate the crowd, nudging him to make small talk and potentially important connections with other attendees, while he complained about the tightness of the bow tie that I'd fastened for him, since he'd never gotten the hang of it. It was kind of funny, how much he hated the public parts of his job. But I knew he'd been indispensable to the queen. After all, she'd chosen him for the role, and he'd spent nearly two decades as her prime minister without any suggestion of him being replaced.

Queen Isadora had adored my father. And she adored me, too, which was why, after the tragedy last year, it was her suggestion that I continue on at the prime minister's residence, the only home I'd ever known, as the ward of Regis Ambrose, my father's close friend and successor.

I'd agreed wholeheartedly, deeply thankful for the opportunity. My father had distant family living thousands of miles away, family I'd never met before, so the chance to stay in the life I knew was a true gift.

I mean, it wasn't all perfect. Despite our fathers' friendship, Celina's dad had never approved of me, believing me to be a troublemaker and a corrupting influence on his daughter. I might like to make a bit of trouble, but the only corruption I was interested in was helping Celina to gain confidence. As the new First Daughter, she was going to need a lot of it.

He wasn't the first person who didn't like me, and I knew he wouldn't be the last. It didn't bother me. Much.

I pulled myself out of the past enough to notice that someone approached me. The someone was six foot two, with lightly tanned skin, black hair, and brown eyes. He had broad shoulders, a muscled chest, and narrow hips that filled out his black-and-gold Queensguard dress uniform like he was some sort of warrior god.

And just like that, my mood had already started to improve.

"Are you all right, Miss Drake?" He held a glass of wine toward me, and I immediately accepted it. "I saw what happened with the reporter."

"I'm fine, thank you." I took a grateful sip of the wine. "Can you please do me a favor, though?"

"What's that?"

"Call me Joss."

He raised a dark brow. "That doesn't seem very proper, does it?"

"Trust me, I'm the least proper girl you're ever going to meet."

This earned a grin. "Is that so?"

"Very much so," I confirmed with a genuine smile.

His name was Viktor Raden.

Commander Viktor Raden.

At only eighteen, Viktor was the youngest person in the Regarian Empire who'd ever achieved the lofty rank.

Two years ago, he'd been named high champion of the biannual gladiatorial Queensgames, making him an instant celebrity throughout the Empire. Viktor was an orphan who had come from nothing and achieved everything by defeating every single opponent who'd faced him in battle. Only the strongest and the bravest won, and nobody had won more matches than Viktor. Seventeen in a row, to be precise, over the four-day event.

Queen Isadora herself had seen greatness in the young champion and immediately enlisted him into her royal guard. Since then, he had achieved every ounce of greatness he deserved.

I'd spoken personally with Viktor on three very memorable occasions, the last of which was at Celina's birthday party last month. I'd heard he would be here tonight, and that *might* have helped influence my decision to attend this year's Gala. A little.

More than a little.

Perhaps Viktor didn't realize it yet, but he was going to fall madly in love with me. And very soon. After all, he was gorgeous, accomplished, and absolutely perfect. And tall. Very tall. All my friends literally drooled over him, which only made him a shinier prize I badly wanted to win.

The moment he'd seen me, he'd brought me a glass of wine and asked me if I was well. That was a very encouraging start, I thought.

I took a sip of my wine, forcing it past the lump in my throat that insisted on lingering. "Is Queen Isadora here yet?" I asked.

"Not yet," he replied.

I guess I wasn't the only one who was late. "She does like to make a grand entrance, doesn't she?"

"The grandest," Viktor agreed.

As pleasantly distracting as the commander was, I now scanned the entrance hallway, searching for Celina. I finally spotted her next to her father, speaking to three men wearing stiff formal suits and stiff formal expressions. She looked deeply pained, which wasn't exactly the "smile and nod" advice I'd given her, as she studied a table featuring a forest of crystal wine bottles and an array of artistically carved, colorful fruits and vegetables that looked far too beautiful to actually eat.

Still, she didn't look like she desperately needed my help just yet. Which gave me a little time to put my Project Viktor plan into place.

"I'm so glad you're here tonight," I told Viktor, turning to face him fully.

"Are you?" he replied.

"Very much so. In fact, I'm thinking that we should make this a more regular occurrence."

"What's that?"

"You and me. Talking. And drinking wine." I sipped from my glass. "Not that you're drinking wine tonight."

"On duty."

"Yes, of course. But maybe next time you'll be off duty." I twisted a long, wavy lock of my blond hair around my finger. "The two of us, a bottle of wine. No reporters. No crowds. I'd love the chance to get to know you better."

"Would you?"

"Yes, I think I would."

Viktor studied me for a moment, his brows drawing together as his gaze moved toward the prime minister. "Unfortunately, I don't think that will be possible."

I frowned. "What do you—?"

"If you'll excuse me, Miss Drake."

And then he was gone, leaving me standing there awkwardly by myself.

I quickly shook off whatever that was. It felt almost like a rejection. I wasn't used to that. Then again, I wasn't really all that focused tonight. It was extremely rare that my social skills failed me when I was fully committed to getting what I wanted.

And I wanted Viktor.

I'd try again another time.

Viktor now stood with the prime minister and Celina, and I decided to give them a wide berth for the moment as I finished my glass of wine and went in search of another, which I quickly found and drained in record time.

I needed a distraction from my grief and my dark thoughts about Lord Banyon, but I knew I couldn't avoid them all night. Queen Isadora had requested that a selection of Banyon's treasures confiscated during the raid be displayed at the gallery tonight. Banyon was an infamous collector of art stolen from the Empire.

And now all his treasures had been stolen back from him, his compound destroyed, leaving him with nothing.

That thought alone was almost soothing.

Not nearly as soothing as Banyon's execution would be. All witches and warlocks were executed. No exceptions. The queen's goal, and the goal of her father and multiple generations before that, was to eliminate every last trace of magic from the world. Only then would the Empire be entirely free from evil.

Lord Banyon was particularly dangerous because he hated the Empire and all it stood for. His greatest desire was to destroy it, to destroy the queen, and to rebuild it all as its absolute ruler, enslaving the entire world with his magic. Thankfully, I'd never been a witness to real magic in any form, but the idea of it, and the legends I'd heard of the horrors perpetrated by those who could summon this ultimate darkness, haunted my dreams.

I hated him. I hated what the evil warlock had stolen from me. And I hated that the mention of him was more than enough to ruin my mood and my night.

But I wouldn't let him ruin my life.

No good could come of standing all by myself with a simmering stew of dark thoughts to keep me company, so I decided I needed a new distraction. Somewhere in this maze of well-dressed bodies under sparkling chandeliers, wandering violinists, and sumptuous displays of food were more of my friends, just waiting to be found.

I needed some fresh gossip to focus on.

I wove through the main hall, past a large orchestra, and made conversation with a few familiar faces on my way, who informed me that my girlfriends were outside. I exited into a beautiful garden courtyard that smelled like lavender and fresh-cut grass, surrounded by a canopy of lush century-old trees. There was another table of hors d'oeuvres and wine out here. I grabbed a fresh glass from a passing tray as I wandered around the large walled area.

"Can you believe she's here tonight? You'd think she'd have

more respect for her father's memory than to show up on the anniversary of his murder. Especially in that dress!"

I froze in place, recognizing Bella's voice immediately. After all, she was one of my very best friends.

The girls had congregated around the corner, and I pressed up against the stone wall just out of their view, clutching my drink, and listened to them talk about me.

"I just saw her throwing herself at Commander Raden. It was so obvious and desperate, it's, like, sad. Especially since he's clearly not interested in her."

That was Olivia.

Another good friend of mine.

"You know she wore red to try to outshine Celina. But Celina has class, natural class oozing from her pores. That's something Josslyn Drake will *never* have."

And then we had Helen.

I'd always hated Helen.

My stomach churned with every poisonous word they spoke.

"I don't know how Celina puts up with her," Bella said. "And defends her, even. All the time! No matter what Joss does or how loud and embarrassing she's being. Imagine having to live with her all the time. Like, she's *always* in your house and there's no escape!"

"Not like she has a choice," Olivia replied. "What was Prime Minister Ambrose supposed to say when the queen asked him to look after Joss?"

"He could have said no, because Joss is a self-obsessed narcissist who doesn't care about anyone but herself," said Helen.

I realized that I'd started to tremble. Every word was a red-hot needle piercing deeper into my soul.

"Where would she have gone?" Olivia asked. "She barely has any family other than her father."

"I say throw her in the Queen's Keep and forget she exists," Helen said.

Bella laughed. "If only it were that easy!"

The Queen's Keep was a walled prison a few hundred miles north of Ironport, where criminals were sent to live out their lives apart from regular society. Once you went in, you didn't come out. For all intents and purposes, you ceased to exist.

And my friends thought I should get a one-way ticket there. Nice.

I wanted to walk away before anyone saw me, but that would be weak. They might like to talk garbage about me behind my back, but nobody could ever call Josslyn Drake *weak*.

With straight shoulders and a lifted chin, I walked around the corner.

"Oh, there you all are," I said with a big smile on my face. "I've been looking everywhere for you!"

"Joss!" Bella exclaimed, sharing an alarmed glance with Olivia. "Wow, you look amazing tonight."

"That dress is gorgeous," Olivia gushed enthusiastically. "You're so lucky. I would seriously kill to have your body."

"You're so sweet," I said. "You all look amazing too. Even you, Helen."

Helen, who wore the same black silk dress she'd worn to Celina's birthday party, was not as effusive with her compliments. She watched me coolly. "You're too kind, Joss."

I regarded the three of them, two of whom were wearing guilty looks. "You know, nights like this make me realize how lucky I am to have real friends like you. Especially after this difficult year."

"You've been so brave," Bella said quickly.

"*So* brave," Olivia agreed.

I turned to Helen. "Do you think I've been brave this past year?"

She smiled, but it didn't come anywhere close to meeting her eyes. "The very bravest. You're an inspiration, Joss."

The murmuring from all around us grew louder, and I turned to see what the fuss was about. The queen herself had entered the courtyard. Queen Isadora Regara, flanked by her personal team of guards. She wore an ornate white-and-gold gown with a tight bodice and layered skirt. It fit her perfectly—the ultimate royal fashion choice—and made her pale skin shimmer as if dusted in precious metals.

"Ah, there she is," the queen said, smiling. She reached out a hand toward me. "Josslyn, come with me, would you?"

I met Helen's eyes again, happy to see a mountain of chagrin had risen in their weaselly depths. "If you'll excuse me, my dear friend Queen Isadora needs me. You all know she's actually more like an aunt to me. Talk to you all later. Try not to miss me too much."

They'd cut me; they'd wounded me.

But I'd never let them see me bleed.

TWO

I curtsied before the queen, sinking as low as my tight gown would allow. "Your Majesty, it's so wonderful to see you again."

She nodded. "You as well. I deeply regret that I haven't reached out in far too long, my dear. It's unforgivable, really."

The last time I'd seen the queen was at my father's funeral, a muddy, gray day I barely remembered a moment of.

I shook my head. "There's nothing to forgive. I know how busy you are."

She sighed, her brows knitting together. "I'm so proud that you found the strength within yourself to come here tonight."

"I wanted to be here," I said, my voice catching. "And I know my father would have wanted me to be here."

"I agree. Yes, your father was a great man and a magnificent prime minister. I feel Louis's loss every single day."

"So do I," I agreed, now desperate to change the subject to something that didn't threaten to make me totally lose my composure.

"You need more wine," the queen said, noting my pained

expression. She gestured toward one of her personal guards to get us two glasses. Once the fresh glass was in my grateful grasp, she took my arm in hers. "Now come with me, my dear. I want to show you something I think you'll find very interesting."

The queen led me back inside the gallery's wide and shining hallways. A few royally approved reporters were nearby taking photos. I focused on standing just a little straighter and smiling just a little wider now that everyone would see me arm in arm with the queen herself.

Choke on that, Helen, I thought.

"Are you getting along well with the Ambroses?" the queen asked as we walked.

"Very well," I said as brightly as possible. "Celina is my best friend; she's like a sister to me. And her father has been so welcoming and so kind."

Hardly. But he hadn't exactly been a monster, either. Mostly, he ignored my very existence, which was perfectly fine with me.

"I know he cared for Louis very much," the queen said.

"He did," I agreed readily.

We moved down a golden hallway that smelled like sweet wine and expensive perfume, and the queen nodded at attendees who turned their smiling faces toward her as we passed.

Then, once we reached an empty stretch of hallway, the queen's expression turned grave. "Josslyn, I'm sure you've heard of the recent raid on Lord Banyon's compound."

My steps slowed. "I know he escaped."

"Unfortunately, yes. For now. Have you seen the exhibit of his stolen art yet?"

So that was where we were headed. "Not yet."

"Me neither." Her jaw tightened. "I thought it fitting we view it together, since that evil man has stolen so much from both of us. I swear, Zarek Banyon will pay for all the pain he's unleashed in this world."

"Good," I said. It was only the tip of the iceberg of what I wanted to say: a diatribe of hatred toward the evil warlock who used his unnatural hold on magic to hurt anyone and everyone who crossed his path.

The art exhibit was in a room at the far end of the hallway, with four armed Queensguards stationed within. At first glance, it looked like any other room here at the gallery—some paintings adorned the walls in ornate golden frames, and some jewelry, statues, and other objects sat under glass.

My gaze was immediately drawn to a small golden box, which reminded me of a jewelry box my father had given me just after my mother's death when I was four years old. The lid of mine was engraved with my name and a drawing my mother had done of a butterfly. I kept my favorite ring and necklace in it to this day.

This box had other engravings on it, deep geometric shapes entwined with each other.

"Dear god," the queen whispered.

I turned to see what had prompted this reaction.

She stood in front of a painted portrait of a handsome young man with dark blond hair and blue eyes.

"Your Majesty?" I said tentatively.

Her face had paled as she studied the painting. "I never

thought I'd see this again, but I'm so grateful it was recovered."

My breath caught as I realized what I was looking at. Or rather, *who* I was looking at.

The queen's son, Prince Elian. Her only child. He'd been my age, seventeen, when Lord Banyon had killed him sixteen years ago. Banyon had summoned dark magic to set the palace on fire, a violent, unnatural blaze that had taken scores of innocent lives, including the prince's.

Queen Isadora had been widowed a decade prior to this when her husband Prince Gregor died after a tragic fall. Elian had been her only living family and the sole heir to her throne.

And that evil warlock had stolen him from her.

"I'm so sorry," I said.

She nodded but didn't take her attention away from the portrait. "You've always reminded me so much of my Elian, you know. You're both strong-willed and very clever young people."

"I would have loved to meet him," I said.

"Yes." Her gaze grew distant. "I would have done anything to save my son's life, anything at all. No matter how great the cost."

"Of course you would have," I agreed.

"Banyon will pay," she said through gritted teeth. "I will take everything he's ever cared for and claim it as my own. And then, when he stands before me once again, I will listen to him beg for my forgiveness, and then I will laugh as I watch him die."

This wasn't the poised ruler that most citizens of the Empire saw on their newsfeeds. This was both chilling and raw, a woman who still grieved for her son as deeply as she had all those years ago. As deeply as I grieved my father.

"I understand completely," I said very firmly.

There was a hardness in her gaze as she regarded me for a moment before it softened at the edges.

"Yes, of course you do." She reached down and squeezed my hand in hers. "Josslyn, I will be returning to my palace promptly following my speech tonight, but I insist that you visit me there very soon. I feel a great need to have a young person such as yourself, full of light and life, near me again. I feel it's my duty to start to keep a closer eye on you, my dear."

"It would be my honor," I said solemnly.

"Take a moment in here alone with the knowledge that even the darkest and most dangerous magic can and will be defeated by all that is good and true. And then come and listen to my speech. It's lengthy, but quite excellent, if I do say so myself."

With that, the queen kissed both my cheeks and departed the gallery showroom.

I looked at the portrait of Prince Elian for another moment. There was something about his eyes, something familiar that I couldn't put my finger on, and I found myself unnerved by how lifelike he appeared, as if he might step right out of the frame to stand next to me. All my life, I'd known Lord Banyon was evil, but this felt excessively cruel, somehow, to steal such a sentimental piece of art from a grieving mother, right after he'd stolen the prince's life.

I wandered along the other paintings, none of them as interesting as the portrait of the dead prince. Then I turned back to the small golden box I'd first noticed. It seemed, oddly, to shine just a little brighter than any other object in this exhibit.

Out of the corner of my eye, I saw another Queensguard enter the small room.

It was Viktor—tall and lean and handsome in his black-and-gold uniform.

Good, I thought. *Another chance at my prize.*

His back was to me as I moved closer to him, pushing away all my sadness and doubt and uneasiness, to appear as charming as humanly possible, determined to focus on my bright future rather than my dark past.

"I'm leaving right after the speech," I said. "Want to come with me to find some of that wine I mentioned earlier?"

His shoulders stiffened, and he turned his tanned face slightly toward me. "Bad idea."

Tall, dark hair, broad shoulders. But that was all that he had in common with Viktor. My gaze moved over him with surprise to now register a slightly crooked nose. A scar on his sharp jaw-line, white under the gallery spotlights. He had a tattoo on the left side of his neck, the outline of a dagger. And his eyes were so dark they seemed black.

A sudden surge of embarrassment made me take a step backward from his black, piercing gaze. "I thought you were someone else."

"Clearly," he muttered.

It seemed like the room had grown abruptly smaller with this Queensguard in it, which made me feel claustrophobic and weirdly exposed. So I left, without another word or a backward glance.

In the main hall, the queen had taken her place on a dais behind a podium and the crowd had formed a cluster before her. I spotted Celina, standing with her father, and made my way to her side.

"Good evening, Josslyn," Regis Ambrose said to me without an actual full glance in my direction.

"Sir," I said, nodding my head. It appeared that I'd successfully escaped his curt sermon about tardiness. Good.

"Joss!" Celina exclaimed, grabbing my hand. "Where have you been? I've been looking everywhere for you. I need to talk to you before the speech."

"About what? How nasty our friends are? Because I think I learned that myself tonight. Thank god I have you." I eyed the periphery of the room, searching for another glass of wine.

"No . . . it's something else," she said. "Something I should have told you before tonight."

This was it. Her weighty secret. I silently reprimanded myself for not staying with her earlier, instead distracted by my own problems. But I was here now.

"It's a pleasure to see you all tonight," the queen said into the microphone, the sound of her voice echoing through the high-ceilinged room.

The crowd fell silent.

"Tell me right after, okay?" I whispered to Celina.

Her gaze held deep uncertainty. "Okay."

I squeezed her hand and turned to focus on Queen Isadora.

"This is a night that marks not only the thirtieth anniversary of my yearly Gala, established during the very first year of my reign, but a much darker anniversary," she said solemnly. "A year ago, the prime minister of Ironport, Louis Drake, an admirable, warm, and intelligent man who gave half his life to serving my Empire, was taken from us in an outright act of war by Lord Zarek Banyon."

I felt Celina's arm around my back and many sets of eyeballs glance in my direction. I pressed my lips together and tried to focus on my breathing.

It's what my therapist told me to do, the one I'd seen after the funeral, before I decided his advice wasn't going to make any real difference in my life. Well, except for the breathing thing.

It really did help to clear the mind and chase any momentary anxiety away.

"I promise you," the queen continued, "the warlock will be brought to justice. Magic, what little remains of it, and those few left who can summon it from darkness itself, are a continued blight on humanity. I pledge to soon finish what my family began over three centuries ago. I will not rest until my Empire is cleansed of the plague of magic once and for all, and every last remaining witch or warlock ceases to exist, for all magic is evil and uncontrollable. And anyone in my Empire who possesses this evil, or channels it, or is infected by it in any way, will pay the ultimate price. There will be no exceptions."

Everyone knew about the dangers of magic—we'd all grown up with the same legends, studied the history in our classes. Magic was the root cause of all darkness, all illness, all cruelty and violence, and witches and warlocks were responsible for countless atrocities throughout the centuries. Queen Isadora and her army worked tirelessly to keep us safe from this darkness, to allow us to come to sparkling galas like this, and listen to inspiring speeches, look at beautiful art, drink delicious wine, and flirt with handsome Queensguards.

I had absolute faith in Her Majesty and her promises about the future.

"The warlock who has struck terror in the hearts of millions for years will soon answer for his crimes. For now, some of the art he's stolen from me, from you, from all of us, is on display here to show that he can be found, and he can be stopped. And that the only prize for evil is death. I know I can count on all of you—my most affluent and influential citizens of this great and powerful Empire, to give generously to help fund this ongoing fight—the ultimate fight of good versus evil."

She paused to let her words sink in, glancing grimly around the silent hall, directly meeting the gazes of her audience.

"Here in the Royal Gallery we stand in the presence of all this great beauty, these priceless pieces of artwork that represent generations past. They are a precious physical symbol of this Empire's rich and powerful history. Each generation since my family first took the throne has valued history, heritage, and legacy. Nothing truly good can be destroyed, and nothing truly evil can live forever. And this is why we choose to focus on the good tonight. On the future. On a brighter day when our children and our children's children will be safe from harm."

The queen spoke about what I also wanted. To focus on the

future, not the past. I was glad I came here tonight, despite any initial misgivings. Of course, it had been difficult. But this Gala marked the first day of the rest of my life.

A good life. A happy and fulfilling life, here in Ironport. I just had to believe in a brighter tomorrow, like the queen did. The pain and loss she'd endured had forged the spirit of the strongest woman I'd ever known.

I wanted to be exactly like her.

"I'm very pleased to share some wonderful news with you all," the queen said, a smile lightening her previously serious expression. "News that is all about moving toward a positive future. Tonight I'm pleased to announce the engagement of two very special young people—Celina Ambrose, the daughter of Prime Minster Regis Ambrose, and the current shining champion of the Queensgames, a young man who has quickly forged a reputation as a fierce and brave hero of my Queensguard, Commander Viktor Raden."

I blinked and looked at Celina.

"Oh my god," she whispered, just before she smiled and nodded as all attention in the room shot to her and the crowd started to applaud the amazing news. At some point, Viktor must have come up behind us, because now he was here, taking Celina's hand in his.

The crowd called out their congratulations. "You make such a stunning couple!" one woman nearby gushed.

The applause eventually died down, and the queen continued her speech, but I couldn't hear a word of it anymore. I felt like I was frozen.

I needed more wine.

"Excuse me," I muttered as I turned walked away from the audience.

Actually, forget wine—temporarily, anyway. I needed fresh air much more desperately.

I exited the gallery into the courtyard and sucked in several big gulps of oxygen.

Celina came running behind me. "Joss, I'm sorry! I thought I'd see you before the speech. I wanted the chance to tell you . . . oh, god. I wasn't totally sure it would be tonight that she'd officially announce . . . well . . . *that*."

"I basically asked him out earlier," I muttered. "And he walked away from me. I guess now I know why."

"I should have told you," Celina said, wringing her hands like she had when she was much younger and even more nervous and self-conscious than she was now.

I searched her strained expression, shaking my head. "Why didn't you? How long has this been going on?"

"A couple of months," she admitted. "This . . . it was Queen Isadora's idea. She thought we would be a perfect match."

They kind of were. The beautiful First Daughter of Ironport and the handsome high champion of the Queensgames. Still, I felt a twist of something very dark and unpleasant inside me. I think it was jealousy.

Or envy.

I'd always gotten the two confused.

Celina had been seeing Viktor Raden for a couple of months.

And now they were engaged. And I knew absolutely nothing about it.

"Why didn't you tell me?" I asked, my voice strained. "We're best friends, aren't we? We live in the same house. We tell each other everything."

"The queen wanted to announce it herself, and she wanted it to be a surprise. I . . . I knew if I told you . . ." She bit her bottom lip as she trailed off.

"If you told me, I would have told everyone," I finished for her flatly.

She didn't have to confirm it; I knew I was right.

A tear spilled down Celina's cheek, and my heart broke. It wasn't her fault I was deeply envious of how perfect and easy her life was, how much other people naturally loved her, and how effortlessly bright her future was.

I hugged her. "I understand. Really. And I'm happy for you, okay? If you're happy, I'm happy."

"I think I'm happy," she managed.

"Good, since that's the most important part. Now go back inside, do that 'smile and nod' thing I told you to do, and I promise everything is going to be just fine."

She nodded and wiped at her face. "Are you coming?"

"I'm going to take another minute. Loving this fresh air way too much to leave it just yet. Plus, I'm searching for the perfect glass of wine. Five's not too many, right?"

She laughed a little at this and finally went back to the speech, which was still in progress.

As for me, I grabbed a glass of wine and downed it as the words I'd overheard earlier echoed in my memories.

I don't know how Celina puts up with her. No matter what Joss does or how loud and embarrassing she's being. Imagine having to live with her all the time. Like, she's always in your house and there's no escape!

The truth of how other people saw me stung like a slap across the face.

Did Celina see me that way, too? A loud and embarrassing ever-present friend she couldn't completely confide in, for fear that I would tell the world her deepest, darkest secrets?

The thought bothered me more than a little, since it wasn't how I saw myself: a good friend, who only wanted Celina to be happy. But if that was my absolute truth, then I wouldn't feel so many unpleasant emotions right now—from doubt to envy, and that undeniably sharp sliver of betrayal.

She could have told me something this big and life changing, and it stung that she hadn't.

I wandered the vacant hallway as the welcome numbness from the wine spread through my mind, looking at the paintings without much interest. These were the stiffly posed men and women who'd made some sort of impact on the Empire over the last centuries.

I should know their names. This was history laid out neatly and artistically in front of me. But I didn't care who they were or what they'd done.

History was so pointless.

I needed to pull myself together. This wasn't the end of the world. Sure, my best friend had kept this massive secret from me, but Celina had always played by the rules. The rules of this particular game were: don't tell anyone, especially Joss, who has a big, yappy, gossipy mouth.

I couldn't even say she was wrong. To be honest, if I'd learned before tonight that she and Viktor were engaged, or even dating, I would have told everyone I knew, starting with Bella, Olivia, and Helen. And they, in turn, would have told everyone they knew, and by now, all of Ironport, if not the whole of the Regarian Empire, would have known before the queen had a chance to announce it officially. I adored the queen, but I knew she wouldn't have been pleased by this disappointment.

Still, just because I understood what had happened and why it had happened, didn't mean it didn't hurt like hell.

I studied a portrait of a stern-faced woman who looked fifty but was probably twenty years younger than that. She had an old-fashioned hairstyle that included a randomly placed peacock feather and a dress with a stiff white collar that went right up to her chin.

She didn't look too happy about posing for this portrait. Couldn't say I blamed her.

My father's most recent portrait was here, too, in a different hallway. I remember the unveiling, which happened at the Queen's Gala five years ago. He'd been so nervous, being someone who didn't like too much attention. He was always so self-conscious about his double chin. He said that my mother had told him every day how handsome he was, hoping that he'd come to believe it for himself.

But my father never cared about being handsome. He cared about being a good prime minister, about serving Queen Isadora, even if that meant he spent most of his waking hours in boring meetings. He didn't think meetings were boring, though. He liked the job, but he didn't like the spotlight.

I *loved* the spotlight. I loved being photographed and having all eyes on me, even if those eyes were filled more with jealousy than with fondness. As long as the people closest to me cared about me, that's all I needed to be happy.

But the more I thought about it, I realized that there weren't many people close to me anymore.

Celina, of course. And the queen.

I knew they cared about me. But everyone else? No one immediately came to mind who really liked me, really understood me, apart from my history and social status. No one, out of the millions of people who made Ironport their home, who I knew without a doubt would stand by me in good times and bad.

This was a surprisingly lonely thought.

I shouldn't have come here tonight. I shouldn't have felt the need to make an appearance, to seem like I had everything under control. Because I didn't. And maybe I never would.

The sound of a crash from around the corner drew my attention. I followed the sound, curious and wanting my increasingly inebriated mind to be taken away from my self-obsessed ruminations.

The sound had come from the Lord Banyon exhibit room, and as I entered, it took me a moment to make sense of what I saw.

Three guards lay on the ground. A fourth fell to his knees,

clutching his throat before dropping heavily to his side.

The fifth stood behind the one who'd just fallen—it was the same guard whom I'd embarrassingly mistaken for Viktor earlier.

His black-eyed gaze tracked to me, and his expression tensed. "You again," he said.

The multiple glasses of wine I'd consumed didn't make it easy to process information, to say the very least, but I quickly came to the drunken realization that this Queensguard wasn't really a Queensguard.

My gaze clumsily moved around the room, resting on each of the fallen guards. I couldn't see any blood, but I didn't see any movement or breathing or any signs of life at all.

"What are you doing?" I said, my words slow and slurred. "What is this?"

His expression darkened. "Listen to me very carefully. Make a move, make a sound, and I promise you'll regret it."

I couldn't seem to summon a suitable comeback for that, nothing to say that would make sense of this.

He turned away from me, giving me another look at the dagger tattoo on his neck.

"Don't worry," he muttered. "I'll be gone before you know it."

Crime in Ironport was nearly unheard of, so I had no idea what I was supposed to do. This sort of thing just didn't happen here.

I wanted to open my mouth and scream, to call for help, but his threat kept me locked in place.

He stood in front of the small golden box I'd admired earlier.

He pushed the glass holder back from it and grabbed the box in one smooth motion. No alarms sounded; no sudden burst of a dozen armed guards flooded the room.

The thief looked at the box for a moment, then glanced at me. "This is all I need. I'm out of here."

Box in hand, the thief strode toward the exit until a hand darted out and grabbed his ankle. It was the last guard who'd fallen—he was still conscious.

The thief tripped, falling to the ground hard, and the golden box flew out of his grip.

It landed right in front of me. Before I could summon my wits to pick it up—or run away—the lid swung wide open, and something rose from inside. It looked like golden smoke. Breath frozen in my chest, I watched as the sparkling, shimmering, swirling golden smoke rose up in a tall funnel, as tall as me. And hung there.

I heard the thief swear, a harsh and guttural sound.

Before I could move, before I could even think, the golden smoke streamed toward me, hitting me with enough force to knock me completely off my feet.

I don't remember landing.

I only remember the darkness.

THREE

*F*ire.

    Fire all around me, lighting up the moonless night.

    People were screaming—adults and children alike, trying to flee the flames.

    They were burning. They were all burning.

                  ▷◁◊▷◁

"Joss . . . Joss, wake up. Please wake up!"

I sat up with a gasp, my heart pounding as I came out of the fiery nightmare.

"Where am I?" I demanded, the words coming out croaky and barely audible.

"You're home. You're safe. I was so worried about you!"

It was Celina. The sound of her voice helped me relax just a little. I squinted to see her sitting on the edge of my bed. My head throbbed from my hangover, and I groaned with pain. "How did I get here? I don't remember coming home." I looked down to see that I was wearing my favorite turquoise nightshirt.

"Oh my god," I said. "Did someone change my clothes like I'm a baby?"

She grimaced. "You were really out of it. A nurse was here overnight to monitor you."

My eyes bugged. "How long was I asleep?"

"Nearly a whole day," she said tentatively.

I stared at her. "Seriously?"

She nodded. "But you're fine. The doctor said you're fine."

I slumped back in my soft, familiar bed. "What happened?"

"You walked in on a robbery," Celina said, her voice strained. "You're lucky you're still alive."

I gasped as jagged pieces of what had happened came back to me. The exhibit of Lord Banyon's stolen art. The fallen guards. The thief wearing the Queensguard uniform.

"Are they dead?" I asked tentatively, my stomach twisting. "The guards?"

Celina shook her head, and something inside me eased just a little.

"The thief escaped," she said. "But my father says there's security footage that might be able to identify him."

"Good," I whispered. "Because I'm not sure I'd be much help. I don't remember very much."

"The guards don't remember a lot, either. The thief had some sort of drug he used to knock everyone out with. Luckily, he was only able to steal one piece of art from the exhibit, and nobody was really hurt." She threw her arms around me. "I'm just so happy you're okay."

The thief drugged me? I did a quick mental scan of my body from head to toe, relieved that everything felt normal apart from my throbbing headache. "I am okay."

"I was so worried."

"If I'd been remotely conscious, I'm sure I'd have been worried, too. Remind me not to drink a whole bottle of wine in less than an hour, especially if some criminal is going to drug me." I tried very hard to smile and seem capable of shaking off what I'd been through. I didn't want Celina to worry about me more than she already had.

"This isn't funny, Joss." She frowned and stood up, crossing her arms over her chest. "You shouldn't drink so much."

"Great, a lecture. Thanks. Just what I need."

"Not a lecture. An observation."

"Is it my fault the queen has the most delicious and potent wine at her Gala?" I forced a grin to combat her serious expression. "Fine, you're right. No more drinking to excess. I think my brain might actually explode."

She shook her head. "You could have died, Joss. And I would have totally and completely blamed myself."

"Stop." I grabbed her hand and pulled her back down to sit next to me, trying my best to shake off my extreme uneasiness about whatever happened last night. "Like I said, I'm fine—and you're saying that the doctor agrees. So I don't want to think about last night. I've decided to officially repress any memories about it." I paused. "Well, except for the part when the queen invited me to the palace for a visit, which is very exciting. It's been years since I was there last. You're definitely coming with me. And, of course, we're going to have to start planning your wedding."

Celina bit her bottom lip. "It's all over the newsfeeds. Everyone knows my secret now."

"And everyone wishes they were you. Or . . . I guess, at least half of them probably wish they were Viktor. You, Celina Ambrose, are going to make a gorgeous bride. Way too young to get married in my opinion, of course. But gorgeous." I sat up higher in the bed against the pillows. "We should go shopping. Immediately."

I'd finally coaxed a genuine laugh from her. "Shopping? No, Joss, you need to rest after your ordeal."

I rubbed my temples. "And I will. At least until this headache fades. Then I'm going to have a really hot, really long shower and wash every remaining memory of that nasty thief out of my mind."

"Then you should eat something," she suggested.

"Good idea. So rest, headache maintenance, shower, eat . . . and then we're going out. I can't stay trapped in this room much longer. I'm already feeling claustrophobic. You don't want me to start climbing the walls, do you?"

"No, wouldn't want that." Celina stood up and wrung her hands, moving toward the windows that looked out at the residence's expansive gardens. "But I'm not ready to shop for my wedding yet. We haven't even set a date."

"That's totally up to you," I said. "I still want to go out, though. And I'd love some company, if you're willing."

I let her ponder this in silence for a full minute without inter-jecting.

"You're sure you want to go shopping?" she asked uneasily.

"Celina, when *don't* I want to go shopping? Besides, my monthly allowance just came in. And you know I can't let it sit in my account for too long before spending it."

Too much wine at parties and no respect for money. Yes, this summed up my life.

Finally, Celina nodded. "Fine, you win. While you rest up, I'll go request a driver and some bodyguards to be ready to take us downtown later for a *short* outing. Okay?"

That was part of being the daughter of the prime minister, and something I'd gotten used to a long time ago. Wherever you went, bodyguards were always a necessary but annoying presence.

"You're so organized," I told her. "It's kind of ridiculous."

She chuckled. "Love you, too."

When she left my room, I closed my heavy eyelids. A mo-ment later, an unwelcome image of the tall thief with his black eyes and dagger tattoo invaded my mind.

Immediately, my eyes snapped open and I swung out of bed. I already regretted my shopping request, since I felt like hell. But if I didn't occupy my thoughts with something, the mem-ories of last night would keep repeating in my head—from the reporter asking incredibly personal questions to overhearing my friends gossiping about me to walking in on a full-blown robbery.

I needed a major distraction, and I needed it now.

⟞◦⟨◦⟩◦⟨◦⟩◦⟞

A few hours later, Celina and I left the prime minister's residence. The sun had already set, and the shops would be open for only a little while longer, so the quicker we got there the better.

Shopping always made me feel normal. My father said my mother loved to go shopping—although her addiction was homewares more than fashion. The sprawling PM residence was still full of the evidence of Evelyne Drake in its every vase, painting, mural, sofa, and bed frame.

My mother had died when I was only four years old, and I always wished I'd had a chance to know her better. The woman clearly had impeccable taste.

My favorite shop was on Promenade Street, well known throughout the Empire for having the best designer boutiques with price tags that definitely *weren't* accessible to everyone.

They weren't all that accessible to me, either. The allowance the queen had set up for me after my father died was generous, but I wasn't dripping in jewelry and wearing head-to-toe luxury fashion every single day.

In fact, I was already about six allowances ahead of myself, now relying on store credit to sustain my little shopping habit. I knew I had to curb myself and pay what I owed soon or I would hit my limit.

Something to think about another day. But not today.

Celina didn't know I lived well beyond my means. She always

suggested that I put some of the monthly allowance away, that I should invest in the future.

Easy for her to say. The Ambroses were filthy rich to start with, so she didn't know what it was like not to be able to buy anything you wanted, whenever you wanted it. Not that she was the impulsive type. She was so sensible, sometimes it set my teeth on edge when I tried to get her to loosen up.

We arrived at the boutique only five minutes before it was set to close, with two armed bodyguards in tow to keep us nice and secure. My favorite sales associate was on the floor, and I gave him my biggest, shiniest smile as I begged him to stay open for us.

"I'm sorry, Miss Drake, but store policy states . . ." he began.

But his words cut off at the sight of Celina, who'd been featured at the very top of today's royal newsfeed with the engagement announcement and a swath of pictures of her and Viktor at the Gala last night.

"Of course, it would be our honor to remain open," he said.

I fought to hold on to my smile, knowing full well that he might not have stayed open just for little old me, the girl who *used* to be featured at the top of the newsfeeds. A single picture of me and my short interview with the rude and pushy reporter would have been barely noticeable if I hadn't been looking for them.

There hadn't been a single mention of the robbery in the news, either, but this wasn't a surprise. Queen Isadora preferred to keep certain unsavory matters away from the public eye until they were resolved to her satisfaction.

The remaining customers left the shop and the lock was turned, the CLOSED sign flipped. The sales associate remained behind and fetched all my selections and put them in the changing room.

"See anything you like?" I asked Celina, gesturing toward a piece displayed on a tall, faceless mannequin. I continued to ignore the presence of my lingering headache. "That shirt would look amazing on you."

She glanced at it without interest. "I'm not really in the mood to shop tonight. But you have fun. And let me know when you want my opinion."

That was fine. I was happy to have all the fun tonight, as I leisurely picked out the equivalent of a whole new wardrobe.

I entered the spacious changing room and surveyed the pieces I'd selected, running my fingers over the silky texture of a purple skirt, the soft cashmere of a teal sweater.

Shimmying out of the casual clothes I'd worn there, I slid on a pair of black velvet skinny-leg pants that hit at midcalf and fit my petite frame perfectly and a silk shirt in an exquisite shade of indigo. A long, gauzy turquoise scarf tied loosely around my neck was the perfect finishing touch.

It felt so good, like it had been made especially for me by the designer. And it brought out the blue of my eyes, like—*pop*.

It was perfect. The shirt, the pants, the scarf, perfect. I grabbed the tag hanging from the sleeve and glanced at the price. My stomach dropped.

So not perfect.

The designer shirt alone was a third of my monthly allowance, and my credit was already close to the max at this store. I knew I should take off the clothes and forget about them. Start saving my money, like Celina suggested.

But that didn't sound like much fun.

And this shirt *was* absolutely gorgeous.

Leaving the rest of the clothes and my purse in the changing room, I went looking for Celina to get a second opinion on the outfit. She wasn't waiting nearby, so I moved along the hallway leading to the main store. Even the sales associate hadn't stayed around to see if I needed anything. Rude.

"Celina?" I called as I walked across the boutique. "Where did you—?"

My foot hit something.

I looked down to see my best friend lying on the ground, her eyes shut.

It took me a moment to fully register this.

"Celina!" I gasped, as I crouched next to her and grabbed her hand. "What happened? Wake up!"

When she didn't move, I stood up in a flash. "Somebody! Help me! My friend is—"

That was when I saw the sales associate and the two bodyguards who'd accompanied us here. Also on the ground.

The thief from last night stood next their bodies, his arms crossed over his chest. He wasn't wearing a Queensguard uniform tonight. He wore a knee-length black leather coat, black jeans, and a black T-shirt.

Fear crashed over me.

"They're not dead," the thief said evenly. He fished into the inner pocket of his leather coat and pulled out a glass vial that was filled with what looked like a sparkling pink powder. "This is called Dust," he said, shaking the vial. "Its magic works really well in getting people out of my way without unnecessary violence. They'll all be asleep for a while, but no harm done."

My entire body hummed with panic, with the urge to choose between fight or flight.

Magic.

He'd just admitted to willfully using magic on four people, including the daughter of the prime minister of Ironport. He'd just signed his own death warrant.

He looked so calm, as if this was something he did all the time. No problem at all. Walk into a space filled with innocent people and use magic on them, as if this were perfectly normal behavior.

It was so utterly surreal that, for a moment, I wondered if I was still asleep and this was only a nightmare—if the thief's face had lodged into my unconscious mind so deeply that it had fooled me into thinking I was awake.

But no. My dreams were never this vivid. I could feel my heart pounding, the cold streak of sweat running down my spine, the lock of long blond hair, still a tiny bit damp from my shower, hanging over my left eye as I stood there.

"What the hell do you want?" I bit out. I was impressed by how irritated I sounded—instead of sounding like the shaky, terrified mess I was inside.

His expression darkened as he swept his gaze over me from head to foot. "Don't you already know?"

"Clearly not, if I'm asking you."

"I need the magic you took from me."

I gaped at him. "What are you talking about? I didn't take anything from you, especially not magic."

I hated even saying the word out loud. It felt so wrong, like something that had no place in my life or my vocabulary.

"Maybe not on purpose, I'll give you that. But you were definitely there when the memory box I was sent to steal opened up. And I watched the magic inside of it flow straight into you."

His words sent blurry images speeding through my head. The unconscious guards. The thief reaching for the small golden box. Then it falling as he tripped, hitting the floor in front of me . . . and opening up.

The golden smoke.

Yes, now I remembered seeing that, even though I desperately wanted to blame my imagination for what I'd seen. I'd thought that was part of my dream, because there was no way that could be real.

"There's no magic inside of me," I managed. "If there was, I would feel it."

"Right," he replied. "Sure you would. I would really love to debate all of this with you, but I'm on a bit of a deadline, Drake."

My gaze snapped to his. "What did you call me?"

He sighed. "Your name. Josslyn Drake, daughter of the former prime minister. Personal friend to the queen. Concerned friend of unconscious girls. I prefer to call people by their last names in my line of work. It makes it easier. Less personal." He hissed out a breath. "Now back to the problem at hand."

"The magic you think is inside of me," I said, shuddering at the words. "From this . . . this *memory box*."

"Yes, so glad you can keep up. I've had a whole day to try to figure this mess out the best I can. It's not remotely ideal, but I know someone here in Ironport who might be able to help."

I lifted my chin and gave the delusional thief the fiercest look I could summon. "So do I. The same people who will arrest you for robbery, assault, and magic possession, if you don't get out of my face immediately."

He blinked. "Get out of your face?"

"You haven't killed anyone," I reasoned. "The guards from last night are still alive. And you said my friend and the other people here are going to wake up soon."

"Well, maybe not *soon*," he said. "But they will wake up."

"Now you need to walk away." I forced a smile to my lips. "And we can go ahead and forget this ever happened."

His expression tightened, his black eyes steely. "Yeah, unfortunately, that's not going to work for me. I understand that you're probably in a bit of shock. But I have a finite amount of time to handle this little problem, and nothing's going to get in my way of fixing it as quickly and easily as possible."

With that, he came toward me, closing the space in three strides. He clamped his hand down on my wrist. "You're coming with me."

Panic surging, I tried to pull away, but he was too strong. "I'm not going anywhere with you!"

The steely look had begun to dissipate, replaced with a flash of impatience. "You're going to—"

That was when I kneed him.

Between the legs.

Really, really hard.

He grunted, let go of me, and doubled over.

I raced for the exit, feeling for my phone and realizing with horror that it was still in my purse in the changing room.

I shoved on the door, but it didn't budge. Right—the sales associate had locked it to give me and Celina an after-hours, private shopping experience.

"Damn it," I cried as I pushed at the lock. And I'd almost got it, when I felt a hand clamp down on my shoulder and turn me around.

The thief glared at me, his gaze pained. "You're seriously trying my patience."

My knee rose again, but he saw it coming this time. He spun me around so I was pressed against the glass door, his arm like an iron bar against my back.

"Don't," he growled into my ear.

"Disgusting lowlife," I growled back, my fear turning to outrage. Nobody pushed me around like this. Nobody. "Who are you working for? Who'd want you to steal from that exhibit? Was it Lord Banyon?"

The very thought made me sick.

"Lord Banyon?" he repeated gruffly. "You think that's who I work for?"

"Who else?" I spat. "It was his stolen art in that gallery. Is he that greedy, that he'd try to steal it back? Why am I not surprised?"

"Listen to me very carefully, if that's even possible for you. I hate Banyon. I want to see him dead. Everything I do, everything I am, is to get closer to that goal. Got it?"

"I don't believe you."

"You don't have to. You don't have to believe anything except the fact that I'm here to get the magic currently swirling around inside of you back into the box. And take that box to my boss, who is definitely *not* Lord Banyon. And then I never have to come back to Ironport again in my entire life, and trust me, that will be far too soon."

While he spoke, I was busy plotting my way out of this. Celina had a phone. All I had to do was get my hands on it and hit the button to connect to the emergency Queensguard line, the button all members of Parliament, royalty, and high-end political dignitaries had. Armed help would arrive here in an instant.

"Fine," I gritted out. "You win. I'd be happy to help you."

He turned me around so I could see he was frowning. "That was a sudden change of heart."

"Anything I have to do to get you out of my face will be a wonderful thing."

I punctuated this with a tight, insincere smile. I'd try flirting, which usually worked to get me what I wanted, but I thought we were well beyond that being a possibility by now.

The thief studied me. I studied him.

My first impression of him last night was that he was attractive. I mean, he'd reminded me of Viktor enough that I thought he was actually him. They shared very similar dark good looks, the same height and presence and ease. The thief brushed his dark hair behind his left ear, letting me get a glimpse of that dagger tattoo I'd noticed at the Gala, which Viktor definitely didn't share.

Wow. Talk about cliché. Like a flashing sign that said: WATCH OUT, I'M THE BAD GUY.

And the black leather coat to finish off the look was so predictable.

Well, actually it was really nice and looked super expensive. He'd probably stolen it.

The shine of a car's headlights drew his attention away from me to the street outside. I took the only opportunity I might get and spun on my heel, ran toward Celina, and dropped to my knees beside her, fishing into her handbag for her phone. The screen lit up immediately, and right there, on the home screen, was the button.

Red. Round. EMERG.

I'd almost jabbed it when the phone flew out of my hand.

The thief had kicked it right out of my grip. I let out a scream of frustration and scrambled to grab it. He got there first, the phone now clutched in his hand.

"Nice try," he said.

Then he tossed it on the floor and, without a moment of

hesitation, smashed it with the heel of his steel-tipped boot. I watched with dismay as the remnants scattered in all directions.

"Are we done with the antics?" he asked. When my only reply was a hateful glare, he continued, "Now, here's the plan. I have an old acquaintance in the city who has a long and deeply sordid history when it comes to magic. I believe he can help us with our mutual problem here. So what I propose is this: We go see him. He helps us. I make my boss happy by delivering what she sent me here to get. And you go back to your happy little magic-free life. Thoughts?"

"You need to get it through your head," I snarled. "There's no magic inside of me. If there was, I'd feel it. So you need to leave me the hell alone. Got it?"

"Why is nothing ever easy?" he muttered. Then he fished into his jacket and pulled out the vial. "Fine. Here's my alternate plan: I knock you out with some Dust, haul you to my acquaintance's establishment, and we deal with this problem while you're totally unconscious. Makes the trip there a bit trickier, but I've dealt with worse."

My gaze fixed on the vial of pink Dust, and a fresh burst of panic shot through me.

Part of the queen's speech echoed in my mind, chilling me right down to my bones.

All magic is evil and uncontrollable. And anyone in my Empire who possesses this evil, or channels it, or is infected by it in any way, will pay the ultimate price. There will be no exceptions.

The thief took a step toward me.

"Touch me and you're dead," I growled.

He cocked his head. "You're gutsy. Delusional, yes. But definitely gutsy. Now let's get this over with."

Perhaps he thought I'd try to run again, but I didn't. When he got within arm's reach, I fought. I lashed out with my fists, with my legs and feet. My fingernails managed to draw blood on his cheek.

The vial fell and smashed the ground, the pink powder spilling out, and the thief swore.

I'd fight until Celina woke up. Until someone walked by the store and saw the commotion through the windows and called for help.

I went at him again. He didn't fight back, didn't try to punch or hit me. He did manage to dodge one of my punches, and I lost my balance. I staggered, tripping over my own feet. I hit the ground hard enough to rattle my teeth.

And suddenly, everything vanished before my eyes.

The store was gone, swept away by a curtain of golden smoke. And then there were flames all around me. Flames as high as the ceiling. A cacophony of screams and wails pieced my ears.

It was just like my nightmare, just before I woke up today.

"Help us! Help, please—somebody help!"

I sprung to my feet and turned in the direction of the voice. It was a woman with two small boys clutching her skirt. Her face was dirty with soot, and she looked at someone standing next to me with panicked desperation.

But then her expression shifted into something harder and filled with hate.

"You," she gasped. "This is your fault. You brought this horror upon us all!"

"No, this is her fault, not mine. Never forget that. She brought this on herself." The man's voice was deep and pained, and I turned to see him, see his face.

I couldn't believe my eyes.

It was Lord Banyon.

The warlock stood not more than an arm's length away from me. His face seemed younger than the last time I'd seen his picture on the royal newsfeed, less lined, but it was pale and gaunt, with dark circles beneath his eyes as if he hadn't slept or eaten in days.

"The queen would never want to hurt her people like this," the woman snarled. "She would never try to kill us."

"You're right," Banyon said, his eyes dark coals in the center of his face. "She was trying to kill me, and she failed. Now run far from here, if you can. For I am about to destroy anything that stands in my way."

The crashing sound of a building collapsing made me stagger backward, and the flames rose higher, blocking my view of Banyon and the woman in a fiery blaze.

And then the fire turned to golden smoke, and then to nothingness. And a moment later, I was back in the boutique.

The thief had me by my shoulders, staring into my face, his brows drawn together over black eyes.

"Your nose is bleeding. Take this." He thrust a white handkerchief at me, and I dabbed at my nose, shocked to see it come away red with blood. A moment later, I realized that it wasn't a handkerchief; it was a lacy camisole he'd snatched off a nearby display table.

"Do you know how expensive this is?" I demanded, my words coming out more like sobs.

"Like I care." He frowned deeply at me. "What just happened?" When I didn't reply, he said, "The magic is in you, Drake. You can't keep denying it anymore, can you?"

I shook my head. It couldn't be true, because if it was, my life was over. "I—I'm just seeing things that aren't really there. The stress is getting to me, messing with my mind."

"Seeing things? What did you see?"

"Lord Banyon," I managed to say.

His expression darkened. "Damn it all."

I drew in a ragged breath. "I need to go home. I need a doctor, or something. I . . . I'm starting to hallucinate."

"No, what you're doing is channeling the memory magic that was in that box. The same memory magic I need back in its holder so I can get the hell out of this city. And full circle back to my plan."

He kept insisting the magic was in me, but that couldn't be true. I fought to steady myself, to find the calm in the middle of this storm, so I could try to understand any of this.

Clearly, he was delusional and desperate. And obviously dangerous. I needed to try to talk some sense into him before this got any worse than it already was.

Perhaps it would be best if we started at the beginning. With the simplest concepts that everyone knew and believed. "Magic is evil," I said almost gently, as if he were a child. "And uncontrollable. And it isn't something that's contained in a little golden box. Magic is used by witches and warlocks who want to hurt people."

"This is seriously painful," he muttered as he regarded me grimly. "In far too many ways to count."

I ignored his unhelpful commentary but knew I had to make him hear me. "There's no way that what you're saying is true. If there was, my life would be over. Do you understand that?"

"Oh, I understand that better than you know. Seems like you need some more proof." He grabbed a mirror from a nearby shelf and held it in front of my face. "You usually have blue eyes, right?"

I frowned as I looked at my reflection. Then I gasped.

My eyes were no longer blue. They were gold. Molten gold.

They were the same color as the golden smoke that I'd just seen appear from nowhere. The same golden smoke that exited the box last night.

"Oh my god," I whispered, my eyes wide.

"You *do* have magic inside of you," he said. "And, surprise, your life didn't suddenly come to a screeching stop. Can we move on now?"

He was right. There was no other explanation. Somehow, the magic from inside that box was inside *me* now. And it was the reason I'd seen that fiery scene starring Lord Zarek Banyon himself, the one torn right out of my nightmare earlier.

Magic—dark, evil magic—had burrowed inside me like some sort of invisible disease, and I hadn't even realized it until now. It was already changing me—changing my eyes. It was in my head, controlling what I saw.

"Get it out of me," I gasped, clawing at my face. "Please."

He grasped my wrists before I could do any damage. "Calm down."

But I couldn't calm down. The horrible truth had hit me like a punch to my gut, and I felt sick—like I was going to throw up. I doubled over, trembling and shaking my head.

"Breathe, would you?" he said. "I think I liked it better when you were trying to kill me."

"I need to go home. I need help." I could barely form coherent words. Tears streamed down my cheeks, and my chest felt impossibly tight. "This magic—it's killing me!"

It was hard to focus on making a plan right now, even harder to contemplate the plan I was formulating, but my life was at stake. I had no choice.

"You're not dying. You're having a panic attack. Breathe, Drake. Or you're going to pass out."

I sucked in a deep breath and wiped at my damp face. "Queen Isadora needs to know what happened. She'll help me."

The thief stared at me as if I'd just grown another head. "You think she'll help you?"

"Of course she will."

"You mean the woman who personally orders the death of anyone remotely touched by magic—both the users and the receivers. The supreme ruler of the Regarian Empire, whose family has spent centuries conquering and enslaving more than a third of the entire world. The one who has an entire regiment of her army dedicated to hunting down witches and warlocks and executing them without the courtesy of a trial. That Queen Isadora?"

I gaped at him. "The queen protects us from evil."

He hissed out a sigh of frustration. "Sure. And right now, at this very minute, according to every strictly worded law there is, you're part of that evil. So take a deep breath, Drake, and think about it. Think about what will happen if the queen—or anyone else in a thousand-mile radius—sees your golden eyes and hears that you've got a box full of dark and evil stolen magic swirling around inside of you. And ask yourself this: Would you give someone like that the benefit of the doubt? Would you help them, knowing what you think you know about magic?"

I wanted to throw his words back at him, to insist that he was wrong.

But he wasn't wrong.

The royal newsfeed often spoke of magic-related arrests throughout the Empire, witches and warlocks who were swiftly executed after intense questioning.

The queen had reiterated this in her speech only last night. All magic was evil. And anyone infected by magic would be seen as a threat to the Empire.

No exceptions.

"I get that this is difficult for you," the thief said. "That you're still fighting this, thinking you might be the exception to the rule because of who you are. But I've known a lot of people who've been executed for magic possession. And not all of them were witches or warlocks."

"Evil people," I muttered.

"Some of them, sure. But not all. And none of them were given a chance to explain or to ask for help. They were seen as enemies to the Empire, a direct threat to the queen, and those threats were erased."

I watched him, searching for some sign of deception, despite his deep voice sounding surprisingly earnest. Then my gaze shot to Celina, lying twenty feet away, her face peaceful in her magical slumber.

If she saw my eyes, if she learned what had happened to me, I wondered if she would help me or run away.

If it had happened to her, what would I do? Would I ever be able to look at her the same way again, knowing what I knew?

"Two hours is all it'll take to find the answers we need to fix this," the thief said. "Then you can resume your normal life, and I get the hell out of Ironport. But you need to cooperate with me and stop fighting this."

Who was this thief? He wasn't old—maybe only a couple of years older than me. But there was a hardness to him that went well beyond his age. He was a criminal. He knew evil people who'd been executed. He talked about magic like it was no big deal and spoke of the queen with utter and complete disrespect.

I hated him. And I feared him.

But his words had wedged their way under my skin like splinters—sharp, painful, and impossible to ignore.

"You said you know someone who can help," I said, fighting to get the words out since they were the last thing I wanted to say to this criminal.

He nodded. "I do."

"Here in Ironport."

"Yes."

I looked directly at him. His cheek was bleeding from where I'd scratched him. His arms were crossed over his chest.

He looked relaxed at first glance, but it was only an act. I could see the tension everywhere—from his tight jawline to his stiff shoulders. And his dark gaze held doubt as he regarded me. And, oddly, what looked like pain. But it was only for a moment before his expression shifted to neutral and unreadable.

The thief towered over me. He could easily overpower me, knock me out, and drag me anywhere, as he'd threatened. But he hadn't. Yet.

From a nearby rack, I grabbed a pair of sunglasses to help shield the ugly truth I couldn't deny any longer.

"I don't want anyone to ever know what happened to me," I said through clenched teeth. "So, fine. You have two hours."

He nodded. "Then let's get going."

FOUR

I reluctantly left the boutique with the thief, my thoughts spinning out of control. I'd love to believe I was simply having a nightmare, that I'd wake up soon and everything would be back to normal. But I wasn't that naive. This was really happening. Doubt slammed through me with every step I took. Maybe I'd agreed too quickly to the thief's plan and been too fast to believe his dire warnings.

But I'd seen my golden eyes. I'd felt how real that fiery vision—or whatever it was—had been.

It had felt like I was really there, in the middle of the chaos.

Had the queen known that there was magic among the stolen art displayed at the Gala last night? She couldn't have. She wouldn't have let anyone that close to such evil, for fear of them being infected by it, like a horrible, unnatural disease.

I'm infected by magic.

And I needed it out of me if I had any chance of surviving this. Before anyone else learned the truth of what had happened to me.

And for that reason, and that reason alone, I was willing to spend a couple of hours meeting the thief's contact and putting this nightmare behind me.

"Keep walking straight," he said. "At the next intersection, turn left."

He sounded as thrilled by this situation as I felt about it.

My hands were cold. My heart thudded. I felt like I was sleepwalking, my body automatically going through the motions without any input from my brain—one step after another. Numb, from head to foot.

The magic was eating into me, turning my insides dark and cold. I couldn't believe I hadn't felt it before now. I thought I'd been perfectly normal, only dealing with a hangover, but I'd been so very wrong.

If this worked—and it *had* to work—I wondered if I'd be permanently damaged from this experience. Would this magic do any lasting harm to me, or could I pretend this never happened?

But it had happened. And my desperation forced me to leave Celina behind, unconscious on the floor of a clothing boutique, while I followed a hardened criminal into dark and unknown parts of the city.

The thought coaxed forth a fresh wave of panic.

"What's your name, anyway?" I asked without looking at him, but needing to say something to help me escape from my inner storm. "You know mine, but I don't know yours."

He didn't answer me.

"Fine, I'll call you Bob," I said, my throat tight. "Does that work for you? Hey, Bob, how much farther is this contact of yours?"

"It's Jericho," he finally gritted out.

"*Jericho*," I repeated. I crossed my arms over the expensive shirt and scarf I hadn't paid for. I still felt the scratch of the shirt's tag at my neck, so I reached back and yanked it off. "I think I like Bob better."

"We still have a few miles to go."

"A car would have helped," I muttered.

"Next time my plans go up in a big puff of golden smoke, I'll make sure I have wheels."

We walked for a whole hour, and Jericho led me to a part of Ironport I'd never been to before. Despite low reports of crime, the city still had its good parts and its bad parts.

"Low" didn't mean *zero*.

Here at the south end of the city, close to the Diamond River—which didn't exactly live up to its name in shining, priceless beauty—there were no trees, no vegetation meticulously maintained by provincial taxes as it was in the affluent midtown core.

This neighborhood was hard and dry and unwelcoming. A skinny black cat scurried down the sidewalk, hissing in our general direction. The few people we passed, sitting on curbs or leaning against walls, watched us silently with glittering, suspicious eyes.

If I screamed for help right now, I doubted that anyone would come to my assistance.

"This brings back memories," Jericho said.

"Don't you mean nightmares?"

He snorted. "Both."

I stumbled over an uneven crack in the pavement. "You lived here?"

He nodded. "For longer than I care to admit."

"Fascinating," I said dryly.

"Thought you'd think so. I'm assuming someone like you has never been this far south before."

"You assume correctly."

Pieces of trash blew along the silent one-way street from a gust of cool wind. There were exactly three streetlamps on this block, and one of them was broken.

A few minutes later, Jericho stopped walking and looked up at a metal door with a symbol sprayed on it in neon green paint—a circle with a line through it.

"We're here," he said.

I knew what that symbol meant; I'd seen a similar one on the royal newsfeed last month. It didn't fill me with confidence.

"This building is condemned," I said. "It's not safe to enter."

"You're absolutely right about that," he agreed. "It's definitely not safe."

He grabbed the handle and twisted. The door opened with a loud creak. No one was on the other side of the door, only a long hallway that seemingly led into nothing but darkness.

Jericho made a sweeping motion. "After you."

I knew I needed to be tough, but all I felt was weak. All I wanted to do was go somewhere and hide, fall into a deep, dreamless sleep, and wait for this to all blow away. Most problems had a tendency to disappear, if you waited long enough.

Most, but definitely not all.

"I don't like this," I said.

"I'm sure you don't."

I shook my head, clasping my hands together to stop them from trembling. "I hate this. And I hate you."

"I'm fine with that. Bottom line, Drake, our answer's waiting at the end of this hallway. And the clock's ticking."

I searched my mind for another option but came up blank.

Jericho sighed. "You agreed to this."

"Under duress."

"I could have Dusted you, thrown you over my shoulder, and carried you here. But I didn't."

I gaped at him. "Gee, thanks so much for not violently assaulting and kidnapping me. Gold star, really. This still isn't okay. None of it."

"I seriously don't have time for this." Without another word, Jericho walked straight into the darkness.

I waited a whole minute, but he didn't reappear.

Damn it.

With gritted teeth, I made my way down the narrow hallway, wincing as I heard the metal door click shut behind me. There were dim lights set into the wall, lighting the way just enough to see another door thirty feet ahead, which was black with no handle.

Jericho waited for me there, and he hesitated for only a moment before he raised his fist. Three knocks, then two, then four.

He smirked at my bemused expression. "Hopefully the secret knock hasn't changed in the last two years."

"What happens if it has?" I had to ask.

"Nothing good. Now keep your mouth shut and let me do the talking. This isn't your kind of place."

Before I could come up with a quality comeback for that, the door creaked open, and we were suddenly engulfed in a sea of noise.

Jericho hadn't told me anything about our destination other than that his contact would be here, so I wasn't sure what to expect. But in this mostly deserted, dangerous neighborhood, I was surprised to see that the room behind the door was packed wall-to-wall with at least two hundred people of all shapes, sizes, and skin tones.

They were all talking, or yelling, and all focused on something in the middle of the large room with a high ceiling. Lights were set into the ceiling, highlighting the wafting, swirling smoke from cigars and cigarettes—outlawed in downtown Ironport a decade ago because of health concerns.

Each hand seemed to hold a drink. The sharp scents of unwashed bodies, cigarette smoke, and alcohol attacked my nose all at once.

The crowd collectively cheered, and I craned my neck to see what the spectacle was, peering at the smoky space through the dark lenses of my sunglasses.

Two men were fighting in a roped-off circle. Bare-fisted, bare-chested. Blood and bruises marred their swollen faces. One took a hit to his jaw, and a line of blood shot out of his mouth and splashed onto a bystander, prompting another cheer of appreciation.

"This is a fight club," I said, my throat tight.

"It sure is," Jericho confirmed.

I'd heard rumors of illegal fight clubs in the city. Someone had mentioned it at a party a few months ago, and the subject had caught my attention. They were like small, dirty versions of Queensgames matches where people could go and drink, smoke, and gamble. And here we were, live and in person.

It smelled far worse than I ever could have imagined.

"My money would be on the skinny one if I was betting tonight," Jericho said, noting my look of disgust with amusement. "The big guy doesn't have the moves."

"Fun," I said without any enthusiasm. "So where's your friend so we can get this over with?"

"I wouldn't really call him a friend," Jericho muttered as we moved deeper into the club.

I noticed that some people had started to watch us with bemused expressions. A few looked surprised. In only a few moments, the buzz of the club had gone deadly silent, and even the fight stopped as everyone turned to look at us.

I did normally enjoy being the center of attention, but this didn't feel all that friendly to me.

"What's happening?" I asked.

"So much for keeping a low profile," Jericho muttered.

"If it isn't Jericho Nox, back from the dead," a deep, accented voice cut through the silence. "To what do I owe this honor?"

A man who looked to be in his fifties, wearing a black three-piece suit, approached us. Lines set into his dark-bronzed skin splayed out from around his gray eyes, and his hair was touched with silver. His gaze was cold.

Jericho smiled, but it was one of those smiles that didn't reach the eyes. "Long time."

"It certainly has been," the man replied.

"I need a favor."

"I don't do favors. You should know that better than most."

"I'm hoping you might make an exception this time." Jericho nodded at me. "This is Josslyn Drake. Drake, this is Rush."

It was a highly unusual name for a highly unusual man. Just like Jericho's. For a moment, I wondered if they were father and son. But they looked nothing alike—not in height, or facial features, or even coloring.

So this man was the answer to my problems. If all went well, I would be asleep in my bed in a matter of hours and wake up tomorrow good as new.

For a moment, I allowed myself to welcome a small but bright sliver of hope.

"Hi," I said as smoothly as I could.

"Hello." Rush now regarded me with interest, from my dark shades to my newly stolen outfit. "This lovely young woman is far out of your league, Jericho."

"It's not like that," Jericho snapped.

I was about to readily agree, as if it even needed to be said, but chose to keep my mouth shut. For now.

Rush laughed lightly. "I see your sense of humor has not improved over the last two years."

"My sense of humor's just fine, thanks."

Rush clasped his hands together, a cool smile on his lips. "It's an honor to meet you, Miss Drake. I'm afraid to say, you're not keeping the sort of company tonight that I'd expect from the daughter of our former prime minister, may he rest in peace."

I flinched at the mention of my father, as well as the fact that this strange man had recognized me immediately. My father would be horrified to know I was here, in this company, seeking help in the last place I ever would have chosen to be.

"It's been an unusual night," I allowed tightly.

"I don't doubt it." Rush turned to Jericho. "Now, what brings your ghost to my doorstep after all this time?"

"Show him your eyes," Jericho said to me.

I hesitated, but only for a moment. Then I slid my sunglasses down over my nose to reveal my unnaturally molten-gold irises.

Rush inhaled sharply, then glanced around at those nearby. "Everyone mind your own business. Start the fight again," he barked. "Now."

As commanded, the fight club returned to its previous level of noise and activity, and everyone's attention was drawn again to the fight in progress.

Rush swore under his breath. "You shouldn't have come back here, boy."

"And yet here I am," Jericho replied.

Rush's gray eyes were stormy and unwelcoming. "Follow me."

He turned and walked away from us.

"That actually went way better than I expected," Jericho said evenly, and started after Rush.

If I wanted an answer to this epic nightmare I'd found myself in, I knew I had to be brave. No problem. I could definitely be brave—or at least *pretend* to be, and no one would know my insides had turned to jelly.

I also had to play along and be nice. That would be more of a challenge, to say the least. More pretending required. I needed to follow this through to the end. I'd come this far, and I couldn't stop now. But following these strange men out of the relative safety of the crowd went against every instinct I had.

I did it anyway.

At the back of the fighting hall there was another door. It opened to a hallway similar to the entry hallway, dark and narrow. At the end of this was an archway that led into a lit room with a tall ceiling at least three stories high. Empty, wooden shelves lined the walls.

To my left was a large ebony desk with a neatly arranged line of rectangular objects on it—at least twenty of them.

I had to look twice to realize what they were.

I'd never seen a physical book made from paper in person, so it was a surprise to see them here. A single spine was three inches in width. I paused for a moment to look at it.

"This was a library once," Jericho explained. "Rush managed to save a few books before the rest were destroyed."

The queen had closed down the few remaining brick-and-mortar libraries before I was born. It wasn't worth the cost to keep them open when nobody used them anymore.

"Interesting," I said, working hard to keep my tone calm and cool. "But useless."

"Debatable." Jericho shrugged. "Now that everything's digitized, the queen can delete or rewrite anything she doesn't like. No one can separate truth from lies anymore."

If I'd been feeling more at ease about any of this, I might have rolled my eyes. "That's quite a conspiracy theory. Do you even remember when there were real libraries? What are you, a hundred?"

"Nineteen, actually. And it's not a conspiracy theory. But you go ahead and believe whatever you want."

"Thanks, I will."

Rush interrupted us, gesturing toward an area with two sofas. "Sit down."

I forced myself to take a seat in the middle of the room, letting my heavy limbs sink deep into the soft cushions. Beneath my feet was a colorfully embroidered rug that looked to be both old and expensive. I focused my attention on a line of purple in the embroidery, willing my heart to stop beating so fast as Rush studied me closely, his eyes narrowed. I tried not to flinch or show how uncomfortable I felt.

"What magic is this?" he asked.

The M-word never ceased to make me flinch.

"Memory magic," Jericho replied, and pulled the golden box from the pocket of his leather coat. I'd have been happy if I never saw that box again. "Have you seen something like this before?"

Rush took the box from Jericho, turning it over in his hand to inspect the symbols on it. "Yes, but rarely. It's a combination of air and earth elementia summoned by a highly skilled warlock that allows the extraction of one's memories. It keeps the memories safe, so that their owner can reexperience them anew. In this form, they're referred to as echoes."

My stomach lurched. He spoke about such horrible things so easily, as if speaking of nothing more important than the weather. "Echoes? And air and earth ele-*what*? What are you talking about?"

He regarded me for a moment. "What do you know about magic, Miss Drake?"

"That it's evil and should be destroyed," I said immediately, finding myself unable to tear my gaze away from the golden box in his grip. "And I need it out of me immediately before it completely destroys my life."

Rush shared a look with Jericho, who shrugged. "She gets all of her information from the royal newsfeed, just like everyone else around here," the thief said. "Are you surprised?"

I hated how dismissive he sounded. It infuriated me.

"No, not surprised at all." Rush sighed. "In any case, memory magic is incredibly rare, but I have seen an engraved container like this before. I sold one for a very high price."

I inhaled sharply. "You sold magic?"

"I sold everything," Rush replied, grinning at my look of horror. "One with eyes as unnaturally gold as yours shouldn't judge too harshly, I think, young lady."

"Fine, whatever. I don't really care," I said, adjusting my sunglasses with shaking hands. "Jericho says you can help. That's the only reason I'm here. I want to get back to my normal life immediately."

"Of course you do," he replied. "If I were you, I'd want the exact same thing." Then to Jericho: "Whose memories are these?"

Jericho didn't reply for a moment, but I'd found my heart had sped up even more as I waited.

"Lord Banyon's," he finally said.

Part of me already knew this, but my mind went blank with shock and denial at the confirmation. What I'd seen—Lord Banyon and the woman in the center of that inferno. His promise to burn everything and everyone in his path.

These were his memories. Lord Banyon's memories. Lord Banyon's magic.

That made everything so much worse.

Rush's eyes widened. "What in the hell have you gotten yourself into, boy?"

"A little bit of a predicament," Jericho replied.

"To say the very least," Rush agreed.

"He killed my father," I whispered. "I can't . . . no, this can't be happening to me. I don't want anything to do with this!"

"Bit late for that," Jericho muttered.

Rush hissed out a breath. "This is what your current employer wanted, is it? This box of Banyon's memories? I wonder who requested these incredibly valuable echoes from the legendary Valery herself?"

Jericho didn't reply to this, but his lips thinned. "I need the magic out of Drake and back in the box. That's all. I don't know more than that, and I don't want to."

Rush shook his head. "You're a damn fool to sign your life, your freedom, away to that witch."

That witch?

"Who are you talking about?" I asked. No, *demanded.* "Who's Valery?"

"Jericho's employer," Rush replied.

I shot a look at the thief. "You work for a witch?"

I hated how scared I sounded, my words raspy and raw.

"I'm not discussing Valery with anyone," Jericho said flatly.

"That woman is evil," Rush said. "Truly and utterly evil."

"Yeah, well, who isn't these days?"

Rush shook his head. "You should have come to me for help long before this."

"I thought you said you didn't do favors."

"Don't be glib, boy."

Jericho spread his hands. "Here I am, here and now. In all of Ironport, I thought you might be the only damn one who could give me some answers. Let me know if I was wrong, and I'll get out of your hair."

I found I was holding my breath, watching this exchange, but that wasn't going to get me what I needed. I had to try to summon my social skills, since sitting there with my mouth gaping open wasn't particularly proactive and was increasingly making me feel like a quivering victim. And I knew making demands wasn't going to earn me any friends, so I had to summon some charm from down deep inside me. "If you can help to extract this magic from me, Mr. Rush, I would so greatly appreciate it.

I'd also personally make sure that you're well compensated for keeping this matter confidential."

Rush's lips quirked as he regarded me. "Yes, I'm quite sure you wouldn't want anyone to know about this." He placed the golden box down on the table in front of me. "Unfortunately, Miss Drake, there are no witches or warlocks in my family line, only thieves and opportunists. I can't help you."

FIVE

I was sure I'd heard him wrong.

"I don't think you understand how important this is to me," I said. "I need this fixed tonight. I said I'd pay you. How much will it cost?"

I could figure this out. I could ask Celina to help me find the funds; I would just have to decide what to say so she would never know the truth.

"It's not a matter of money, Miss Drake. It's a matter of skill. I'm very sorry to have disappointed you." Rush then turned to Jericho while I stared at him, stunned. "If Valery wants this magic so much, why don't you take the girl to her?"

"I'm currently looking for other options," Jericho replied.

"I suppose I can guess why that is."

"Don't strain yourself too hard."

"What is this, Jericho?" I snapped. "You said that Rush could get this magic out of me and put it back in the box in two hours. Were you lying?"

"That's not exactly what I said, Drake." Jericho snatched the golden box off the table and turned a glare on the old man.

"I'm not walking away this easily. There must be someone out there, someone you know who can help me fix this mess without Valery needing to know anything about it."

Rush narrowed his gaze. "You are in so far over your head, boy, that you don't even know you're drowning."

"I need a name, not an intervention." Jericho's expression was strained. "Come on, Rush. You always had the answers I needed to make sense of it all. Don't stop now."

"Two long years, Jericho." Rush's expression had only hardened. "I thought you were dead and gone all this time. Imagine my surprise when I recently heard that you'd begun working for someone like Valery. It was like a stab to my own heart. The ultimate betrayal."

Jericho didn't reply. The two stared at each other in silence.

As much as I enjoyed a bit of family drama, which was what this sure felt like, despite Jericho and Rush not looking remotely related, I didn't give a minuscule crap about their history.

"This is ridiculous," I said tightly. "Whatever problem the two of you are dealing with has nothing to do with me. I need answers and I need them now. Could this Valery person help me?"

"No," Jericho said immediately, the word like a gunshot.

"Then who else? What witch or warlock can fix this?" I shuddered at the very thought of it, but I'd have to consider it a necessary evil—*literally*. When they didn't look at me, I slammed my fist down on the table. "I need a name and I need it now!"

Jericho and Rush both regarded me with surprise.

"She asked you a question, Rush," Jericho said. "Are you going to answer her?"

"Certainly," Rush replied evenly. "Here's a name for you: *Lord Banyon*. He's the most powerful and influential warlock alive today. I'm sure he'd appreciate this magic safely returned to him before it truly falls into the wrong hands."

"Fantastic suggestion," Jericho said. "Know where he's currently hiding? I'd love to get his help before I slit his throat."

My previous fear had faded to the background. Now I was seething. "Who else?"

Rush didn't speak again for a long moment, but his gaze grew faraway. I wasn't going to beg for his help, even if every fiber of my being screamed at me to do just that.

Oh, who was I kidding? As soon as this fresh burst of red-hot anger faded, I'd start begging like a hungry dog. I figured I had about two minutes left.

"The only other living warlock capable of this level of elementia is Vander Lazos," Rush finally said.

A name. Finally, a name.

"Tell me more," I pressed.

"Lazos is a former associate of Lord Banyon himself," Rush said. "For a time, Queen Isadora kept him at the palace as her resident expert on the subject of magic, due to both his skill and his photographic memory. It's rumored that she had him commit volumes of ancient magical tomes to memory before burning them."

My mouth had fallen open in shock. "That's the most ridiculous thing I've ever heard. The queen has warlocks executed; she doesn't hire them on as staff."

"Ignore her," Jericho said. "She's been living under a very posh and fashionable rock for seventeen years. Where's Lazos now?"

I scowled at him, but he wasn't even looking at me.

Rush nodded. "The queen and Lazos had a falling-out a decade ago. I don't know the details of what happened, but it was something big. Big enough that anyone else—especially a powerful warlock—would have been swiftly put to death. But the queen is known to be practical, and Lazos had a head full of valuable magical history. So she chose to imprison her problem rather than kill it."

I sorted through all this information as quickly as I could. My initial protests had faded as everything began to make sense to me. Of course the queen would want to be educated about the dark topic of magic. She would never choose ignorance about something that threatened her Empire. And of course she would keep this education private, since so many citizens might not approve of such a choice—but to defeat great evil, one had to understand it.

"So he's in a prison somewhere in the Empire," Jericho said, nodding. "Not ideal, but whatever. Which one?"

"The queen wanted him gone, but not far. Vander Lazos is a current resident of the prison closest to the palace."

"The Queen's Keep," Jericho replied. He raked his fingers through his dark hair as he glowered at me. "Seems like my two-hour estimate might have been a bit optimistic. It'll take us until the morning to get there, if we leave now."

"Are you kidding me?" I stood up from the sofa, every muscle in my body tense. "I'm not going to the Queen's Keep."

"Let's not start this again, Drake."

"No, I said I'd come here. Meet your friend—or whatever the hell he is to you. And I did that. And now this?"

"We have the name of a warlock who can help."

"A warlock who's a prisoner of the Queen's Keep." I turned a glare on Rush. "I don't know you. How do I know you're not lying about all of this?"

"You don't," Rush said. "Your skepticism is entirely understandable."

I wrung my hands, my gaze shooting everywhere in the cavernous room, in the middle of a fight club, in the middle of a seedy, dangerous neighborhood. "What am I doing here? Why did I listen to a word you said?"

"Drake . . ." Jericho began, but I didn't let him speak another word.

"No," I snapped. "I let you prey on my fear. I let you get into my head and scare me even more than I already was. But I'm not some random evil witch who stole a box of magical memory echoes to use against the Empire. I am Josslyn Drake, ward of Prime Minister Ambrose, and like family to Queen Isadora herself."

"Great," Jericho snapped back. "Maybe you should go ask Aunt Issy for help, then, if you think she'd be so understanding."

"Maybe I will."

"There's just one problem. That magic isn't yours. It's mine."

"Actually," Rush said, "it's Lord Banyon's."

"Shut the hell up," Jericho growled. "My patience is wearing thin with both of you."

"Mine too," I retorted. "And your two hours are officially up."

I turned away from them and left the room, headed back to the crowded club. To the exit. To freedom, and a totally different direction I'd decided my night would take.

Screw this, and screw Jericho.

This wasn't ideal in any way, shape, or form, but I had to swallow my pride and trust in the queen's mercy, which was what I should have done in the first place. If she'd secretly consulted a warlock to better understand how to fight back against scum like Lord Banyon and the threat of magic, then she would know how to help me better than anyone else.

I could only hope no one else would find out. But if they did, I'd just deny everything until my last breath. I'd dealt with painful rumors and gossip in the past, and I knew I'd deal with more in the future. I didn't see a long list of choices here; I had to do whatever it took to survive this.

If only I had my phone, I could contact Her Majesty immediately.

I pushed my way through the crowd of sweaty bodies, focused only on that black door. On this side of it, there was a handle, which I grabbed, twisted, and pulled on, relieved when the heavy door opened inward.

And I found myself looking directly at Viktor, who stood on the other side.

His eyes widened. "Miss Drake. You're here."

"*Joss*," I corrected, breathless with surprise. "What are you doing here?"

Before he had a chance to reply, another man in uniform nudged him aside. I recognized him immediately: Viktor's superior, High Commander Armel Norris. He was a good friend of the family—both Drake and Ambrose. A high-ranking Queensguard who had always been kind to me, even giving me birthday gifts over the years when he'd visited my father to brief him on high-level military business matters.

"This is a relief." Norris nodded at me. "Stand aside, Miss Drake. We will handle this from here."

I watched with shock as Commander Norris and Viktor entered the smoky fight club followed by eight other guards. The Queensguards' crisp black-and-gold uniforms contrasted with the faded clothing, unshaved faces, and scent of sweat and cheap wine. Immediately, I felt at my face to ensure that my sunglasses were still firmly in place to shield my eyes.

Norris's brows were drawn together as he peered down his pale, sharp nose at his unsavory surroundings. "Should I ask how you even knew this cesspit existed and never said anything about it until tonight, Commander?"

"It'll be in my report, sir," Viktor replied tightly, and then to me: "Are you all right?"

I blinked, not sure how to answer him. "Not even slightly."

I didn't know how to feel about this. Only a moment ago, I'd had a fresh new plan on how to deal with my horrible problem, but this wasn't it. Too many people, too many witnesses.

I needed a chance to contact the queen privately. A part of me knew I should feel relief, but I felt only numbness and uncertainty. I didn't know if I could trust this many Queensguards with my awful new secret. I wasn't even sure if I could trust Celina.

"Wait—Celina!" I exclaimed. "Oh my god. Is she all right?"

"She's fine," Viktor replied. "She's recovering from her ordeal. But she's extremely worried about you."

That made two of us. A dozen more questions bubbled up in my throat, but I swallowed them back down when the loud music that had been playing came to a stop and the club fell into silence, apart from breathing and whispers of alarm. Obviously, the presence of an armed military squad invading an illegal establishment hadn't gone unnoticed.

Norris grimly scanned the faces of the suddenly nervous crowd. "Where is the Blackheart, Miss Drake?"

I blinked. "The Blackheart?"

"The criminal who kidnapped you," Norris clarified.

"Hi there," said Jericho. To my surprise, he had stealthily come to stand next to me in the shadows. "You can call me Jericho. *Blackheart* is more of a job title, really."

A flash of silver guns in the hands of the surrounding Queensguards raised to point directly at Jericho's face.

"Don't move," Norris told him. "You're under arrest."

Jericho eyed the guards with disinterest. "No shit."

I couldn't help but let out a choked laugh at his response, not to mention his audacity to stroll out here like he didn't have a care in the world.

Norris was far less amused. "We identified you from the security footage from both the Gala and the boutique earlier tonight. We know who you work for, Blackheart, and I don't underestimate what you're capable of. Make any move, and my men will shoot you."

"Noted. But let's put a pin in that for a moment, shall we?" Jericho crossed his arms over his chest, still seemingly unfazed by the full arsenal directed at him. "I'm floored by being in the presence of the famous Commander Raden here. Even more radiant and glorious in the flesh, I see."

My surprised gaze flew to Viktor, who didn't reply to this, but his jaw tightened.

Jericho continued, so casual it was as if we were chatting at a cocktail party. An extremely sarcastic cocktail party, leaning toward *acidic*. "I hear things have been really swell for you these last few years," he said. "Really moving up in the world. *Commander Viktor Raden.* Wow. Should I kneel or something?"

Viktor still hadn't said a single word in reply, but the tension between the two was so thick, it was as if a blanket of fog had rolled into the club.

"You know each other?" I asked. I mean, clearly stating the obvious here, but it was an obvious that was difficult for me to believe.

"Little bit," Jericho said with a nod. "But that was a long time ago. Congrats on your engagement, by the way, Vik. And sorry I magic-Dusted your shiny new fiancée earlier. Just business. She took it well, didn't fight back at all. Nice and docile and obedient, which is perfect for you."

I shot a dark look at him, not that he noticed. Not that he cared.

Viktor clenched his teeth into a smile—which was more like a snarl, if you asked me. "Sir?" he said, addressing Norris. "Shall we proceed?"

Norris nodded. "Restrain the Blackheart. He'll be questioned at length."

"That sounds like fun," Jericho said. "But I'm going to have to pass. I already have a very full schedule tonight."

This flippant attitude had to be just an act, a show of strength when he was completely outnumbered. False bravado to try to throw off his opponents. If it wasn't, he was a complete and utter fool.

I hadn't known Jericho very long at all, but he didn't strike me as a fool.

Blackheart. I turned the word—the job title, he'd said—over in my head, and it made an icy chill run through me. It didn't sound friendly. It sounded just as dangerous as my first impression of him had been.

Norris said crisply, "Who runs this illegal hall?"

Utter silence fell across the club, but a moment later Rush strode forward through the nervous crowd.

"I do," he said simply, and his gaze flicked to Viktor. "Hello, young man."

Viktor's jaw tightened.

Wait. They knew each other, too?

I eyed the standoff uneasily and with confusion, hating how much uncertainty I felt about every moment of this. How I wished I could just go home and forget tonight ever happened, but I knew that wasn't possible. This wasn't over yet—far from it.

Norris gestured forward a pair of nearby Queensguards. "Arrest both of them. And everyone present will be charged with patronizing an unlicensed and unsanctioned gambling hall."

The guards shoved both Jericho and Rush toward a wall, turning them roughly around to restrain their hands behind their backs. I felt the heat of the Blackheart's gaze on me, and I searched his face for some sign of what he was thinking but came up totally blank.

High Commander Norris held a hand out to me. "You're safe now, Miss Drake. Come with me, and I'll take you home."

Safe. What a small word for such a very big lie. I wasn't safe, not anymore. Not even the promise of man I'd known since I was just a little girl, a man who'd spent his life in service to Queen Isadora, could ease a fraction of my inner turmoil.

I wanted to end this nightmare easily and quickly. But there would be nothing easy or quick about this. So for now, I'd have to play along until I had a chance to personally contact the queen. I guessed I'd better get used to wearing these sunglasses.

"Of course, sir," I said.

I took his hand, and a moment later, a stream of golden smoke appeared out of nowhere and swirled around me, obliterating the fight club from my view in an instant.

Swirling, swirling, until I was dizzy. Until I couldn't see straight.

No, I thought with rising panic. *Please, no. Not again!*

Disjointed, fractured images appeared before me. Only pieces—like a puzzle I desperately didn't want to put together. I couldn't let this memory magic take a deeper hold on me—from what little I understood about any of this, these were Lord Banyon's memories, echoes of his life, which made this even more of a curse. I didn't want to see anything to do with the man who'd murdered my father.

But it seemed I didn't have a say in the matter, and regardless of how much I fought against it, the images didn't disappear; they only grew clearer.

"I won't help her." A pained voice, weak and raspy, rose from the smoky scene unfolding before me. It was Lord Banyon himself, every bit as pale and gaunt as he'd looked when he'd been surrounded by flames. His hands were tied above his head, the rope secured to a hook attached to the ceiling.

Seeing the legendary warlock shocked me, and for a moment, I didn't believe my own eyes. He looked far more like a victim than a villain.

"You will do whatever she commands you to do or you die." It was Commander Norris who said this, his voice so loud it was nearly a roar. Younger than he was now, his face red with anger.

I gasped as he slammed his fist into Banyon's stomach. The warlock grunted in pain, spitting blood, his lips peeling back from clenched teeth.

"Kill me, then," he snarled.

"No," Norris said, his gaze cold. "Not yet. Not nearly yet. You will summon the magic she's asked of you, and you will do the ritual until it works. Until he's restored."

Banyon shook his head. "I can't do what she wants. No mere mortal can control the level of dark magic required. The risk is too great that something will go horribly wrong. The price is too high, even for me. Even for her, but she's stubbornly ignorant to the risks."

Norris loomed closer. "The price you will pay for defying her will be much worse, I assure you. She will make you suffer like no one else has ever suffered."

Banyon raised his chin, red blood sliding over his bottom lip. "She can go to hell."

His words held bottomless hate and so much cold defiance that they made me shiver.

Norris's eyes flashed with frustration. "Don't say I didn't warn you," he hissed.

The golden smoke returned, obliterating the fractured scene before me, leaving me gasping for breath.

The dark club came back into view, and I found myself doubled over, the drip of blood from my nose hitting the tiled floor.

Norris had let go of my hand, and he regarded me with shock. "Miss Drake, do you need medical assistance? Are you injured?"

"No, I . . . I'm fine," I replied, despising the unfamiliar edge of weakness in my voice as I bit out the lie. I wasn't fine. So very far from it.

What the hell had I just seen? If these were Lord Banyon's memories magically trapped inside me, that had been him being interrogated and . . . and tortured.

By High Commander Norris.

For "her." There was only one "her" in the Regarian Empire who held that kind of power over someone like Norris. But what magic had the queen wanted Lord Banyon to summon?

None of this made any damn sense.

The sudden and acrid scent of smoke made me tense up, thinking I might be swept into another nightmarish, disjointed vision.

"Something's on fire," Norris said with annoyance. "Go. Check it out."

He gestured toward a couple of guards, who did as commanded. They moved toward a metal door behind the fighting ring where a line of smoke wafted out.

The next moment, the door blew open and a wave of fire crashed into the center of the club, lighting everything in its path ablaze. I staggered backward, immediately reminded of my first memory vision. Only here, I felt the searing heat of the flames.

The crowd, previously frozen in collective fright, all began to scream and run for the exit.

Norris tore his attention from the raging fire to look at Rush with shock. "What the hell is this?"

Rush shrugged, but there was a hard, grim look in his gray eyes. "I knew the day would come that my club would be raided and burned to the ground like all the others who dared to defy Her Majesty's laws. Years ago, I acquired a single matchstick from a witch, containing enough fire magic to turn this building to ash. My choice, not yours. Never yours. Please give my regards to Queen Isadora."

Before Norris could respond, a wall of flames rose up between the two. Norris snarled orders at his men to control the swarm of terrified, screaming people now fleeing the club, but there were too few guards and too many desperate people who were fighting against the guards and each other to escape.

"Get Miss Drake out of here," Norris barked at Viktor before he moved closer to the struggle and disappeared from view.

I turned toward Viktor, the heat from the flames close enough to singe my new, unpaid-for outfit, but Jericho grabbed my wrist, pulling me in his direction. He'd somehow escaped from his restraints.

"We need to leave," he snapped "Now."

"Let go of her," Viktor snarled. He'd drawn his gun and had it pointed directly at Jericho.

Jericho groaned. "Really enjoying our reunion, Vik. So much fun. But I think it's time to leave the burning building before we burn with it. Drake is coming with me."

"The hell I am," I snapped.

"Where are you going to go?" he asked. "Home sweet home? Or to the palace, to beg Aunt Issy to help you? Sorry to break it to you, but she won't."

I shook my head. "You don't know her like I do."

His eyes flashed with anger. "You're so delusional I almost feel sorry for you. You know what? Let's get Vik's opinion on our little problem, shall we?"

"What do you—?"

He snatched the sunglasses right off my face, and I gasped.

Viktor stared at me for a moment before his gaze went wide, and he staggered backward.

"Your eyes . . ." he said. "My god . . . you're a witch."

Shit! I shoved Jericho away from me. "I'm not. Of course I'm not!"

"What the hell have you done to her?" Viktor demanded, and I was deeply disturbed to see that his gun now wavered between the two of us.

Jericho's jaw tensed. "The magic in the box I stole last night is in Drake. It was an accident. One that I'm highly motivated to fix as soon as humanly possible. I have a name, someone who can help us."

"No, Viktor, you need to take me to the queen," I said, the words tripping over themselves. "She'll help me."

"You know damn well that's not true, Vik," Jericho snapped. "Tell her the truth. Tell Drake that if she strolls into the palace with gold eyes and chock-full of dangerous magic, she'll be executed on the spot."

I turned a look of horror on the commander. "That's not true!"

Sure, I'd imagined life as I knew it ending as I was shunned and shamed by everyone I knew, exiled from any social possibility as I dealt with this nightmare, but real death hadn't even occurred to me. Not until this very moment. Executed like an evil witch or warlock, or another horrific threat against the queen and the Empire.

"Damn you, Jericho," Viktor snarled. "You made this mess; you need to fix it."

"That's the plan."

Finally, Viktor met my gaze. "Go with Jericho. He'll protect you. Do whatever it takes to get this poison out of you before it's too late."

I was shaking my head so violently that it made me dizzy. "Wait, Viktor—"

"Go now, before I change my mind." Viktor swore under his breath, and then he turned and left the burning club before I could say another word.

"Come on." Jericho took my arm and yanked me in the opposite direction, shoving the sunglasses at me that he'd snatched up off the floor.

I was too stunned to fight him this time and allowed him to navigate us through the maze of flames devouring the fight club until we came to another hallway. Another metal door.

"Looks like Rush left without giving us a heartfelt farewell," he muttered. "Shocking, really."

He swung open the door, and we swiftly exited into a dark, garbage-strewn alley. Once I was outside and had gulped in some clean air, I could finally think clearly enough to violently wrench my arm out of his grip.

"Congratulations, asshole," I snapped. "You've ruined my life."

Jericho turned to stare at me for a moment before he chuckled darkly. "Oh, Drake, you have no idea how true that is. But you're stuck with me awhile longer. We're going to the Queen's Keep, and we're going to get Vander Lazos to help end this once and for all."

Viktor hadn't confirmed what Jericho said—that the queen would have me executed. But he hadn't denied it, either.

His first thought when he'd seen my golden eyes was that I was a witch.

A witch!

But it meant that anyone else might come to the same horrifying, knee-jerk conclusion.

No exceptions, the queen had said.

Oh my god. I was so screwed.

This wasn't my fault. I hadn't asked for any of this. But it didn't make any difference. I was officially out of options.

"Who is Viktor to you?" I managed, forcing the question out from my tight throat. "How do you know him?"

Jericho looked away. "We need to get going, Drake. It's a long drive. The clock's ticking."

I shook my head. "No. Tell me who Viktor is to you. Tell me now or I'm not moving a single step, which means you're going to have to knock me out and carry me. And that's not going to happen without a hell of a fight first."

He swore under his breath, then glared at me. "You really want to know?"

"If I didn't, I wouldn't have asked." Not a single thing had gone right tonight, but this was a war I would win. It would show him that I didn't back down from a fight—physical or verbal. "Is he an old friend? An old enemy? How does he know you so well that he'd tell me to go with a . . . a Blackheart? What kind of a job title is that, anyway?"

"An extremely accurate one," he bit out, his dark eyes glittering under the moonlight. "So be careful, Drake. You don't want to push me too far."

I ignored the fresh shiver that coursed through me at the cold warning.

"Careful isn't going to get me what I need," I retorted. "Now tell me who Viktor is to you."

I waited as Jericho's gaze raked the alleyway before it finally landed heavily on me.

"Viktor Raden, the shiny and glorious champion of the Queensgames and loyal commander of the Queensguard," he said darkly, "is my brother."

SIX

With that jaw-dropping revelation, Jericho turned away from me and started walking out of the alley so fast that I barely was able to keep up with him.

"He's your *what?*" I asked.

He didn't even look at me. "Brother. A year younger. Do I need to draw you a diagram?"

I opened my mouth to argue as I jogged just behind him and his ridiculously long legs. Every part of me wanted to scoff, wanted to call him a liar. It seemed impossible.

But it also explained why they were so similar in looks, enough that I'd mistaken Jericho for Viktor when I first saw him at the Gala. Their height, their hair color. Their jawlines and sharp chiseled cheekbones.

The noses were different, but I'd already decided Jericho's had to have been broken before, which made it a little less perfect than Viktor's.

But Viktor's eyes were light brown. And Jericho's were black.

"You lived here with Rush. Both of you," I said, trying to

fill in the empty pieces for myself. "That's how Viktor knew to come here, looking for you."

"Our parents were killed sixteen years ago. Someone found us and brought us to Rush. He took us in. Fed us, clothed us. And later, when we were older and more valuable to a place like this, he taught us how to fight for money. That part obviously worked out a bit better for Vik." His jaw tensed. "That's it, Drake. That's all you're getting from me on the subject. I don't talk about my past with anybody."

The small glimpse of Jericho's past turned my stomach and made me feel something for him, against my will. A weird gut punch of sympathy for the innocent little boy he'd been.

I'd been only four when I'd lost my mother to cancer. I didn't remember much at all about that time; I was too young. But I remember feeling like my home was emptier without her in it, that there was a great sense of loss. That my father was sad. He never let me see him cry, but I remember him having red-rimmed eyes a lot of the time.

"I'm . . . sorry you went through that," I said.

Jericho hissed out a breath. "Yeah, life sucks and then you die."

A flash of light made me turn sharply to see a car round the corner and drive down the street toward us.

Jericho eyed it. "If you're finished with the interrogation, let's get on with this."

He stepped right in front of the car, and I shrieked. The wheels screeched as the car came to a lurching halt. The driver, a man of about fifty, threw the door open, his expression furious.

"What the hell do you think you're doing?" he demanded. "I could have killed you!"

"If you say so." Jericho grabbed the man and tossed him aside. "Get in, Drake."

He got in the driver's side. The man stormed toward him, but as soon as he saw the gun in Jericho's grip, he threw his hands up.

My heart nearly stopped at the sight of it. I hadn't even known he was armed until this very moment.

"Don't—don't shoot me!" the man gasped. "Please!"

I opened my mouth to say something, although I wasn't exactly sure what. Of all the people I'd ever met, Jericho was the one who left me the most tongue-tied and flat-out stunned by everything he said and everything he did.

"Drake." Jericho shot me a dark and chilling look that made me shiver. There was not even a glimmer of humor in his gaze anymore. "Get in the damn car or you're going in the trunk."

I gaped at him, equally scared and outraged at the suggestion. He'd do it, too. He'd throw me in the trunk.

Letting out a loud snarl of frustration, I got in the car. "I hate you."

"Good."

Jericho didn't wait until I'd shut the door to slam his foot down on the gas, leaving the man behind us in a cloud of exhaust fumes, a hand to his chest, a look of shock and outrage on his face.

I was sure I wore a similar expression.

After a minute, Jericho glanced at me. "I know, right? So surprising that a lowlife criminal like me would carjack a decent, taxpaying citizen of Ironport. Someone should probably stop me."

"Somebody probably will," I gritted out.

"They're more than welcome to try." He was quiet for a moment. "Now back to the matter at hand. I know a Queensguard who's one of my boss's contacts stationed near the Queen's Keep. I get in touch with him, bribe the hell out of him so he goes into the prison and yanks Lazos out long enough for us to have a good chat about magical memories and how to get them out of you and back in the box."

I blinked. "Your boss has a contact who's a Queensguard?"

"Yes. Scandalous, I know, but even Her Majesty's perfect soldiers can be bribed by black market masterminds when the situation calls for it. And this situation is actually shouting so loud my eardrums hurt."

I crossed my arms over my chest and slunk back into the seat of the stolen car. "Disgusting."

"And potentially helpful to you getting your happy, diamond-studded life back. So. Off we go. Any further arguments?"

"No," I muttered.

"Any escape attempts or more random attempts to crush my balls planned?"

I cringed. "Not currently."

"Super." The Blackheart didn't spare me a direct look; he

kept his attention on the road. "Now shut up, let me drive, and we'll be there by morning barring any further catastrophes."

I turned my face away from him, staring out the passenger-side window. Then I squeezed my eyes shut.

This was a nightmare I was never going to wake up from. I felt like I'd been swept away by an unexpected tide and suddenly I'd totally forgotten how to swim.

I would fix this; I would get this rancid magic out of me and make it a distant, horrible part of my past, and I would go back to my familiar life where everything made sense and I didn't doubt everyone and everything. I liked seeing everything in the bright light of day. At night, there were too many shadows, too many questions.

I would tolerate Jericho since he was helping—in the roughest and most unpleasant way possible—to get what I ultimately wanted.

And he was Viktor's brother.

I still couldn't believe it. Brothers. But so different from each other in everything except looks; they were like night and day.

Go with Jericho. He'll protect you.

I didn't feel all that protected. In fact, at times, I felt distinctly threatened. But I was still breathing. I guess, after the night I'd had—magical visions, fight clubs, and fires included—that had to be a step in the right direction.

I opened my eyes and watched the tall buildings that made up the skyline of downtown Ironport grow smaller in the rearview mirror as we sped along the highway, headed north. After an hour of silence, the hum of the car's engine lulled me, finally, into a sleep I didn't bother trying to fight.

I hoped it would be a dreamless sleep, but no such luck.

And it wasn't one of Banyon's memories I was forced to see in my unconscious mind.

No. It was one of mine. One that was branded into my memory and would be forever.

The Ironport Royal Gallery. Last year's Queen's Gala.

I saw it all vividly and crystal clear, including the amazing amethyst-colored dress that my father had wanted me to change out of because he thought it was too short and too tight for a sixteen-year-old. The subsequent fight we'd had because of my fashion choices and my overall stubbornness about everything, but I won by wearing him out.

The moment we exited the chauffeured car and began ascending the stone stairs leading to the grand entrance.

The second he fell to his knees and I saw all that blood.

I was right there at his side, holding him in my arms, the delicate silk of my dress soaking up the bright red blood pouring out from somewhere on his chest.

So much blood.

"Daddy!" I cried.

Our security team swarmed around us.

"I'm all right," my father managed to rasp out. "It's just a flesh wound."

I grabbed his face, staring deep into his eyes. "You're sure?"

He grasped my shoulder, giving me a tight smile. "Yes, I'm sure. I'm fine. Everything's fine, Jossie. Don't worry."

I woke up from the nightmare and lurched forward. "Please, no!"

"Drake." Jericho's tone was alarmed and his arm was across my chest, trying to stop me from thrashing about in the passenger seat. "You were just dreaming. Calm down."

I gulped in a mouthful of air as my heart thudded wildly. "Easier said than done."

"What was it?" he asked. "Did you experience another echo about that bastard?"

I shook my head. "No. A nightmare of the night my father was assassinated. I've had it before—lots of times. It's so real, it's like I'm living through it again."

I viciously wiped at my damp eyes with the sleeve of my shirt, angry and frustrated that I'd let myself cry in front of the Blackheart. "I still can't believe he lied to me. He told me he was fine, but he wasn't. They took him away, and the next time I saw him was at . . ." I inhaled raggedly. "At his funeral."

Jericho turned to the road ahead again, his knuckles whitening on the steering wheel. "I'm so sorry, Drake."

His response surprised me, since it sounded so painfully earnest compared with everything else he'd said to me. But then I remembered he, too, had lost his parents.

"I miss him so much. Nothing's been the same since he died. Nothing will ever be the same again." I rubbed my face and dragged fingers through my tangled hair. "Why am I telling you any of this?"

"You strike me as someone who likes an audience."

I wanted to shoot back an insult, but then I realized he wasn't exactly wrong. He was just making a very obvious observation. I deflated. "Last night, I overheard my friends saying I was a self-obsessed narcissist."

"A self-obsessed narcissist," he repeated. "Sound a bit redundant to me."

"One of them even said I should be thrown in the Queen's Keep like all the other social rejects. And here we are, on our way to that exact place. Funny, right?"

"Hilarious," he replied dryly.

"Oh my god, is it morning already?" I asked. There was most definitely a sunrise happening to the right of the road, which had changed from a paved highway into a more narrow dirt lane.

"Rise and shine."

"I can't believe I slept that long."

"For the record, Drake? You snore."

I stared at him, aghast. "I do not."

"You do."

He was lying just to make me feel self-conscious. I wouldn't let him get to me.

I pulled down the sun visor to look at the mirror there, which reflected my frightening golden eyes. I shivered at the sight of them. "I can't believe this is happening to me."

"Me neither," Jericho agreed under his breath.

"I keep waiting to feel different," I said quietly, my throat tight. "I will, won't I? Magic is evil, diseased. It's going to permanently change me if I don't get it out soon."

Jericho kept his eyes on the road, but his expression turned grim.

"What?" I prompted, even more alarmed now.

He shook his head. "I'm trying to decide how much I want to say right now that you'll actually willingly listen to."

"About what? Magic?"

"Yeah, that."

"I already know about it," I told him. "It's the cause of all pain and suffering in the world."

He sighed. "And yet you're full of it right now, and you don't feel any different than you did yesterday. Right?"

I wasn't sure where he was going with this. "That's probably just an illusion. It's festering inside of me. That's what magic does."

"Sure it is." He rolled his eyes. "Obviously, it's gnawing away at your very soul right now. You've had, what? Two echoes so far? Both strong enough to trigger a bloody nose, which is a very common magical side effect. Your eyes have changed color, which is way more rare, so congrats on that. It's in you, Drake. Deep. But you're still you. Trust me, I should know."

I clenched my fists at my sides while he spoke, my nails biting painfully into my palms. "What are you saying?"

"Nothing you're ready to hear. And it doesn't even matter. You believe what you believe. What everyone believes because your beloved Aunt Issy wants it that way. So let's just leave it at that. It keeps everything very simple."

"You are making absolutely no sense," I told him, annoyed now.

"Story of my life."

"How much longer am I going to have to put up with this nonsense?" I asked sullenly.

"Not long at all," he replied. "We're here."

I sat bolt upright in my seat. "We're at the Queen's Keep already?"

"Close enough. We're pulling into Silverside."

Silverside was the closest town to the Queen's Keep, the place where the small army of Queensguards who monitored and maintained the walled city lived.

It wasn't much. A small town of about three thousand residents. There was a main street. A local theater. A park where they held small fairs and celebrations. Tons of farmland. A whole lot of cows.

I'd visited this town only once, a few years ago. It was during one of my father's visits with the local mayor, and he'd suggested I come along since the mayor had a daughter around my age.

I'd forgotten her name, but she'd looked at me with awe despite her nearly debilitating shyness. The big city girl with the awesome life and wardrobe, according to her, anyway, coming to meet a simple girl from the country. And then she'd made her excuses and went out with her local friends, leaving me alone with my father and the mayor for a very boring dinner where they discussed politics and I secretly fed the mayor's friendly cat under the table from my plate.

Only fifty miles northeast of here was the palace city. I'd been there several times over the years to visit Queen Isadora. While the population was similarly low, the sparkly streets and high-end restaurants and stores that made up the palace grounds were a stark contrast to the small-town atmosphere in Silverside.

"We're so close to the palace," I said wistfully.

"Still counting on the queen to save you?" Jericho asked. "Because she won't."

"So you keep saying." I crossed my arms over my chest and went quiet, trying my best to avoid the tangle of thoughts that his question created. "If Rush was telling the truth, that means she didn't execute Vander Lazos. That's proof that she's willing to make exceptions."

"Rush also said the warlock's photographic memory made him too valuable to execute. He's got volumes of magical encyclopedias tightly locked up in his head. And even with that going for him, he still got tossed in the Keep like a bag of garbage. Do you want to head to the palace and take your chances?"

I hated to admit that he had a point. But so did I.

Still, Viktor hadn't eased my mind enough to avoid coming here with Jericho, and I couldn't seem to shake off the way he'd reacted to my golden eyes.

With that thought, I slid on the dark sunglasses.

"We'll try it your way first," I said.

"Good decision."

Without the queen as an absolute certainty, I had no one else I could depend on to help me with this. I had no family, not anymore. A distant aunt or uncle I'd never met before, who'd never even bothered to meet me in seventeen years, didn't count. My father was all I'd had, the only one I'd known loved me uncon-ditionally.

And Celina . . . she didn't have any power, any say in the matter. I couldn't lean on her, I couldn't draw her into this nightmare. I had to figure this out for myself without putting the burden on anyone else.

And I would.

Jericho parked the car next to a cluster of small buildings that made up Silverside's downtown area.

"Go get us some breakfast," he said.

I eyed the money he shoved at me with confusion. "Break-fast."

"You know, what you eat soon after you wake up to give you energy to face the day."

"I know what breakfast is."

He pulled out his phone. "I need to contact Tobin." When I didn't make a move to exit the car, he eyed me. "Problem?"

"I'm not used to being told what to do," I said.

"I gave you money to get us breakfast. Not exactly barking commands, Drake. If you don't want to do it, feel free to go hungry. I'll get something for myself later."

My stomach growled then, as if making a counterargument.

"Fine." I straightened my sunglasses, got out of the car, and scanned my surroundings. Motivated by my vocal abdomen, I strode into the closest bakery and bought an assortment of sweet and savory pastries, using up most of the Blackheart's money and leaving the remainder as a tip.

When I returned to Jericho, who'd also exited the car, he looked pleased. Or smug. I wasn't sure which.

"What?" I asked.

"We're good," he said. "Tobin says he'll meet us just outside the southern entry point and give us a chance to question Vander Lazos."

I crossed my arms, expecting to feel some sort of elation, but only sensing a swirling anxiety in my gut. "You trust him?"

"I don't trust anyone, Drake. But Tobin is one of those people I mentioned before who really likes money."

The thought that a Queensguard could be bribed turned my stomach. "I hate this."

"Well, I'm certainly open to other options on how to end this delightful partnership between us in another easy way."

My eyes narrowed. "Do you ever say anything that isn't dripping in sarcasm?"

"Do you?" he countered.

I shook my head. "I can't believe you're Viktor's brother."

"Yeah, well, feel free to forget that little piece of inside information. I'd certainly like to." Jericho studied the stolen car for a moment. "We're leaving this here and walking the rest of the way. A car would get us spotted too easy, and nobody's supposed to come within five miles of the wall unless they're with the military."

I cringed at the thought. "How far is it from here?"

"Seven miles." At my look of shock, he shrugged. "Time to hustle, Drake."

I was about to say something else, but Jericho just started walking away from me without another word. And he wasn't trying to walk at a slow enough pace for me to easily keep up with him.

He was fast. But I was determined. At his pace, I didn't have any energy, or breath, left to do any talking, so I focused on my footsteps over the uneven ground.

Seven miles later my legs ached and my lungs burned, but I knew I was that much closer to regaining control over my own damn life. After we crested yet another hill, I looked up and finally saw it.

The wall stretched from east to west, a metallic, serpentine structure a hundred feet tall, as if one of Ironport's steel sky-scrapers had fallen on its side and been stretched out from one horizon to the other.

Except a skyscraper had windows. This didn't.

It seemed so modern and out of place after seven miles of nothing but tree, tree, tree, rock.

It was awe-inspiring, that's for sure.

"Speechless again," Jericho said. "Good. I won't have to tell you to shut up when Tobin gets here."

"You could tell me, but it wouldn't make me." I cut a side-long glance at him, tearing my attention away from the impres-sive barrier. "Let's get one thing straight, Blackheart. You can try to bully and intimidate me, but I don't obey you and you don't scare me. This partnership, or whatever you want to call it, is out of dire necessity only. Got it?"

"Got it." His dark eyes glittered. "Oh, and just for the record, Drake? I don't give a damn what you think about me—if you think I'm rude, a scumbag, a piece of garbage beneath your shiny designer heel. I don't think about you at all. All I care about is fixing this epic mistake as soon as humanly possible."

"Good," I said, disappointed in myself for not having a better comeback at the ready.

"How about we go back to not talking?" he said. "I liked that a lot."

I glowered at him.

But not talking was fine with me. Instead, I focused on how much I despised this criminal, how I didn't owe him anything, and how I was counting down the minutes until my life returned to normal and only a few people knew the terrible truth.

I still fought the idea that the queen wouldn't make an exception for me, like she had with Lazos, even if I didn't come with valuable extra skills that made me entirely indispensable. However, I knew she hated Lord Banyon to the very bottom of her soul. If she learned that I had Banyon's magic—his very memories—inside me . . .

The only guarantee I had of returning to my normal life was to rid myself of this magic.

Not talking lasted a while for me. But not forever.

"If this doesn't work," I said, a half hour of silence later, wrapping my arms around myself now that a cold wind had started blowing. "If Rush was wrong—"

"Rush is never wrong."

"But if he is. If Vander Lazos can't help us." The words tasted bitter. "What then?"

Jericho scanned the barrier through a pair of binoculars he'd pulled from the depths of his seemingly magical leather duster. "Then I'll take you to Valery."

My heart skipped a beat. "Rush suggested that. And you said no."

"That's right."

"Why did you say no?"

He cut a look at me. "Because she'd kill you to get the magic out of you."

I gasped. "What?"

"She deals with problems in a very decisive way, like a hammer with a nail." Jericho's tone was flat. "She'd kill you and get on with her business without missing a beat."

I could barely breathe now. "And knowing that, you'd take me to her?"

Jericho shrugged without glancing at me. "One thing at a time."

"No. Screw that and screw you," I snarled, my anger and frustration rising to the surface in a heartbeat. "You're not taking me to Valery, no matter what happens today. I'll kill you first!"

He lowered the binoculars and glared at me. "Don't push me, Drake. I might seem all nicey-nicey at the moment—"

"You actually don't," I said.

"But I'm annoyed and frustrated and moving toward pissed off the longer we sit here waiting." His gaze moved behind me. "Finally."

I turned to see a dark-haired, pasty-faced man about ten

years Jericho's senior, wearing the black-with-gold-accents Queensguard uniform with enough military pins to tell me he ranked very high, walking toward us.

So this was Tobin. A traitor who'd pledged his loyal service and obedience to Queen Isadora, yet was happy to take bribes on the side from common criminals.

Sickening.

And yet, at this very moment, also super helpful.

"Jericho," Tobin said in greeting. "I was surprised to hear from you."

"Tobin," Jericho replied with a nod. "Not as surprised as I was to contact you. But here we are."

"Should I ask why you want to talk to Vander Lazos?"

"Best you don't know."

"I don't want to know." Tobin glanced at me. "Who's the girl?"

I was still trying to calm myself after learning what would happen if Jericho took me to see Valery, who easily sounded like the most evil and dangerous woman in the world.

This Queensguard didn't recognize me, but I wasn't overly surprised. I wasn't wearing makeup. My long hair was a tangled mess. I rarely left home without being "on" when it came to my looks. That had to be why nobody, here or at Rush's club earlier, could pick me out of a lineup—apart from Rush himself. As annoying as it was, not being recognized right now was a huge relief, not an insult.

"This"—Jericho put his arm around my tense shoulders and pulled me against his side—"this is my girlfriend, Janie. She tags along wherever I go lately. True love, you know? What can I say? Right, Janie?"

I eyed him with shock before I managed to compose myself. "Yeah. Right. The truest ever."

Tobin looked like he couldn't care less. "Do you have what you promised?"

"Half transfer now, half when we talk to Lazos."

"All of it now," Tobin said firmly. "My word is good, but yours isn't."

"Well, that's rude." Jericho studied the man as a hungry beast might study a smaller beast thinking it could be its next meal.

"I can leave and we can forget all about this," Tobin said. "I guess it all depends on how much you need to see Lazos."

"Give him the money," I urged under my breath.

"Shut up," Jericho bit out through clenched teeth. Then to Tobin. "Fine. I'll make an exception this one time."

The Blackheart pulled his phone from the inner pocket of his jacket and performed a money transfer very quickly.

"Always nice doing business with one of Valery's most valuable employees," Tobin said, glancing down at the screen of his device with satisfaction. "How is she, anyway?"

"Just fine, thanks so much for asking," Jericho replied.

"I assume you're here on her orders."

Jericho smiled thinly. "You can go fetch Lazos for me now. That would be super."

Tobin frowned. "Fetch him?"

Jericho hissed out a breath. "That was the deal."

"Actually, the deal was that you wished to talk to him." Tobin looked very calm, very smug.

"And?"

"You should be careful what you wish for," Tobin said. He raised his hand, and I watched in horror as a half dozen Queens-guards broached the hill with weapons in hand.

Jericho swore, his silver gun out and now pointed at Tobin. "What the hell are you doing?"

"Giving you a chance to talk to Lazos, as per my end of our deal."

"I'm going to kill you."

"No, you're not," Tobin said evenly. "If you shoot, you will die and so will your pretty little girlfriend here. You won't see Lazos and Valery will be pissed, which is never a good thing for anyone. I'm giving you what you asked for. Now drop your weapon."

This wasn't happening.

"Jericho . . ." I whispered, panic clawing at my throat.

Part of me wanted to throw my arms up in surrender and beg for assistance, revealing who I was. I was Josslyn Drake, daughter of the former prime minister and ward of the current one. A dear friend of Queen Isadora who would have to, *have to*, think twice about blaming me for this unfortunate situation. None of this was my fault!

But I didn't say any of that.

The growing fear of what would happen to me if my truth was revealed now shadowed every word I spoke, every move

I made. Two days ago, I never would have questioned Queen Isadora. But today, I overflowed with doubt.

"You're going to regret this, Tobin," Jericho said as he placed his gun on the ground and kicked it forward.

Tobin picked it up and inspected it. "Illegal possession of this military-grade weapon alone gives me the right to execute you, here and now."

I swallowed down a whimper of panic.

Tobin gestured toward Jericho with the tip of the gun. "Now the coat."

Jericho hesitated. "But it's my favorite."

"And now it's *my* favorite," Tobin growled. When Jericho didn't immediately shed the coat, Tobin pointed the gun at me, and I went cold inside. "Give it to me it *now*."

By the look in Tobin's hard eyes, I knew he wouldn't hesitate to pull the trigger.

"*Now*, Nox," Tobin said.

Jericho grudgingly shrugged the leather coat off his shoulders and let it puddle to the ground. "Did I mention that you're going to regret this? Valery is going to eviscerate you. Slowly. With a toothpick."

"Really? I'd think Val would be angrier that one of her minions got himself into a situation like this in the first place. She doesn't suffer fools; you know that. And she most certainly doesn't keep them on her payroll."

"I'm special," Jericho said.

"Keep telling yourself that. It might help." Tobin's gaze grew thoughtful. "Tell me something, Nox, and maybe I'll change my mind about this . . ."

My heart lifted and I watched them closely.

"What?" Jericho prompted.

Tobin leaned closer. "There's a rumor that Valery is an immortal goddess; that's why she's so damn powerful. Is it true? The queen's obsessed with that witch. Some inside information like this would get me a promotion."

Jericho held Tobin's curious gaze for a moment, then chuckled. "I thought you were too old to believe in fairy tales, Tobin. Do you sleep with a cute stuffed bear, too?"

Tobin scowled. "We're done here."

Jericho shook his head. "It doesn't have to go like this."

"Doesn't it? Let me refresh your memory. A mission, six months ago. I pushed back when you asked for help, since it could have exposed me as a traitor. You complained to Valery about me." Tobin held up his right hand, encased in a black glove. "She cut off my hand."

He pulled off the glove to reveal a metal prosthesis.

I inhaled sharply.

"Didn't know that," Jericho said flatly. "Where should I send the sympathy card?"

I glared at him. "You making this worse."

He shook his head. "It can't get worse than this."

"Oh, but it can." Tobin's thin smile remained throughout this exchange. It chilled me to my core. "Anyway, you asked me for a favor today, and you paid well for it. You're welcome to go and talk with Lazos. I'll even open the door for you."

We were marched down to the barrier itself, to where a door slid open in the silvery surface. The realization of what was about to happen weakened my knees.

"I'll escape," Jericho said darkly.

"No, you won't."

Tobin raised his gun and pulled the trigger. Jericho staggered back, his expression filled with shock, his hand clamping over his chest. Blood oozed through his fingers.

Tobin smiled. "Nice doing business with you."

With that, Jericho and I were shoved through the doorway and into the Queen's Keep.

SEVEN

The door slid shut behind us, locking with a metallic, bone-chilling click.

Jericho dropped to his knees, his face paling in an instant.

"Really should have expected that," he managed.

No, no, no. No!

The sight of someone right in front of me. Shot. Bleeding. My vision darkened at the edges as a wave of panic crashed over me.

I grabbed his arm, trembling now. "What do we do? Oh my god, are you going to die?"

"Probably someday very soon," he mumbled. "But I can't die today. Damn it. That son of a bitch, I'm going to kill him for this. I need . . ." He drew in a ragged breath. "I need—"

"You need help. A doctor . . . a nurse!" The Blackheart was struggling to get to his feet, and I tried to assist him. "There's got to be someone in here who can help you."

This was a walled prison, filled with prisoners of all sorts of backgrounds. I cursed myself for not learning more than the absolute basics about the Queen's Keep. Had I known ahead of time that I was going to be tossed in here like a discarded apple peel, I might have studied up.

However, I was going to go ahead and assume that they had to be able to treat injuries here. We just needed to find someone who could help. I scanned our immediate surroundings to register that we were in a clearing. A hundred feet of dirt and rock, leading to a thick forest.

"Asshole would have gone for a head shot if he really wanted me dead," Jericho gritted out.

My heart lifted despite the horrific imagery that presented. "So you're going to be all right?"

"Not saying that." He grimaced. "I'm bleeding bad. Check my back for an exit wound."

I didn't resist. There was no time to resist any of this.

I yanked up his black T-shirt to look at his back, grimacing when I saw the bloody wound. "Yes, there's an exit wound."

"Good," he muttered.

"That's good?"

"It means the bullet's not still in me. Damn it, it was a mistake to go to Tobin. Huge. I know he hates me."

"Does anyone *not* hate you?" I asked.

"Great question, Drake. Not helpful at the moment, but really great."

"You did what you thought you had to do to get what we needed," I said. "And guess what? We've now got the chance to find Vander Lazos in here and talk to him."

"Cue the celebration."

A slick layer of Jericho's blood now coated my hands, and I

absently wiped them on my blue silk shirt. "Just don't die yet. Later, I don't care. But not until we find the warlock."

"Your bedside manner leaves a lot to be desired." His face tensed. "I need your scarf."

I hesitated only a moment before I untied my scarf and handed it to him, and then watched as he wrapped it around his chest, tying it in a snug knot, grimacing as he did so.

"This hurts like a bitch," he bit out. "Get moving."

Even now, he was barking orders at me. But I wasn't going to argue this time.

Shoving all distracting memories of the last time I saw my father, who'd had a very similar injury, out of my mind, I started across the clearing after Jericho. To his credit, or perhaps simply because of male pride even when dealing with a bullet wound to the chest, he didn't lean on me for support.

I'd never really tried to picture what the Keep looked like on the inside. Mostly, I supposed, because I never imagined in a million years I'd ever be here. First impression of it after we left the entry clearing? There were a lot of trees.

Sure, there had been plenty of trees on the walk here, but they had been growing sparsely, not side by side. I'd never seen anything like this. The trees in Ironport's wealthier communities were more manicured and strategically placed, not this wild, random mixture of tall, short, leafy, and pointy.

Jericho now walked slower than I did, his hand pressed to his wound, so I took the lead, following a narrow path that cut through the forest.

Paths always led somewhere.

Birds chirped and squawked loudly, as if protesting our arrival.

Something alarming suddenly occurred to me. "Tobin took your coat. Does that means he has the box now?"

Jericho answered this with a pained grunt that I took as an affirmative.

It wasn't the answer I wanted. "I only ask because I'm a bit busy worrying about everything else at the moment, and there's not that much room left."

"He has the box, Drake. As well as my phone, my wallet, and about five knives of various sizes. I loved that damn coat."

I sent a glance over my shoulder at him. His dark hair fell onto his forehead, covering his eyes. He studied the ground as he trudged along. I couldn't help but notice with a sharp twinge of concern that he was leaving a spotted trail of his blood on the dirt path.

"What does that mean for us?" I prompted when I found my voice again. "Don't we need the box?"

Jericho shook his head. "It was only a container. We could suck the memory magic out of you and put it in a tin can, if necessary. Well, not we. *Lazos*. And before you ask, I don't know what happens next, if he can't do it. Especially now that we're in here."

Lord Zarek Banyon's memories were swirling around inside me and sometimes bubbling to the surface, forcing me to have insight into that monster's history. And there was nothing I could personally do to stop it.

I hated feeling so powerless. I hated every minute of it.

I didn't understand why I couldn't *feel* the magic corrupting me. If I didn't know I had this magic inside me, if I hadn't seen my golden eyes, I wouldn't be able to sense it at all. But I had gotten a nosebleed after both of the echoes I'd experienced so far. That was a sign of the darkness at work, devouring me from the inside out.

The thought made me shudder.

While I walked along the dim, twisting path through the thick trees, I busied myself by trying to remember everything I knew about the Queen's Keep, wishing I'd paid more attention to any mentions of it in my history classes.

I knew only that it had started as an experiment by Queen Isadora's father, King Dannis, just before his death thirty years ago. He'd been trying to find a solution to the over-crowded prisons across the Empire. Too many prisoners and not nearly enough guards. So the king commissioned this walled community—three miles wide by three miles deep—because it was much more cost-efficient than a stone-and-mortar construction.

Here the prisoners had access to farming, both livestock and crops. It was a self-sustaining entity where everyone would play a part in making a better life for themselves and their neighbors. No technology, no phones, no access to outside communication. It would be, King Dannis said, like taking a step back to a simpler time, away from the temptations that had caused these prisoners to turn to lives of crime in the first place.

And that, pretty much, was all I knew about my current location.

"How do we get out of here?" I asked aloud, giving voice to another of my current worries on a very long list. "After we talk to Lazos and get him to help us, what's the plan then?"

Jericho didn't answer me.

I stopped walking and looked back to see that he'd stopped twenty paces ago and fallen to his knees. Blood pooled at his side.

He raised his pained gaze to mine. "Sorry, Drake. Not feeling so hot at the moment."

I ran to him, my heart pounding. "You need to get up."

His black eyes were glazed, unfocused. "Can't."

"No, Jericho." I grabbed his shoulders and shook him. "Don't even think about checking out on me. You're supposed to protect me. Viktor said so!"

That earned the curve of a pained smile. "My little brother's good, you know. Born good, through and through, not like me. Tell him I'm sorry, okay? Tell him I'm sorry for everything that happened between us. It was my fault; it always was."

His eyes rolled to the back of his head.

"No, stay with me." I grabbed hold of his shoulders and shook him. "Get on your feet, or I'm going to knee you in the balls again. Seriously."

But he didn't. Instead, he slumped forward and I caught him.

He had to outweigh me by at least eighty pounds. I wasn't going to be able to pick him up and carry him anywhere.

Just then, I heard a rustle through the trees. My gaze snapped to my right, where three people were emerging through the foliage. The leader was a girl who looked to be in her early twenties. Tall, with dark brown skin and a mass of black curly hair. A scowl on her lips.

A big-ass knife in her hand.

"Problem here?" she asked.

I swallowed back my surge of fear and lifted my chin. "You could say so. Who the hell are you?"

"We're the Keep's welcoming committee." She smiled thinly, then raised a brow. "What happened to your friend?"

"A Queensguard shot him," I said.

"Is he dead yet?"

I cringed at the flat question but looked at Jericho, who was most definitely unconscious. My blood turned to ice. I pressed my fingers against his throat, relieved to feel a slow pulse.

"Not yet. But he's lost a lot of blood." I shot a look at her two companions, both grown men and both large enough to flip cars if the mood struck them. "You two," I said, loudly and commandingly. "Grab him and help me take him somewhere for medical attention."

They collectively took a step forward, but the girl frowned and raised her hand to stop them. "You're not in charge here," she told me.

"He's dying," I snarled.

"And . . . ?"

"And you're going to help him."

"Why would I do that? Why do I care if a newbie drops dead on entry after getting shot by a guard? It's happened before; it'll happen again."

The admission stunned me, but I shook it off.

"I need him alive," I said.

"You're together," she said. It wasn't a question; it was more of an observation.

I knew what she meant and wanted to say no, but I quickly decided it wasn't in my best interest to distance myself from the Blackheart. "Yes. I . . . can't lose him. Not like this, not after all we've been through together. I . . . I love him."

The words tasted bitter on my tongue, but I'd told worse lies in my past. This one, at least, might help somebody.

Mainly me.

She studied me for a moment, and I focused on looking as sincere as I could.

Finally, she sheathed the knife in a leather holder attached to her belt.

I didn't breathe a sigh of relief just yet.

"Names?" she said.

"This is Jericho," I said, and then without hesitation: "And I'm Janie."

"I'm Mika," she said. "This is Otis and Arlo."

"Charmed, I'm sure," I said tightly.

"Nice sunglasses," she said.

I slid them higher up on my nose. "Thanks, they're new. Now how about some help?"

Mika waited another long and unpleasant moment, her expression not shifting from cool curiosity, before she gestured to the men.

They moved forward without argument and hoisted Jericho off the ground.

"Take him to Tamara's cottage," she said.

"Yes, Mika," they said in unison, and started moving through the forest again.

"Come on, then," Mika said to me, her gaze moving over me from head to foot. "Let's see if Tamara can save him."

She turned without another word and started following the men. I hurried to keep up with them.

The dirt path soon turned into a cobblestone one, which widened as the forest cleared, and I could see a group of buildings ahead of me. A squawking sound drew my attention to my left, where there was a fenced-in area that held dozens of pigs and cows, and too many chickens to count.

An old woman with white hair and a pale, lined face, wearing an outfit that looked like it had been stitched together from old rags, crossed in front of us, holding a gigantic basket full of corn husks. She eyed us unpleasantly, her mouth a thin, tight line. She didn't even flinch or react when she saw the unconscious, bleeding Jericho.

"Mika," she said. "I have a bone to pick with you."

"What else is new, Gloria? It'll have to wait. I have business to attend to with some newcomers."

"That's unacceptable. I need to speak with the Overlord."

"He's busy," Mika said tightly as we moved past her.

I glanced over my shoulder to see Gloria's brows were drawn together, outrage in her gaze.

"What's her problem?" I asked.

"What isn't her problem," Mika muttered. "She's always whining about something around here."

"Who's the Overlord?"

"Consider him your king here," Mika replied.

I scoffed. "There's a king of a prison?"

"Oh, yes. Don't worry, you'll learn respect soon enough. Keepers stay healthier that way, newbies and veterans alike."

"Keepers?" I repeated. "Is that the clever little name you have for the prisoners in here?"

"It sure is." She eyed me. "You've got a lot to learn, Janie."

My knee-jerk reaction was to snap back something unpleasant and insulting, but I held my tongue. I was off to a rough start, but I knew I had to try to be nice. I had to be charming, even with uncharming people. That's how I always got what I wanted, making friends wherever I could. I didn't have the luxury of making enemies right now.

"Mika, have you heard of a man named Vander Lazos?" I asked as sweetly as possible as we continued through the small town, dotted with buildings no more than fifteen feet wide. On my left, we passed a larger building constructed of stone and long wooden logs. "I need to find him immediately."

"No, what you need to do is be patient," Mika replied "And not make demands the very first day you arrive here. Got it?"

I bit back a sharp comeback before it escaped, and forced a smile. "Of course. My apologies."

I watched with concern as the men took Jericho into a small wooden cottage with a thatched roof.

"Let's see what can be done for your boyfriend," Mika said.

She pushed through the front door. I followed, and I could tell immediately that there was no electricity here, the darkness even more profound because of the sunglasses I would not be removing anytime soon. The only light inside came through a tiny window and several lit lanterns on tables around a small bed. The men had put Jericho on that bed, and his blood had already soaked into the wool blanket.

A fresh well of concern rose inside me, and I watched him carefully for any sign he was conscious, but his eyes remained shut. His chest hitched as if each breath was a struggle. How odd it was to watch someone who'd seemed so intimidating, so strong, so utterly indestructible until now, fight for life itself.

Was he going to die? He was the only person I knew in here, and it would be the last place anyone would think I'd end up all on my own.

A woman entered the cottage, her cheeks flushed. She had curly red hair and green eyes that widened as she scanned the group of us.

"Mika, what are you —?" Her gaze fell on Jericho and she gasped.

"Got a brand new patient for you," Mika said. "Shot by a Queensguard just before entry. Doesn't look good."

A shiver went down my spine at the emotionless way she said it.

Tamara sat on the edge of the bed and placed her tanned hand on his forehead. "Give me your knife," she said, gesturing to Mika.

I was sure Mika would refuse, but she pulled the weapon from its sheath and handed it over. Without hesitation, Tamara cut open Jericho's shirt and pulled the scarf away to bare his bloody chest, and I winced at the sight of it.

"The . . . the bullet's not still in him," I offered weakly, the sight of so much blood making me light-headed.

"Good," Tamara replied. "Otis, help me get his shirt off completely."

The man did as she asked, tossing the bloody garment into a nearby wooden bucket.

"He needs a doctor," I asked, my throat strained.

"That's exactly what I am," she said. "Or *was*, anyway. Now, quiet. I need to concentrate."

She held her hands over his chest, moving up and down without touching him, only an inch away. When she got to his abdomen, she paused.

"I sense magic inside of him," she said. "Powerful magic."

I stifled a gasp. "You can sense that?"

"I can," she said.

Jericho didn't tell me he had any magic. I think I'd remember something like that. But I suddenly remembered what he'd said in the car . . . about how this magic wouldn't change me like I expected it would. That I was still me.

Trust me, I should know, he'd said.

Oh my god.

"What kind of magic is it?" Mika asked.

Tamara frowned. "I'm . . . actually not sure yet. It's different from anything I've sensed before."

I eyed them both, confused. They didn't seem nearly shocked or frightened enough. They even made this sound like a regular occurrence—sensing magic in people.

Tamara took Jericho's bare arm in her hands. "Look at this."

In the dim light of the room, something glowed faintly on Jericho's forearm, so faint I almost doubted my eyes. It was as if someone had etched symbols on his skin and those symbols now glowed with an inner light.

"What the hell is going on?" I whispered, my chest tight.

Tamara gasped and drew her hand back from Jericho as if it had been plunged in ice-cold water. "This isn't simple elementia. It's so much darker than that."

"What does that mean?" Mika asked.

I wanted to know, too. It sounded like this magic was even worse than the regular kind, which didn't seem possible.

"I—I'm not sure," Tamara said, hugging her arms around her as if trying to warm herself up.

I felt Mika staring at me, and I turned to face her.

"Your boyfriend seems to be chock-full of unidentifiable dark magic," she said. "And you don't know anything about it?"

I blinked. "I don't. I swear I don't."

"Who are you two? What did you do to get in here? Magic like this gets you killed, not thrown in the Keep."

"Like I said," I began tightly. "I'm Janie. That's Jericho."

She glared at me for another moment. "Tamara, can you help him?"

"I'm certainly going to try," Tamara replied. She held her hands, which now trembled, over the wound itself, and they began to glow with golden light.

Instinctively, I recoiled, scrambling backward so fast I hit the wall hard.

"Oh my god," I managed. "You're a witch." That explained

her attitude, the way she treated magic like something normal instead of deadly, soul-sucking evil.

"Please don't be afraid," Tamara said with a pained expression. "My elementia is pure earth magic, and I swear I've only ever used it to help others."

She was the first witch I'd ever met. The first witch I'd ever been in the same room as. I couldn't breathe.

"Why are you in the Queen's Keep?" I forced out the question.

"Because I healed the wrong patient this way at the hospital I worked for," she said. "And she reported me."

That didn't make any sense at all. "Wait. You . . . saved her. With your magic.

"That's right," Tamara said tightly. "Now, please, I need to concentrate just a moment longer, or it may be too late to help your friend."

The glow from her hands intensified, and Jericho gasped and arched off the bed as if experiencing intense, shattering pain. Now I instinctively took a step forward, my hands fisted, ready to pull this witch off him before she did any more damage.

But then it was all over.

Tamara took a damp washcloth and wiped off Jericho's chest to show that the wound was nothing more than a reddish mark now.

I gaped. Literally gaped at this, mouth open, eyes bugging out. I'd never seen anything more astonishing in my entire life.

Jericho inhaled again, raggedly, and slowly opened his eyes.

He surveyed the room, face by face, until he came to mine. Our gazes locked.

The knee-weakening relief I felt, knowing that he was going to survive, surprised me. I'd fully believed he was mere moments from death and was going to leave me here all alone to try to fix this by myself. But he was alive. He was going to recover. And all because this witch used her magic to heal him.

But that didn't make sense.

Magic didn't heal. Evil couldn't heal. It could only hurt. It caused pain; it didn't relieve it.

Yet I'd just witnessed exactly that. Tamara had healed Jericho with only her magic. *Elementia*, she'd called it. It was the same unfamiliar word that Rush had used.

But all magic was evil, dark, and forbidden. All magic, with no exceptions.

"Drake . . ." Jericho whispered, his brows drawing together.

I stumbled back a step as the walls of the small room felt like they were closing in all around me.

I needed air. I needed time. I needed this to all be an epic nightmare I could still wake up from, but unfortunately I wasn't that delusional. Too bad.

Without another word, I turned and left the cottage.

EIGHT

Denial was a wonderful thing.

It had served me very well in the past. Even the therapist I saw after my father died commented on my amazing ability to compartmentalize—just shove my problems into separate rooms and lock the door on them.

I saw my ability to ignore problems as an asset. The therapist saw it as something I needed to "work on" in order to be "happy and fulfilled."

Whatever.

To me, it made perfect sense to not dwell on thoughts or problems that caused somebody pain.

Especially if that somebody was me.

So I was going to ignore everything I'd just seen, everything I'd just learned about Jericho and about the way prisoners in this place were so keen on using evil, soul-corrupting magic. And about how I felt when I learned Jericho would survive.

Mika followed me out of Tamara's cottage. I braced myself for whatever she planned to say to me—about the mysterious dark magic Tamara sensed inside Jericho, about who we were and where we'd come from.

But she didn't ask any of this.

"Follow me," she said instead.

And I followed her to another cottage a short walk away. If anything, it was even smaller than Tamara's.

"Not to your liking?" Mika observed my automatic sour look, which I tried to shield immediately. "Too bad, since this is where you and your boyfriend will be living now."

"It's great, really," I said, forcing a tight smile. "Thanks so much. Now, I know you said you didn't want questions today, but I'm hoping that—"

She cut me off. "You can go to the lodge for food. Newbies are given a few days to settle in before we'll put you to work, so take the time to accept where you are and try to make the best of it."

My head spun as I attempted to situate myself and not get completely overwhelmed. "All right. Where can I get new clothes? I've been wearing this outfit for almost a day and . . . well, there's some bloodstains on it."

Blood on my clothes made me think of the Gala. My father in my arms . . .

"There's a small lake a half mile to the north and a river nearby where we get fresh water. Those are two places where we wash clothes and bathe. A good scrubbing should get any fresh stains out of what you're wearing. You'll also be able to spot the outhouses on your way. Word to the wise, newbies usually get the job to clean them twice a day." At my look of chagrin: "No luxury fashion boutiques here, sorry. And no showers or spa facilities. Feel free to complain to the management."

Fine.

I could deal with this because I had to.

"Where can I find Vander Lazos?" I asked.

But Mika was already walking away from me without a backward glance. I watched her with disbelief.

And I thought my fake friends back in the real world were frustrating.

Luckily, Mika wasn't the only one here. The Keep was a fully functioning and self-contained community with lots of people who might have the answers I needed. I could talk to anyone.

That was what I did best: talk. I would rely on my greatest skill to get what I wanted. It worked outside the Keep. Why wouldn't it work inside the Keep?

I pushed open the door of my little shack—because, let's face it, calling it a "cottage" was far too generous—and took a good look inside, sliding my sunglasses up to the top of my head.

Just like Tamara's, it was only one room. The floor was wooden slats that looked old and worn. The shack had a thatched roof that looked positively archaic compared with anything seen in the prime minister's residence—or any modern dwelling, really.

A small window, no curtains or blinds.

A small table with only one rickety-looking wooden chair.

A small wood-burning stove.

And one small bed.

I stared at the bed for a whole minute, my mind blanking, then shook it off.

The Blackheart would have to get used to sleeping on the floor. Or in the woods. Or somewhere else that wasn't here.

I mean, I was relieved he was still breathing, but the sleeping arrangements were nonnegotiable.

On the small table was a half-melted candle with a box of matches next to it. The matches felt positively luxurious to me. I struck one and lit the candle, taking some small comfort in its flickering glow, allowing myself a moment to let it hypnotize me and take me away from this disaster my life had become literally overnight.

I would be all right. I would survive this and come out stronger in the end.

Why? Because I was Josslyn Drake, that's why. And I was a winner.

"I'm a winner," I told the candle.

The candle had nothing to add to the conversation.

The magical golden smoke that quickly swirled into the periphery of my vision took me so much by surprise that I wasn't even able to brace myself or fight against it.

Suddenly I wasn't there in my tiny cottage, staring at a flickering candle.

I was in the middle of a blazing fire, just like the first time, the first echo I'd experienced in the boutique. A cacophony of sound and chaos pressed in all around me.

Heart pounding, I spun on my heel until I spotted Banyon

standing there, looking as worn and bruised as he had in both my previous visions. In this one, however, he also looked enraged.

He stood there, fists clenched, fire swirling around his ankles, as he watched the people running away from burning buildings. A mix of hate and madness blazed in his eyes.

I inhaled sharply as I realized where this was. The tall glittering palace rose up before me, flames rising from its roof and turrets. I hadn't seen it in the previous visions.

It was the queen's palace. And I instinctively knew that this was the night that Banyon escaped from his cell while awaiting trial, using his evil magic to burn everything in his path, sixteen years ago. Dozens of people had been killed, including Prince Elian, and it had taken years to restore the palace city to its former glory.

Fresh hatred for my father's murderer rose up inside me and spilled forth.

"You're a monster!" I screamed at him.

He didn't look at me. He didn't hear me, because I wasn't really here. I couldn't feel the heat of the fire, like I had in Rush's club. I was only a ghost walking through the past.

Forced to walk through Banyon's memory of this night.

I heard something—the cry of a baby.

Banyon's head whipped in that direction, and he frowned into the smoke and flames as if seeking the source of the sound.

He moved in the direction of the crying baby, and I clawed at him, trying to stop him from whatever he planned to do next, but my hands went through him as if I were nothing more than smoke. And then smoke was all there was. Golden smoke, which swirled in and cleared out in a matter of moments, revealing the interior of the small cottage once again.

"Oh god," I whispered, the nightmare of Banyon and the fire and all the people who'd perished slicing through my brain like razor blades.

I ran my hand under my nose to wipe away the blood.

Now desperate to breathe clean air, I blew out the candle and burst out of the dark cottage, back into the sunlight, shoving my sunglasses back on my face.

Lord Banyon had escaped from the palace, where he'd been held awaiting trial for his crimes. That was the night Prince Elian had perished, leaving the queen without an heir but determined to find the warlock and bring his evil to an end once and for all.

Yet sixteen years had gone by, and he was still free.

Witnessing the destruction he caused had shaken me. I couldn't believe somebody could be that evil. And the memory I'd seen when I'd touched Commander Norris still bothered me, too. Banyon, weak and tortured, refusing to help with some request made by the queen herself.

What had she wanted him to do? Had she wanted to offer him some mercy, like Lazos? Had she asked for him to surrender?

It didn't matter. He'd said no. Definitively. And I'd seen the horror of what happened next.

I needed these echoes out of me. I didn't give a crap if they went into another box or container or if they were simply released into the air itself to vanish forever. I wouldn't continue to be a vessel for the memories of a monster. I'd rather die first. And I sure as hell wouldn't say something like that if I didn't mean it.

On the dirt road that wound through the town, I saw many Keepers going about their daily business. Carrying vegetables to the lodge, chopping wood, and hauling buckets of water. One of these prisoners had to have answers that could help me.

But then I saw Tamara. The witch had changed out of her bloody clothes into a white cotton dress. It actually wasn't horribly unfashionable, and it also proved to me that Mika had been lying about not having any new clothes available in town. I didn't need a full-on boutique. Any talented and willing seamstress would be more than enough for me. But that was very low on my list of problems at the moment, to say the least.

I hesitated only a moment before I made a beeline directly toward her.

"How is Jericho?" I asked.

"Recovering," she said, and something tight eased inside me. "He'll need plenty of rest for the remainder of today. Otis and Arlo are taking him to your cottage."

I nodded. "Thank you."

"You're welcome." She said it with the kind of sincerity that some people naturally had. The kind of sincerity where you knew that they meant what they said and said what they meant.

People like that were few and far between. I sure wasn't one of them.

"Janie," Tamara said tentatively. "I know you're unnerved

by what you witnessed, but please know that I mean no harm with my magic. Not to you or to anyone else."

I tensed and searched her face, looking for some sign of deception, but there was nothing there. "That literally goes against everything I've ever believed."

"I'm well aware of that."

"Magic is evil," I said. The three words had been repeating over and over again in my head. I'd said this aloud so many times over the last day that my throat was raw.

I kept waiting for someone to agree with me.

"Elementia is neutral," she said gently. "The magic I have— that most witches or warlocks possess—draws from the natural elements all around us. Air, earth, water, fire. Elemental magic. It's as pure as the air we breathe or the earth we stand upon."

I had an image of Banyon standing among the flames. "Or the fire that burns down a city and everyone in it? Like Lord Banyon did?"

She grimaced. "A bolt of lightning can turn a forest to ash and burn any creature trapped within. It's still natural."

"Lord Banyon is evil," I bit out.

"Perhaps he is," she allowed. "But elementia isn't. It's as easy as that."

I shook my head. I might not have paid much attention in history class, but I knew enough to know that witches and warlocks were responsible for the greatest atrocities in human history. "This isn't easy," I told her. "None of this is easy."

"You're right; it's not. Especially not to someone who has never had a chance to expand her knowledge on the subject. It's shameful that the queen continues to perpetuate this horrific lie her ancestors began—a lie that's harmed far more people than it's helped."

I glared at her, ready to defend Her Majesty, but I bit my tongue so hard I nearly drew blood.

I couldn't make enemies here. I desperately needed friends. Even if those friends believed the exact opposite of what I did.

"It's true," I allowed, summoning whatever charm I had left back into my tone. "There isn't much information about magic, is there? Jericho told me about all the books being burned and how digital information is easier to change than ink on a page."

"That young man is wise beyond his years," she said. "So much history on the subject of elementia has been destroyed or altered. But try to keep your mind open, Janie. What I did in there to save your friend? I swear that that magic didn't come from a dark place. You must be able to see that for yourself."

I had to admit, that much seemed to make sense, but even thinking about it felt sticky, like walking through a room full of taffy.

"What about the magic you sensed inside Jericho?" I asked as evenly as I could. "You said that was dark. And those symbols—whatever they were—on his arm. I don't understand."

"That . . . was different," she said, her brows drawing together. "How can I explain this when I barely understand it myself? There is elementia, pure and natural and ever present like an invisible flowing river, and then there is the magic that lurks in the shadows of what is known, what is accessible to most witches or warlocks. The kind of magic only spoken about in legends, passed from generation to generation."

"What kind of legends?" I asked, my throat tight. Every instinct I had wanted me to turn away from this, but I forced myself to stand my ground. I had to know more.

Tamara's face paled and she seemed hesitant, as if she didn't want to say another word. As if that would stop me.

I grabbed her hand to get her attention again.

"Should I be afraid of Jericho?" I asked, breathless.

She frowned down at my hand in hers, then her gaze moved up to my face. To my sunglasses.

"I sense magic within you, too," she said with surprise, and I let go of her immediately. "But yours . . . it's pure elementia. Why in the world are you in the Queen's Keep, Janie?"

She sensed the memory magic, just like that. So easily. It unnerved me even more. "It's complicated."

"I'm sure it is."

"I don't want to talk about me," I asked. "I want to talk about Jericho. What magic does he have in him? Please, I need to know."

"The darkest magic there is." Tamara took a breath. "Death magic."

I stared at her, speechless for a moment as I struggled to breathe.

"What does that mean?" I whispered.

"I honestly don't know, since it's far outside my expertise," she replied. "All I know about your friend is that he's alive and he's recovering from nearly dying from a Queensguard's bullet that pierced his chest. Now, if you'll excuse me, I need to go check on him."

I watched her walk away and then stood there, stunned, her words echoing in my ears.

The darkest magic there is. Death magic.

For someone who'd always believed *all* magic was dark and evil, something to be avoided at all costs, to now learn there might be something even worse . . .

I mean, forget avoiding it. I'd never even considered the possibility I'd come this close to it. I hadn't for seventeen years. All these years, I'd only heard it mentioned on the newsfeeds and in the queen's speeches, like some sort of deadly plague that threatened to wipe out humanity if it wasn't contained.

Magic had always been the monster hiding under my bed that I feared would grab my ankle with its clawed hand if it slipped out from beneath the sheets. But I never actually saw that monster since I'd always stayed tightly tucked in until morning.

It was a metaphor, of course. I didn't believe there was a monster under my bed.

Well, not anymore.

But *death magic*. In *Jericho*. Tamara had sensed it immediately, but I sure hadn't. Not even for a moment.

The sound of crickets chirping brought me back from my daze, and I nervously scanned my surroundings. Despite all the world-shattering and painfully confusing information I'd gathered so far today, I couldn't help but notice my stomach had started growling. I was starving.

I headed to the lodge, the largest building in town. It was constructed of long logs of wood. Inside, roughly hewn tables stretched from one wall to the other, each with wooden benches. On the wall opposite the entryway was a large, blazing fireplace.

Mika had said to come here for food. A server behind a counter watched my approach, and before I even asked for anything, she slid a bowl of soup and a package of crackers toward me.

I stared at the crackers with surprise.

"Leave your bowl on the table when you're done, and toss the wrapper in the bin near the exit," she told me. "Welcome to the Keep."

"Thanks," I managed. Then I turned toward the tables and immediately saw another face I recognized. It was the old woman who'd wanted Mika's attention when we'd first arrived. I thought her name was Gloria.

She sat at a table, alone, with a wooden goblet in front of her. She seemed very interested in whatever was inside the goblet, staring down into the depths of it.

I took a seat across from her, and she looked up at me with surprise.

"Hi," I said, pushing a smile onto my face. "I'm Janie. I'm new here and hoping to make some friends."

Yes, friends who could fill in a whole bunch of blanks for me, since information was going to be my weapon to help me stop feeling so utterly ignorant about how to save my own damn life.

Gloria cocked her head. "If you say so."

I tore open my package of crackers and took a small, dry, and salty bite before I ate a spoonful of the soup.

"What is this?" I asked. "Chicken noodle?"

"Rats and worms," Gloria replied.

I spat out the mouthful of soup and stared at her with disgust. "What?"

She cackled. "Just kidding. But it's not chicken. We don't have nearly enough livestock to feed all these hungry fools meat every day. We get a large delivery of supplies monthly, with meat substitutes that taste like chicken. That is, if you've got a good enough imagination."

I took this in as I ate the rest of my not-rats-and-worms soup, which wasn't very good, but wasn't terrible, either. "How long have you been here, Gloria?"

"Long enough." She peered at me. "Why are you wearing sunglasses inside?"

"Because I want to," I replied firmly.

"Fair enough."

I put down my spoon and regarded Gloria very seriously. "I'm looking for someone named Vander Lazos. Do you know where I can find him?"

"No idea," she replied.

I deflated. "He's supposed to be in here. He's been here for, like, ten years."

She shook her head. "I don't know anyone by that name."

"Really?"

"Really. Anything else you want to know?"

My stomach started to churn, and I pushed the bowl of soup back from me. Maybe he went by another name. "How do I escape from this place?"

Gloria stared at me for a moment before she cackled again. "Is that what you want? Young people, so full of strange ideas."

"It's not strange. This is a prison; why wouldn't I want to escape?"

"It's risky. A few months ago, a young man managed to scale the wall but was shot down when he reached the top. I wouldn't wish a death like that on anyone. Such a waste."

I cringed at the thought of it, since it reminded me of what that traitorous Queensguard had done to Jericho. "But there must have been others who've found a way out."

"Of course. There have been twelve Keepers who've escaped over the last few years, although don't ask me how they managed it. It's a mystery to me." She studied me for a moment. "You know, you remind me of someone, Janie."

While encouraged by the confirmation that escape was possible, I froze at the sudden change of subject, certain she was about to identify me. I didn't want anyone to know who I really was if I could help it. I'd decided to temporarily become this Janie person, the girl most likely to get thrown into prisons with her criminal boyfriend.

"Who?" I asked tentatively.

"Mika. She was full of plans of escape when she first arrived, too. But look at her, a year later, still here, so I suppose she hasn't figured out the trick yet. By the way, don't trust her." She leaned forward and lowered her voice. "She's a spy."

"A spy?" I repeated.

Gloria nodded. "For the Overlord."

"And who is the Overlord?" I asked. "Mika says he's the king here."

"He is. And a king has his spies with their listening ears and watching eyes. And whispering mouths. Et cetera. Et cetera." She took a sip of whatever was in her goblet. The sharp scent of alcohol smacked me right in the face.

"What is that?" I asked.

She ran her fingertip along the lip of the goblet. "This is my sole salvation in a world that has turned upside down."

Well, that explained how jumpy her train of thought was. Not that I was going to judge. It sure didn't smell like wine poured from crystal bottles at fancy galas. But, after the day I'd had, I really didn't care.

"I think I may need some of that," I said with growing enthusiasm.

Gloria signaled to a server across the room, who brought over another goblet.

"Don't think about it; just drink it," she suggested.

I raised the goblet. "Bottoms up."

And I took a full mouthful of the beverage before immediately spitting it back out, shuddering. "That is disgusting."

"Yes. Yes, it is," Gloria agreed. "Which is exactly why it earned the nickname pisswater."

I almost gagged. "That's a terrible name."

"It wasn't my idea."

"Do you get used to the taste?"

She smiled knowingly. "Never. But you'll come to appreciate the effects it has on you in the years to come."

The very thought turned my stomach. "I'm not going to be here for years."

Her smile faded and her gaze grew faraway. "That's very possible, too."

I knew I needed to keep my questions fairly neutral and friendly, especially now that it was clear to me that this woman wasn't exactly sober. Gloria might be a good source of information in the future, but tonight I'd pace myself until I got my footing. "How many prisoners are in the Keep?"

She drained her goblet. "No idea whatsoever. Quite a few."

"It's weird. I kind of expected to see children around," I admitted.

Gloria looked at me as if I'd just grown another head. "Children? In the Keep?"

I spread my hands. "I mean, men and women. Confined. Together. You know. Things happen, I'm sure."

"Oh, Janie." She leaned across the table, and I heard the unmistakable slur to her words that confirmed this had not been her first goblet of the day. "Things most certainly do happen. But no children ever result from it."

"Why not?"

"Because Her Majesty, the high and mighty Queen Isadora, ruler of the great Empire of Regara, has put something in our food supplies that prevents any pregnancies. Young ladies such as yourself have their monthly visits halted indefinitely. I'm well past that nonsense myself, thankfully. So messy and unnecessary, really."

Birth control in the food supplies.

It made sense, of course, for population control, but something about it didn't sit right with me.

"Someone is watching you," Gloria said.

It took me a moment to realize what she meant. I turned in my seat and scanned the room, realizing only now that Mika sat a couple of tables away, her eyes narrowed. She gestured for me to join her.

"If you'll excuse me," I said to Gloria. "It's been a pleasure."

But the old woman wasn't looking at me anymore; she was signaling for her goblet to be refilled. I guessed I'd been dismissed.

Rude.

I went to Mika's table.

"Have a seat, Josslyn," she said. "And take off those ridiculous sunglasses."

My heart doubled its pace in an instant. "The name's Janie."

"No, it's not. Now sit down," she said more firmly. "We're going to have a little chat, you and me. Very brief, but very focused."

She knew who I was.

Normally, I'd take it as a compliment. I'd always loved being recognized. But here, and especially after I'd lied about my name, I'd rather remain anonymous.

Uneasy now that I'd been exposed so quickly, I took a seat. I couldn't let her think she had the upper hand. "If you think you're going to intimidate me, think again."

"You're pretty ballsy. Do you know what would happen to you if everyone here found out you're the daughter of the prime

minister? They hate him for allowing this hell on earth to continue existing, and I guarantee that you wouldn't live through
the night."

I regarded her with horror, confused for a moment, but then
it occurred to me that she'd been in here more than a year without any access to daily newsfeeds.

"You don't know, do you?" I said.

"Know what?"

"My father was assassinated a year ago." It hurt my throat to
say it out loud. "Shot by someone working for Lord Banyon to
send a message to the queen."

Some of Mika's bluster, her hardness, faded. Only some, but
it was noticeable.

"I despised your father and everything he stood for," Mika
said, frowning. "But I'm sorry for your loss."

I realized I was hugging myself.

"Thank you, I think," I replied, my throat tight.

Mika regarded me for a moment in silence. And then: "Why
are you here and who is Jericho? And before you lie to me, I can
tell he's not your boyfriend and you're not in love with him."

I didn't like Mika, but I couldn't help but admire her bluntness. I'd found most people danced around the edges of topics.
She jumped right into the center of them.

"He's a Blackheart," I said.

"What's a Blackheart?"

It was an excellent question. I was only starting to figure that
out for myself.

"He's a thief who works for a powerful witch who apparently buys and sells magic on the black market, and if anyone gets in her way, she rolls right over them."

That was basically what I'd learned so far. Saying it out loud sounded like complete nonsense, but it didn't make it any less true.

"I like her already," Mika said. "How is it that you, Josslyn Drake, are associated with someone like Jericho? To the point that you're here, right now, in the last place in the world I'd expect someone like you should ever be?"

I considered my options and found them to be greatly lacking.

So I decided to go for the truth for the first time in forever. Slowly, I removed my sunglasses and put them on the table in front of me before looking directly at Mika.

To her credit, she didn't react to my golden eyes with shock or fear. She did, however, raise an eyebrow.

"As you can see," I began, "I got in the way of a box of magic, and now that magic is in me, and I need it out before it destroys my life more than it already has. And I'm told the only one who can do that for me is Vander Lazos. So I'm here to find him and ask him very nicely for his help so I can get back to my normal life."

She blinked. "Interesting."

"Maybe one day I'll share that opinion. But that day sure isn't today."

"What kind of magic is it?" she asked.

Again, I found no solid reason to lie. "Memory magic, which

gives me a random screening every now and then and a nasty nosebleed afterward."

I didn't think it necessary to mention *whose* memories they were. Saying his name once during a conversation was more than enough for me.

Mika studied me carefully, as if trying to determine if I was telling her the truth.

I studied her back. "Who are *you*, anyway? Gloria says you wanted to escape when you first got here. Have you had any luck?"

"I'm still here, aren't I?" she replied dryly. "More than a year now and I have no idea how other prisoners managed to do it. It's not ideal, but I suppose it could be worse. I've made a life for myself here, such as it is. I have a purpose now, which I didn't really have on the outside."

"What purpose? Gloria also says you're this Overlord's spy."

"Gloria has a big mouth," she snapped. "I'm not his spy so much as law enforcement around here. It's given me certain perks around town. Respect, for one."

"Respect? People look at you like they're afraid of you."

"My definition of respect may be different than yours."

I hesitated. I didn't regret telling Mika what I did, since she struck me as someone who could be a very valuable ally. At least, that was my first impression, but it could change at any time. "Are you going to tell anyone who I really am?" I asked.

She considered this. "No. Not yet, anyway."

It was a relief, albeit one with a bit of a time crunch by the sound of it. If I wanted to make friends with these unsavory outcasts of society, I'd rather not have anyone else learn who I really was.

"Thank you," I said. "And are you going to tell me where to find Vander Lazos, or do I have to keep asking anyone else who crosses my path?"

"You'll be seeing him tomorrow," Mika replied.

It was the last thing I expected her to say. "I will?"

"Yes," she said. "Because Vander Lazos *is* the Overlord."

NINE

I thought I'd forgotten to breathe for a moment.

"Vander Lazos, the queen's ex–magic advisor," I said to clarify, even though saying it out loud didn't make it sound any less ludicrous to me. "I mean, that's what I've been told he is. Did you know he's a warlock?"

"I know everything," Mika replied smoothly. "Now, why don't you go back to your cottage and get some rest. You can ask the Overlord the questions you have tomorrow, but I warn you, be respectful if you want any answers."

ᗐᗝᗝᗝᗕ

The sun had nearly set completely as I quickly made my way back to my cottage. I swung the door open to immediately see that Jericho was in bed.

My bed.

The Blackheart regarded me wearily, his dark eyes glittering in the candlelight.

Even though what Tamara had said about Jericho haunted

me, the sight of him hit me with an unexpected and nearly over-whelming wave of relief. I guess I'd honestly thought he was going to die and leave me here all by myself to figure this out.

But he wasn't dead. He was very much alive.

I could only stand there and stare blankly at him for several moments as I felt my eyes well up with hot tears. I turned toward the window before he could see them.

Pull it together, I scolded myself.

"She's returned," Jericho said, breaking the silence. "I thought you might have dug your way out of here already."

"It's on the list of possibilities," I replied quietly.

His formidable height was barely contained in the small bed, the off-white bedsheet tightly molded against his bare chest.

"How are you feeling?" I asked.

"Like hell."

"You nearly died."

He nodded. "I'm getting that impression. You almost suc-ceeded in getting rid of me."

"I'm not done with you yet," I said.

"Noted."

I clasped my hands together, uncertain where to begin. "So. While you've been busy not dying, I've learned a little about our temporary home away from home."

"Such as?"

"Vander Lazos is here, and he's calling himself the Overlord of this place."

Jericho pushed himself up into a sitting position. "Overlord, huh? Anyone who'd call himself that has a very high opinion of himself."

I sat down on the wooden chair, and it made a creaking sound. "I don't care if he has a mountain-sized ego, as long as he can help me. I can't handle this any longer. I experienced another of those echoes. More fire, more pain." I tried not to think about it, but it kept flashing through my mind. "And I didn't tell you this, but at the club when I touched Commander Norris, I saw Banyon tortured. The queen wanted him to do something, but he refused. All the memories seem to be the same time—the day of the fire at the palace city when he escaped, sixteen years ago."

Jericho didn't say anything, but his face had paled.

"What?" I prompted, alarmed now.

"You're sure your echoes have been about that fire?"

I nodded. "Why?"

"That was the night my parents were killed," he said, and I looked at him with shock. "We lived in the palace city—me, my brother, my mother and father. My father was a Queensguard stationed at the palace. Banyon killed him. I was young, so I don't remember much, but I know my father loved his job. Sometimes I think that's why Viktor became a Queensguard himself, even though he was definitely too young to have remembered anything specific about our parents. Maybe it was his destiny or something."

"Oh my god, I'm so sorry," I said. I had no idea that Lord Banyon had been the cause of his parents' death, too. It seemed like we had more in common than I'd thought.

"It was a long time ago," he said.

"Doesn't matter how long ago it was. It's all so horrible."

I didn't see pain etched on his face, just a hard blankness in his black eyes. But I knew he cared. He wanted Lord Banyon dead for it. Someone with vengeance in their heart wasn't totally immune to the raw emotion behind it.

Jericho actively and consciously repressed any emotions that he thought might weaken him. I recognized this in him, since it was also one of my many talents.

"So you've now seen real live magic at work, summoned by a real live witch," Jericho said, and it didn't escape my attention that he'd swiftly changed the subject. "And, surprise, it didn't make the world implode and fall into eternal darkness. Food for thought, Drake?"

"Oh, I've been thinking about it, all right."

"And what have you been thinking?"

"Tamara says it was earth magic. *Elementia*," I said, tasting the word in my mouth and cringing.

"Earth magic is healing magic," he agreed. "Very handy when a bullet makes a quick trip through your chest."

"She told me she sensed death magic in you," I said bluntly, watching him carefully for his reaction, my body tense. "She said it's the darkest magic, like the opposite of elementia. Is that true?"

Jericho didn't reply for a moment.

"Well?" I prompted.

"Does it matter if it's true or not?" he said quietly, his deep voice low.

I suddenly sensed a shift in the small cottage. We'd already been having a conversation about important things. But this was different. This suddenly felt dangerous, as if I'd just crossed a line with Jericho that I hadn't even known was there. As if I'd allowed myself to get too comfortable around him and forgotten what he was.

It was then that I realized this cottage was way too small for the two of us. The Blackheart's presence alone felt like it strained the very edges of the limited space, invading my own. I could hear him breathing, nearly sense his heartbeat, as he watched me. Even from the bed, recovering from a massive injury, he seemed like a predator watching every small move his prey made. Waiting for the perfect time to strike.

I had to remember that Jericho wasn't my friend. He was someone who'd taken down multiple armed guards without breaking a sweat, both at the Gala and at the boutique. Who'd drugged my best friend without a second thought. Who used magic fearlessly and shamelessly and entirely for his own gain. Who'd suggested that if this plan didn't work out, he would take me to his witch boss, who would kill me for the magic currently trapped inside me.

Jericho hadn't killed anyone, I reminded myself.

But it didn't mean he wouldn't. Or couldn't.

No. I refused to be intimidated by him. Or—at least, *show* my intimidation.

"Does it matter that you're chock-full of death magic?" I repeated. "Kind of. Yeah, it definitely does. So I need some information to help me understand."

His lips thinned. "You can't understand this, Drake. I don't even understand it."

"And yet, here I am. Wanting to know more about a subject that I've never wanted any part of before. That's got to count for something, right?"

I felt pinned by his gaze, heavy and searching, filling with dark curiosity with every word I spoke.

"Suddenly interested in magic, are you? Be careful what you ask for. You might get it."

I glared at him. "Don't patronize me."

Jericho sat up and swung his legs to the side of the bed.

I tensed.

But he didn't get up and lurch toward me. He was hunched over and paler than normal. Predator or not, it was still a strange relief to see him vaguely functional after everything he'd been through.

"You wouldn't believe me if I told you the truth," he said.

"Try me. I've had to start believing a whole lot of unbelievable things since yesterday. I need to know why you have death magic in you. Because the very idea of it makes me really uneasy to be around you, to say the least. Since we're currently forced to share this cottage, and I want to sleep as much as I can, despite the vicious nightmares I know I'll be having, I need some information. Now talk."

It looked like he was going to stand up, but had second thoughts. He pressed his hand against his chest, where the wound had been, and lay back down.

"I hate being weak," he said.

"You're not weak," I replied. The very thought of it was laughable. "You're recovering from being shot in the chest and nearly dying. And don't try to change the subject."

"Fine." Jericho hissed out a sigh, not speaking again for a long moment. "Remember how Rush called me a ghost, said I'd come back from the dead?"

"Yes," I said.

"That's because I did. I was dead. And then Valery used the darkest magic that exists in the whole damn universe to bring me back to life, which is why I work for her now. That's the debt I have to pay back to her before I'm free. Death magic, real death magic, is rare as hell, and it doesn't come cheap. Val's the only one I know of who can channel that kind of magic without breaking a sweat. Don't ask me how. She's a mystery, that's for sure."

I tried to make this make sense in my head, but couldn't. Possibilities like this didn't fit into my world, and I wasn't sure I wanted them to.

"What do you mean, you were dead?" I said. "How? When?"

Jericho's expression was haunted. "Two years ago. The Queensgames. Me and my little brother were natural-born fighters, but we'd fallen out by then, hadn't talked in almost a year. Rush bought me a place in the fights, hoping to make a bunch of money in the process and draw a wider and more affluent clientele to his club. Vik—I don't even know how he qualified, other than the fact he'd just turned sixteen, but I wouldn't doubt he could do anything he put his mind to all on his own. We weren't matched together, thank god. He watched my last match, and I remember seeing that pained look on his face at being in the same place as me again. When I spotted him on the sidelines, my attention . . ." He shook his head. "I forgot where I was for a second, and that's all it took."

He touched his bare chest, drawing a line along a barely noticeable three-inch scar. "Sword right to the heart. Impaled all the way through. I don't remember anything except waking up screaming in pain. But I woke up. And Val was there, smiling. Saying she'd chosen me because she liked my moves, that she'd been studying me since the games began, every one of my matches. And that I was going to work for her now."

I listened to him silently, stunned by every word he spoke.

I'd attended those games. I had watched Viktor with great admiration as he was crowned champion.

Other opponents were killed during the matches sometimes. It happened, and it wasn't against the rules.

Blood and death meant more views as the event was broadcast throughout the Empire. And more views meant more advertising revenue.

It was simple math, really.

I'd seen several fighters drop onto the sand, never to get up again, but had always justified it because they'd signed up of their own free will. They knew the risks and they'd wanted in anyway.

No risk, no reward.

"You were badly injured," I said, trying to rationalize it. "And Valery healed you with powerful earth magic, like Tamara's."

"No. I was dead," Jericho said flatly. "And she brought me back to life."

He held out his forearm, where the glowing symbols had been. Now it was just smooth, tanned skin. "When I agreed to work for her in payment for my resurrection, she used this special dagger of hers to literally carve more of her magic into me. She said it was our contract, written in blood."

"Was it elementia?" I asked, still unsure about the strange and unfamiliar word. "Or something else?"

"Something else," he said quietly. "Don't ask me how, but Val's different from other witches. Her magic is deeper, stronger. More powerful. Scary as hell. I guess that's why there are rumors out there that she's a literal goddess. I know you think all magic is evil, and I know you're not just going to wake up tomorrow suddenly thinking differently from what you've always believed. But most magic isn't evil—not regular elementia, anyway. Sure, it can be used by evil people for evil reasons, but mostly it isn't. Kind of like how a knife isn't evil, no matter how sharp it is. It can cut rope or bandages or whittle a piece of wood into a toy. But it can also kill someone. It all depends on who's holding it and what their intentions are. Elementia's kind of the same as that."

I listened to all of this without interrupting, suddenly hungry for more knowledge. "And death magic?"

"Death magic . . ." Jericho's voice went quiet, his brows drawn together. "I don't know. I hate to say it, but I don't know for sure if it's pure evil or not. I've never found any solid information about it anywhere. And Val isn't the most forthcoming. All I can say is I'm alive and I don't feel all that different than I did before the sword went through me."

It was what he'd hinted at in the car. If he'd admitted any of this to me then, I probably would have thrown myself out of the moving vehicle to get away from him.

A whole lot can change in a day.

"Maybe Lazos knows more about it," I said. "He's the living and breathing magical encyclopedia."

"Yeah, maybe." He sighed. "Anyway, after Val brought me back to life and had me agree to work for her, she marked my arm with this special dagger she uses on all her Blackhearts."

I blinked. "You mean, there's more people just like you?"

He grinned. "There's nobody just like me, Drake."

"You know what I mean. So what are these magical marks for?" I managed to say this smoothly, as if we weren't talking about witches and magic and people being brought back from the dead.

"It means that my senses are better than most regular people's. That I'm stronger. And I can take a beating if I have to, and it won't slow me down much. I also heal faster than regular people. It's probably how I survived that bullet today long enough to get to Tamara." He cocked his head. "You don't look so good, Drake."

"I'm processing," I said quietly.

"Sorry to ruin your shiny, perfect life with a whole heap of nasty magic."

"My life wasn't all that perfect before this," I said under my breath, surprising even myself with the truth of it. I frowned and met his gaze again. "But it will be when this is all over."

"I have no doubt," he replied.

"Is that why you have that tattoo on your neck?" I asked. "Because of Valery's dagger?"

He brushed his fingers over the tattoo and smirked at me. "No. I got this when I was fifteen because I thought it looked badass."

I didn't know why I trusted him about any of this, but I didn't think he was lying. Everything about this felt real. Too real.

"Were your eyes always black?" I asked.

"No. My eyes used to be the same color as Vik's. So that's something else we have in common, Drake. We're both so full of magic we never asked for that it shows on the outside." He studied me for a moment in silence, his brows drawn together. "Got to say, you're holding up better than I thought. Overwhelmed yet?"

"I'm way beyond overwhelmed," I replied. "Overwhelmed was hours ago. It was followed by panic, and then a large serving of denial."

"And how do you feel now?"

"I honestly don't know." I couldn't help but wonder if Queen Isadora knew any of this or had even considered that there was more to the story than all magic being pure evil.

"You look tired," Jericho said.

"I am," I admitted.

He made a move to get out of the bed.

"No," I said, holding up my hand. "You keep it. I can sleep on the floor tonight. I guess there's a first time for everything."

I grabbed an extra blanket from the foot of the bed and curled up on the hard wooden floor.

After all I'd learned, all I'd seen and experienced today, I was sure it would take me forever to get to sleep, especially in the presence of Jericho.

But I was out in mere moments, embraced by the mercy of a dark, dreamless sleep.

▷◁◇◁◇▷◁

When I opened my eyes, I could see the glow of the sun through the small window. I'd slept straight through the night, and it had felt like only seconds.

I wasn't sure what had woken me, but then I heard the sound.

Someone was pounding on the door. A moment later, it swung open.

"Morning," Mika said, leaning against the doorframe.

"What do you want?" I managed.

She smiled thinly. "The Overlord will see you now."

TEN

Heart pounding, I followed Mika out of the cottage, sliding my sunglasses onto my face. Jericho followed behind me. He looked so much better than he did yesterday, which was a great relief. Stronger, less pale, and ready to take on the world.

But he didn't look happy. Instead, he looked grim and determined.

We followed Mika down the cobblestone road toward a larger building that sat all by itself at the edge of the forest. Mika walked quickly, her strides confident and swift. I had to hustle to keep up with her, but that was okay. I saw my destination. The answer I needed was in that building.

"Drake," said Jericho.

I glanced over my shoulder at him. "What?"

"Let me do all the talking."

"And why should I do that?"

He glared at me.

"Seriously," I said. "Why should I do that? This is my life, my problem."

"Our problem," he corrected.

"Our problem is currently in *me*. Which makes it *my* problem."

"*Our* problem," he said again, firmly. "I just figured you'd be uneasy about conversing with an actual warlock capable of doing, well, *actual* magic."

"You figured wrong," I lied. "I'm fine."

"Glad to hear it. I don't believe it, but I'm glad to hear it. Onward, then."

Yes, Vander Lazos was a warlock, but I would ask him for his help. And he would help me. And why would he do that? Because I always got what I wanted, if I wanted it bad enough. And I desperately wanted this. I couldn't live with the echoes of Lord Banyon's life trapped inside my head. Not for another damn day.

In front of me, Mika pushed open the door to the building, which was about half the size of the lodge, and gestured for me and Jericho to enter.

I scanned my suddenly darkened surroundings, made only darker by the sunglasses covering my golden eyes. A wooden floor stretched out before me. The stone walls held lit torches that sent their flickering light across the mostly empty space.

At the far end of the room, about thirty feet from where I stood, there was a single piece of furniture. A large wooden chair with a high back. A man with olive-toned skin, dark hair a couple of inches past his shoulders, and a long beard threaded with gray sat on the chair, watching us.

"Welcome to my palace," the man said. "I am the Overlord of the Keep. Come closer, so I can see you."

My steps faltered, unsettled by the warlock so near to me and this twisted mirror image of a throne room. The queen's throne room at the palace was full of color and light. Large portraits and tapestries adorned her walls. A domed skylight allowed sunshine to stream down on the throne itself—a magnificent chair carved from mahogany and edged in gold that had seated the ruler of the Regarian Empire for centuries.

This room was dark and dreary and depressing, yet still incredibly intimidating.

Choosing to ignore that unhelpful thought, I pushed a smile to my face. It was the same one I used at the seemingly endless political functions I'd attended with my father, needing to make a good impression as the daughter of the prime minister.

I could fake it with the best of them.

I turned my practiced smile to the man who called himself the Overlord as I drew closer to him. Jericho stood to my left, his arms crossed over his chest.

"It's a great pleasure to meet you," I said, then added, "my lord."

I mean, anyone who called himself Overlord probably expected such signs of respect. Like Lord Banyon, who wasn't actually a real lord, at least not to my knowledge. Rumor was he'd taken that title on himself because it made him sound more important.

Lazos nodded at me. "Mika has already told me who you are. Josslyn Drake, Louis Drake's daughter. However, I'm sure I would have recognized you anyway."

I shot a look at Mika and she shrugged.

My smile held. "That's right, my lord."

"This is the last place I would have expected to find someone like you, Josslyn."

"To be honest, my lord, this is the last place I ever expected to be."

"I'm so sorry to hear of your father's death." He shook his head. "I liked Louis very much. He was a good man."

"Thank you." I couldn't let the mention of my father throw me off, or let myself get distracted wondering what my father would have thought about the queen having a warlock as a magic advisor, despite her own unbendable laws against magic. After all, if she needed information about magic because it helped her fight against such a weapon in the hands of her enemies, then why wouldn't she have been more transparent about it?

I hated that I'd begun to question Her Majesty's intentions, but I couldn't help it.

"I met you, Josslyn, when you were just a baby," the Overlord said, then raised an eyebrow. "But I'm sure you don't remember that."

I tempered my uneasiness with a steady smile. "Babies don't really remember much, do they?"

"Often, that's for the best." Lazos grasped the arms of his chair. His makeshift wooden throne was very roughly carved, as if by an ax more than a chisel. His gaze moved to Jericho. "And then we have you."

"I don't suppose you met me as a baby, too, did you?" Jericho said.

"I don't believe so." Lazos eyed him slowly from head to foot. "You're Jericho."

"I certainly am."

"And you're a Blackheart." He cocked his head. "I've never met an actual Blackheart before."

Jericho didn't speak for a moment. "I wonder how you'd know something like that about me already? It's certainly not something I advertise, nor have I mentioned it to anyone here yet."

I felt Jericho looking at me now. A hot, searing sensation on the side of my face.

I tried not to cringe or feel guilty about saying something I hadn't realized was supposed to be top secret. "I may have mentioned it to Mika last night."

"Figured," he said, and a whisper of annoyance slid through his black eyes.

He'd obviously never gotten the message not to share gossip with me if he didn't want it spread far and wide in record time. Not that it mattered. A criminal like him landing in the Queen's Keep wouldn't be a surprise to anyone here.

"A Blackheart and the daughter of a prime minister," Lazos said, tearing my attention away from Jericho. "What a truly unlikely pairing, especially in a place such as this."

"Couldn't agree more," Jericho replied. "Now, before we continue, let's just get one thing cleared up. You're Vander Lazos, right? A warlock, formerly the magical advisor to Queen Isadora?"

The Overlord's eyes narrowed, and he was silent for several very long moments. "I am."

"Excellent." Jericho smiled now, but it wasn't a pleasant expression.

"My lord," I cut in, not wanting to waste another moment. "We come to you today to ask for your help—"

"No." Lazos held up his hand to stop me from speaking. "I will ask the questions. I will make the requests. I am Overlord here, and if you don't want to respect that, Mika will see you out."

I tensed, unsure what to do for a moment. However, at the political functions I'd attended, I'd been faced with many egomaniacs and rude men (and plenty of rude women, too) who loved the sound of their own voices so much that they didn't want to listen to anyone else speak.

The best thing to do to get on their good side was to let them talk until they ran out of steam. Then it was easier to swing the conversation back in the direction one desired.

I nodded, my smile steady and true. "Of course, my lord."

"We'll start with you, Josslyn. What crime did you commit to be thrown into the Keep? Answer honestly, for I will know if you lie."

He looked like a perfectly normal middle-aged man, but I had to remember that this was a warlock. For all I knew, he could use his magic to sense deceit.

Magic is evil. The words still echoed in my mind.

Oddly, though, the words had grown quieter since meeting Tamara. Since hearing the knife theory from Jericho. But they were still there. And Lazos wasn't doing too much to refute them.

"I committed no crime," I replied. "I'm here in the Queen's Keep because I needed to find you."

"Mika informs me that you have memory magic within you."

I glanced at Mika, whose defiant expression reflected absolutely no remorse for shamelessly sharing everything I'd told her last night with the Overlord.

"It's true," I said. "Which is actually the reason why we're—"

"Silence." Lazos gestured at me. "Remove your sunglasses and give them to me."

I sent a beseeching look at Jericho, who grimly gave me a small nod. Reluctantly, I took off the sunglasses and handed them to the warlock as requested without argument.

He nodded. "While you're in my presence, you won't hide what you are."

"This isn't who I am," I told him tightly.

"Mika," Lazos said, and Mika drew closer. Then he broke my sunglasses in half and handed her the pieces. "Dispose of these immediately."

"Yes, my lord," Mika said. She didn't even glance at me or Jericho as she left the room with the only thing I had to shield my golden eyes from the world. I watched her leave with shock.

"Now." Lazos returned his attention to me and my stunned expression. "We can continue."

"Everyone will know I have magic in me," I whispered.

"Not everyone. Only those who understand such matters, and frankly, those people are few and far between. Most choose to live in ignorance of even the boldest signs of magic. Many of those possessed by magic show no physical signs like this at all. Such a change is usually triggered by a strong surge of exterior magic, which seems to be what has happened to you."

All the more reason for me to get that exterior magic out of me.

Lazos steepled his fingers and leaned back in his chair. "You say you wanted to find me, but how did you know I was here?"

I fought to regain my composure, which was a struggle, but it was my only chance to control this conversation in the slightest. "A man named Rush told me."

"I don't know anyone by that name."

"He said you were my only hope to remove this magic so I could go back to my normal life. So no one would know what happened to me."

Lazos watched my mouth as if he could see every word I spoke hanging in the air like smoke.

"Tell me, Josslyn. What memory magic is this inside of you? Whose echoes are these?"

I pressed my lips together. Speaking the name was difficult for me, so I needed a moment to compose myself.

Jericho groaned. "Goddamn, can we move this along a bit? Lord Banyon's memories are in her head. She needs them out and I need them contained. Rush says you can help us, which is why we're here. You might not know him, but he knows everybody operating on the wrong side of normal. It's kind of his thing. And as soon as we fix this mess, we need a way out of this hellhole."

Well, that pretty much summed it up.

Still, it was like watching a wild bull charging through a jewelry boutique: no finesse, no grace. Just obliterating everything in its path without a single care to the carnage it left behind.

"My apologies for Jericho's manners, but it's been a difficult couple of days," I said, trying my best to salvage whatever damage the tactless Blackheart had already done. I guess nobody had ever taught him to use honey rather than vinegar to get what he wanted.

I was surprised when Lazos didn't give his attention back to me, instead focusing still on Jericho.

"You need this memory magic, do you?" he said.

"That's right."

"Lord Zarek Banyon's memories."

"Again, yes. Rush says you and Banyon knew each other once, not that it really matters."

"It seems this Rush person knows far more about me than I know about him." There was a tenseness to his expression now that hadn't been there before as he regarded Jericho. "I've heard much about your kind before."

"My kind?"

"A powerful witch's personal army of Blackhearts."

"Hardly an army."

"How many willing servants does she have at her beck and call these days?"

"A few." Jericho's expression had gone blank, unreadable. It seemed like it was his way to deal with conflict. He gave nothing away—no weakness, no fear, not even a show of strength. No sign of how to approach him if one wanted the upper hand.

Lazos's attention shifted back to me after he'd studied the Blackheart for another moment. "Josslyn Drake, filled with the echoes of Lord Zarek Banyon's life." He shook his head. "It seems as if destiny has intervened, since such odds are truly astronomical."

I tried to make sense of this, but came up empty. "I don't think it's destiny. I think it's just an epic case of wrong place, wrong time. Lord Banyon had my father murdered. I can't have him in my head another day. I hate him with every fiber of my being."

"Of course you do. What possible choice have you been given in all of this to feel any differently? Tell me, are you able to access these echoes at will?"

I shook my head. "No. They come randomly. I've only had a few so far."

"What did you see?"

I forced myself to remember what I didn't want to remember. "I think all three were from the night that he escaped from the palace sixteen years ago. Two were him in the fire. And one . . ." I grimaced at the memory. "He was being tortured by a Queensguard who wanted him to do something for the queen. I don't know what it was. But he refused."

Lazos watched me so closely as I spoke, and it started to make me feel uncomfortable. I was used to being admired in public for how I dressed, how I looked. But I had to say I wasn't a big fan of being inspected like something small, helpless, and squirming on a glass slide under a microscope.

"I see," he said, then his gaze flicked to Jericho. "And this memory magic is something you were sent to obtain for your enigmatic employer."

"Pretty much," Jericho agreed.

"Valery," Lazos said, letting the name hang there in the air between them.

Jericho gave him a tight grin. "You've met?"

"No. But her reputation precedes her, as well as the reputation of her Blackhearts. A very rare breed indeed. All raised from the dead with death magic strong enough to have been summoned by the god of death himself. Or perhaps Valery is the goddess of death? That would explain a great deal."

Jericho's expression turned icy. "It would, wouldn't it?"

"Is she a goddess?"

"Not that I'm aware of. She's just a damn powerful witch who's a genius at selling magical things that people want to pay a lot of money for. And sometimes there's a little life and death thrown into the mix. That's all."

Lazos shook his head, his expression fierce. "No one in this world can channel death magic as easily as it seems that she can. The price to be paid is far too great for any mere mortal. What price is it that you pay, Jericho?"

I found that I was now holding my breath, waiting for his answer.

"Other than my good looks and devastating charm?" Jericho replied easily. "Can't think of a thing."

"Very well." Lazos nodded, unamused. "I need to test you. I need to be sure of what you are." He stood up from the throne and raised his voice: "Arlo, Otis. Come here."

A few moments later, the two hulking men who had helped bring the injured Jericho to Tamara's cottage yesterday entered the room.

Jericho eyed them. "Good to see you guys again."

Lazos flicked his hand at the men. "Kill him."

I watched in shock as the torchlight glinted off the sharp silver blades the two held. They didn't hesitate; they went directly for Jericho, who immediately shoved me away from him. I staggered back a few feet.

"What's happening?" I demanded. "My lord, you don't want to do this!"

"Silence," Lazos hissed.

Jericho eyed the two men, both bigger and more muscular than he was. Their expressions were focused, their gazes fixed. And they didn't look the least bit friendly.

"Can we talk about this?" he asked. "Here I thought we were all good friends now."

Apparently not. Otis and Arlo lunged for Jericho, their blades aimed for his throat.

Jericho dodged the attack so fast that I could barely follow his movements. He kicked Arlo back from him, the sole of his boot slamming into the larger man's chest. And then he grabbed Otis's pale, freckled arm, wrenching it around until I heard a sickening snap. When the knife fell, Jericho snatched it before it even hit the ground and in the next instant had it against the brown skin of Arlo's throat as the man returned for another attack.

"Drop it," Jericho growled. A thin line of blood trickled down his assailant's neck.

Arlo dropped his knife.

"Should I kill them?" Jericho asked tightly. "Would that satisfy you?"

"No. I'm already satisfied." Lazos returned to his throne and sat down. "Arlo, take Otis to see Tamara to have his arm healed."

Arlo, his face red and sweaty, eyed Jericho with trepidation as the Blackheart released him, then went to help his associate off the floor. The two limped out of the Overlord's throne room without a word spoken.

Jericho wiped the blood off the blade on his black jeans. "I think I'll keep this," he said. Then he glanced at me. "You okay, Drake?"

I just gaped at him. He'd easily taken two large, armed men down in mere moments without even breaking a sweat. I'd never seen anyone move that fast before.

He'd said that Valery had given him special abilities. I guessed I'd just witnessed that for myself.

"I'm good," I managed.

"Great," he said, flicking his attention to Lazos. "Now back to the subject at hand. We're here because you're going to help us get the magic out of Drake and into a container for me to deliver to my boss. And then you're going to help us get the hell out of here. Simple, straightforward. We can end this in a matter of minutes, really."

Lazos studied him, his brows drawn together. "You're fascinating. So much strength, so much power, so much life emanating from you. Yet you're filled with pure, unadulterated death magic."

"I'm a shiny teapot full of rattlesnakes. So what?"

Lazos nodded. There was no distrust in his gaze now, no challenge; there was only awe. "You are going to help me with a problem I have," he said.

"Let's not get it twisted," Jericho replied. "You're going to help us. I mean, unless you can't do what Rush said you could do. In which case, tell me now. I won't be very happy if you waste any more of my time."

A part of me wanted to intervene. I didn't want Jericho to push the warlock too far, to piss him off. But I couldn't quite form cohesive words at the moment, still processing what I'd just witnessed with Jericho's fighting ability.

I guessed I now understood how he'd so easily taken out half a dozen highly trained and highly armed Queensguards along the way.

Lazos nodded. "Of course I can help you. Both of you."

Something tight and tangled inside me finally eased. "Really? That is so good to hear. When can we do it? Now? Now is good for me."

"The problem is, I don't do favors. I never have." Lazos casually leaned back in his throne. "I make deals. There's something I want, something I need, before I will do as you've requested of me."

The tension was back inside me, tighter than before. "What is it?"

"For the first time, I now have a Blackheart in my kingdom, one who's asked a large favor of me," Lazos said. "And if you want my help, you must agree to my terms."

Jericho's expression was unreadable, but his black eyes glittered unpleasantly. "This is your lucky day. I just happen to be an amazing problem solver and highly motivated toward a successful resolution. What do you need?"

Lazos stroked his beard for a moment. "What I'm about to tell you can't go beyond these four walls. No one else can know the truth."

"Well, then, you probably shouldn't tell Drake here," Jericho replied. "She doesn't seem to be too great with keeping secrets."

I shot him a dark look. "I can keep a secret if I have to. My lord, you can trust me. This is my future we're talking about here. I'm not going to jeopardize it for anything."

I said it; I meant it. And when I made a promise, I always kept it.

Lazos nodded. "Very well. The problem is this: The Queen's Keep is cursed. On seven occasions over the last three years, these walls have been breached by a creature of darkness. Under the shield of night, this hungry beast stalks its prey among the prisoners here. In the morning, those prisoners have disappeared, never to be seen again. Twelve prisoners have fallen victim so far."

I realized my mouth was hanging open. Twelve was the same number of prisoners Gloria told me had escaped. "A hungry beast. Here. You're got to be kidding."

Lazos shook his head gravely, his brow furrowed. "Unfortunately, I'm not."

I sent a stunned look at Jericho, but he didn't seem nearly as shocked by this news as I was.

"Maybe those prisoners just found a way out of here," I reasoned.

"That's what my Keepers think. And in the beginning, I, too, thought that was the case." Lazos shook his head. "I know what it is because it's begun to haunt my dreams. And I can now prophesize when the beast will arrive next. I had such a dream last night. It will return on the night of the next full moon, two weeks from tonight." He held Jericho's gaze heavily. "On that night, I need you to find it and kill it. That is the deal I want to make with you, Blackheart."

"Interesting," Jericho said.

"Interesting?" I repeated. "Are you serious? This is like something out of a nightmare. Or a . . . a ridiculously far-fetched fairy tale. Monsters like this don't really exist."

"Sure they do," Jericho replied smoothly. "There's so much magic in this great big universe, Drake. And you've only experienced the tiniest taste of it."

I found I had absolutely no rebuttal for that for a stunned and silent moment. "I can't accept this."

"Then it's probably good the Overlord here asked me to be the one to kill it. I've dealt with worse assignments, believe me."

"You've killed things like this," I said.

His jaw tightened, and he now studied the base of Lazos's throne. "I've killed lots of things, Drake."

It wasn't a confirmation that set my mind at ease. At all. "If this horrific possibility is actually real, why doesn't anyone else know about it? Why would you want to keep this a secret?

Wouldn't you want to warn the other prisoners about the danger, especially if you know when it's coming again?"

"It's only very recently that I fully realized what was happening," Lazos replied tightly. "And now, to strike panic and fear in the hearts of those trapped here would only lead to chaos. I've been carefully considering my options in how to deal with this problem." His attention fixed on Jericho again. "And here is a Blackheart before me, another undeniable act of destiny. The perfect solution to end this swiftly and easily two weeks from now. No one ever has to know the horrible truth."

"How does this thing get in?" Jericho asked. "If there's a way in, there has to be a way out, right?"

"That, I don't know." Lazos shook his head. "All I know is that the very special magic inside you will give you the edge you need to slay such a creature. You proved with the demonstration earlier that you are stronger, faster, and deadlier than anyone else inside these walls."

"Maybe," Jericho allowed. "But you're a warlock. Why can't you take care of this problem yourself?"

"I planned to do just that, but here you are before me, a skilled Blackheart who wants a favor in return, presenting me with another option." Lazos spread his hands. "Are you saying no?"

Jericho rolled his eyes. "I'm not saying no. But I think I have the right to ask a couple questions, given what you're asking of me."

"The moment you stepped foot into the Keep, you forfeited any rights you may have enjoyed on the outside. This is the deal. Slay the beast on the night of the next full moon, and I will do exactly what you've requested of me. Everyone wins. So do we have a deal, Blackheart?"

By now, Jericho appeared almost bored by this conversation. As if this was the sort of request he got every day. It was an act; it had to be. This was what he did when someone turned up the heat—he appeared not to care one way or the other.

It was his form of self-protection.

It was his way to control the situation.

Finally, Jericho nodded, his eyes black and cold and seemingly without a single shred of emotion. "We have a deal."

ELEVEN

The Blackheart turned and left the Overlord's makeshift palace without another word. I watched him leave, stunned.

"You don't have to worry about him," Lazos said. "Someone who's already well acquainted with death no longer has any reason to fear it."

Worry about Jericho Nox? A death-magic-filled criminal I'd known all of two days, who'd been instrumental in turning my life upside down just because my path randomly crossed with his?

"I'm not worried," I said, but the words tasted false. "Where did it come from? This monster? What does it look like? How big is it?"

"All I know for sure is that it's very dangerous."

I shook my head. "That's not enough. I need to know more. You said you saw it in your dreams, so you had to have gotten a good look at it. Tell me more so I can try to wrap my head around this and have it make some kind of sense for me."

Lazos regarded me stonily for a very long and unpleasant moment, his brows drawn over his gray eyes.

"You remind me very much of your father," he finally said. "He was always inquisitive to a fault. Fighting his way toward the truth, even if that truth had sharp teeth and claws ready to tear him apart from top to tail. Unfortunately for him, he also had to learn such lessons the hard way."

I frowned. "That doesn't sound like my father."

"No, I'm sure it doesn't."

The father I'd known was one who was almost always too tired after a full day of meetings to eat dinner with me, instead taking his meals in his study most of the time. Working hard to maintain civility with all those he dealt with, no matter what their opinions were.

I'd always assumed I'd gotten my passionate streak from my mother.

But maybe my father had been different when he was younger.

"Echoes of Zarek Banyon's memories have found their way into Josslyn Drake, of all people," Lazos mused, drawing my attention and making me cringe. "How incredibly curious."

"Could have been anyone who'd been there when the box opened," I muttered. "I'm just extra unlucky, I guess."

"No. Not anyone, not at all. Only someone already touched by magic can attract magic to them."

I almost laughed at that, even though it was the least funny thing I'd ever heard in my life. "Obviously you're wrong, since I have never been touched by magic in any way, shape, or form before this."

Lazos nodded. "If you say so."

"I didn't attract this," I said, as if to reiterate how wrong he was. "I hate this. I want it out of me. Lord Banyon murdered my father, and now his memories are in my head and I can't control it."

My cheeks were flushed, my fists clenched at my sides.

"Why do you think you can't control it?" Lazos asked.

My frustration with this warlock threatened to overwhelm me and I wanted to turn and leave, but I stood my ground. He was playing with me—an imprisoned cat who'd cornered a mouse. But I was no mouse.

"All magic is uncontrollable," I said, finding myself quoting from the queen's speech at the Gala.

"Certainly, in the beginning, it can feel that way. But with practice, there's no reason why you can't control these visions." He raised an eyebrow. "For all its over-the-top theatrical appearance, memory magic is really quite straightforward. And this memory magic is contained in you."

"I *can't* control this," I said again.

He spread his hands. "Very well. I won't continue to argue with you about this. When someone has emphatically decided what they can't do, they're usually right. We're done here, Josslyn."

I had an endless list of questions that had been running ceaselessly through my mind, but I didn't stay a second longer. I emerged from the dark building into the sunshine, and I stood there for a moment, my legs shaking.

The warlock was trying to mess with my composure and my confidence. And he'd done an excellent job.

Jericho waited nearby, watching me. I made a beeline for him.

"Have you lost your damn mind?" I demanded.

"That happened a long time ago, I'm afraid. Can you be more specific?"

"You just agreed to kill some sort of magical monster? Like it's that easy? Just stick a knife in it and it's all over?"

"That's usually how killing works. The great and powerful warlock has spoken, and he has made his deal very clear. Don't worry, Drake; it's not nearly the first big, scary magical thing I've killed. I can handle it."

"What if you can't?" I found I was wringing my hands, pacing back and forth in short, quick lines. "I need this over."

"Me too. More than you even know."

I looked up at the sudden grimness in his tone. "What do you mean?"

Jericho hissed out a breath, and I realized he was rubbing his forearm. "Don't worry about it," he said tightly.

Then he turned away from me and walked the short distance to our cottage. I followed closely after him, slamming the door behind me.

He'd taken a seat in the single chair, and he looked up at me darkly. "We definitely need to look into getting separate cottages."

"You don't get to walk away from me when the questions get hard and you get uncomfortable. You do that, you know."

He glared at me. "Do I?"

"Yes, it's quite annoying. Can you ever just answer a question fully without your cryptic nonsense?"

Jericho leaned back in his seat. "Fine. Here's all I know. On the night of the next full moon, I've agreed to go monster hunting," he said. "Until then, you're going to have to give me some space, because the next couple of weeks might get a bit messy."

I shook my head. "What are you talking about? Messy how?" I realized he was still rubbing his forearm. "What's wrong with you?"

"What isn't wrong with me? This entire experience is a damn nightmare, that's what's wrong with me." He blew out a breath, his frown so deep it looked painful. "Fine. Here's a heads-up for you if you're that concerned, which I doubt. My marks . . . the ones Val gave me. Along with all the fancy perks and enhancements they give me, which you just got a tiny glimpse of, they bind me to her in some seriously epic ways. They ensure I do my job, that I follow her command to the letter whether I want to or not." He grimaced and looked down at the ground. "And they keep me on deadline."

I shook my head. "What does that mean?"

"It means, if she expects me to report back to her on a certain day, at a certain hour, then I better damn well be there. And she expected me back yesterday at the latest with Banyon's memory box in hand."

"What happens if you're late?" I asked quietly. "Or if you don't show up at all?" I didn't know much about this witch Jericho worked for, but she didn't sound like someone up for the best boss of the year award.

Jericho laughed darkly. "Motivation to return, in the form of some nice searing pain, pain that gets worse with every day that passes. But don't worry too much; I can deal with a little pain for a couple of weeks."

Valery sounded like the most evil person in the world. I hated her and I'd never even met her. I never wanted to meet her, especially after hearing the goddess-of-death rumor. It was enough that I had to deal with warlocks and witches. I wasn't ready to add the possibility of goddesses to the list.

"I can't wait two weeks," I said, feeling like I was confessing a weakness to him. "I can't have Banyon in my head that long. It—it's too much."

Jericho stood up and moved closer to me, frowning. "Are the visions causing you pain?" he asked.

"Not physical," I admitted honestly, and only because he sounded really sincere in the asking. If he'd been flippant about it, I would have lied and said it was torturous every minute of every day. "I just hate seeing anything about that monster. I don't want this strange and unnatural connection to him. I hate him more than anything in the world. When you left, Lazos said that I can control this magic, but he's wrong. I can't."

I let out a shuddery sigh, suddenly feeling on the edge of tears.

"It's going to be all right. I promise you that, okay?" Jericho gently brushed my hair back from my face and tucked it behind my ear. He frowned. "Never noticed this mark before. It's shaped like a heart."

"Yeah." I touched my neck. "Another thing we have in common. I have a birthmark on my neck, and you have a tattoo."

"Yours is much better than my tattoo. Hearts beat daggers any day."

He brushed his fingers against the small mark on my neck,

his brows drawn tightly together. My breath caught.

I suppose most people would be intimidated or frightened by the Blackheart, especially after witnessing him take down two large armed men in mere moments. But it seemed I'd moved well beyond that now. Still, it suddenly felt dangerous to be this close to Jericho. And yet, for some reason, I didn't pull away from him as his gaze moved from my neck to my face, and then my lips.

The warmth of his touch made me shiver, and I looked up at him, my gaze locking with his, and for a moment I forgot how to breathe.

Then he blinked and looked down at his hand with shock, as if it had acted totally against his will.

He pulled away from me completely.

"Sorry," he said.

I shook my head. "It's okay."

"No, it isn't okay. Not at all," he said, harsher now. "Anyway, it's only two weeks. Suck it up, Drake. There are worse things in this world, I assure you. Memories can't hurt you, no matter how bad they may seem—especially when those memories belong to someone else. Hell, maybe you can control them. You should give it a try and see what happens."

Before I could say anything else, not that I was sure what it would be, the Blackheart turned and left the cottage without another word.

TWELVE

I'd hoped this would be over in a matter of hours. Now I had to wait two weeks. Two weeks trapped in the Queen's Keep, surrounded by prisoners, while everything Vander Lazos said buzzed around in my head like a swarm of angry wasps. The worst thing, really, was that it seemed I had absolutely no say in what would happen next. I was expected simply to wait and leave my destiny in the hands of others.

Namely Jericho.

He hadn't returned to the cottage yesterday. Or last night. I had no idea at all where he'd gone, but I wasn't going to search for him or run after him.

He was so strange, so secretive. He could have his secrets; I didn't really care. I mean, I was wildly curious what they were, but that was just the way I was. If one of my friends tried to keep a secret, it would become my mission to find out what it was. I rarely failed.

Well, except with Celina's secret.

I hated that I'd had to leave her with no idea where I'd gone or if I was safe. I didn't have a clue what Viktor would have told her, if anything.

I'm so sorry, Celina, I thought. *I promise I'll make this up to you.*

Even after a night to sleep on it, Lazos's request still seemed so incredibly bizarre. None of this sat right with me, but I had to remind myself that this wasn't my world. From the knife-wielding, death-magic-infused Blackheart, to the witch who used to be a doctor, to some kind of wild animal that would magically appear on the night of the next full moon and completely devour a few prisoners who were foolish enough to wander into its path. And, of course, the magical echoes of an evil warlock's past stuck in my head.

I tried to sense that magic in me—to feel its presence.

But I couldn't feel anything. Maybe it would have been better if I could, if there was some ache or pain or heaviness associated with the nebulous thing that had derailed my life. It would be back to give another viewing of Banyon's past when I least expected it.

Unless . . .

Unless Lazos was right and there was some way I *could* learn to control this, like a light switch—on or off. If I had that choice, I would definitely keep it in the off position. I didn't know how to even start to learn such a thing. It seemed dangerous, like diving into dark waters without knowing what lurked beneath the surface.

No, that wasn't true. I knew what lurked beneath the surface:

Lord Banyon. If there was any way I could stop these horrible visions from happening, then I couldn't ignore that possibility. But I didn't have any idea where to start.

This whole situation was a nightmare, but at least it was one I knew I would escape from. I just had to be patient. Unfortunately, patience had never been one of my greatest strengths. So instead, I would have to distract myself. My favorite distractions had always been shopping and going to parties—not likely in here—and spending time with friends. And gossiping, of course.

Which meant one important thing. I needed to make some friends so I could learn some gossip.

Most of the prisoners here seemed to keep utterly to themselves, spending a great deal of time in their cottages or focused on their assigned chores around the village. I tried to engage a few of them in conversation, but they only looked at me with wariness before quickly ending our chats.

I didn't push. What Mika had told me weighed heavy in my mind, that they wouldn't take kindly to learning I was the daughter of the former prime minister, a man who represented the very government who'd sent them into this prison in the first place. Some would hate me. Others might even want to hurt me. I just had to hope that no one else recognized me.

At one point, I spotted Jericho at a distance and realized his gaze was focused on me. Our eyes met briefly, and I raised my hand in greeting. I swear I saw pain cross his expression for the briefest of moments, before his face went blank and he headed into the forest.

He was so weird.

After spending the day exploring the village, I headed to the lodge to get some dinner. There were a few dozen Keepers spread around the long tables, their metal plates filled with rice, beans, and some sort of paste. I watched as it was slopped down onto my own plate by the server.

"What is that?" I asked, scrunching my nose.

"We call it slop," the server replied.

"Fitting. But what is it?"

"A protein-and-vitamin mix to keep us all alive for a bit longer, courtesy of Her Majesty. May she rot in hell."

I cringed. "I mean, I guess she could provide nothing, right?"

"Nothing might taste better." The server gave me a tight smile. "Enjoy your meal, Janie."

I moved away from her, looking down at my plate. It literally had no smell at all, which made me nostalgic for the watery soup from last night, which sort of smelled like chicken if you really used your imagination.

I spotted Gloria at what seemed to be her usual seat. She was watching me and gestured for me to join her. I slid onto the bench across from her.

"Pisswater?" she asked.

It was as good a greeting as I was likely to get. "Please."

She obtained another cup from a passing server and poured me a drink from the bottle next to her. I swallowed down the burning liquid, remembering that drinking wine was another activity I enjoyed very much in the outside world. This wasn't wine, but it would do the trick. I downed the entire cup and allowed the warmth to flow through me.

"Tell me about yourself, Janie," Gloria said. "I make it my business to get to know all the newcomers."

Finally, someone who wanted to chat.

"What do you want to know?" I asked.

"Anything you want to tell me. Where do you come from? And where did you meet that handsome young man who can't keep his eyes off of you?"

I laughed nervously at that. "The handsome young man who has been hiding from me all day, you mean?"

"Same one. If there's one thing I know, Janie, it's men. They think we're hard to figure out, but they're the true mysteries of the universe. Perhaps he's hiding from you because he wants you to come find him."

"I doubt it," I replied honestly.

"You would know better than me, I suppose. Have you two been together long?"

"Honestly? It feels like forever," I said. "But it hasn't been very long at all. There's not a lot to know about me, Gloria. I'm just a girl who fell for the wrong guy, and he led her headfirst into a life of crime and danger. And here we are, on the wrong side of this prison's wall, the last place I ever thought I'd be."

Gloria patted my hand. "Story as old as time."

She poured me more of the drink and I sipped it uneasily, hoping it would renew my courage to pretend that everything was fine. Or, at least, appear that way.

While I sipped, Vander Lazos himself entered the lodge, walking along the rows of tables to speak with the prisoners.

The sight of the queen's former magic advisor made me

tense, and I remembered what he'd said—suggesting that I'd been touched by magic.

I needed to talk to him again, to ask him his advice on how to control this magic. Even just a little control would help me survive the next two weeks.

Gloria's attention moved to him immediately. "The Overlord blesses us with a rare public visit. This is a special evening."

Despite my distaste for the warlock, I knew I needed to learn more about him. I'd decided yesterday that information was my power, and since I felt pretty powerless, I knew I had to gather as much information as I possibly could.

"Who decided that he would be the leader here?" I asked.

Gloria shook her head. "I don't know. When I arrived five years ago, he was already here. The Overlord has such a command to him, such a strong presence, that he is the perfect man to make sure this place runs as smoothly as possible." She eyed me. "You sound like you doubt his authority."

"Not at all," I replied quickly. "Just getting the lay of the land."

"Understandable."

"Do you know who he is?" I asked. "Did you get to know him as well, like you're getting to know me? What's his real name?"

Gloria's brows drew together. "I don't honestly know. But it doesn't matter, does it, Janie? I suppose we could all use false names in here if we were so inclined."

"I suppose we could," I admitted.

"All I need to know about the Overlord is that he watches

over us all. Without him, I can only imagine the chaos that would rule here. All of these strange people with strange personalities, many with a tendency toward violence, and no hope of ever returning to a life beyond these walls."

"But you mentioned that people have escaped. About a dozen or so, right?" I said, thinking of those who were, according to Lazos, victims of this mysterious beast.

"That's right."

"Do you know how they did it?" When she shook her head, I continued: "Couldn't you have figured it out after being in here five years?"

"Perhaps I could have," she allowed. "If I was interested in escaping, but I'm not. The outside world never appealed to me very much, and I've made peace with my life inside the Keep. It's simple and steady with very little drama, thankfully. Clean air, beautiful nature surrounding us. I like to think of it as a sanctuary for lost souls. However, if there's anyone who is actively trying to find a way out of here, it's Mika. I'm honestly surprised that she's still here." Gloria gave me a conspiratorial look, then leaned closer and lowered her voice. "She used to be a Queensguard, you know."

I gasped. "Are you serious?"

She nodded gravely. "A Queensguard among all these prisoners. Can you imagine what would happen if her secret was revealed?" She made a twisting motion at her lips. "Promise me that you won't say a word."

"I promise," I replied immediately.

Now that was some seriously good gossip.

I sat with Gloria for a little while longer while I ate my sub-standard dinner, full of protein and vitamins but lacking any taste. Lazos didn't stop by our table to chat. Gloria looked disappointed by this, but I took it as a sign that the Overlord was avoiding me.

He should join Jericho's club. There might even be a secret handshake by now.

But I wasn't about to let Lazos escape me that easily. I had more questions for him, and one was whether he might consider working his magic on me a little earlier than originally scheduled. I could charm him; I knew I could. I'd have him eating out of my hand before the night was over. I just had to think positively because the alternative wasn't helpful in the slightest.

When Lazos left, I said goodnight to Gloria and followed him out of the lodge.

"My lord," I called out to him.

He glanced over his shoulder at me. "Josslyn."

"I wanted to apologize if I seemed rude yesterday. It's not every day I hear about such . . . fantastical possibilities." Yeah, that was a gentle way of saying that my worldview had been irreparably upended. "I wanted to thank you for the advice you gave me."

He raised a brow. "What advice is that?"

I lowered my voice. "That it's possible for me to control this magic. Can you share the steps to take to start doing that?"

"Unfortunately, there isn't a learner's manual, Josslyn. But I would suggest that you start with mindfulness. And acceptance— letting the magic flow through you without resistance."

I blinked. "Mindfulness and acceptance. You want me to accept that piece of murderous scum's memories in my head?"

He frowned. "Perhaps you should focus on the mindfulness first. Good day, Josslyn."

He walked away from me, leaving me there stewing in my own frustration. That was it? He'd just brushed me off as if I'd asked what the weather would be like today.

I was about to pursue him to demand more answers with much less honey involved this time, when something else caught my attention.

Jericho and Mika were nearby, speaking together. My curiosity piqued, I walked over to them. Jericho tensed at the sight of me.

"And there she is. Tell me, Drake, were your ears burning?" he asked.

I glanced between the Blackheart and Mika. "You were talking about me?"

Mika nodded. "Jericho's requested his own cottage."

This surprised me for a moment, but I wasn't sure why it would. Jericho had already mentioned this yesterday. "Great news. I could use the extra space."

"Didn't think you'd fight it," Jericho said. "I figure if anyone asks, not that they probably care, we can say our true love didn't last long after incarceration. That we've parted ways since we can't be in the same room for long without fighting."

"Fine with me," I said evenly, giving him a tight smile.

"Good. So that's that."

"That's that," I agreed.

I didn't know why this annoyed me so much. Maybe because he'd gone to Mika behind my back. He was actively avoiding me, again. Funny how it started after last night, when we'd gotten a little too close to each other.

"Problem, Drake?" he asked.

"So many problems I can't count them all," I replied.

"Two weeks."

"Too long."

"You're going to have to take that up with the Overlord. I got my assignment and the rules were clear."

"You seem to follow rules really well."

"Sometimes I do. Sometimes I don't."

We glared at each other and I heard Mika sigh.

"I'm out of here," she said wearily. "You go ahead and sort your issues out between the two of you. I want nothing to do with it."

I grabbed her arm. "Wait a minute."

She tensed and sent me a dark look. "What?"

"Gloria told me what you are. Seems like a strange thing to me, a Queensguard stuck in the middle of the Keep."

She wrenched away from me. "Gloria has a big damn mouth."

"So it's true."

"Mind your own business, Josslyn. It's healthier that way for you, especially in a place like this. There are some very dangerous people in here. Don't trust everyone you meet."

"Like you?"

"This might shock you, but I'm likely the most trustworthy person in this pit of despair. Gloria, on the other hand . . . do you know why she's in here?"

"No idea."

"On the outside, Gloria was a very popular woman in her day who was married three times to very wealthy men. Each of her husbands ended up dead."

I blinked. "She killed them."

"She says she didn't, but it seems like a bit of a coincidence, doesn't it?"

Jericho's arms were crossed over his chest. "Forget Gloria. Are you really a Queensguard?" he asked, his voice low.

Mika looked at him, unflinching. "I was. Once. But not anymore."

"What did you do to get in here?"

"None of your business, that's what I did. Now, why don't the two of you talk out your problems. Or whatever. I don't really care. Tomorrow I'll be assigning you both chores to keep you out of trouble and make you vaguely useful around here. You've already had an extra free day. This conversation is over."

She walked away from us without looking back.

"And then there were two," Jericho muttered. "Anyway, great talk, Drake. I'm going to check out my new home away from home now."

"So that's it, is it?" I said.

"What do you mean?"

"You're just going to avoid me for the next two weeks?"

He hissed out a sigh. "Sorry, I didn't realize you were so

needy. Did you want us to schedule playtimes? Maybe date nights? That might get in the way of the story that the two of us broke up and need separate accommodations."

"I'm not needy." His unexpected harshness took me by surprise, but I tried my best to shake it off. "What's wrong with you today?"

"Nothing."

"Something's wrong. You're acting like more of a jerk than before, and I'm pretty sure I didn't do a damn thing to deserve it. But maybe I'm wrong. What happened yesterday that made you run away from me?"

He scoffed. "I didn't run away."

"You walked. Quickly. And now, the moment I talk to you again, you're being an epic dick to me. Don't forget, we're in this together, Jericho."

"No, we're not. We're not in this together. We're not a team. You have something inside of you that I need back. That's it. Try to get that through your head. So for now we'll play by Lazos's rules. We'll keep on believing that Rush was right to send us here and he wasn't just messing with me because he's pissed I didn't send him a 'wish you were here' postcard for the last two years. But if he was lying, and if Lazos can't work his magic on you, then I think you know what plan B is."

I couldn't believe what was he was saying to me. It took me a moment to find my voice. "I do. And it's not going to happen." I raised my chin. "You think I'm scared of you? I'm not."

"You should be. And you should understand something very important. My boss gets what she wants, no matter what it takes.

She sent me out to get that golden box at the Gala, nothing else. No paintings or statues—nothing else that was in that entire gallery full of priceless works of art. Just the box. And she's not going to accept failure from me."

My heart started to pound hard and loud in my ears. "You're not taking me to her. So I guess you're going to fail."

He studied me intensely, his brow furrowed. "I did another job for her not so long ago that didn't go exactly according to plan. I tried to fight against the magical command she'd carved into me. And in return, she locked me in a small room for a week—no lights, no food, no water. If it wasn't for my marks that give me just a little edge on a regular human, I would have died in there instead of nearly losing my mind. She'd be even less forgiving for a second mistake. So don't pretend you know what the cost of failure would be." He swore and looked away from me. "I don't know why I'm telling you this."

I glared at him. "You know what? Your little story from hell might mean more to me if you didn't just threaten to offer me up on a silver platter so she can cut this magic right out of me. Is it that damn important to her? One little job that went wrong?"

"She wants what she wants."

"Yeah, that's as clear as mud, thanks. So here's what I'm understanding—no matter which option we choose, if Lazos won't help us, one of us ends up dead?"

I waited for his confirmation, but he stayed silent.

"Sorry, but no," I said, doing my best to ignore the wave of panic rising inside me. "That's not how this is going to end. For either of us. How do you get away from this horrible witch?"

"I don't." He shook his head. "At least, not until I finish paying off my debt to her. And that's going to be a while."

"Until then, you have to do whatever she says. And if you fight, if you give her any problems, your boss tortures you to the edge of death."

He hissed out a breath. "Well, on the bright side, the health plan is amazing."

He might be able to play it off with a quip, but I couldn't. Not this time. "It's just not fair, Jericho. It's not—"

But then a thick column of golden smoke swirled in before I could say another word, and Jericho vanished before my very eyes.

THIRTEEN

No, this wasn't going to happen again. I wouldn't let it.

Lazos said I could learn to control this. And it seemed like class was officially in session.

As the smoke swirled around me, revealing only disjointed images beyond it that hadn't formed a cohesive picture yet, I braced myself and held up my hands.

Mindfulness and acceptance, Lazos had said.

Sure. If I wasn't currently standing in the middle of a raging magical storm made from golden smoke and jagged images, that might be a possibility. I didn't have long to figure this out, a couple of seconds at most.

"No!" I said out loud, as if this magic might actually be able to hear me. "Stop right now. I don't want this. I don't want to see anything else to do with him. Leave me alone!"

I concentrated on a light switch. On shutting this down, denying its access to my mind. The storm began to swirl stronger and faster, but it didn't transition to a clear vision yet.

Now I thought of a door, like at Rush's fight club. A tall, heavy metal door with no handle. I pictured slamming that door shut on this magic, closing myself off from it and not letting it get any closer to me.

And for a moment, the storm began to wane. I couldn't help but grin, feeling a flash of victory that I'd managed to figure this out so quickly and easily without relying on anyone else's help.

But the moment my concentration slipped, the door in my mind burst open and the violent magical storm of memories slammed straight into me.

And it was different this time. Instead of a scene I could walk through like a ghost, it was as if huge, vivid images shot right through me. Jagged, disjointed pieces of a larger puzzle that sent my mind into a spiral of confusion and searing pain.

Lord Banyon. He was just a child, maybe eight years old. Outdoors, with a blue sky and a bright sun shining down. He had a net in his hand and was chasing after a butterfly.

"Mama!" he called out, laughing. "Mama, look at me!"

And then it was gone, golden smoke obliterating my view of this happy scene.

Next, Banyon stroking a baby's cheek. "My angels," he said, his voice filled with pain and regret. "Both of you. I'm so sorry this happened."

Gone in an instant. I gasped as the memory was wrenched out of my head, replaced by another. I barely had a chance to catch my breath.

Fire. An angry sea of flames rising up as tall as buildings. Consuming everything in their path. Someone screamed for help, and Banyon's head whipped in that direction. There wasn't even an ounce of pity or mercy on his face, only pure hatred.

Gone. On to the next.

A beautiful woman in a white dress, purple and blue flowers in her golden hair. And Banyon gazing adoringly at her as if she were the center of the entire universe.

"Are you sure about this?" he asked.

"I've never been more sure about anything," she said, before taking his face between her hands and kissing him.

Gone. On to the next.

A younger Vander Lazos faced a bruised and beaten Lord Banyon.

"Zarek," Lazos said, his voice tight. "A tree that doesn't bend in a storm will break. You've always been a damn stubborn tree, Zarek. But today you finally need to bend."

And then another.

Banyon standing on a stone balcony, wearing a billowing black cloak, looking down at an audience of thousands.

"Follow me. Pledge your devotion to me, and only me, your lord and savior in this cruel world. I will bring elementia back to this world, and we will watch as the Empire of Regara shatters into a million pieces at our feet."

Gone.

Being whipped from one memory to the next like this had made me dizzy, made me nauseous. I couldn't bear it. It felt as if I would lose my hold on reality and be swept away completely into this storm of memories with seemingly no end to it. Nothing to ground myself from the painful onslaught.

But then I felt something. Someone held on to me, hands gripping my shoulders. And through the golden storm, I heard him.

"Drake, come back. Come back to me. Focus on my voice, okay? Don't think about anything but my voice."

And I did just that. I focused on Jericho's voice, deepened with a pained gravity I hadn't heard before from him. A seriousness very different from his usual sarcasm, one that worked like an anchor for me. He kept talking, and I latched on to that anchor and pulled myself back to him, out of the searing golden haze. Back to reality.

My vision cleared enough to see the Blackheart in front of me, gripping my shoulders so tightly that I was sure he'd leave bruises. His dark brows knit together over coal-black eyes.

He let out a deep sigh of relief and cupped my face between his hands. "Talk to me, Drake. Say something."

"I . . ." I began, my head still spinning. "I need a nap."

He laughed, the sound short and sharp and full of relief. "There she is. What the hell just happened? You looked like you were having a seizure."

"I tried to control it, but it didn't work. Memories. A bunch all at once. Too much, too many. It . . . it hurt so bad."

Concern slid though his dark gaze. "I thought I lost you."

"Not that easy," I managed.

"Good." He shook his head. "You really want to make this difficult for me, don't you? I'm going to have to keep an eye on you now, whether I like it or not."

"Got to make sure the merchandise isn't damaged."

He rolled his eyes. "Yeah, that's exactly why."

"I need this magic out of me, Jericho. I can't deal with something like that happening again."

I still felt weakened, like I'd just run a marathon. I wiped my hand under my bloody nose and tried to take a step, but my legs gave out beneath me.

Jericho caught me before I hit the ground, sweeping me up in his arms as if I weighed next to nothing. "Time for that nap," he said.

I didn't protest. I let him carry me back to my cottage, resting my throbbing head against his shoulder. He gently placed me down on the bed and pulled the blanket up over me.

"We will fix this," he told me. "Lazos will fix this."

"And Valery . . ."

He shook his head. "Valery can go to hell. Knowing her, she probably already vacations there. Plan A is alive and well, no need for plan B. Okay?"

"Okay," I replied.

He stroked my hair off my forehead, an anguished expression on his face. I reached up and absently touched the scar on his jawline, desperate to focus on something tangible. Something real.

"How did you get this?" I asked.

"My brother gave it to me as a going-away gift." He smirked down at me. "Let's just say a broken bottle and a difference of opinions were involved. I don't think he meant to cut me; my worthless face just happened to get in the way of his dramatic exit from my life."

"Not a worthless face," I murmured. "A very worthy face."

Again, that now familiar pain slid though his dark eyes. "You definitely need a nap. Go to sleep, Drake."

I didn't argue. I fell asleep almost immediately.

When I woke the next morning, I found Jericho sleeping on the floor next to the bed, his arm behind his head.

I watched him for a moment, silently, before his eyes opened and met mine.

"Morning," he muttered.

"Morning," I replied. "You didn't stay in your new cottage last night."

"A brilliant observation." He slowly got to his feet and scratched his shoulder. "Get up. We're going to see Lazos again about that magic stuck in your head. And he's damn well going to make sure what happened yesterday doesn't happen again."

Jericho tried the door to the Overlord's residence only to find it locked. Apparently, it was the only building in the entire Keep that got to have a lock.

He slammed his fist against it instead. "Open up!"

"What the hell do you think you're doing?" Mika demanded from behind us.

My arms were crossed very tightly over my chest. "I need to see Lazos."

"You saw him yesterday."

"I need to see him again."

"Doesn't work that way."

"How does it work?" Jericho growled, turning to face her.

"You make your request. I take that request to the Overlord. Then he decides when and if he's going to talk to you. The rules are very simple."

"You're right," Jericho replied. "I've always appreciated it when the rules are simple. My rules are pretty simple, too. If I have a question for you, you damn well better answer it. And if you're in my way, you better get out of it."

He turned and kicked the door hard. It splintered and swung open.

"After you, Drake," he said.

I glanced at Mika, who stared at us with wide eyes. She reached for her knife and swiftly moved to block us from entering.

"Don't take another step," she snarled.

"It's fine, Mika," a voice said from within. "They may enter."

Her shoulders tense, she reluctantly stepped aside and allowed me and Jericho to enter the darkened room. My gaze immediately fixed on the bearded man, who sat on his wooden throne.

"I apologize for this failure, my lord," Mika said.

"Apology not accepted." Lazos flicked his wrist at her. "Leave us now."

She did as he commanded and shut the broken door behind her as much as a broken door could be shut.

It smelled like alcohol in here. And not just any alcohol. *Pisswater.* The sharp, cheap, nasal-clearing scent wasn't one that could easily be forgotten. A dozen empty bottles were scattered across the wooden floor.

"Did somebody have a party last night?" Jericho said. "I didn't get an invite. Should I take that personally?"

Lazos glowered at him. "No party here, Blackheart."

I couldn't help but notice the drunken slur to his words. I stepped forward before Jericho could say something insulting.

"I tried to control the magic," I said. "But it didn't work. Instead, it showed me too many echoes, one after another, and they were incredibly painful and . . . disorienting. I'm here to ask you to please consider removing this magic from me ahead of schedule."

He picked up a bottle from the floor, checking to see if there was any liquid still inside. When there wasn't, he sighed and tossed it over his shoulder.

"Our deal is already set," he said. "I won't be doing anything of the sort until the beast is dead."

I fought to retain my composure. "Surely we can renegotiate. It felt like my head was splitting in two."

"But it didn't, did it? Your head is still in one single piece."

"That's not the answer we came here for," Jericho said evenly, his jaw tight. "I know everyone around here treats you like some sort of king, but I know you're not. *You* know you're not. I've gone along with your deal, and I'm true to my word. I'll slay the beast, whatever the hell it is, but you're going to help Drake today."

"Will I?" Lazos said, his eyes narrowed.

"You sure will."

"Leave us," he said. "I wish to speak to Josslyn in private."

Jericho shook his head. "I'm not going anywhere."

"Then this conversation is at an end. Goodbye."

Jericho took a menacing step forward, but I put a hand on his arm, holding my pleasant expression as steady as possible.

"It's fine," I said. "Let me talk to him alone."

Jericho glared at me.

"Seriously," I said. "It's fine."

"Fine," he bit out. "Ten minutes and I'm coming back in here, and things are going to get a lot less civil."

He left the room and slammed the broken door behind him.

"Please excuse Jericho's manners," I said to Lazos. "Surprisingly, he actually means well."

"He cares about you."

I wanted to argue, but it seemed that the evidence spoke for itself. "He mostly cares about the magic in me and getting it back to his boss."

The Overlord peered at me then, through the shadows. "It's been a long time since I've come into contact with memory magic. As I told you before, it's a straightforward magic, but it requires an astronomically high proficiency in both earth and air elementia to capture one's memories perfectly."

"Is that you?" I asked hopefully. "Rush said you could extract this magic from me, so you must have a high, uh, *proficiency* for earth and air elementia, right?"

"I do indeed."

The confirmation was a relief. "Is it like how Tamara can heal people with earth magic?"

"Her magic is much less powerful than mine. But, still, incredibly useful."

I shook my head. "I don't understand any of this."

"Of course you don't. No one does. Elementia is ancient, as ancient as the universe itself. Most witches and warlocks are born with a mild hold on such magic—one or two elements at the most. Very rarely, one is born with much greater control than that." He leaned back in his seat. "Do you want to learn more about magic? Or are you only seeking a solution to your current problem?"

I desperately wanted to get back to my request, but I had to pace myself. I couldn't push him too far and risk dismissal.

"I'm seeking a solution that will help me return to my normal life as soon as humanly possible," I replied honestly, but then frowned. "But I do want to learn more. And I want to learn how to control this. Will you help me?"

Until he'd asked the question, I hadn't known the answer. But it felt true. It wasn't just something I said to stay on the warlock's good side. My whole life I'd been taught that magic was evil, and that all witches and warlocks were enemies of the Empire, but I'd seen and heard glimpses of another truth in the Keep that had nagged at me, refusing to let me ignore its existence.

"I'll help you." Lazos nodded. "I feel, in many ways, that it's my duty to offer you a small education on elementia. I believe your father would be proud of your tentative interest in this very maligned subject."

I almost laughed. "My father would be horrified by all of this, from beginning to end. He was a firm believer in the evil of magic and those who use it."

"It's more accurate to say that magic is *channeled*, rather than used, like one would use a napkin or a toilet," Lazos said tightly. "A witch draws her magic from the natural elements. It doesn't exist within her in a vacuum."

"But this memory magic is in me, not outside of me."

"Yes, but that magic was not originally channeled by you; it's simply contained." He nodded. "Contained magic is much more advanced, such as earth- or water-magic-based potions and elixirs: virility, health, fertility enhancements, mostly. The types of commodities that the Blackheart's employer deals in. I have come across silver amulets infused with air magic, which when worn can give the wearer the illusion of beauty. I've also heard of seeds infused with earth magic that could cure the most dire of diseases when ingested. Nearly anything can be had for a price. The vast majority of magic practitioners don't possess the depth of skill or control to create such containments, so they're very rare and very expensive, which is why Valery is so interested in obtaining this magic currently within you. Not to mention whose memories are involved. Priceless, really."

My head had started to spin. "Valery has a dagger that she used to carve magic into Jericho. Would that be the same sort of thing?"

Lazos went very still. "She has a dagger? What sort of dagger? Is that the secret to her death magic?"

The air chilled all around me, and it became so quiet that I could hear the sound of my heart beating. I realized I shouldn't have said anything.

More gossip, only unintentional this time. Oops.

I pushed an easy smile onto my lips. "Honestly? I have no idea. This is all new to me."

I mean, it was the truth.

Lazos studied me for a moment before he nodded. "Of course you wouldn't know more about such things." He blew out a breath. "It's all such a mystery, really."

"You seem like you know a lot."

"I do. But not about death magic. Once, I was foolish enough to think I did. That I was worthy of channeling such ultimate power." He shook his head, his gaze growing haunted. "To be able to control life and death itself like a god—it was a heady prospect. But death magic is a crime against nature itself. And one pays a very high price for such a crime."

"Is that why you're here? Because you tried to channel death magic?" I asked.

Lazos shot me a look so cold it turned my blood to ice. But then his harsh expression relaxed.

"I did try once. Only once. The results were . . . disturbing."

I shivered. I didn't know what he meant by that, and I honestly didn't think I wanted to know.

"My lord, please forget I asked such a personal question. It has nothing to do with me or the magic in me."

He sought another bottle while muttering, as if to himself: "Such dark fate this is, as black as pitch. It seems there's no way for me to escape from it."

"My lord?" I prompted when he seemed to fall into a bit of a trance, staring dully at the bottle in his hand.

"Enough talk of death magic." His gaze met mine again, and he seemed clearer now, more present. "I have to wonder why Zarek would choose to contain his memories. He's a man of endless secrets, so why would he risk revealing them in this way?"

"Good question." I knew he wasn't really asking me; he was pondering aloud. "Rush said you were associated with him, but I don't know how closely."

"Close enough to have once been considered a friend." Lazos had successfully found another bottle with some alcohol still in it, which he quickly drained. "I've always found it difficult to be friends with any highly gifted warlock. But I suppose with Zarek, I came close for a time." Lazos noticed me eyeing the bottle he tossed away from him. "Drinking makes coping with my many mistakes a bit easier."

"I understand," I said, even though I was surprised by this confession.

"No. You're far too young to understand such things, Josslyn. Now, why would Zarek want to contain his memories? Memories that, in the wrong hands, might be used against him in far too many ways to count? Only one reason comes to mind. He wanted to see the truth."

I shook my head. "What do you mean? If he wanted to remember things, couldn't he just . . . you know, remember things? Naturally?"

"That is the charm of memory magic, though. When we use our natural ability to recall events, we see them through a distorted reality. It's the reason why no two people will remember an event exactly the same. We view the past through the lens of our own desires, prejudices, and misconceptions. But when one contains their memories, steps into the echoes created with magic, they can see with more objectivity, as if watching a recorded event. Do you understand?"

I nodded slowly. "I think so. You mean, there wouldn't be any room for error—for misremembering? It's like when I was at my friend's party, I swear I remembered wearing a pink dress, but when I saw photos from it, I was clearly wearing blue." I cringed. Suddenly, the many trials and tribulations of my life before this magic seemed a bit insignificant. "I guess that's a pretty bad example."

"The important thing is, you understand the concept."

I did. So I supposed that was a decent enough start. "I can walk around in Banyon's memories, at least the first few that I had. The ones from yesterday that I tried to control were different, though. Disjointed and hard to follow. And they really hurt." I winced. "It felt like I'd been swept up by a tornado and thrown all over the place."

"Tell me more about the memories you saw."

I twisted a lock of my hair around my finger. "I'm trying

not to dwell on anything to do with that warlock."

"Humor me. And then I promise to help you with your control so this won't happen again. Unless you want it to."

"As if I'd ever want that." Still, I was encouraged enough by his promise to force myself to remember my disjointed vision from yesterday. "I saw Banyon as a child. Then I saw him furious and full of hate. In another, there was a beautiful woman with him who kissed him. And then he was speaking in front of an audience, telling them that they would destroy the Empire. That was more like the Lord Banyon I'd been expecting to see." I shuddered. "It was chilling, actually."

Lazos watched me, listening silently. "Is that all?"

"No, actually. You were in one of the memories."

Silence fell for several uncomfortable moments. "What memory?"

I shook my head. "Just a snippet, just a moment, but it was disturbing. He was bruised and bloody. And you were saying something to him about being a tree that didn't bend, that he might break."

His jaw tightened. "That's all?"

I nodded. "Yes, that's all I saw."

Lazos studied my face, his eyes narrowed. "And you saw all of these memories, all at once."

"One after another. I tried to fight them, to make them stop, but they kept coming at me."

He nodded. "This was right after I told you to accept the echoes. And yet, you fought against them, which is the exact opposite of my advice."

And now I fought to maintain my composure. "It sounds like you're blaming me for what happened."

"I am." The warlock stood up from his makeshift throne and moved toward another bottle a few feet away, one that had a couple of inches of pisswater still at the bottom. He tipped it back and drained it, then tossed the bottle away from him. It shattered against the wall. "You disrespected the magic and tried to dominate it. The results don't surprise me at all."

I almost laughed. "And, what? The magic got angry with me?"

"In a sense."

"That's ridiculous. Magic isn't sentient. It doesn't have a mind of its own."

"You are very certain for someone who's lived her entire life believing every lie you've been told about the subject without ever asking a single question to help refute it. Yet now that it has infringed upon your life, you're suddenly open to learning more."

Before I could say anything to that, and I couldn't guarantee anything I did say would include any honey at all, he raised his hand. "You can't fight magic when it rises within you. You can't repress its power. These may not be your memories, but it is now your magic to control, with effort and practice. Think of it like a wild dog that needs to be tamed. If you kick that dog or try to cage it, it will bite you. But if you're gentle and patient, it will learn to obey your command. This is the first lesson any young witch should learn, no matter what element she is able to channel."

I was quickly growing impatient with this tutorial and the warlock's ramblings. "I'm not a witch." I fought to hold on to my composure. As frustrating as this warlock was, and as much as he made my skin crawl, I still needed him on my side. I had no other options to fix this horrible mess I'd found myself in.

Lazos's drunken gaze grew distant. "This Empire has struck such great fear into the hearts of its citizens—fear that has evolved over centuries to a point that it's a tight knot in the soul of humanity, one I'm not certain can ever be untangled. Because of this fear, there are few born today who wouldn't naturally and unconsciously repress any signs that they may be sensitive to elementia. But I sensed it from the moment I first saw you. You, Josslyn Drake, are most certainly a witch."

He'd said it again.

He'd given voice to this ridiculous and offensive idea.

"You're drunk," I bit out.

Lazos was still talking. "If you weren't a witch, you would not have drawn this magic into you, and you would not be able to access it as you so clearly can."

I wanted to put my hands up to stop him from saying anything else. Or stick my fingers in my ears so I wouldn't have to hear him. What he suggested shook my world at its very foundation.

I sucked in a shaky breath. It felt like I was starting to suffocate. "Why would you lie to me about something so horrible?"

"I'm not lying. You can deny it, you can fight it, and you will continue to suffer from it. But if you accept this fact into your reality and know that this magic will not hurt you even if the images you see are jarring and unwelcome, then you can lean into the magic and let it flow naturally through you. Only then can you truly control it."

I just stared at him, shaking now. Wishing I'd never come here, wishing I'd never listened to Rush. Wishing I'd never gone to the Gala in the first place, never started down this long, dark, and frightening path.

It felt like he'd backed me into a corner. My first instinct was to come out fighting. "Why did Queen Isadora exile you ten years ago? What did you do to her? What's your big dark secret that keeps you here, cowering in your sad little makeshift palace, drowning yourself in pisswater?"

"We're done here." Lazos's eyes glittered in the shadows. "Today's lesson is over, young witch. Now leave me alone."

He went through another door at the back of the room and slammed it shut behind him.

FOURTEEN

I didn't even try to see if the door was locked; I knew he had nothing else to say to me. Numbly, I staggered outside, Lazos's claims still loud in my ears, to find Jericho pacing nearby.

"What happened in there?" he asked. "Did he help you?"

I didn't reply to him. I couldn't find my voice.

"Drake. Are you listening to me?"

I'd started to shiver, as if all the warmth in the world had disappeared, leaving me surrounded by ice. "It's not true," I whispered.

Jericho took me by my shoulders, peering down at me with concern. "What's not true?"

I shook my head, inwardly grasping at my ability to compartmentalize my problems, hoping that I could lock this one away in a small dark room where I could forget about it. But all my small, dark, locked rooms were currently occupied by the plethora of world-shattering information that had been thrown at me this week.

"Drake," he growled. "Now you're starting to piss me off.

Talk, would you? What did that bastard tell you that has you acting like this?"

I lifted my chin, searching the Blackheart's face. His world hadn't been shattered. He'd weathered every twist and turn we'd faced, deflecting each hit as if it didn't faze him. He dealt with magic every day; it was normal to him to the point that hunting a monster was just another item on his to-do list.

I wondered if he'd always been like that, or if he'd been broken first.

No, I didn't have to wonder. I knew he had been. He had the scars to prove it.

"He said I'm a witch," I whispered. "That I wouldn't have this magic in me if I wasn't."

Jericho's jaw tightened. "That guy doesn't pull any punches, does he?"

"It's not true," I said, as if it had to be said. "He's just a pathetic old drunk with a vivid imagination. Right?"

The Blackheart didn't answer me right away.

My heart pounded. "I'm *not* a witch."

"Of course you aren't," he finally agreed.

I really wished he had put far more certainty into that statement than he did.

I suddenly noticed that Mika now approached us and I hoped she hadn't heard anything.

"All done?" she asked.

I nodded, forcing myself to appear calm and unfazed. "For now."

"Good." She gave me a sinister smile. "Now I get to assign you both your chores. Time to make yourselves useful citizens of the Keep."

"Bring it on," I told her, strangely grateful to her for delivering some sort of normalcy into my life again. "I seriously need a major distraction."

I really should have been more specific.

My first assigned chore, the same one she'd warned me about when I first arrived, was outhouse maintenance. This dire job involved inspecting the ten outhouses across the town and keeping them clean. And, when they were full, collecting and emptying buckets that contained horrors I'd never experienced in my lifetime into a deep hole dug into the ground on the far west side of town. The stench of other people's waste would haunt the rest of my life like putrid, screaming ghosts.

Still, as bad as it was, it did keep my mind off my other problems, and I forced myself to try to forget my conversation with the drunk and delusional warlock. Over the next couple of days, I fell into a routine. Meals at the lodge. Work during the day. Brief conversations with Jericho. I still caught him giving me a strangely guilty look from time to time, like he had our second day here, and he usually kept our chats light and quick, mostly focused on whether I'd had another memory vision, before he moved off in another direction.

He didn't bring up the topic of either witches or monsters. And neither did I.

Lazos rarely emerged from his residence, which I realized only made him seem more important and elite to the other

Keepers. The main rumor that circulated around town was that the Overlord had been a wealthy, powerful king from a far-away country, a country that Queen Isadora wanted to conquer. He'd fought. He'd lost and he'd surrendered, offering to be a prisoner if she allowed his kingdom twenty more years of independence before being added to the Empire. Apparently, she'd agreed to this, in this fantasy version of the truth. The oddest thing about the rumors regarding Vander Lazos, though . . . none mentioned his magic.

Apparently, the warlock liked to keep his secrets extremely close to the chest.

Also, I quickly learned that Mika had lied to me. There was a way to get new clothes. Or . . . at least, old clothes that could be mended when necessary. I now was the proud owner of exactly two outfits—the expensive but stolen one I'd arrived in, and a simple cream-colored dress that I wouldn't have been caught dead in on the other side of these walls but was super comfortable and kind of cute in a minimalist sort of way.

Despite all these distractions, one thing kept repeating in my mind, taking over my mantra of "magic is evil."

I'm a witch.

◄◦◦◦◦◦►

It was impossible. Lazos had to be wrong. There was another explanation for why this had happened to me, other than being in the wrong place at the wrong time, and I would find it.

On day seven—which was thankfully the last day I had to

clean outhouses—I experienced another memory echo, my first since the rapid-fire deluge. I dropped my bucket on the cobblestone road as the golden smoke came at me fast and furious, and my first inclination was to resist what came next, to try to stop it before it even began.

Instead, I decided to welcome it. And to breathe through it, just like my therapist had taught me.

Breathe in, breathe out.

Mindfulness and acceptance, not fighting and denial.

And I allowed the vision to appear before me without trying to resist it.

The golden smoke dissipated, and a cliffside appeared before me, a multicolored sunset over a sparkling ocean to the left. To my right, a handful of well-dressed people were seated in rows of chairs. At the front, Lord Banyon stood before the golden-haired woman I'd seen before, holding her hands.

Another woman standing before them wearing dark-blue robes spoke. "Zarek, will you take this woman as your wife? As your truth, as your light. As your greatest love. A bond that will begin this day and go forth unto eternity."

"I will," Banyon said, smiling. His eyes shone with tears. "I love you, Eleanor. More than anything else in this entire world."

"Eleanor, will you take this man as your husband? As your truth, as your light. As your greatest love. A bond that will begin this day and go forth unto eternity."

She smiled up at him, her attention nowhere else but on the warlock. "I will. I love you, too, Zarek."

"Then I pronounce you husband and wife. Today, tomorrow, and forever."

Eleanor held a bouquet of colorful flowers and, as the two kissed, she rested it against her swollen belly, her pregnancy very evident under her gauzy white dress.

The audience applauded as the pair, smiling and laughing, turned to greet them as husband and wife, and the golden smoke swept in and took me away from the wedding and from Lord Banyon's memory.

I was in the Keep again, the dropped outhouse bucket spilling onto the ground next to me. It took me a moment to get my bearings, to steady myself, as I ran my hand under my nose to wipe away the blood.

Blood, like usual. But the pain I usually felt after these was much duller, only a faint sensation at the back of my head.

Huh. Maybe this wild dog could be trained not to bite after all.

"You, Drake," Jericho said from nearby, "look like you've seen a ghost."

"That pretty much sums it up." I turned to him to see that he had an armful of firewood. "Remind me. Why did you get lumberjack duty and I'm the outhouse attendant?"

He shrugged. "Mika loves me?"

"No, she hates you."

"Well, I guess she hates you more." He frowned. "You saw another memory, didn't you?"

"How can you tell?"

"Lucky guess. Was it bad?"

"No." I shook my head. "I mean, *yes*. But—it didn't hurt this time. Not as much, anyway. I didn't try to fight it. I accepted it, like Lazos suggested."

"Good."

"Not good. Not really. Banyon was happy in this memory, Jericho," I said. "It was his wedding, on a gorgeous cliffside under the sunset. His wife was pregnant. They were, like, a normal couple, madly in love."

His pleasant expression faded. "And?"

"Lazos said this magic allows for an objective account of memories, moments trapped in time. And in a few of these memories, Banyon . . . he's not the evil man that I always expected. He's just a man who's experienced pain and suffering and hope and love and loss. All of it. Just like anyone else."

"Listen to me, Drake. Listen to me carefully. I don't care what you see in these echoes. Banyon is the devil, okay? He killed my parents, burned them alive, and made me and my brother orphans. It's a damn miracle that we survived."

I deflated immediately. Of course, I'd seen the memories of him burning down the palace, too. "I know. And I'm so sorry. He killed my father, too."

He turned his face away, shielding the pain that immediately crossed through his dark eyes. "I have to go."

"But, Jericho—"

"I have to go," he said again. And then he was gone.

Now with a heavy heart, I finished my chores, relieved that it would be the last day I was on outhouse maintenance, at least for a while. I had dinner—rice, beans, and tasteless, odorless slop again—at the lodge. Gloria entertained me and several other Keepers with tales of her younger days, a sparkling life of parties and handsome suitors and travel to all corners of the Empire.

She didn't make any mention of murdering her three husbands. And I didn't ask. Some things, I was better off not knowing for sure.

I went to bed with a bit of a buzz from drinking too much substandard alcohol, and a stomachache from too little substandard food, and I fell asleep immediately.

That night, I dreamed about a monster. One that tore through the Keep, hunting all of us trapped inside, until Jericho appeared to face it. As the beast and Jericho fought, I saw Lazos's face, repeating over and over: "No one ever has to know the horrible truth."

The only monster I woke up to in the morning was a hell of a hangover from all I'd drunk the night before. But I also woke up with one very clear thought, something I should have realized much earlier: I didn't trust Lazos. He hid the truth from the Keepers—he admitted as much. So what guarantee did I have that he wouldn't do the same to me? Something smelled really bad here, and I didn't think the outhouses were the only thing to blame.

Jericho and I had believed Lazos when he told us that he was a powerful warlock, and when he told us that he'd help me if Jericho slayed the beast.

But I didn't see why Lazos hadn't found a way to slay it already. He was a warlock. This prison was full of hulking men like Otis and Arlo who could yank full-grown trees out of the ground and use them for toothpicks. Yet he apparently waited for someone like Jericho to come along to take care of this problem. And we had to keep it all a secret. It sounded more suspicious by the minute.

What the hell was going on?

Jericho had gone along with it, agreeing to the deal, so I guess I'd been swayed by his confidence. After all, he was the well-traveled Blackheart that dealt with nightmares and violence on a daily basis.

But even a Blackheart could be wrong.

I needed to talk to Jericho. But first, I'd have to find him.

I left my cottage and walked down the main cobblestone road, my cream dress tucked under my arm. I'd spilled some vegetable stew on it during lunch yesterday and wanted to wash it in the river. Most people I passed nodded at me in greeting. I nodded back, grateful that no one else had recognized me yet. I guess I looked as far removed as I could get from the Josslyn Drake who regularly appeared on the royal newsfeed. She was glamour and sparkle and flirtatious smiles. This Josslyn was tomato-sauce stains, nightmares, and feigned friendliness.

I followed the path into the forest that led to the lake and the river, a walk I'd taken every day since our arrival. I knelt at the side of the river and scrubbed the stain, stubbornly working at it until it faded away to almost nothing. Which was still something. Just like my outfit with the faint traces of Jericho's blood still on it, a harsh reminder of how close he'd come to dying. Again.

Wringing out the wet garment as much as I could, I resigned

myself to the fact I'd be wearing stained clothes all the time. And I started back to the village to track down the Blackheart.

Then I spotted a familiar face at the edge of the lake.

Tamara.

She had some laundry in her arms but had stopped and was looking intently at the lake. I drew up beside her.

"Something interesting?" I asked

She jumped. "Oh my god. Janie . . . you startled me."

"Sorry." For someone filled with healing magic, who'd previously been a doctor, she was a nervous little thing. I looked past her to the lake to see what had captured her attention so much that she hadn't noticed my approach.

"Oh," I said, blinking with surprise.

A hundred feet away, up to his waist in the lake water, was Jericho. His dark hair was wet and slicked back from his face. He had a washcloth in hand and he was . . . well . . .

He was bathing.

Shirtless.

And probably pantsless, too.

The sun hit his smooth, bare skin, his muscled chest, his broad shoulders, and I found that I couldn't quite look away.

"I wasn't spying," Tamara said, but she sounded guilty as hell.

I tore my gaze away from the naked Blackheart to regard the sheepish-looking witch.

"Sure you weren't." I cleared my throat. "I mean, can I blame you? Not really. He's kind of hard to ignore, isn't he?"

Her cheeks flushed red. "He's very handsome."

Well, of course he was. Painfully and distractingly so. And, annoyingly, I'd noticed this more with every day that passed.

I shrugged. "I guess. If you like that type."

"Who wouldn't?" She laughed nervously. "Can we forget this ever happened? I'm honestly not someone who spies on young men bathing in lakes. I mean, I haven't been with a man in years. Didn't even think I liked them anymore, since I fell in love with a woman."

I actually hadn't expected that. "True confessions, huh?"

"It's not really a secret." Tamara laughed lightly and twisted a lock of her red hair around her index finger. "I know you and Jericho have broken up, but I hope you reconsider. I see the way he looks at you."

I frowned. "And how exactly is that?"

"He looks at you so intensely, like . . ." Tamara shook her head. "Like he's sorry for what happened. Like he wants your forgiveness, but he's desperately afraid to ask for it."

I'd noticed the same thing. That pained expression that crossed his gaze, at least once a day. I'd assumed it was due to the magical marks on his arm. The reminder that he was late returning from his latest mission for the boss from hell.

"Should I forgive him?" I told Tamara. "Maybe we're destined for a happily ever after in the Keep."

She didn't laugh; her expression only got more serious. "You do have a way of deflecting earnest statements."

I shrugged. "It's part of my charm."

Now I was worried about Jericho and his built-in Blackheart signal. I hoped he wasn't in constant pain as we waited out this two-week sentence.

"Can you do me a favor?" Tamara asked, cringing.

"Sure. What?"

"Don't tell Mika I was spying on your ex-boyfriend?"

It took me a moment, but then my eyes widened as her meaning became clear. I couldn't believe I hadn't realized it before now. I was usually way better at homing in on romantic pairings. *Mika.* "Oh. Well, yeah. Sure. Jealous type, huh?"

"She seems so strong, but she can be paranoid when it comes to loyalty. My love and loyalty to her are unmatched. I'd follow her into the fires of hell itself, just like she followed me here."

"Wait. Mika followed you here?" I asked with surprise. "I thought she was thrown in here for committing a crime, like everybody else. That's not true?"

A shadow crossed Tamara's face, and pain flitted through her gaze. "She sneaked in, joining a group of other prisoners. Nobody questioned it. I mean, who would sneak into the Queen's Keep, right? She shouldn't have, but she was so sure we could easily escape together."

I guess Mika and I had more in common than I thought.

"No escape yet," I said.

Tamara shook her head. "The Overlord promised to help us, which is why Mika works so closely with him. He asked for her help in keeping the peace here as payment. But it's been over a year, and we're still waiting for his help."

Maybe I'd misjudged Mika. Well, not for being a straight-up bitch. But for following her heart. At least now I knew why she was so loyal to Lazos—because, just like me, she believed he held the answer to her problem.

"I know she was a Queensguard," I said, lowering my voice.

Fear flashed in Tamara's eyes. "She was. But please don't tell anyone that."

"I won't," I promised. "Her secret is safe with me."

And I meant it, too. I knew without a doubt that I would never share this gossip with anyone. Even though the ex-Queensguard in question seemed to take great pleasure in making me clean disgusting outhouses.

"Does she think the Overlord can use his magic to help you escape?" I asked.

She frowned. "Magic? What do you mean?"

I frowned back at her. "He's a warlock."

"What? I didn't know that."

That seemed highly unlikely to me. "You didn't?"

She shook her head. "He knows that I'm a witch, but he never said a thing to me about having elementia of his own. Although, to be honest, I've never been close enough to him to be able to sense anything of the sort. Why do you think that about him?"

My heart pounded. More questions had now been raised about the enigmatic Overlord, questions that didn't seem to add up to any satisfying or comforting answers.

"Oh, I don't know," I said as lightly as I could, sending another look toward Jericho and his ridiculously admirable torso. "I heard that rumor the other day in the lodge. People talk. Doesn't mean what they say is true. Does everyone know you're a witch around here?"

"No," she said quietly. "There are definitely a few prisoners in here who believe that all witches are evil."

"You're not evil," I said, shaking my head.

She eyed me warily. "You reacted quite strongly to my magic last week. I was worried I'd frightened you. That I'd said too much. I wouldn't normally have been so quick to use my healing magic in front of you, but Jericho was in bad shape."

The talk of magic had quickly set my nerves on edge. But I wanted Tamara to feel comfortable with me, since she might have information I could use. I wanted to tell her I wasn't frightened anymore, that I'd quickly come to accept the idea of elementia, and that magic wasn't as horrible and wholly destructive as I'd always believed.

But a brick wall built from seventeen years of certainty didn't crumble to the ground in a single week.

I'd been presented with facts, with counterarguments, and I had a lot to think about and consider. Meeting Tamara had definitely helped me see there was more to the story than I ever would have believed.

"Jericho has this really nifty explanation of magic that's helped me start to understand it better," I said. "How it's like a knife, only as dangerous as the person using it."

"That's a good metaphor," she agreed.

For days now, I'd tried to forget what Lazos had said to me about being a witch, even though my new mantra played constantly in the back of my mind. I couldn't understand why such a ludicrous claim had bothered me so much.

But hiding from it wasn't making it go away.

"You sensed magic in me when I arrived," I said.

She nodded. "I did."

My stomach clenched, a signal that I wanted to end this conversation just as it was getting started. But instead, I squared my shoulders and forged ahead. "Do you sense magic in many people?"

"No," she replied. "Not many at all."

"Did Mika tell you anything about my . . . situation?"

Tamara frowned. "Not a word."

I hated how tentative I'd become. This wasn't me. Fear had installed a permanent lump in my throat that seemed to block my former bluntness. But dancing around the edge of subjects wouldn't get me anywhere.

I had to stop being so damn afraid.

"The magic you sensed in me is from an outside source," I said. "A box of memory magic opened up and flowed right into me."

"I'm not familiar with that kind of magic," she said. "I only really know my own. But, yes, that would certainly explain your golden eyes."

I had to appreciate the fact that she'd taken this admission in stride, not even blinking. I drew in a long, shaky breath, trying to balance myself before I asked my next question.

"Can what happened to me happen to a normal person?"

Tamara shook her head. "What do you mean?"

"Someone told me that I'm a witch." I said this so quietly, so under my breath, that half of me hoped she wouldn't hear me. "That I couldn't have elementia like this in me if I wasn't."

I waited for her reply, my chest tight, my stomach tense.

"Do you really want the truth?" Tamara asked.

I met her serious gaze as I considered my incredibly limited options.

Then I nodded.

She cocked her head. "The magic I sensed in Jericho wasn't like yours. I immediately knew he wasn't a warlock. The death magic in him can't be channeled in any way; it's been integrated into his very being. I'd like to say like a sponge with water, but water can be extracted. It's more like a sponge saturated with permanent dye. If that makes sense. But you . . ." She pressed her hand against my cheek, holding my gaze intently. "This possibility pains you greatly."

I nodded, my eyes stinging. "But I still need to know the truth, Tamara. Please. The ugly, unedited, painful truth. Am I a witch?"

Tamara held my gaze firmly, her expression gentle. "I knew the moment I sensed the magic within you that you were a witch."

I just stared at her.

She smiled sadly. "I'm sure that wasn't the answer you were hoping for."

"It's just not possible," I whispered, letting the hot tears I'd been fighting to hold back splash to my cheeks.

I wanted to shove Tamara away from me, scream at her, accuse her of being a liar, and run away from her as fast as my legs could carry me.

I wanted to keep denying it, to keep searching for someone who would confirm that it couldn't be true. That I hadn't lived for seventeen years without knowing this dark secret about myself. I wanted to look at Tamara like one of my friends at the Gala who liked to spread hurtful rumors and gossip about me behind my back.

But the worst thing—the absolute worst thing about this . . .

I knew, deep down in my soul, in those small, dark, locked rooms I'd collected over the years of things I didn't want to deal with, things that hurt me, made me feel weak, made me feel doubt, made me feel like I didn't fit in with my friends or my life, and that I never had and I never would . . .

I knew it was true.

I staggered away from Tamara as my stomach lurched and I threw up at the base of a tall, leafy tree.

Tamara didn't come near me; she stayed silent, waiting. After a few minutes of kneeling there, sobbing, I wiped my eyes, and then my mouth, and looked at her over my shoulder.

"You won't believe me," she said, "but you have a gift. This magic inside of you is as old as the universe itself. It's quite beautiful."

My golden eyes began to sting again. "You're right. I don't believe you."

She tentatively moved toward me to give me a hug. And I let her. "I understand how you feel. This is a frightening world for people like us. But it's not all bad. There are leaders out there, leaders like Lord Banyon. He is trying to change the world and bring magic back to it. One day I know he'll succeed, and we'll be safe again to be who we are without living in fear."

I recoiled from her, searching her face, but saw only sincerity there.

"I'm sorry," she said, her cheeks flaming with color. "I shouldn't say such things so openly. I know he has a terrible reputation, but I honestly believe it's false. He's been accused of many crimes he isn't responsible for, so everyone views him as evil without question."

"He had my father murdered," I gritted out.

Her eyes widened. "I'm so sorry, Janie. I didn't know. Please . . . don't tell Mika I've been spouting my conspiracy theories again. She always tells me to keep them to myself, even in here. I've said too much and upset you. I only wanted to help. Please forgive me."

"I . . . I need to go."

I turned from her and began making my way back to the village, lost in a thick and violent swarm of thoughts.

With my stained, damp dress clutched tightly in my arms and my mind far, far away, it wasn't long at all before I slammed right into a very firm chest.

FIFTEEN

Jericho took me by my shoulders. "Daydreaming, Drake?"

He still wasn't wearing a shirt. My gaze sped down his tanned bare skin.

"You could say that," I managed.

"By the way, I couldn't help but notice you were spying on me just now. You and Tamara. See anything interesting?"

I tried to ignore the heat that flooded into my cheeks. "Not spying. We were having a serious conversation. Which just happened to be close to where you were having a bath."

"Totally understandable, I suppose." He slung his wet shirt over his shoulder. "Walk with me back to town."

I didn't immediately follow him, so he glanced over his shoulder at me. "Problem?" he asked.

"Many."

"Care to share?"

"No."

Tamara's confident confirmation about my witch status felt like a far too intimate confession, since I was still processing it for myself. I wasn't ready to talk about it with anyone. And that went double for conspiracy theories about Banyon. Jericho hated him, wanted him dead. Mentioning Tamara's personal opinion on the matter would do nothing to change his mind.

As we walked, I noticed the Blackheart watching me curiously.

"What?" I asked.

"Now I'm dying to know what you're hiding from me. After all, you're not someone to keep any secrets to herself."

"Gee, thanks." I chose to pivot to something that might be easier to talk about—something to distract myself from all of this, the reason I'd been looking for Jericho in the first place. "I think Lazos has been lying to us."

"I'm sure he has. But about what in particular?"

"Tamara didn't know that he's a warlock," I said. "If anyone would know, you'd think that she would, right?"

"Agreed."

"Have you seen him do any magic?" I asked. "Or elementia, or whatever?"

"I haven't exactly been spending a lot of time with him."

"So, no."

"No, I haven't seen him summon a tidal wave, or create a windstorm, or make a tree grow, or start a bonfire —or whatever. Nothing. No elementia. But that doesn't mean he can't."

"He seemed pretty fixated on death magic. *Your* death magic. When I talked to him, he hinted that he'd tried to channel that magic before and it didn't go so well."

"I'm sure a lot of witches and warlocks dabble in the darkness from time to time. Forget death magic; I know many who use blood from animal sacrifices to supercharge their regular ele-mentia. Make it, like, ten times more powerful for a short time."

I stared at him. "And you're trying to convince me that magic isn't evil?"

"Remember the knife, Drake. It's all about that knife. I'd never suggest that people aren't evil. People can be evil as hell, and you can't tell it just from looking at them. Take Valery, for example. She's the most beautiful woman I've ever seen in my entire life. And I bet she's sacrificed more than a few bunnies over the years to help take her magic up to the next level."

It annoyed me deeply that out of our entire conversation so far, learning that Jericho found Valery incredibly beautiful bothered me most of all.

And the immediate and unexpected stab of jealousy that fol-lowed wasn't the least bit helpful.

"How are your marks?" I asked tightly, grasping at some other random topic.

"Searingly painful, thanks for asking. But I can handle it for a bit longer. Anyway, you feel free to investigate Lazos. I'm going to continue on with plan A as previously scheduled. Update me if you get any new intel."

"Fine," I said.

"Oh, and Drake?"

I raised my gaze to meet his. "What?"

A smile played at his lips. "I take a swim in the lake every day around this time. You're free to watch, if you like."

Maybe he expected me to blush again and run away. But I wouldn't give him the satisfaction.

"Thanks," I said, without missing a beat. "Maybe I will."

He didn't have a witty retort for that parting line, but I felt his gaze heavy on me as I walked away.

Over the next three days, I experienced two more short memory echoes, and I tried to use everything I'd learned to control them. That control didn't mean stopping them, which was always my first inclination. No, it meant mindfully allowing this magic to flow gently through me, and accepting what it needed to show me.

When I did that, there was no storm, no fight. Only a clear view into another time and place. Another moment that had forged its place in Lord Banyon's memories.

The first:

Banyon stood over a cradle, gazing down at a baby sleeping peacefully. "She's very nearly as beautiful as you are," he whispered in Eleanor's ear.

And the second:

Banyon stood outside the burning palace as two little boys, not much older than toddlers, crossed his path. The younger one was sobbing. The older one stared up defiantly at the warlock, his young face dirty with ashes, his arm protectively around the little one.

Some of the hate fell from Banyon's expression, and regret filled his eyes.

"I'm so sorry," he whispered as he walked past them.

I slowly came out of that vision, wiping the blood from under my nose and the tears from my eyes, knowing without a single doubt that those two little boys had been Jericho and Viktor, right after their parents were killed.

It broke my heart. Jericho's life would have been so different had his parents lived. He wouldn't have had to rely on a morally challenged criminal like Rush growing up. And his path never would have crossed with Valery's.

Who would he be, then? At nineteen years old, having not experienced even a fraction of the pain and grief and challenges he'd faced?

I believed he could have been anything he wanted to be. But that hadn't happened. In his escape from the palace, Lord Banyon had burned everything in his path, including mothers and fathers, daughters and sons—including Prince Elian.

A tragedy. And though these glimpses of the warlock's past added much more dimension to his story, it didn't change what he'd done and who he'd killed.

Lord Zarek Banyon may not have always been a power-driven monster. And maybe the fire magic he'd summoned wasn't evil all on its own. But he was a dangerous warlock who wanted to destroy the queen and her Empire, who wouldn't let anybody stand in his way, not even the innocent. So far he'd failed in his mission, but that didn't mean he wouldn't try again. I had to remember that. I had to keep reminding myself of that. And I had to get his poisonous memories out of my head.

Everything I'd been through over the past week had started to distract me from my purpose. But from now on, I wouldn't let myself be distracted by anything that happened, any conversations I had, or people I'd met along the way. My one and only goal had to be to return to my life. To Celina. To my friends—at least, the ones who actually weren't horrible. To my bright future in which I could do anything and be anything I wanted to be.

Even though you're a witch? a little voice asked inside my head.

That little voice was the part of me that couldn't sweep everything I'd learned under a rug.

One way or the other, my future currently hinged on a deal made with a habitually drunk supposed warlock with a very sketchy past and an extremely frightening request. None of it sat right with me. It didn't make sense. Lazos had to be hiding something big, but I had no idea what it was.

But I was damn well going to find out. I pledged to uncover Lazos's secret, because he definitely had one. He wouldn't be here if he didn't.

⚬⚬⚬⚬⚬⚬

The enigmatic and private Overlord kept mostly to himself except for the few times he emerged from his residence to walk through the village. Every time I saw him I immediately went up to him, trying to ooze with my social charm.

"My lord, it's so wonderful to see you out," I said to him on one of these occasions.

"It's wonderful to be out," he replied.

"I'm hoping we can continue my education that we started the other day. It gave me so much to think about."

"Of course," he said, scanning the faces of other Keepers who passed us, smiles on their faces at seeing their leader. "But not now. I will have Mika bring you to my palace when it's time."

It did bother me deeply that he called that shack, with its rickety wooden throne, a palace, but I held on tightly to my pleasant expression.

"Of course, my lord," I said with as much grace as I could muster. However, my grace tank was nearly empty.

Not too shockingly, that time to come to his "palace" never came. And subsequent conversations with him were even briefer before I was dismissed as he moved on to talk with someone else.

My friends might have liked to gossip about me behind my back, but I'd rarely been given the complete brush-off in person. It didn't feel very good at all.

"He's hiding something rotten," I told Jericho at the lodge one night at dinner. "Some secret, some piece of information that I need to know."

"Isn't everyone hiding something rotten?" he muttered.

"What?"

The Blackheart seemed fascinated by the tasteless slop on his plate. "Everyone's in here for a good reason, Drake. Everyone has secrets. And I'd assume that the Overlord has more than most of us, given who he used to work for."

"The only reason I'm in here is for answers," I told him firmly. "And I'm going to get them. Starting with what Lazos is hiding and what this beast actually is."

I wasn't sure why Jericho was so willing to go along with Lazos's strange deal without the drive to find out more. Maybe he was used to taking orders without questioning them, since disappointing Valery came with a harsh punishment.

"You do that," he said. "Best of luck to you."

Then he got up and left the lodge—which was *so* Jericho, to remove himself from a conversation he no longer wanted to be part of—and I wanted to be mad at him. But I wasn't mad. After seeing that memory vision of him and Viktor—so small, so innocent. It made me want to help him. Both of them, really.

Unfortunately, I had no idea how, so for now it would have to take a lower position on my to-do list.

For the second week of my unplanned stay in the Queen's Keep, Mika had assigned me to the chicken coop. I got to feed, clean up after, and care for scores of chickens.

Gloria had also been assigned here for the week, and she spent most of the time telling me all about the chickens, as if each one had a personality of its own, and how they were weren't used for their meat until they stopped providing eggs. Poor chickens.

"Except for that one time last year that Otis stole and cooked a perfectly fine young hen for dinner over a bonfire," Gloria shook her head with annoyance. "Can you believe it? He said he needed meat to stay as strong as an ox. What a brute. He was reprimanded by the Overlord, assigned to outhouse duty for two months. Yet if you ask Otis, he says it was all worth it."

I was only half listening to Gloria. She liked to talk a lot, and my mind was busy coming up with ways to see Lazos again and find a way to draw the answers I needed out of him.

I realized that the old woman was studying me with a deep frown on her wrinkled face.

"Are you even listening to me?" she asked.

"Of course." I straightened my shoulders as I tossed bird feed from my bucket toward the chickens. "Otis loves barbecued chicken enough to break all the rules to get it." I cocked my head to the side. Something had occurred to me as she shared the tragic tale of the unknown chicken. "Have any other chickens gone missing?"

"What do you mean?"

Of course, I was thinking about the horrific beast Jericho had agreed to slay, based solely on Lazos's prophetic dream and a handful of prisoners who'd disappeared. "Are there larger wild animals in the Keep that might come into town to prey on the livestock here?"

"There's never been any missing livestock that I'm aware of." Gloria shook her head. "And there are no wild animals to speak of here, other than birds and insects. Any small mammals were made extinct by the first residents of the Keep, who would have hunted them and made a meal of them just like what Otis did."

No missing chickens, pigs, or cows. That was odd. It didn't seem likely a ravenous animal would go after humans while ignoring a free, pretrapped meal like livestock in a pen. This wasn't adding up.

But if Lazos was lying about this beast, about his own magic that no one else seemed aware he even had, then I needed to know what his agenda was. If I went directly to him, I had no guarantee of getting to the truth.

Since I knew the powerful warlock would dodge me and my bottomless ocean of questions, I decided to seek out his administrative-assistant-slash-law-enforcement.

Mika stood outside Tamara's cottage, her arms crossed over her chest as she eyed my very determined approach. "What's your problem today?"

"It's a long list, actually. But let's start with your boss and whether or not he's really a warlock."

"It would be great if you could lower your voice when you say things like that," she said tightly. "Or even better? Don't ask questions about the Overlord at all."

"Why?" I turned in a circle, holding my arms out to either side of me. "There's no one close enough to hear us. I could throw a rock and probably not hit anyone except you. Want me to try?"

"Not necessary."

"Great. So. No one around here thinks he's a warlock. But you do."

"I don't want to talk about this." Mika turned away, but I grabbed her arm. She glared at me, but she must have seen the desperation on my face, since she didn't storm off. I wasn't going to use my social skills with her, since I knew they wouldn't work. She saw through that sort of thing, just like Jericho did.

"My entire life hangs in the balance here," I told her. "My future is on the line. Lazos promised he would remove the magic in me, but if he's not a warlock, if he can't do magic, then he lied and I'm screwed."

I didn't share the current opinion held by both the Overlord and the witch-in-residence that I had more than temporary memory magic in me. For all I knew, Lazos had already sent out a memo on the subject.

Her hard expression softened, but only a little. "He is a warlock, Josslyn. I know he was the queen's advisor, that she trusted and valued him for quite some time. I don't know a lot about it, but she wouldn't put her faith in just anybody on such a delicate subject."

I stared at her with shock. "How do you know he was Her Majesty's advisor?"

"The higher your rank as a Queensguard, the more access you have to classified documents. I got a bit of a taste for information when someone I loved was arrested and put in shackles, all because she used her magic to save someone's life."

"Tamara," I said.

"Yeah." More of her hardness eased. "So I dove in and read a lot. Too much, maybe. But part of it was about Vander Lazos, a former friend of Lord Banyon's, and how he became Queen Isadora's advisor, living at the palace in the inner circle."

"What's the inner circle?" I asked.

"The heavily guarded part of the palace where the queen's chambers are. So to have the Overlord living there meant that he was a major secret, even to most of the queen's own army. And also that the queen wanted him close to her. And it wasn't because any romance was involved."

Surprisingly, the thought hadn't even occurred to me. "No matter how I look at it, I just can't rationalize the queen ever keeping a powerful warlock so close to her, especially one who was friends with the man who killed her son."

"You're right, it doesn't make sense," Mika said, her voice sharp and pitiless. "Especially since Her Majesty is actually someone who'd have a witch put to death who's only ever summoned healing earth magic. Tamara doesn't have an evil bone in her body."

We agreed on that much. "But Tamara wasn't executed."

"Only because I changed the file. I had Tamara sent in here to spare her life. It was the only choice I had."

I searched her pained expression, trying to understand. "Tamara was going to be executed for saving someone's life?"

"That's what your good friend Queen Isadora does to witches, no matter who they are. She kills them. But for some reason, she didn't kill Vander Lazos."

A shiver sped down my spine. "Why not?" When she didn't answer me right away, a thought occurred to me. "You're investigating him, too, aren't you?"

Her gaze shot to mine, but then she laughed. "Is that what you're doing, too? An investigation?"

"Absolutely."

"And I'm your latest witness."

"Seems like you're a better witness than I thought. So, what? You've gotten close to him so you can learn his secrets?"

She nodded. "That's the plan."

"Why?"

"Why?" she repeated. "Because when I get the hell out of

here, I'm going to do everything in my power to expose the queen's lies to the world, even if it means I need to take what I know to Lord Banyon himself, not that I have any idea how to find him."

I stared at her with horror. "You're kidding, right?"

She shook her head. "Not even slightly. I saw plenty of files on him, too. Most of what the queen's accused him of is nothing but lies. Lies she broadcasts on the palace-controlled newsfeeds, tampered video and pictures, showing him as a terrorist who wants to bring down the Empire—her precious Empire, built from stolen lands and conquered people. It's a crime against humanity. Nearly everything Banyon's accused of is something the queen did herself, all to build this gigantic lie to brainwash everyone."

"Oh my god." I physically winced, since the accusations against a woman I'd always admired were painful to me. But they only built on what I'd already learned about Queen Isadora since the night of the Gala.

I couldn't ignore what Mika said. She wasn't a random prisoner with a beef against Her Majesty. She was a former Queensguard who'd had access to classified information.

Mika swore under her breath. "Why am I wasting my time here? I can't think of anyone worse to complain to about the queen. You adore her."

"I do," I whispered.

"Feel free to continue. It doesn't make a damn difference to me. You asked if Lazos is a warlock. Yes, he sure is, and I fully believe he can help you get that magic out of your head, just like

I believe he can help me and Tamara escape from here. The only question is, when? Now get away from me. I have work to do."

She turned and started walking in the opposite direction, but after everything she'd said and everything she'd hinted at, there was no way this conversation was over.

"Mika, wait!" I called out.

It was then that something large and heavy dropped from the sky. A wooden crate the size of a car slammed down right in front of me, shaking the ground beneath my feet.

SIXTEEN

I scrambled back, falling on my butt, and stared at the crate in shock. I heard screams from other Keepers and more thuds from nearby.

Mika's hand appeared before my face, and I grabbed hold of it to help me get back to my feet.

"What the hell just happened?" I demanded.

"It's our monthly delivery of supplies," she said, a grim look on her face. "A bit too close to town. Let's hope there's no casualties this time."

I gaped at her. "*This* time?"

She gave me a very tight smile that looked more like a grimace. "Yes. This time. Her Majesty's monthly benevolence upon us lowly, caged creatures has flattened at least a dozen people over the years. You'd think whoever's piloting those planes might take a moment and aim. Or . . . hell, maybe they *are* aiming. They don't care about anyone in here. I'm surprised they even bother with the supply drops at all. Why would they care if we all starved to death?"

Behind Mika, five prisoners were prying open one of the

crates. They didn't seem to be freaked out by this near-deadly delivery; instead they were cheering and laughing.

Mika glanced at them over her shoulder. "It's not all bad. There's always lots of extra goodies to keep the Keepers happy for a night or two. Get ready for a celebration tonight."

⋈⋄⋄⋄⋄⋈

I tried to ask Mika more questions, but it seemed that she'd remembered who she was spilling all sorts of secrets to: the ward of the current prime minister and a girl who literally got her generous monthly allowance from Queen Isadora herself.

I guess I was the enemy here, and that sudden realization felt strange and unpleasant.

It shouldn't matter to me what Mika thought, I reminded myself. My goal was to save myself, get back to my real life. That was what I'd been working toward for nearly two weeks. But along the way, things had gotten complicated.

To say the very least.

Thanks to the near-deadly supply drop, the Keep had enough dry goods and protein packs to last the next month, as well as cloth for new clothes, extra blankets, more candles, and plenty of feed for the farm animals. And there were cratefuls of fresh fruit, pastries, chocolates, and other treats.

It took me a while to shake off the fact that murderously heavy objects had been dropped on a populated area—especially so close to *me*—but everyone else seemed to take this in stride and was excited for the chance to indulge tonight.

After nightfall, nearly all Keepers—at least those who didn't have chores that prevented them from being part of the celebration—filled the lodge from wall to wall like some sort of an imprisoned wedding reception to enjoy the fallen bounty.

When I entered, I scanned the area, spotting Gloria, Tamara, Mika, and dozens of other familiar faces. Even Otis and Arlo were at a table to the far left, their plates filled with nonslop food items and their cups filled with alcohol.

But my gaze settled on Jericho, sitting by himself in the back of the hall near the fireplace. He'd had the black T-shirt he'd worn upon our arrival mended after it was cut off of him to tend to his wound. That shirt of his didn't do much to hide the rather admirable lines of his body, which were now branded into my brain after seeing him in the lake. I hadn't asked for the image of Jericho's naked body to be permanently lodged in my head, but it seemed to have taken a front-row seat.

His black eyes watched my approach.

"Did you save me a spot?" I asked lightly, among the noisy buzz of conversation all around me.

"The most popular girl in the Keep wants to sit with me." He gestured toward the log bench across from him. "I'm deeply honored."

"Is that what I am here? Popular?" I asked, taking a seat.

"Isn't that what you are anywhere you go?" He raised his hand to flag down a server, who delivered a glass bottle and two wooden cups. "You're just in time to help me drink this."

I peered at the bottle, which had a very attractively designed label. "This is wine. Like, real wine, not pisswater."

"It sure is." He poured some of the dark red liquid into both of the cups, then pushed one toward me.

"This is the best day of my life," I told him, positively giddy.

"I doubt that."

"I'm exaggerating, of course. But this is still so great."

He raised his cup. "A toast."

"To what?"

"To the full moon tomorrow night." He tossed the entire contents of his cup down in one swallow.

"To the full moon." I drank mine, but my grip on the cup increased. How was it possible that the last two weeks had felt as long as a year, but also as short as a single day?

And here we were. Tomorrow my fate would be decided, one way or the other.

"Good?" Jericho asked.

"Delicious," I admitted. "Reminds me of being home and drinking far too much on a regular basis."

"I usually don't drink," he said. "Valery forbids it."

"Really?" My gaze shot to his as he poured us more of the wine. I drank my portion without hesitation, allowing the smooth, sweet liquid to slide down my throat.

"Really. She likes her Blackhearts to be stone-cold sober, which makes sense. You can make a lot of mistakes when you're drunk."

"True enough." The warmth from the wine already started to slowly spread to all of my limbs. "How much do you owe her?"

"Why? Are you going to give me a loan?"

"Maybe." I shrugged. "I know people."

Jericho sighed. "It's not really a literal price that can be paid with money. Money actually doesn't matter that much to Val, which means she already has more than she can spend. No, her price is loyalty, control, and power. She'll let me go when she's ready to let me go. When she thinks I've earned my freedom."

"When's that?"

"No idea. But the way this mission's going . . . it's sure not going to earn me any bonus points with her."

Something disturbing caught my eye. The marks on Jericho's arms were usually invisible except for when they'd glowed that first night to show their existence. Tonight, I could see the outline of the marks, thin red lines that looked alarmingly like fresh scars.

"Jericho!" I reached across the table and took hold of his left wrist, turning his arm over so I could fully see his bared fore-arm. "What's happening to you? Is it getting worse?"

He pulled away from me. "Don't worry about it." He swallowed another mouthful of the wine. "This'll help. And in a few days, it won't matter. One way or the other, this will be over."

"Let me see," I said quietly. Suddenly the buzz of activity around us became nothing but faraway background noise.

"Why?"

I glared at him for making everything an argument with me. "Let's call it morbid curiosity."

This answer made the edge of his mouth quirk, as if he were repressing a smile. "Fine. Be my guest."

Jericho presented his arm to me again, laying it across the

table between us and giving me a chance, albeit only by candle-light, to really take a good look at what that evil witch had done to him.

I guess it *was* morbid curiosity, or just plain old regular curiosity, but I couldn't help but gently trace one of the scar-like symbols with my index finger: a circle inside a circle.

"That's the symbol for earth magic," he said. "Valery put all four symbols on me—*in* me—and some other writing. I don't understand it, but I don't really need to for it to work."

"So this is elementia, not death magic."

"It's a mixture. I don't know. I didn't ask, and she didn't offer up any answers."

My fingertip moved over a wavy line, a triangle, and a spiral. Seemingly simple shapes for some seriously complex magic.

For someone who'd believed that magic, *all* magic, was evil until very recently, I was overflowing with curiosity about how it worked, what it meant, and why Queen Isadora felt that she needed to execute all witches and warlocks who were arrested—including Tamara, but excluding Vander Lazos. And why everyone seemed to just go along with this as if it made any sense at all.

I'd witnessed magic. I had magic inside me. And currently, I was touching magic.

It wasn't evil. *Jericho* wasn't evil. Despite his current job and his shady boss, and the fact that he'd kind of kidnapped me, that much I knew for sure.

"Does it hurt right now?" I asked the Blackheart.

"Not right at this very moment."

His voice had turned husky. I glanced up at him curiously, meeting his dark gaze full-on.

"Finished your inspection yet, Drake?" he asked, but he didn't pull his arm back from me.

"Yes," I said. But I didn't pull back, either. I sought answers in his expression, in those bottomless black eyes of his. No matter how much time we spent together, the Blackheart was a continuing mystery to me. Most people I'd met weren't. I could figure them out in a heartbeat. Jericho Nox, however . . . he was an enigma, and I couldn't seem to figure him out no matter how hard I tried.

"Tamara says that you look at me sometimes like you're sorry about something," I said. "What are you sorry about, Jericho?"

"Nothing. She's obviously seeing things that aren't there," he replied tightly.

I shook my head. "I've seen it, too. I've seen pain in your eyes when you look at me. I thought it was just the pain from these marks."

"That must be it, then." He nodded gravely. "Most of the time, I don't look at you, Drake. Don't mistake me for one of your many drooling admirers out there in the real world. Because I'm not."

"You're looking at me right now."

"Can't really avoid it, can I?"

"Sure you could."

"I came here to drink tonight, Drake," he said. "And you sat down across from me, smack dab in my eyeline. That's why I'm looking at you."

I glanced at the bottle of wine, realizing foggily that it was already empty and I had definitely helped in draining its contents. "I think I'm drunk."

"That would explain a lot." He flagged down a server, who brought over another bottle.

"Like what?"

"Like why you're touching me right now when you don't have to."

I drew my hands back, folding them instead on my lap, and laughed nervously. "So sorry. Didn't mean to offend you."

"Forget it." He poured us both another cup, his expression dark as he drank from his. "So, what else is new in the world of Janie?"

I slid my index finger along the rim of my cup. "Mika confirmed that Lazos is a warlock."

"Huzzah. So he's telling the truth."

"Something is still off with his story about the beast. That this hungry, murderous thing slips into the impenetrable Keep and gobbles down a few prisoners before slipping back out again, but leaves the livestock alone, for some reason? Not even grabbing a single chicken along the way for a snack? And Lazos knows when it's going to be here thanks to his dreams."

"Well, when you put it like that it does sound a bit hard to believe. But that doesn't mean it isn't true." He leaned closer to me. "I got this, Drake. Whatever happens tomorrow night, I can handle it."

"Okay," I whispered. "So you head out into the forest and track this thing down and put a knife in its heart. Lazos is thrilled, and he holds up his end of the bargain. What then?"

"Then I go back to Val, and you go back to your happy, shiny life."

I drained my cup of wine. "Even if I'm a witch?"

He hissed out a breath. "I thought you'd dismissed that as the ramblings of a drunken idiot?"

"Tamara confirmed it. I've been fighting it, Jericho. All this time. Fighting everything, but I don't think I'm strong enough."

"You're strong as hell, Drake. Stronger than you even think you are. Maybe you are a witch. Doesn't matter. It doesn't change you. It just makes things more interesting."

I envied how easily he'd taken this earth-shattering news in stride. "You make it sound so simple."

"It is simple. Magic always runs along a family line. Is there anyone in yours who might have qualified as a witch or warlock?"

I shook my head. "I don't know anything about my family history. I never even thought to ask. Like, it never, not once, occurred to me."

"Of course it didn't. Why would it?"

I searched my mind, even though it was currently dulled by the wine, to try to find some clue, something. Anything that might help me make sense of this.

Something rose up from the depths, from where I'd shoved it down as deep as it could go.

"Wait. The night of the Gala," I said. "Last year's Gala, my father said he wanted to tell me something. He seemed really stressed out that night, which was probably why we ended up fighting about my damn dress and how short it was. He—he said he wanted me to know the truth, that I was old enough, and that he'd held on to it for too long already. My god, I haven't even thought of that again until now."

Jericho had gone very still in the center of the boisterous lodge. "What truth?"

My eyes had started to sting. "I don't know. Maybe about magic in my family? Maybe something else? I'll never know now, will I? We were already late, and I was pissed off at him. I told him to tell me later. But later never came, did it?" I looked down at my hands as a tear splashed to the tabletop. "A half hour later he was dying in my arms. And it was over, just like that. I can't go back. I can't make it different. He died thinking I was a brat who gave him a hard time, who didn't appreciate him when I should have."

Jericho poured more wine, and I noticed his hands were shaking. He swore under his breath. "I don't know what to say, Drake. You're not a brat. You were sixteen years old. A kid. And you shouldn't have had to go through any of that. Damn it. I'm sorry. I'm so sorry."

He swallowed the wine, and when he put down the cup, I reached for his hand, entwining my fingers with his and inhaling sharply at the feel of his warm skin against mine.

"Thank you, Jericho," I said softly.

"Don't thank me," he muttered.

Only a moment later, he withdrew his hand and swore again under his breath.

"I need to go. I need to rest up for my hunt tomorrow." He

stood up and grabbed the half-empty bottle of wine, taking a quick swig from the bottle.

I nearly said something to stop him, but he was moving swiftly toward the exit. He was done talking. I got that. He had a lot to think about when it came to his task tomorrow night.

Kill the beast.

Save the girl.

But was this the only way, the only choice? I'd finally reached the point that I thought would never come—I could no longer totally ignore everything in my life that didn't make sense, or lock it all away to sort through when I was ready. And I couldn't look away from everything I'd learned. It was like someone had cleaned windows inside me that I hadn't realized were covered in years of grime, windows that previously had let in only a little light from the outside world.

When the windows were at their grimiest, I never would have spoken to someone like Jericho. He wouldn't have even been on my radar—someone literally raised from the dead, someone marked by magic that had changed him, that controlled him, that forced him to obey a boss from hell.

But I could see him crystal clear through my newly clean windows.

And, despite his annoyingly passive-aggressive tendency to leave rooms where he felt uncomfortable, this conversation wasn't nearly over yet.

I left the crowded lodge and caught up to him when he reached his cottage.

"Jericho," I said.

His shoulders tensed as he pushed open the front door.

"We're done, Drake. Go get some sleep."

He went inside, and the door shut behind him.

As if that was going to stop me. The alcohol now coursing through my veins seemed to have a mind of its own. And the doors here didn't have any locks.

Jericho groaned darkly when I entered the small cottage.

"What now?" he growled.

"Why didn't the queen have Lazos executed? She executes everyone else who has anything to do with magic. She was even going to execute Tamara, and she's literally the least evil person I've ever met in my life. And don't tell me it's because he's a magic encyclopedia. What would she care? She destroys magic; she doesn't archive it."

"Honestly? Who knows? Maybe because the queen's just a shameless, power-hungry hypocrite and always has been, even if you don't see that fully for yourself quite yet. Keeping Lazos alive but contained, only a short trip from the palace, must serve her in some way."

I still flinched whenever anyone disrespected the queen, even now. Even armed with more knowledge about her past decisions.

"She's always been kind to me," I said. "But I'm starting to see her flaws."

"That's a start, I guess."

"Jericho, something really strange is going on here, and I don't know what it is."

"You don't have to know what it is. Just let me find and kill this beast, whatever it is, and be done with it. Then you can sort your life out in the comfort and luxury of the prime minister's residence."

I raised my chin. "What if this beast kills you instead?"

He glowered at me. "Unlikely."

"But not impossible."

"I've killed before, Drake, whether you like it or not. Both beasts and nonbeasts."

"Who have you killed?" I asked tentatively, then with more force: "I get that you're this badass Blackheart with your badass dagger tattoo, and you have to do what your witch boss tells you to do. And, well, I assume things can get messy."

"You assume right. Very messy. Don't worry about me, Drake. I can handle anything that's thrown at me all by myself with nobody's help. I've been doing it since my parents died. And even when *I* died, I still came back for more."

Jericho turned toward the small window that showed a sliver of the night outside, a darkness that obliterated even the view of the forest. There was no moon tonight; the skies were covered in a blanket of thick clouds. Only candlelight kept the room from being plunged into total darkness.

I watched him, searching for a clue to understand him better. "So I'm supposed to go back to my normal life, even knowing I'm a witch and that magic isn't evil and that most witches and warlocks executed over the last century and beyond didn't deserve to die."

"Simple, right?"

God, he was so frustrating. "And you're just going to go back to Valery?"

"I suppose I could always chop off my arm, stay here in the Keep, and keep eating slop and drinking pisswater until I die of natural causes." He drank more from the bottle of wine, then wiped his mouth off on the back of his arm. "That sounds like fun."

"What about Viktor?" I asked.

His expression darkened. "What about him?"

"He thought you were dead. You're not. You could reconcile, have a family again." I wanted to tell him about the echo I'd seen of him protecting Viktor when their path crossed with Banyon's, but I held it in. That memory wouldn't help right now; it would only hurt.

"Vik wished me dead during our last face-to-face before the Queensgames." Jericho ran his finger along the scar on his jaw. "He told me I was standing in his way—that staying with me would ruin any chance he had to reach for the stars. Or . . . whatever cliché you want to pick for having a successful life. That my way of dealing with the large, rotten lemon that life had handed us was a waste of his potential. Vik didn't want to fight in dirty, secret clubs for money, handing over ninety percent of the winnings to Rush. He always had his eyes on the prize. My eyes were only focused on surviving."

I shook my head. "It was a fight. Like the one I had with my father. It doesn't mean you didn't love each other, that you couldn't have worked it out."

"No. He was right. He's better off without me. He's achieved so much in such a short time. And me? I work for the devil herself, shoveling whatever garbage she needs me to shovel, just like the rest of her Blackhearts. And if I refuse, I suffer." He groaned and raked a hand through his hair. "Damn, I definitely drank too much. This wine's making me way too talkative about things that don't matter anymore."

"Maybe they're things that matter more than anything else."

"After two long weeks forced to be in my presence, you might think you know me, but you don't. And despite chasing me all over the Keep, you don't want to know me."

My cheeks flamed. "I'm not chasing you anywhere."

"You're in my cottage right now after chasing me from the lodge."

"Only on a search for the truth."

"Truth," Jericho repeated. He took another deep drink from the bottle, draining the rest of its contents. Then he slammed it down on the small wooden table. "Here's the truth, Drake. I am counting the hours until tomorrow, until I can face this beast, whatever the hell it is; I don't even care anymore. I'm going to kill it because that's what I do. I kill the things that I'm told to kill. And when that's done, it's one step closer to never having to see you again."

His words were like a slap, and I actually cringed. "Ouch. Thanks for that."

"We're not friends, Drake. I'm not sure what you think is happening here, but this is not any sort of shiny friendship blossoming between us. I don't need you. I don't need anyone. And I prefer to be alone to sort out my shit. Got it?"

I lifted my chin, defiant. "Well, with that attitude, I'd be surprised you have any friends at all."

"I guess it's good that I don't. Not here, not anywhere else. So is that enough truth for you tonight? Did you learn anything that helps to make the world make sense again?"

"I learned that when things get too personal, you like to push people away. Which explains a lot when it comes to Viktor."

"Great, let's talk about him again." He rolled his eyes. "Viktor. Shiny, handsome, glorious Viktor. Here's another truth for you to add to your growing collection, Drake. I always envied my little brother—how he got anything he wanted because he believed he deserved greatness and glory. Like, deep, dark envy. The kind that buries itself into your soul and starts gnawing away at it. He was always better than me, and he wasn't even trying to be."

"Yeah? Well, it sounds to me like you did the hard work to keep you two alive, working for Rush, giving Viktor the opportunities he wouldn't have had to start with. And he took you for granted. Viktor wouldn't have achieved anything he has if he hadn't had you as a brother."

"I don't believe that." He shook his head. "Viktor was always destined for success. And me? I got what was coming to me."

I watched him, shocked by how he talked about himself. "Why do you hate yourself so much? You deserve better than that from yourself."

"Do I?" He laughed, but there was no humor to the sound. "You don't know me, Drake. You don't know who I am after only two weeks or the terrible things I've done."

"I do know you," I said firmly. "And you're wrong. We are friends. I care about you, Jericho. Whether or not you want me to."

"No, you *don't* know me." He stepped toward me, which was all it took to close the distance between us in the small cottage. I took a shaky step back, which meant I was now pressed against the closed door. "And trust me, you don't want to know anything about me. So stop trying to figure me out. I'm not worth it."

When he turned away from me, I grabbed his hand to stop him and he froze.

"You're so wrong," I told him, my voice thick. "So incredibly wrong. You are worth it."

"Drake . . ." he began.

But he didn't have a chance to say anything else because that's when I kissed him. I took his face between my hands to pull him closer to me, feeling the roughness of his stubble against my skin, and then my mouth was on his, his mouth was on mine.

I'd never kissed anybody like him before. Jericho wasn't a shiny prize I wanted to win to make other people jealous. He wasn't a champion, a celebrity that all my friends—and the entire Empire as a whole—drooled over.

Meeting Jericho, having my path cross with his, had destroyed my life in so many ways. Changed it. Shaped it into something different, a shape I didn't even know existed less than a month ago.

His sarcasm matched my own. He didn't take anyone's shit, especially not mine. He was strong and brave and stubborn as hell. He walked his own path, holding true to his own moral compass despite every horrible thing he'd endured and who he was forced to work for.

Jericho was a fighter—inside and out. Figuratively and literally. His whole life had been one long fight to survive.

But he didn't fight this.

It did take a moment, with his body stiff and resistant against mine, but then I felt something give way in him and he uttered a dark groan, pulling back just a moment to stare into my eyes, his brow furrowed, his expression deadly serious. He searched my face for answers. His hand pressed against my cheek, his thumb sliding across my lower lip.

"Drake . . ." he whispered.

I was barely able to catch my breath when he crushed his mouth against mine, stealing whatever breath I had left. He pressed me against the door, his hands at my waist, sliding down over my hips, pulling me closer against him.

And I felt something deep inside me—something I had never felt before, not with anyone. Not at this level.

I wanted Jericho.

I *needed* Jericho.

In every way someone could need someone else, I needed him. And it was a dark, aching need that encompassed everything in my life in that moment so completely that nothing else existed anymore.

Only Jericho.

His demanding mouth, his warm skin, his hard chest beneath my hands.

And then, suddenly, there was only air between us as he pulled away, swearing darkly and staring at me, the back of his hand pressed against his lips.

What was that look on his face? I couldn't quite figure it out, since it was so chaotic.

Anger. Desire. Pain.

Regret.

"Jericho . . ." I managed.

"Damn it, you shouldn't have come here," he growled. "Just stay the hell away from me, Drake. It's better for both of us that way, trust me."

With that, he left the cottage. And this time, I didn't follow him.

SEVENTEEN

Mornings, especially the ones following a great deal of wine, happened whether you were ready for them or not. I woke up with both a hangover and a whole heap of uncertainty looming over me like a dark and angry storm cloud.

I fed the chickens. I collected eggs. Gloria milked the cows, and I took the buckets of milk to the kitchen at the lodge.

Tonight was the full moon.

I tried to keep my mind busy as I waited for my path to cross with Jericho's, so we could talk about what had happened last night when I'd decided to drunkenly climb him as if he were a black-eyed, grumpy but gorgeous nineteen-year-old tree.

A black-eyed, grumpy but gorgeous nineteen-year-old tree that *did* kiss me back with a level of passion I'd never experienced before in my entire life.

But I didn't see him anywhere, and as the day quickly faded and turned to dusk, I started to get worried. More worried.

And finally, there he was, headed toward the forest, a knife in his grip.

"Jericho!" I called after him.

His shoulders tensed, and he turned to face me. "Drake. Get inside for the rest of the night. Barricade your door."

"You really think you're going to kill whatever you find out there?"

"Hope so."

"You didn't even give me a chance to wish you good luck."

Jericho sighed, a heavy, impatient sound in his chest. "Drake . . ."

"I just wish you wouldn't run away from me whenever things get uncomfortable."

"I don't run away."

"Sure you don't." I raised my hands. "It's fine. We're not buddies. Got that message, loud and clear. And I'm a-okay with that. I just want you to be safe."

Something flitted through his gaze, some dark, painful emotion I couldn't read. "I need to go," he muttered. "Don't try to stop me."

"I wouldn't dare."

"Good. This is almost over, Drake. Now I'm going to go find something to stick this knife into."

I glared him, at his impossible and impenetrable attitude. "You're so frustrating, you make me want to scream, you know that?"

His jaw tightened. "Go to your cottage, and stop giving me a hard time."

"Fine." I hissed out a breath. "Try not to get yourself killed."

With that sentimental parting wish, I turned away from the

Blackheart and walked to the lodge, literally shaking with exasperation over his stubbornness.

Clearly, there was something he wasn't telling me. That look in his eyes, that intense pain that he shrugged off whenever I called him out on it . . .

I kept thinking it was his magical marks that caused that pain, but this was different. Jericho had a secret that was killing him, and I didn't know what it was. A secret he would never tell me in a million years.

And I didn't know why I cared so much.

No, scratch that. I did know. It was because I liked Jericho, more than a little. I'd started to feel deeply for that frustrating, sarcastic, dangerous, death-magic-filled Blackheart when he was the last person in the world who fit easily into my life.

I just didn't know what it meant. What it could lead to, outside the Keep.

Nothing, probably. And that thought made my heart hurt.

Most boys were usually easy to figure out. They didn't confuse me or make me doubt everything I thought I knew. And they definitely didn't challenge me. Maybe that's why I'd set my sights on winning Viktor's attention, because he was a challenge. Someone who I wanted to be seen with, photographed with, and envied for being with.

But I'd known nothing about Viktor except how he looked and how other people looked at him. Surface information, nothing deeper than that. And nothing that pulled at me to try to learn more.

Jericho was literally the opposite. The more I got to know

him, the more I wanted to know him—what made him tick, what interested him, what he liked, what he hated. What his dreams were.

Shit. I was in deep with the last person in the world I ever would have chosen to fall for. And he'd just run off to face something that might tear him apart.

That was, *if* Lazos wasn't manipulating us into believing something that didn't exist. My gut told me he was, but I didn't know why. The opposite was far too frightening for me to fully accept.

I needed to find Mika. I needed her to fill in some more blanks for me about the warlock. Something here didn't make sense. Actually, honestly? Nothing about him made any sense. And my life—and Jericho's—was on the line.

The more I thought about it, the angrier I got. So when I entered the lodge, my blood was boiling.

And when the golden smoke swirled in, it came so quickly that I didn't have a chance to focus on allowing myself to accept whatever echo it wanted to show me.

Vander Lazos stood at the side of a sparkling blue lake, throwing bread crumbs at some enthusiastic ducks. He was clean-shaven and wore a suit and tie, and he looked like a normal businessman from Ironport. Maybe even an accountant.

Lord Banyon approached him from behind. He didn't look like an accountant. He wore all black—an expensive black suit, tailored perfectly for his tall frame, and black leather shoes—and his light brown hair was brushed back from his handsome face. A smile quirked up the side of his mouth.

"Well, I'm here," he said.

Lazos turned to face him, a smile on his face as well. "You are."

"Are you surprised?"

"Not at all. I'm very glad to see you."

Banyon's smile widened to show straight white teeth, and he opened his arms. "My old friend." He embraced the other warlock. "It's been far too long."

"I agree." Lazos took Banyon by his shoulders. "You look happy, Zarek."

"I am happy."

"I'm sorry I couldn't make it to your wedding."

"It's fine. But know that you were missed. I would have liked to introduce you to Eleanor. She's an incredible woman."

"I have no doubt. Eleanor gave birth, what is it now? A year ago?"

Banyon nodded. "Almost a year. Yes, believe it or not, my friend, I'm a family man now." He chuckled. "Everyone can change if given enough time and a second chance. And this is my second chance." When Lazos didn't smile in response, Banyon's pleasant expression faded. "What's wrong? Why did you want to meet me in person?"

Lazos took a deep breath, his expression grim. "Prince Elian died two weeks ago."

"What? How?" Banyon gasped.

"He drowned."

"Dear god. This is terrible news. I didn't see any mention of it in the newsfeeds."

"No, it is to remain a secret for now. The queen is beside

herself with grief. She reached out to me to help find you. I wasn't sure if you'd come, but I'm very glad you did." Lazos nodded. "I'm very sorry about this, Zarek, but I had no choice."

Banyon frowned. "Sorry? Sorry for what?"

A moment later, a dozen armed Queensguards surrounded the pair, and the golden smoke swirled in to obliterate the scene.

As my vision cleared, I braced my hand against the lodge's wall and wiped my bloody nose. Before I even tried to process what I'd just witnessed, I realized someone was studying me.

It was the large and brutish Otis, who usually kept his distance after Jericho had broken his arm in Lazos's residence the day after we arrived.

"It is her," he said, but he wasn't talking to me. He was talking to a couple of his large friends. "I thought it was, but I wasn't sure. But look at her. Imagine her with a dress and makeup and looking much fancier than this."

Oh no.

"Josslyn Drake," one of the other men said, frowning deeply.

"Yeah. Prime Minster Drake's daughter is here in the Keep." Otis leaned closer. "Is that who you are? The spawn of that piece-of-garbage prime minister?"

"I don't know what you're talking about," I said evenly. "I'm Janie, remember?"

"No, you're definitely Josslyn Drake," Otis's friend said. "You're spying on us. Is that right? Are you spying on us for your piece-of-shit father?"

"She's a favorite of the queen," Otis spat. "I wish the queen was here. I'd roast her for dinner. Best protein there is. But you'll do just fine, Josslyn Drake."

"It's Janie," I said, glaring at him, my heart pounding loud and fast. "And if you take one more step toward me I'm going to scream."

"Go ahead." He smiled, and it was a very sinister smile. "I do like a challenge."

I curled my hands into fists, ready to fight for my life. "Great. So do I, you muscle-bound moron."

"Enough." Mika stepped between us. "Is there a problem here, Janie?"

"Nothing I can't handle," I bit out.

She raised her eyebrow. "Really?"

Then I reconsidered. "No, actually I'd really appreciate a little help."

"Figured." She turned to the men. "Go back to your corners, boys. The little show of testosterone isn't necessary tonight."

Otis gestured toward me. "That's Josslyn Drake."

"Where?"

"Her!"

"You need glasses, Otis. Janie here isn't nearly as attractive as Josslyn Drake. And why would Josslyn Drake, of all people, be in the Queen's Keep? Wouldn't she be at some VIP party desperately trying to get her picture taken with her rich friends?" She rolled her eyes. "Use your head."

Otis narrowed his gaze. "I'm using my head. Don't you worry

about that. I've followed your rules, the Overlord's rules, all this time. I came to trust you, Mika. And what do I hear from Gloria? A rumor that you were a Queensguard outside of here?"

My chest tightened and I held my breath.

"Gloria's spreading rumors about me, is she?" Mika said without missing a beat. "Sounds like her. You know she can't stand me. I'm surprised it took so long for her to say such a nasty thing about me."

"So it's not true."

"Of course not. Me, a Queensguard? I hate the queen. And I despise her army. And now you need to get the hell away from me. Come on, Janie."

Mika took me by my arm and directed me away from my would-be attackers, who stared after us, bemused.

"Well, we're screwed," Mika began. "That won't fool them for long. Damn that Gloria and her big mouth. I need out of this prison or it looks like I'm going to have to kill somebody. I'm sick of waiting."

"You need to know something." I met her gaze. "Lazos has been keeping a secret from you." And I told her everything. His claims about the beast, the prophetic dreams, his deal with Jericho. My increasing doubt over his magic.

After I finished, Mika didn't say anything for a very long time. And then: "I knew who he was when I arrived, so I didn't question his magic. But I have to admit that I've never seen him use it here."

"What does it mean?"

Rage sparked in Mika's brown eyes. "It means we need answers. And we need them now."

As we made our way to the exit, I couldn't help but notice the dark, distrustful, and, frankly, *hateful* looks I got as I moved through the lodge. They were the same people I'd had friendly conversations with over the last few weeks.

Otis had been spreading gossip about me to the rest of the prisoners. Everyone knew the truth of who I really was, and continuing to deny it wasn't going to fix this. They saw me, Josslyn Drake, as the enemy. Part of the queen's entourage, a queen who'd exiled them into this prison without any hope for escape.

Their stares weren't any friendlier when they were directed at Mika.

We left the lodge and quickly made our way to Lazos's residence. The Overlord himself stood outside the front door, his arms crossed over his chest, watching our approach. I noticed several empty bottles by his feet.

"Lazos," Mika barked. "What is Jericho hunting tonight?"

His annoyed gaze moved to mine. "You told her."

"I sure did," I replied.

"That wasn't part of our deal."

"I don't care. The deal doesn't matter if you're lying, and you have to be lying. Because it doesn't make sense. None of this makes any sense to me."

"Has any of your life made sense, Josslyn?" Lazos studied me through narrowed eyes. "I can't imagine that it has. Not really.

Not when you take a step back and look at it from a reasonable distance. Does treading this close to magic feel as foul and evil as you always thought it would? Or does it feel right? Like suddenly everything in your life finally makes sense?"

"I hate people who speak in riddles," I snapped. "Just say what you mean."

"Can't do that, I'm afraid."

"Can't or won't?"

"Won't."

"You're drunk," Mika said with disgust.

"Oh yes," Lazos agreed. "I'm very, very drunk. And I've found it's in my best interest to remain that way as long as possible."

"I hate that I was wrong about you," she said, her expression pinched. "All this time, I believed in you because of what I read in the files. But you're not even a warlock, are you?"

"I am a warlock," he snarled. "But how I wish I wasn't. Then none of this would have happened. And that beast would not have tormented me for all these horrible years."

I shared a confused look with Mika.

"Is there really a beast like you said there is?" I demanded. "Is Jericho in danger?"

He turned to face me, his gaze haunted. "Do you want to see? Do you want to see what I did? My greatest crime? My most ardent regret? Do you want to see what I created?"

He grabbed my wrist before I could pull away.

"Concentrate, Josslyn. Draw upon that well of magic inside of you, both the magic you were born with, and the new magic that destiny provided to you. Use it to see a memory of Zarek's that I also hold in my mind."

My first inclination was to yank my hand away, but I didn't. I made a choice, right then and there, to lean into this, not to argue with it. Not to run from it or try to hide.

I was done hiding, since I knew it would find me—this wild dog within me that could either bite me or yield to my command.

So I didn't pull away from the warlock. Instead, I locked gazes with him, and I opened myself to the magic inside me. A moment later, the golden smoke arrived, at my summoning this time instead of by random chance. A thick swirling curtain that obliterated my view in an instant, spinning me back in time to see a vivid memory. An echo of Banyon's past.

When the smoke cleared and my mind stopped spinning, I found myself on solid ground. Literally solid.

I looked down to see a stone floor beneath my feet. At the clomping sound of boots on the stone floor, I whipped my head to my left to see a squad of uniformed Queensguards coming straight toward me down the narrow hallway. I couldn't get out of the way in time and braced myself for them to slam right into me. But instead, they moved through me, as if I were only a ghost.

In the center of the six Queensguards was Lord Banyon, his hands shackled behind his back. Despite the weariness in his expression, his dark blue eyes were sharp, intelligent, and alert. An angry-looking purple-blue bruise circled his left eye.

The long black chains attached to his shackles dragged on

the floor behind him, making a scraping noise. The guards led him into a room at the end of the long dark hallway. When he hesitated at the open door, they shoved him inside.

Heart pounding, I followed.

The room Banyon had been forced into had smooth stone walls, and I moved to stand to the side of a metal table in the center so I could see everyone and everything clearly. Cabinets lined the walls. And on a long table beneath the cabinets on the far side of the room were sharp medical instruments.

Also in the room were two faces I recognized.

Lazos—who looked the same as in my last vision by the lake. And the queen.

Queen Isadora's face was more youthful than it was now, her hair dark and shiny. Their attention moved to Banyon, not a whisper of sympathy between the two of them.

Banyon's eyes narrowed. "Finally, a personal appearance from both Her Majesty and her obedient new lapdog. I'm honored, really."

Lazos's shoulders stiffened, his expression bleak, but he said nothing.

The queen raised her chin, her gaze narrowed on Banyon. "I'm sorry it had to come to this, Zarek. And I'm sorry you've been so terribly mistreated since your arrival."

"I highly doubt you're sorry about any of this," Banyon replied. "You could have cordially invited me here, rather than yanking me so unceremoniously from my life using my trust in my good old friend Vander. Very sneaky, Issy."

I frowned. Did he just call her Issy?

"My grief has made me desperate for a solution, Zarek. I've come here myself to ask for your help. No, that's not quite right." She frowned. "I find I am begging for it. I am begging you, Zarek, to find it in your heart to save our son."

Hold up. Our son?

I felt as if I'd been dropped into the depths of a swirling ocean with no idea which way was up. I'd heard her wrong, right? The queen had had only one son, Prince Elian.

"It's too late." Banyon shook his head. "Even if I could summon the magic necessary, it's far too late now for an intervention like this."

"It's not too late!" The queen's voice rose to a shout. "You are the most powerful warlock alive today. I knew from the moment we first met that you were capable of absolutely anything. You can do this. I know you've done it before!"

Banyon's expression was bleak. "Experiments only. Experiments I never should have done. They cost me part of my very soul. And they were performed on animals, not people. This is the darkest magic, Issy. And the darkest magic comes at a steep price."

"I don't care what price I have to pay!" Her eyes flashed with pain and outrage. "You are simply being petty now. Trying to deny me what I want the most because I didn't tell you the truth about him long ago."

"You should have told me," he snarled. "I should have known I had a son before I learned of his death."

"You can know him. Raise him, Zarek. Bring him back to life, and I promise that you will know him."

"He's been dead over two weeks. He's gone. If it were a few minutes. A few days, perhaps. But it's too late. Let him rest now."

"No, never. He is my son, my heir. The next king. He is my legacy!"

"People die, no matter who they are. It's the natural process."

"There's nothing natural about this. He was only seventeen years old! I am the supreme ruler of an empire of billions. I will not bow to nature!"

Banyon turned his face away. "I can't help you."

"Zarek." Lazos stepped forward, wringing his hands. "A tree that doesn't bend in a storm will break. You've always been a damn stubborn tree, Zarek. But today you finally need to bend."

Banyon's expression only hardened more. "Then I will break. What you risk bringing back to life would likely be something dark and unnatural. I never had the chance to know my son, but I feel I owe him peace. I won't be a part of this."

The harshness in the queen's expression softened, and she placed a hand on Banyon's chest. "Don't be petty. Not today. I swear I will make everything up to you, all the poor choices I've had to make over the years to uphold my name, my legacy. I would choose you this time over Gregor; I swear I would."

"I don't need your apologies, Issy. I haven't for a very, very long time. I love my wife. Our child. It's my second chance to make everything right. I swore to Eleanor I would never, not for any reason, attempt such dark magic again that risks my very soul in the process. My word is my oath."

"So you're saying no." The queen's words were barely audible.

"I'm saying no."

The queen stepped back, her face returning to its rigid mask of civility. "I do understand, you know. I understand why you would refuse me. I even admire your certainty about it and the incredible loyalty you have toward your new family."

Banyon took a deep breath and let it out slowly, his expression skeptical. "Thank you, Issy."

The queen nodded. "Family is the most important thing in the world. I understand that now much better than I ever have in my entire life. I would do anything for my family. Besides, I don't need you. Vander has already promised that he will help me if you refuse."

Banyon laughed then, although the sound held no humor. "Are you serious? He has only a fraction of the skill I have."

"I've read everything on the subject," Vander protested, actually looking hurt by Banyon's words. "Ancient tomes, crumbling in my fingers as I turned the pages. I hold it all vividly in my memory, everything necessary to summon this magic. I know I can do this, with or without you."

"You utter, absolute fool," Banyon muttered. "You've always been cocky, always thought yourself better than everyone else. Your memory got you by, made people believe you were more skilled than you actually are. But you're not. Your magic can't hold a candle to my own, and deep down, I think you know it."

Lazos's lip curled back from his teeth. "You're wrong. I can do this, and I will."

Banyon now leveled his gaze with the queen's. "Whatever you do, do not let Vander attempt to channel this level of death magic. It could so easily go horribly wrong. You'd take that risk?"

"I'll take whatever risk necessary to get what I want," the queen spat.

"Then I pray that Vander fails," Banyon snarled back. "You impossibly ignorant bitch."

This earned him the butt of a guard's gun smashed into his temple as he was forced to his knees before the queen. He tried to get up, and he was beaten down until he kneeled there in silence, dazed, his face bloody, one eye swollen shut.

"Vander," the queen said, and now her voice was quiet, measured, and deeply frightening.

"Yes, my queen?" Lazos said.

"Are you ready to begin?"

Lazos's words came without hesitation. "I am, my queen."

She was quiet for a moment, contemplative. Then she nodded. "I want you to witness this, Zarek."

Another pair of Queensguards entered the room. They pushed a metal gurney covered with a white sheet, concealing a shape that could only be a body.

The queen drew in a shaky breath as the guards transferred the draped body to the metal table in the middle of the room.

"Fear not, Your Majesty," Lazos said thickly. "I won't let you down."

"You damn well better not," she whispered. Then to the guards: "Leave us."

The guards didn't protest. They left. Quickly.

Lazos moved to the table and took hold of the edge of the white sheet, peeling it back.

Death had distorted Prince Elian's handsome face, making his skin translucent and deadly white, his cheeks and eyes sunken. The sickly sweet scent of roses wafted toward me.

"My magic has held," Lazos murmured. "There are no signs of decomposition."

Tears streamed down the queen's cheeks as she neared the corpse, placing her hand on the side of its cold, colorless face.

"My baby," she managed. "My sweet, darling Elian. Come back to me."

I watched all of this with horror, not believing my eyes. Banyon kneeled nearby, chained and beaten. I was surprised he was still conscious. But that didn't even begin to measure up to my surprise at the scene unfolding in front of me.

This was proof that Lord Banyon hadn't killed Prince Elian. That the heir to the throne hadn't died in the palace fire.

The queen had lied—for sixteen years she had lied. To me, to everyone.

"Do it," Queen Isadora said.

Lazos didn't argue, didn't stretch out the conversation for even a moment longer. He got to work.

He peeled back the sheet even more to reveal the corpse's skeletal torso, the dark lines of the dead prince's ribs showing through the thin, translucent flesh. Lazos took one of the sharp silver instruments in hand.

"Perhaps you should look away," he advised the queen.

"No," she said. "I want to witness every moment."

"Very well."

I didn't draw even a single step closer. It seemed my ghostly legs weren't working so well anymore. Frozen in place, heavy with dread, I looked on in horror as Lazos carved a series of symbols on Elian's chest. Bloodless cuts made with a precise, practiced hand.

"No . . ." Banyon muttered, blood trickling from the corner of his mouth. "It's not right. You're summoning darkness itself. Don't do this. Please."

Lazos ignored him, and Banyon didn't have the strength to rise to his feet.

This lasted for what honestly felt like forever. And then Lazos went silent, his brows drawing together.

Nothing happened.

He cast a wary glance at the queen.

"Keep going," she snarled.

It was all the encouragement he needed. Lazos carved more symbols. He started speaking strange and unfamiliar words. The more he spoke, the louder his voice became. The more confident his words. He spoke until his voice became hoarse and he needed to clear his throat.

"The room is so cold," the queen said, shivering.

"Fools," Banyon whispered. "You will regret what you've done here, what you are bringing back."

Silence fell again. A boundless, dark silence that stretched to every wall in the cold, stark room.

And then the sharp, rattling intake of a single breath broke through the silence.

Elian sat bolt upright on the metal table and opened his black, black eyes. And then he opened his mouth and screamed.

Golden smoke streamed in from all angles to obliterate my view of the queen's heir, risen from the dead, and swept me back to the present moment in an instant.

EIGHTEEN

"Did it work?" Lazos asked, his voice hoarse. "Did you see the truth?"

"Oh my god." I staggered back from him, wiping the blood from under my nose. I could barely breathe. "Prince Elian . . ."

Pain flooded his expression at the confirmation. "It's all my fault. All of it. And tonight is my reckoning." He turned away from me and went into his palace without another word.

"What the hell just happened?" Mika demanded.

I stared at the closed door. "He raised Prince Elian from the dead after Banyon refused. And the prince, he's—he's Banyon's son."

Her eyes went wide. "What?"

She tried the door to find it unlocked, and I followed her into Lazos's palace. The Overlord sat wearily on his wooden throne.

I didn't understand how any of this was connected to Lazos's claims about the beast, but I could barely think straight after what I'd just witnessed.

"You raised the prince's corpse with death magic." Saying

it so flatly, so matter-of-factly, didn't make it any easier. "I watched him wake up. I heard him scream."

Lazos's forehead was deeply lined as he frowned at me; then he rubbed his hand over his mouth. "I was cocky, only wanting to please Her Majesty. I betrayed my friend's trust in me, all to gain the favor of the queen, as if she ever gave a damn for me."

"What happened to Prince Elian after that?" Mika asked evenly.

"He was conscious for a few horrible minutes that first night, before he fell into a deep coma." He shook his head. "Zarek warned me, but I didn't listen. I should have listened."

I'd come here for the truth but found this unexpectedly rancid and rotten version of it extremely hard to navigate. Everything inside me wanted to deny it, to turn away from it and pretend this was only more lies. "I can't believe the queen would do this. She opposes all magic, even magic like Tamara's, yet she'd voluntarily want death magic summoned?"

"The queen cares for no one but herself," Lazos spat. "And her legacy. And her absolute control over the Empire. I honestly thought she cared for me, but she didn't. She only wanted access to my magic, but after what happened with Elian, my access to any elementia was blocked. It's like the darkness eclipsed the light."

I gasped at the confirmation of what I'd suspected for a while now.

"So you did lie," I said, my voice shaky. "The bargain you made us was a lie. You can't help me."

"You don't need help, Josslyn. Not with this."

"Go to hell." It was another blow, but I was already bruised and bloodied from everything I'd seen and learned. I knew it would hit me harder later. For now, it just left me empty, with a quiet fury swirling in my chest.

I turned toward the door, wanting to leave. Never wanting to see this shameless liar again.

But something made me pause.

"Is Prince Elian still in a coma?" I asked quietly.

Lazos didn't speak for a moment. "He was unconscious for years. *Years*. And yet, he didn't change. He didn't age a day from the moment of his resurrection." He grasped the arms of his wooden throne. "And then, one night, I felt it in my very soul. I felt the moment that he woke up."

"You felt it," Mika repeated.

"The magic I summoned to raise him created a strange and frightening connection between us. Prince Elian returned from the dead with a darkness within him, a darkness that needed to feed on life itself."

He stood up and started pacing back and forth. Mika and I watched him in shock as he shared his horrific tale.

"Regular food didn't satisfy the prince, so the queen tried animals—living, breathing sacrifices that helped slightly ease Elian's insatiable hunger. But he still wasn't himself. The queen felt the need to experiment, so she began to offer up human sac-rifices."

I found I was shaking my head. "She wouldn't do that."

"She would," he replied flatly. "And she did. Queen Isadora

still saw this dark and unnatural creature as her son, a son she hoped would one day return fully to her. But when I started to lose hope, and when she learned my hold on elementia had faded, she no longer saw me as an ally. And that's when she exiled me here."

I tried to understand the queen's grief and pain driving her to make such horrible decisions when it came to helping her son, but found it impossible.

I'd come to accept that the warm and caring woman I'd admired my whole life wasn't perfect, but to realize that she could also do such horrible, evil things . . .

It was almost too much for me to bear.

I thought Lazos was finished, but he'd only taken a breath. He had more to confess. "Even here, I was still connected to the prince. I felt his hunger spike, and then ease. And with that ease came a great relief, a calm that lasted months at a time until it began to rise again. And then, a few years ago, I began to dream about him. My dreams showed me a door opened for the prince, a door that led into this very prison. A door that led to a vast resource of sacrifices that wouldn't be missed. And vanishing prisoners, every time his hunger was sated."

I thought I'd already heard the worst. I'd been wrong.

I hadn't understood why Lazos's confession had been about Prince Elian, as incredibly horrible as the tale was.

"Prince Elian is the beast," I whispered. "Oh my god. What have you done? Jericho's out there right now. He doesn't know what he's facing."

Lazos turned his drunk, haunted gaze to me. "The Blackheart

is a deadly weapon in the shape of a young man. Sharp, unyielding, hard, and cold. And I need that weapon to help me end this once and for all and finally send the prince back to his grave, where he belongs. I believe this curse will be lifted, that I will be restored. That nature itself will finally forgive me for my sins."

"You're mad," Mika said, breathless. "How did I never see it before?"

"You trusted me all this time," Lazos replied, his brows knitting together. "I promised you a means to escape, and I meant it. The door in my dream—it's only unlocked while the prince hunts within these walls. You will find it on the northeast corner of the wall. It's the only means of escape from this cursed prison. Go now, leave here, and never return."

With that, he sat back down on his wooden throne, grasped the arms, and closed his eyes.

Prince Elian is the beast.

Mika grabbed my arm. "We need to leave. I need to get Tamara, and we need to get the hell out of here. Come on."

She pulled me with her out of the Overlord's residence without looking back, practically dragging me along the cobblestone street that ran through town, until she spotted Tamara, who'd just emerged from her cottage.

Mika ran to her and grabbed her hands, speaking earnestly to the witch for a few moments. Tamara's face paled under the light of the full moon, and she nodded. They embraced tightly and hurried toward me hand in hand.

"Come with us now," Tamara urged me as she approached.

But I backed away a step. "I can't go. Not yet. I have to find Jericho."

It wasn't even a question for me. I wouldn't leave without him, not knowing what I knew. He was out there, somewhere, with absolutely no clue what waited in the shadows.

A monster in the shape of a prince.

"Don't wait for me," I told them, sharing a tense look with Mika. "I know where the door is."

The ex-Queensguard nodded. "Good luck."

Tamara hugged me quickly before letting me go. "Be careful."

"You too," I told her. "Both of you."

I shared another heavy look with Mika before she grabbed Tamara's hand and the two ran toward the forest.

And then I tried to still my thoughts, knowing I couldn't allow my panic to overtake my senses.

I had a jumble of puzzle pieces in my head that revealed the deeply frightening truth about the queen and her empire of lies. I hadn't come in search of this, but here it was, laid forth before me. I couldn't dwell on what I'd learned, the incredible impossibility of everything. I couldn't keep trying to deny impossibilities anymore. They seemed to multiply like rabbits when ignored.

Laughter rumbled in my chest at the absurdity of it all, and hot tears spilled down my cheeks. So much for not panicking. I braced my hands on the fronts of my thighs as I stood in the middle of the road that ran through town, and I laughed and cried at the same time.

"Damn, Drake, you okay?"

My head shot up at the sound of his deep, familiar voice. Jericho stood a dozen feet away from me, his arms crossed over his chest, a confused look on his face.

"Jericho!" I hurled myself at him, throwing my arms around him, and I held on tight. He stiffened, then I felt his hands press against my back.

"This is unexpected," he said. "Given our last conversation."

I looked up at him through my tears. "I was so worried about you."

His brows drew together. "What's wrong?"

"Everything's wrong." And as fast as I could, in a spilling of words that I hoped made some sort of sense, I told him about what I'd seen and what Lazos had confessed to.

Jericho studied me gravely when I finally fell silent. "Well, shit."

I laughed again, a sharp bark of a sound. "Yeah. It's a lot. We need to leave. I know where the door is. Mika and Tamara wanted me to go with them—"

"Why didn't you?" He cut me off, his words suddenly harsh. "You should have gone with them when you had the chance."

I gaped at him. "And leave you here? It's over, Jericho. Lazos can't help us. We'll find another way. We'll figure this out together."

"Haven't you heard a word I've said to you? Are you that damn stubborn?" He swore again. "Have you already forgotten plan B?"

I winced, but then my own anger rose up. "Why are you such an asshole to me all the time?"

"Because I am an asshole, that's why."

"Thanks for the confirmation. I stayed to warn you because I care about you. And you can't tell me that you don't care about me. I see it in your eyes, Jericho. And I felt it in our kiss last night. That was real; I know it was."

"This has to end." He shook his head back and forth. The anger had left his expression, and there was only pain there now. "This is torture, and I can't do this anymore. I can't pretend any of this is okay. Nothing's okay about this."

"What the hell are you keeping from me?" I demanded. "What secret is tormenting you so much? Tell me, you jerk!"

He laughed then, literally threw his head back and laughed. The sound chilled me to my core.

"You are relentless, you know that?" he snarled. "You want to know what my secret is? Why kissing you last night tore my heart right out of my chest? And why I need you to leave me here and never look back?"

"Jericho . . ." I tried to grab his hands, but he pulled away from me.

"It was me, Drake," he said, his voice breaking. "Last year at the Queen's Gala. It was my assignment, my mission. Valery's test of my obedience that she'd carved into my skin so I couldn't resist completely even I wanted to. And I did. I did want to."

I looked up at him with wide eyes.

"No," I managed, the word like a blade scoring my throat.

He turned away from me. "You were wearing a purple dress that night. I saw you get out of the limo at the gallery. Saw it through my scope as if you were standing only five feet in front of me. You were upset with your father. You didn't look at him, but he was trying to get your attention."

I stared at his back, not speaking. Not wanting to say a single thing to stop him from continuing.

"I hated it. I hated being there. I hated Ironport because it reminded me too much of Viktor, of Rush, of my past. But Valery, she insisted that this be my mission. She knew I was a great shot, and she's right. I am. But she wanted to test me— test her control over me. She drilled the command into me, and I felt my soul grow colder and darker with every word she spoke, every slice of her blade. Searing her will into me, what I was to do for her rich client who'd contracted the hit. Drake, I . . . I fought against it. I *did*. I don't kill innocent people. And despite everything I'd heard about the prime minster, every corrupt decision he made under Her Majesty's thumb, the way he looked at you that day . . . he loved you."

I was shaking my head, hot tears spilling down my cheeks.

Jericho drew in a ragged breath. "The orders were to kill both of you. Both, Drake. Going in, I thought I could do it. But seeing you . . . I fought it as hard as I could. I tried not to pull the trigger even once, to resist, but I . . . I couldn't. And every single day since, I've thought about you. Your face, your pain, your grief, burned into my brain forever." He turned his black-eyed gaze to me, pain etched into his face. "I'm sorry, Drake. I'm sorry. I'm so sorry."

A sob rose in my throat, but I was numb with shock. I couldn't feel anything for a moment.

"Now leave here," he said, his pained voice quiet now. "And don't ever look back."

Knife in hand, he turned and walked away from me.

NINETEEN

Stunned into absolute silence, I watched the Blackheart disappear into the darkness.

I didn't have to repeat it out loud to clarify what he'd told me. Or yell it. Or scream it. Or fight it. Or try to deny it.

Jericho was the assassin. A year ago, his mission had been to kill both me and my father. I lived. But my father died.

I clasped my ice-cold hands together to try to stop them from trembling and forced myself to start walking. I couldn't break down and allow my shock and my grief to consume me. I didn't have that luxury. I had to do what Jericho said. I had to follow Mika and Tamara out of here. Maybe I could catch up to them before they got too far.

I couldn't stay here another minute.

By the lodge, I spotted Gloria and her familiar halo of white hair. She was speaking with someone else, and her back was to me. Probably gossiping some more, spilling more secrets. But it didn't matter anymore if everyone found out Mika was a Queensguard. She and Tamara would escape from this place tonight, leaving the Keep far behind them.

And it didn't matter if anyone knew I was Josslyn Drake and hated me for it—for the pampered life of privilege and ignorance I'd lived for seventeen years. Let them hate me.

I didn't even know who that Josslyn Drake was anymore.

Gloria seemed to be entirely focused on her cloaked companion. His hands gripped her arms, and her face was turned up to his.

Wait. Was she kissing him?

The next moment, she turned in my direction. I opened my mouth to say her name, but then stopped.

Her face. Normally, it was lined with age, but full and healthy, her eyes sparkling with the gossip she wanted to spill. But now, even at a fair distance, I could see her cheeks were hollow, her skin as ghostly pale as the full moon itself. Her eyes were black holes in her face.

A corpse, I thought with horror. She looked like a corpse. Her mouth was open, her lips nonexistent, and it looked as if she was frozen in a scream. And then she fell, like a tree toppled in the forest, collapsing heavily to the ground.

Gloria's mysterious companion's hood was pulled up around his face, but I could see his eyes—coal black, but somehow burning in the darkness.

"Prince Elian," I whispered.

The prince cocked his head to the side, then raised his face as if scenting the air. And then he looked directly at me.

I felt as if I'd been locked into place, a scream trapped in my throat, as he began moving toward me. The closer he got, the colder I felt—a coldness that seemed to turn my blood to ice.

And then Jericho was in front of me, his knife in his hand.

"Prince Elian," he said evenly. "Let's not make this more difficult than it needs to be. You and me, it seems we have a lot in common. Who would have thought? And one of us is going to die right now."

"Jericho," I gasped.

"Stay behind me, Drake. Let me do one damn thing right in my life, okay?"

Before I could say another word, the Blackheart lunged at the prince. The prince calmly watched his approach, then reached out and grabbed Jericho by his throat and in one quick motion threw the Blackheart twenty feet through the air to hit the side of the lodge hard, knocking him out cold.

I staggered back from the prince as he drew closer to me again, and eyed Jericho's still form with shock. I'd seen Jericho take down Otis and Arlo without breaking a sweat. He was the strongest and fastest fighter I'd ever witnessed.

And Prince Elian had knocked him unconscious in two seconds flat with a mere flick of his wrist.

"Stay away from me," I snarled, holding my hands up in front of me as if that would help.

This wasn't a prince, raised to be regal and well-mannered. This was a hungry beast hunting for his prey.

"I can help you," I said, randomly reaching for anything to say that might be useful. "It doesn't have to be this way. You're not a monster; you're Prince Elian, the son of Queen Isadora, supreme ruler of the Regarian Empire. Something bad happened to you, and I'm so sorry. It's not fair."

He wasn't listening. Maybe he couldn't hear me.

He took another step toward me, and I braced myself for his attack. But it didn't come. He cocked his head to the side and stared at me with those pitch-black eyes.

"Elian." Vander Lazos's voice came from nearby. "Look at me, Your Highness."

Elian's gaze moved to the warlock.

"Do you remember me?" Lazos asked. "Because I remember you. You can't keep doing this. You have to fight back against these urges. The queen was wrong to allow you to hunt here. These are people who don't deserve to die for the mistake I made so long ago. I don't blame you. I never did. But it's time this stopped."

I realized he held a knife in his grip and was going to attempt to kill the beast himself. Had he completely lost his mind?

It seemed that way, since he moved toward Elian without another moment's hesitation.

"Don't do this," I warned.

"I told you to leave," Lazos snarled at me. "Just as stubborn as your father, you are. I hope somehow he knows how sorry I am for all of this."

With that he charged toward Elian. And just like with Jericho, the prince grabbed the warlock by his throat. But instead of tossing him away like a rag doll, he drew Lazos closer to him, and I swear the air chilled to freezing in that instant.

Lazos screamed, but the sound cut off abruptly.

I turned and ran toward Jericho, pulling at him, trying to wake him up and get him to his feet, but he was out cold. I sent a nervous look over my shoulder at Elian and Lazos, but only Lazos was still there, lying on the ground, his face a dried-out husk like Gloria's had been.

He was dead. And Prince Elian was nowhere to be seen.

And then, in the very next moment, chaos descended. Two huge military helicopters landed in front of the lodge, their blades creating a whirlwind that swept up dirt and debris and tossed it around the street, the thundering noise making it hard to even think.

Bright spotlights shone in my eyes as four Queensguard soldiers went directly to Gloria's and Lazos's bodies, swiftly depositing the corpses into black body bags.

Heart pounding, I felt the urge to run, but a hand closed on my arm. I spun around, my fists clenched, shocked to be faced with Viktor Raden.

"Joss," he said, grasping my shoulders and sweeping his relieved gaze over me. "We've been looking everywhere for you. I thought you were dead."

"Viktor, the prince—" I said, my voice strained. "Prince Elian was here. He's alive—he's . . . he was raised from the dead. He's been killing prisoners!" I stumbled over the words, trying to speak as quickly as possible. There was so much to tell, and I couldn't keep it to myself anymore.

This was a dream. It had to be a dream. No, a nightmare.

"You're safe now," Viktor said firmly, his gaze landing on Jericho. "Dear god. Is he dead, too?"

"No. Just unconscious. But, Viktor, he's . . ." I could barely think the words, let alone say them. "He's the one who shot my father." My voice broke. It was hard to see through the thick tears welling in my eyes. "He just confessed the truth to me. He was supposed to kill both of us, but he only killed my father."

Viktor stiffened. "No. Joss . . . I'm sorry. I'm so sorry."

His words were an eerie echo of Jericho's, which only made everything worse.

Viktor instructed a group of guards to restrain Jericho and put him in the other helicopter.

"You need to find Prince Elian," I urged. "You need to stop him, before he kills someone else!"

"Come with me." He directed me toward a helicopter. "This is over. I'm taking you to the palace."

I grabbed hold of his uniform. "Viktor, didn't you hear me? Prince Elian—"

He clamped his hand over my mouth, and I looked up at him in shock.

"Joss, stop," he said gruffly. "Whatever you think you saw, forget it. Cast it permanently out of your mind."

I wrenched his hand away from my mouth. "Viktor—"

"Listen to me," he hissed, his expression hardening. "This is your one and only chance to return to your former life, to forget any of this ever happened. To *survive* this. Do you understand? Don't mess this up."

I wanted to scream at him, to shake him and hit him. None of this was news to him.

He already knew about the prince.

I fell utterly and completely silent as this painful realization settled over me, followed by another.

Viktor was right. I hated it with every fiber of my being, but he was right.

I'd spent my weeks in here fighting to get out, to get back to my normal life. It had been my one aim. But along the way, I'd learned things that had turned my world upside down. If I wanted to go back to my normal life, if I wanted to be Josslyn Drake again—not Janie, a prisoner in the Keep—I had to make a decision. I had to decide what to do with this knowledge.

My entire existence pivoted on this moment. There would be the before, and there would be the after. Could I go forward as if nothing had changed? As if I hadn't seen what I'd seen, learned what I'd learned? Felt what I'd felt?

Or would I fight back and risk burning my life to the ground all around me?

Queen Isadora was the leader of an empire consisting of two billion people, a woman who stood for truth and justice and fairness. She was someone who fought for peace, whose ancestors had quashed countless rebellions, a woman who lived with the constant threat of Lord Banyon's desire to destroy her with his powerful magic.

Evil magic, she told us. Soul-withering, unnatural magic. Forbidden, illegal, the use of which was punishable by death, all to ensure peace and safety and freedom.

A woman who had her son raised from the dead, only to create a monster, whom she allowed to feed on unsuspecting prisoners who had no escape from their dark fate.

Had my father known any of this? He'd worked closely with the queen for over twenty years, enough that she claimed to consider us as close as family. Would he have said what Viktor said to me now and asked me to forget everything I'd seen and everything I'd learned?

It was all too much to absorb in such a short time. So much that my mind had gone numb to the horror of it all. I could fight, resist, like Banyon had. And like Banyon, I would break.

Viktor watched me carefully for my reaction, not a sliver of surprise on his face. He was a commander of the Queensguard, with access to top-secret information. Information like Elian. And it made no difference to him. Viktor was driven by his quest for greatness, turning his back on everything in his past in order to achieve his goals.

And it seemed that those goals had come at a staggeringly high price.

It was time to pivot, to make my choice about how I wanted to proceed. I had to summon the Josslyn Drake who navigated the world with a smile, who no one saw as a threat. I had to survive this. I had no other choice.

I lifted my chin to meet Viktor's gaze full on. "I understand," I said firmly.

He nodded. "Good. Now let's go."

I didn't resist as he led me onto the helicopter and to the uncertain future that lay beyond the walls of the Queen's Keep.

TWENTY

A half hour later, I caught sight of the palace—a massive building that seemed as if it were carved from one solid piece of alabaster, a jewel rising from the dark horizon. As the helicopter touched down on the roof, all I could see for a moment were the flames that rose out of it in the echo of Banyon's memory, but the mirage quickly cleared away. Not a blemish, not a scorch mark was left behind. Any reminders of that deadly fire sixteen years ago had been removed forever.

Surrounding the palace was the sprawling and entirely self-sufficient compact city, which was devoted to keeping the palace running smoothly. Everyone who worked here, from the queen's personal chef to the chambermaids to the person who shined the shoes of Queensguard commanders, made their home here for security reasons.

After two weeks of outhouses, watery soup for dinner, piss-water, and minuscule cottages with scratchy sheets and leaky roofs, stepping foot onto the shining silver tiles of the palace hallways should have felt like a dream.

But I already knew all too well that this was a nightmare.

Viktor had stayed by my side since we left the Queen's Keep. "The queen wishes to speak with you immediately," he told me.

I nodded stiffly, and he led me along a labyrinth of hallways toward the courtyard, which was the inspiration for the one at the Royal Gallery. This courtyard was far grander, far bigger, a lush garden in the center of the stone-and-glass building. From the velvet black sky, studded with stars, the huge full moon shone down on us as we emerged through arched doors to the warm, sweetly perfumed air.

The air in the Keep definitely hadn't been perfumed.

But the sight of the full moon made me think of Prince Elian again, and I shivered. I tried to focus on the marble fountain before me. On the butterflies that had been captured from throughout the Empire and let free to flutter around this carefully manicured space full of tall green trees and flowers in every color imaginable. I looked down at the water to see a distorted reflection of myself—pale, messy hair twisted into a makeshift braid that lay along my left shoulder. The heavily worn blue silk shirt and velvet pants I'd taken from the boutique. And my eyes . . .

I'd almost forgotten about my eyes, but there was no chance to cover them up now. Panic ignited in my chest.

Viktor straightened his shoulders and bowed from the waist. "Your Majesty."

I turned slowly to see Queen Isadora approaching us. Tonight, she wore a fitted gold gown. Her hair was intricately twisted into an elaborate bun.

Before, I might have admired how effortlessly fashionable she always appeared. The woman had never tried to embrace casual fashion. She always dressed impeccably. It was one of the things about her I'd always marveled at the most, and likely the reason I had a whole heap of debt when it came to keeping up with royal standards of beauty.

But tonight, the sight of her made my heart start to pound, fast and loud, and the fear that had been low on my list of emotions only moments ago swiftly rocketed to the very top. Every muscle in my body tensed, as if ready for me to bolt at any moment if she called for my arrest. For my immediate execution.

Instead, she smiled and, without hesitation, grasped my hands in hers. Any trace of my last manicure was long gone, my nails short and rough, compared with her flawless polish and jeweled rings on each of her fingers.

"My dear, dear Josslyn," she said. "I am so relieved to see you. What absolute horrors you must have endured since I last saw you."

For a moment, I couldn't speak. I waited for something terrible to happen, for her expression to change to one of disgust and accusation. For her to be able to sense that I now knew her darkest and most dangerous secrets, secrets she would never want revealed to the world.

"Your Majesty," I said slowly and evenly. "I'm very relieved to see you, too."

She cupped my face in those cool, elegant hands, her brows

drawing together into a deep frown. "Dear god, it's true. Your eyes . . ."

I winced, forcing myself not to pull back from her. "I can explain."

"You don't have to. I already know."

I gasped. "You do?"

"There are no secrets in my Empire, Josslyn. The man who operated the illegal fighting hall was arrested and questioned. He confessed everything."

Rush. Now I knew why he'd disappeared during the fire he set.

"I'm furious about it," the queen hissed.

I tensed, prepared to recoil from her, to turn and run as far as I could.

"No one told me there was a piece of magic displayed at the Gala. I never would have allowed it. Such fools I put in charge of organizing the display. They are going to be punished very severely for letting this happen. I don't care if they didn't realize their mistake. You never should have been exposed to such a thing. Please forgive me, Josslyn. I swear I will find a way to purge this poison from you fully and completely."

I couldn't believe what I was hearing. I almost asked her to repeat herself, but then thought better of it. I'd heard once that when you were given a pass on some transgression, you shouldn't try to argue with or overexplain to draw even more attention to it. Just accept it and move on.

My worst fear for most of the last two weeks had been that the queen would learn my terrible secret.

But she knew practically the whole time.

"It's been horrible," I admitted, and I didn't even have to fake the tremble in my voice. "I was so worried that you would blame me."

And execute me, I added internally.

"Not at all. It's not as if you sought this magic freely. You are an innocent in all of this."

I wanted to relax into her words, to believe her sincerity. And part of me did. After the horrible night I'd had, I wanted the comfort of trusting someone again.

But I'd seen far too much—of the world, and of the queen herself. My faith in Queen Isadora had been rocked to its very foundation.

Viktor stood nearby attentively.

"Where is the prisoner?" the queen asked him.

"He's been taken to a holding cell," Viktor replied.

Again, I tensed.

Jericho.

"Commander Raden called ahead to fill me in on the situation with the Blackheart," the queen said. "I don't want you to worry, Josslyn. I will take care of everything. You have nothing to fear any longer, especially now that we have him in custody. He will be held accountable for all of his many crimes—against you, and against my Empire as a whole."

Now that my fear for my own immediate safety had subsided just a little, thoughts of the Blackheart rose in my mind—confusing and painful thoughts.

Nothing about Jericho Nox was easy to understand or accept.

I wanted to hate him for his horrible confession. But it was so much more complicated than that for me.

My eyes started to sting. "Jericho says he was under the influence of his employer's magic. That he tried to resist pulling the trigger. His assignment was actually to kill both of us."

I couldn't let her think he was a cold-blooded killer. Because he wasn't.

Her eyes widened slightly. "I'm certainly glad he failed in that regard. But it doesn't change the fact that you lost a father and I lost a dear friend. And the person who ended Louis Drake's life on Lord Banyon's command will pay dearly for those losses."

But wait. Jericho didn't work for Banyon; he worked for Valery. He hated Banyon.

But Banyon was the one who'd ordered my father's death. It was common knowledge reported on the newsfeeds that everyone, including me, had accepted as the truth.

I watched Viktor out of the corner of my eye. I couldn't tell if he had any reaction to this. Probably not. It was as if he'd written Jericho off long ago, like a tick he'd pried from his skin and tossed to the side, hoping it died, but annoyed that it still continued to move around.

"What will you do with Jericho?" I asked the queen carefully.

"Tomorrow he's to be interrogated in my presence. I need to know more about this witch employer of his who hides in the darkest shadows of my Empire. Beyond that, I don't want you to worry about a thing. Justice will be served, Josslyn. I assure you of that."

"I want to be there, too," I said firmly.

The queen didn't respect mincing words or begging for what someone wanted. She respected a flat, clear statement. At least, that had been my experience with her.

Maybe that was why we'd always gotten along so well, since I liked the same thing.

The queen looked at me for a long moment before she nodded. "Of course you can be there." She took my arm in hers. "Now come with me. I have chosen an excellent room for you, one I only make available to my most valued guests."

I searched for some edge of deviousness in her steady gaze. Like the way she'd regarded Lord Banyon in my vision—that coldness and hatefulness when he refused her command to raise their son from the dead.

Instead, all I saw was concern. It was seriously unnerving, given all that I now knew about her frightening secrets.

Arm in arm, just as we'd been when we'd left the courtyard at the Queen's Gala, we walked back into the palace and along shining floors, turning left and right, passing palace guards who squared their shoulders and stood straighter and taller as the queen moved past them with Viktor following behind us.

Finally, the three of us arrived at the most luxurious suite of rooms I'd ever seen. And I'd been in a few luxurious suites of rooms in my life. All silver and blue and white, with a huge, fluffy canopied bed and a sitting area with bright and colorful cushions. Floor-to-ceiling windows looked out at the brightly lit palace city spread out beneath the night sky.

"I know you'll get some well-needed rest here," the queen said. "And tomorrow will be a fresh, new day."

There was a mirror attached to a large dressing table on the far side of the bed. It was the first time I'd seen myself so clearly in weeks. I looked disheveled, my long blond hair tangled and matted. My face was pale with shadows under my eyes.

Golden eyes.

I hadn't seen them this clearly since Jericho held the mirror to my face in the boutique. Compared with my regular blue color, they seemed like two otherworldly dots of molten lava in the middle of my face.

I'm a witch.

My mantra had returned right on schedule.

But that particular revelation wouldn't be shared with either Her Majesty or Commander Raden tonight. Or ever, if I could help it.

The queen's voice cut through to me and made me tense. "I've arranged for my personal stylists to visit you first thing tomorrow. A little glamour, a little gloss, and you'll be feeling like your old self again, Josslyn. I will suggest they include some contact lenses to match your natural eye color."

"Thank you," I said. The offer would have made me literally drool in the past. The queen's stylists working on me, helping me to look my absolute best. And I had to admit, a tiny fraction of myself greatly looked forward to being pampered again.

Maybe more than a tiny fraction.

"Now I will leave you to your rest." She paused at the doorway where Viktor stood stiffly before glancing over her shoulder. "I do have some questions for you, Josslyn. But they can wait until tomorrow."

I nodded, my heart thundering. "Of course."

"Good night. Sleep well."

When she left and the door closed, my questioning gaze moved to Viktor.

"Tell me about Celina," I said. "Is she all right?"

He nodded. "She's fine. And she's arriving here with her father to see you tomorrow," he told me.

To see Celina's face again, to have my best friend back after so long apart, was a major lifeline that I grasped hold of.

Then a jarring thought occurred to me. "Does she know? About what happened to me? About . . . my eyes?"

His jaw tightened. "No. The queen wishes to keep your condition private for now."

My condition—infected by evil magic. Actively seeking a cure so I could return to my regularly scheduled life.

It almost sounded quaint now.

"Good." The tightness in my chest eased. I'd never wanted to keep a secret from Celina, but I'd have to make an exception. I loved her, but I knew she wouldn't be able to handle this. It would irrevocably change how she saw me. "I've missed her so much."

"I'm sure you have," Viktor agreed, then turned to leave.

"Wait," I said, and his shoulders tensed.

I couldn't let him leave as easily as that. This was the first time we had enough privacy to really talk. And I really needed to talk. Despite all that I'd told him in a rush of words before we left the Keep, his reaction had remained stoic. I needed to know why.

"When did you learn the truth about Prince Elian?" I asked.

He turned back to face me, his expression grim. "I can't talk about that with you or anyone else."

"Can't? Or won't?"

"You need to forget what you saw," he advised.

He wanted me to forget? Impossible. What happened had been permanently burned into my brain.

"The queen brought the prince back from the dead and allows him to hunt for prey in the Keep. I don't understand how you can act like any of this is business as usual."

Hearing it out loud made it sound like the ramblings of a madwoman.

"You have been given a chance to put everything behind you now, Joss," Viktor said. "I strongly advise you to take it."

I distantly realized that he'd been calling me Joss like I'd asked him to the night of the Gala. Like a friend would.

But Viktor *wasn't* my friend. We'd spoken only a handful of times, so I knew I couldn't press him for answers. I couldn't make demands or have any expectations of him. So I wasn't really sure why his demeanor pissed me off so much. Maybe because I'd held him in such high regard before tonight. He'd been the handsome champion of the Queensgames, someone who represented strength and perfection.

Viktor Raden might have been strong, but he was far from perfect.

"Goodnight, Joss." Again, Viktor turned toward the door.

"Does the queen know that Jericho's your brother?" I asked.

He froze with his hand on the doorknob, and a muscle in his cheek twitched. "No. She doesn't. And she won't."

He didn't stick around after that. He left and the door clicked shut behind him, leaving me all alone in my luxurious suite. Alone with only my racing mind as company.

I wasn't sure how it was possible to feel more claustrophobic in this large suite of rooms than I had in the minuscule cottage in the Keep. But I did. The walls felt as if they were closing in on me.

I returned to the mirror, sitting down in the silk-upholstered chair in front of it and staring at my disheveled appearance. I touched my face, running my fingers under my golden eyes and down my cheek to my jawline.

I didn't know what Rush had said to the queen about the magic in me. He knew it was specifically Lord Banyon's memories. Would she care that I might have access to the truth about what she'd done?

Queen Isadora saw me as a victim in all of this, someone she wanted to help.

Did I trust her? How could I after what I'd seen?

There were a half dozen candles next to the side of the bed, and I picked one up, staring into the flame. Fire had triggered the memory magic before.

Every echo I'd experienced so far had been like a piece of a puzzle that showed me what Lord Banyon had endured and survived, and revealed a bigger picture about the Empire and the woman who ruled it.

I realized that I was thirsty for another piece.

My last echo with Lazos had been the first I'd consciously summoned. Perhaps it had been so clear and definitive because the warlock had held the memory in his mind to allow me access to it. But could I summon one of Banyon's memories on my own?

I gazed into the mirror, into my own golden eyes, flickering with candlelight. And I breathed in, and out. Calming myself. Accepting this strange magic inside me. My mind open and ready to see another piece of this puzzle.

"Show me the truth," I whispered.

Only a few moments later, I saw it at the edges of the mirror. The golden smoke moving into view, twisting and winding through the room. The smoke thickened and brightened, obliterating my view of the palace chambers, of my own reflection, and it cleared to reveal a bright white windowless room.

Silver bars sectioned off the holding area, and Lord Banyon stood behind them, gripping them. Behind him was a pristine cot and a toilet.

It was a different room, but he seemed to be the same age he'd been in the last echo, when he'd refused to raise Elian from the dead, leaving the task to the much less skilled Lazos.

Everything was so white and clean in this strangely elegant holding cell. Except for his face, which was marred by bruises and cuts. He looked thinner, his cheeks hollow, his eyes glazed as he watched the closed door, as if able to will it open with the power of his mind.

When the door swung open, I thought for a moment he'd done just that. But in walked Queen Isadora, followed by High Commander Norris.

"Where is my wife?" Banyon demanded, slamming his palm against the silver bar.

The queen shook her head. "Such impatience, Zarek."

"I need to see her. It's been weeks now. You promised I could see her."

"I did, didn't I?"

"It's over, Issy. You must have proved by now that what you seek is impossible in the hands of a warlock like Vander Lazos. Death should not be tampered with in this way. Even when such dark magic works, there is a harsh price that must be paid."

She hissed out a sigh. "You think you're so smart, so wise. But you don't know what I'd do to achieve what I want. A mother's love is unlike any other love I've ever felt. I would have done anything for Elian."

"I know," he said, his voice softening slightly. "There was a time, Issy, when you were a kind girl who would never want to harm a fly. When you allowed yourself a fascination for magic, rather than wanting to destroy it or use it selectively for your own gain."

"Sometimes I wish you could have been at my side for all of this, Zarek. What an incredible partner you would have made me. Unfortunately, we all must live according to the rules of the Empire. It is my legacy."

"And my legacy is to leave here, and I promise not to return. I will never darken your doorstep again if you free me and my family."

"I always admired you, Zarek, perhaps more than I should have." She moved closer, brushing her hand against his as it clenched the bar. "Part of me thought you might be strong enough to escape from here. It was Commander Norris who suggested starving you to repress your magic. Such an interesting experiment. Without that, I'm sure you would not be quite so pleasant with me right now."

"All I want is to see my family." His voice broke. "Please, Issy. You promised."

"Of course. I always fulfill my promises." She gestured toward Commander Norris, and he went to the door, opened it, and ushered in Eleanor, Banyon's beautiful wife. In her arms, she held their baby.

Eleanor cried out and moved to the bars, grasping her husband's hand. "Zarek, oh god! What have they done to you?"

"It's fine, my love. I look much worse than I feel, I promise." He reached through the bars to stroke the baby's cheek. "My angels, both of you. I'm so sorry this happened."

The queen stepped forward. "Your husband is a very stubborn man, Eleanor."

"I know that very well," Eleanor agreed quietly. "But he's a good man."

"You're such a lovely young woman. Quite honestly, I think you could have done much better when it comes to husbands." The queen chuckled and gazed down at the baby's face. "May I hold her? I haven't held such a sweet baby for far too long."

Eleanor hesitated and shared a worried look with Banyon, before she reluctantly handed the baby to the queen.

"Such a beauty, just like her mother," the queen said. "I always wanted more children, but unfortunately it wasn't to be. My darling Elian is my one and only."

The way she held the baby, there was no edge of cruelty to

it. She cradled the child in her arms, humming a gentle melody for a few moments.

Then she looked up at Banyon and his wife, their hands clasped through the bars. "See, Zarek? Despite how you've disappointed me and caused me so much grief and anguish, I wanted you to see your beautiful wife and child one last time."

Banyon's gaze now held only cold dread.

"Issy . . . no," he began.

The queen nodded at Norris, and without hesitation, he took a step forward and pulled Eleanor away from the bars, away from her husband. She shrieked, reaching for Banyon, but her struggles were short-lived.

I didn't even see the blade in Norris's hand until it sliced across her throat. He released her, and she dropped to her knees. Banyon roared her name as his wife quickly bled out and died on the pristine white floor of his holding cell.

I stood there, in the midst of this horror, stunned silent. Not that anyone could have heard me anyway if I'd started screaming as well.

The queen adjusted the now crying baby in her arms and coolly surveyed the murder scene. "You chose this, Zarek," she said. "You refused to help me resurrect our son. It could have been so easy for you; I know it in my heart that you are the most powerful warlock in my Empire. Now your wife and daughter will pay the price for this failure. Seems only fair, really."

"I will kill you," Banyon snarled. "I will watch you die for this."

The baby started to wail at the top of her lungs. And as she flailed, turning her head from side to side, I saw something I hadn't noticed before. A mark.

A small, heart-shaped birthmark on the left side of her neck. Just like mine.

I touched my own, brushing my fingers over the mark I'd always had, that I'd once considered having removed.

It was the same birthmark. Same position, same shape.

"It's not possible," I whispered.

"Goodbye, Zarek," the queen said, before she turned and walked out of the room with the baby.

With *me*.

I couldn't move, couldn't think, could barely breathe.

Banyon stared out at Norris, shaking. "Don't kill my daughter. Please, I beg of you."

"I'll do exactly what the queen wants me to do," Norris replied. "Don't worry, your grief won't last long. You'll be following your young family into death very soon."

Banyon grasped the bars, shaking them as if he could pry them open enough to allow him to choke the killer before him. "I will destroy you for this," he promised.

"Such ferocity," Norris mocked. "Too bad you have barely the strength of a baby yourself at the moment. I might be a bit worried otherwise. But I know how to deal with your kind, warlock. No food and no water equals no magic."

"Hide your own family," Banyon snarled. "Hide everyone you love from me, because I swear on my very soul itself, I will burn your entire world to the ground for this."

Finally, I saw a flicker of fear in the high commander's eyes.

But then he stepped over the body of Eleanor and left the room without another word spoken.

Now alone, Banyon stared at the closed door for a full minute in absolute eerie silence before he leaned back his head, opened his mouth, and let out a spine-chilling roar of pain and grief.

Fire raced down his arms, snaking across the ground, and covered the walls in an instant. The door blew off its hinges. And the inferno began to rage as the warlock left his melted cell and walked directly into the flames.

The golden smoke blew in and blew away this dark echo of the past, returning me to my palace chambers. To the mirror before me that reflected a blond girl with a heart-shaped birth-mark on her neck and haunted golden eyes.

A girl who'd opened herself up to the magic inside her and asked to see the truth. And the truth had been shown to her.

TWENTY-ONE

I didn't sleep that night. In fact, I feared I might never sleep again. The crystal-clear image of what I'd seen remained with me. The fire that tore through the palace sixteen years ago had indeed been ignited by Lord Banyon's magic during his escape. That much of the story I already knew was true. But everything else . . .

He'd watched his wife murdered while Queen Isadora stood by, relishing her cold-blooded revenge over someone who'd refused her outrageous demands. They'd tried to starve the magic out of him, thinking him weak and helpless. And then he'd burned everything to the ground. So many people had perished in that fire—including Jericho and Viktor's parents.

They had a villain to blame—the evil warlock Lord Banyon, enemy to the Empire. A terrorist who would stop at nothing to destroy the queen and steal her power.

But now I'd seen the truth with my own eyes.

Nothing was simple about this. Banyon had taken innocent lives, but the queen's unrelenting need for vengeance had triggered his fury and his fire magic.

Banyon believed both his wife and daughter had died that night. But I was still here. I was still alive, hidden in plain sight all this time without a clue who I really was.

Vander Lazos knew the truth about me from the first moment I spoke to him. All that talk about fate—now I knew what he'd meant. It was fate that I'd walked into that art display at the Queen's Gala, right when Jericho was trying to steal the memory box. It was fate that it had opened up and that very specific magic had homed right in on me.

My birth father's memories had led me to the truth that had been kept from me all my life by a woman I'd always thought of as family. But then, all the people I'd thought of as family had lied. I wasn't the birth daughter of Louis and Evelyne Drake. They also had lied to me.

Everyone had lied to me, all my life. But now I knew the truth—the twisted, sharp, and thorny truth.

Lord Banyon, my father. I'd spent the last year believing that Lord Banyon had ordered the assassination of my father—the father I'd known all my life, who'd raised me and loved me and given me a home. But after everything I'd learned, I wasn't sure of anything anymore.

⋈⋄⋈⋄⋈

In the morning, a huge breakfast arrived at my chambers. Trays of eggs, scrambled, fried, and poached; chocolate pastries; and freshly squeezed fruit juices. After so long surviving on the Keep's limited menu, it all seemed like a dream come true.

I couldn't stomach a single mouthful of it.

True to her word, Queen Isadora sent her "glamour squad" to my room to help me get ready to attend the interrogation. There was a hairstylist, a makeup artist, and a fashion expert who rolled in a rack of beautiful clothes. A month ago, this would have been a dream come true.

The makeup artist said nothing as she helped insert the blue contact lenses over my golden irises. This morning, they appeared more like a unique honey-brown color than molten gold. I'd learned some people knew what eyes like mine meant, but most didn't. She did. I saw fear in her gaze at being so close to someone filled with magic, but I didn't say a single word to assure her I wasn't a threat.

Maybe I was, maybe I wasn't. The day was still young.

When the squad was finished and I took it all in via a gilded full-length mirror, it was like looking into the past. Perfect hair, falling in golden waves past my shoulders. Flawless skin, glossy lips, smoky eyes. They put me in a flowy, silk dress in shades of blue, which hit just above my knees, and matching cobalt sandals—a high-end outfit that I'd seen in the boutique last month and knew I couldn't afford even in my most lofty of dreams.

I realized in that moment that I looked just like my birth mother, Eleanor Banyon. I could still see her, dead on the white floor, surrounded by a pool of her own blood, while her infant daughter was stolen away.

After forcing out words of thanks, I followed the squad out of the chambers, which was where I discovered Viktor waiting in the hallway.

He didn't look happy. "I don't think you should be a part of this interrogation."

That was his greeting to me. No *Good morning, Joss. How are you doing after your world has shattered all around you? Feeling good?*

"Then I guess it's good that I don't have to ask you for your permission," I replied stiffly.

"You shouldn't torture yourself with any of this any longer. What Jericho did . . . it's unforgivable."

"I'm going to the interrogation, Viktor," I said tightly. "So either lead the way or get out of my way."

His jaw tensed. "Very well."

Jericho.

In such a short time, I'd gone from hating him, to begrudgingly partnering with him to help solve our mutual problem, to trusting him, to . . .

Liking him. More than a little.

For a moment, as his confession had crashed down on me last night, I thought those feelings would quickly become only a distant, regrettable memory. But they hadn't. They were still here, locked in my heart, but now edged in pain.

Now I knew why he'd resisted liking me back, why he'd walked away when conversations grew more intense, more difficult. Why being close to me had been something he'd avoided and why he'd tried to push me away every opportunity he got. He'd known the truth from the moment he first saw me at the Gala, and it tormented him.

There was so much information swirling in my head, I

couldn't process it all. So, with every ounce of strength I had left, I pushed past these thoughts toward what was happening right now. Right here. My future and my very life were in jeopardy. Deep, deep jeopardy, if I didn't properly hold myself together.

The queen knew I was Banyon's birth daughter. She'd known all these years.

I had to wonder: What was her ultimate plan for the secret daughter of the warlock she hated more than anyone else in the world?

Viktor led me down hallways peppered with uniformed guards and servants. I recognized other faces as well, men and women who were part of the Parliament and of the queen's royal council.

"Where do they keep Prince Elian?" I asked Viktor, eyeing every door that we passed and wondering what lay inside.

He didn't reply.

Along with everything else, Prince Elian had most definitely secured his own high-level position in my mind over the last twelve hours. As had one other thing.

If Elian was Lord Banyon's son, that meant he was my half brother.

All my life, I'd wished I had a sibling. I should have been careful what I wished for.

"Is the prince escorted to and from the Keep for his hunts?" I pressed. "I have to assume so, since you were all there last night, ready to swoop in and escort him back here." I felt the desperate need to keep talking, even if it meant I was talking to myself.

"What does one do with a monster like that on a regular day at the palace, though? Does he eat normal food or just snack on hapless prisoners? What does he do for fun? Since he's the undead apple of his mother's eye, I'm guessing he'd have special accommodations with satin sheets and lovely views, not some dusty dungeon cell."

"You're trying to bait me," Viktor growled.

"Just trying to get answers to frighteningly important questions."

"You don't want answers. Leave this subject alone; it's much healthier that way for you."

I searched his face, trying to understand even a fraction of this. "Did you sign away your soul when you signed up for the Queensguard?"

"Something like that," he bit out.

I was surprised. It was the closest I thought I'd get to a straight answer on the subject, but it only served to infuriate me even more.

We descended a flight of stairs and entered a circular room that had several cameras on the walls as well as a large display monitor. Black upholstered chairs—a dozen of them—were stationed around the circumference in a single line. And in the center of the room, a silver chair was fused to the floor.

The interrogation room.

There was only one other person already in the room.

"Miss Drake," High Commander Norris said with a nod. "I'm so relieved to see that you are well. I've been extremely worried about you."

I froze, my heart thudding. The memory of him slitting my birth mother's throat was as vivid now as it had been last night.

He'd always been kind to me, and I'd liked him whenever he visited the prime minister's residence to speak with my father—my adoptive father, I corrected myself. He seemed nice and sometimes told jokes to make me laugh. I remembered once he let me look at pictures of his family's cute dog on his phone.

Commander Norris had always known who I really was, and he'd helped keep the secret without argument or complaint.

Behind that friendly smile, he was an evil, dangerous man.

"Thank you, sir," I said with a practiced, polite nod. "I'm recovering very well."

Thankfully, that seemed to end our bone-chilling reunion as Norris moved away to speak to some other guards. Viktor gestured for me to take a seat, and I did. A cool trickle of perspiration slid down my spine.

Several guards entered and stood around the periphery of the room, preceding the queen's entrance. Today she wore a stunning dark blue gown threaded with silver that shimmered as she walked.

For a moment, I half expected her to peel off her mask of human skin to reveal a monster beneath it all. A monster who ordered the deaths of innocent women with a mere nod of her head. A monster who allowed her undead son to hunt in a walled prison full of defenseless victims.

"Josslyn, you look lovely," she said. "Yes, your eyes are much better like this. Almost normal."

"Almost," I lied. "And thank you. I feel so much more like myself today."

I searched her face for any sign of the horrible, vengeful woman I'd witnessed in the visions, a woman who would look at me as the daughter of her archenemy. But I saw nothing at all other than warmth, not even a flicker of disdain or cruelty.

This confused me deeply.

The sound of metal chains drew my attention to the doorway as Jericho entered the room, flanked by guards. He looked disheveled, his face bruised and swollen, and he wore the same black jeans and black T-shirt he'd worn last night.

Our gazes met and locked and everyone else in the room seemed to disappear. There was only me and Jericho and the pain that slid though his black eyes for a moment before he looked away from me, frowning deeply.

I'm sorry, Drake. I'm sorry. I'm so sorry.

I know, I thought. *I'm sorry, too.*

Then the world came back. He was forced to sit on the metal chair. A guard fastened his shackles onto a hook at the base of the chair so he wouldn't be able to stand.

I glanced up at the cameras. "Are you recording this, Your Majesty?" I asked.

"No," the queen replied. "This is to remain a private questioning."

Yeah, I'd seen her private questionings before. It didn't surprise me that they weren't recorded for future reference.

Jericho's gaze moved to Viktor, his brow still furrowed. But then his lips stretched into a sinister smile.

"What luck," the Blackheart said. "Two face-to-face meetings with the grand champion in less than a month."

Viktor said nothing—which seemed to be his trademark now—and his expression remained unreadable.

The extra guards left the room, so only the five of us were in attendance for the interrogation—me, the queen, Viktor, Norris, and Jericho.

"So this is the Blackheart," the queen said with distaste.

Jericho's black eyes tracked to her. "Your Majesty. What an absolute honor this is."

"Your Majesty?" said High Commander Norris. "At your command."

"Commander Norris, you may proceed," she replied with a nod.

"More questions?" Jericho asked. "Didn't I already help you wonderful people out enough last night? By the way, I think I have about two dozen broken ribs. A quick trip to the infirmary, and a whole pile of drugs, would be much appreciated."

Sarcastic Jericho. Yes, I was very familiar with that version by now. It was his default survival mode, a way to not show vulnerability. We definitely had that much in common.

It bothered me that he'd obviously been beaten—although some of those bruises likely came from his altercation with Prince Elian.

Jericho had faced so much pain in his life.

And now he was a prisoner of the Empire, about to be treated like a murderer. Not just a murderer, the assassin of a prime minister.

But to paraphrase Lazos from last night, a Blackheart was only a weapon. Everyone already knew the real assassin of my father was Lord Banyon.

But the question I had, the question I'd been turning over in my mind all night, was why would Lord Banyon hire Valery, a shadowy black market witch, to send someone to assassinate a prime minister and his sixteen-year-old daughter at a gala that Queen Isadora herself—the true object of his hatred—would attend? Why wouldn't she have been the target? And wouldn't the most infamous warlock in the world have used magic as his weapon, rather than a hired assassin with a gun?

Why was my father targeted? And why me?

Removing Louis Drake from the government had been only a hiccup of inconvenience. Nothing had changed. And Celina's father had swiftly been appointed his successor. Other than some grief, and perhaps a bit of inconvenience, such a loss hadn't affected the queen's ability to rule at all.

That night was still all too clear in my mind's eye. We'd arrived at the Gala with Celina and Regis Ambrose. And Ambrose had gone with my father to the hospital while Celina stayed with me.

I'm all right. It's just a flesh wound.

You're sure?

Yes, I'm sure. I'm fine. Everything's fine, Jossie. Don't worry.

I shook the memory away, quickly swiping at the tear that spilled down my cheek.

My father had been lying to me. Everything wasn't fine. He was dying in my arms, but he hadn't wanted me to know the truth. His vital signs had flattened only minutes after reaching the hospital because the bullet had found his heart.

"Let's start with your name," Norris began, and I could tell by the confidence and almost singsong quality to his voice that he was used to questioning criminals in front of an audience and he enjoyed it very much.

"Jericho Nox."

"Is that your real name?"

"Real enough."

"Jericho Nox, you are in royal custody with a long list of crimes attached to that name. Assault, drug possession, magic possession, trespassing, burglary, kidnapping, and murder."

"It's been a busy couple of weeks," Jericho admitted.

"You are accused of the assassination of Prime Minister Louis Drake."

Jericho's lips thinned. "Should I have legal representation at this point, or are we just going to forge ahead without it?"

There was a cold smile on Norris's lips, a cruel expression that showed how much he liked it when the accused gave him a difficult time.

"Here's what we know about you, Jericho, and admittedly it isn't very much at all," Norris said, walking a slow circle around Jericho's chair, his hands clasped behind his back. "You are a Blackheart, working for a notorious and very powerful witch known only as Valery. One who works outside of polite society, and one who has been of great interest to the royal council for many years. We know that Blackhearts are tainted by this witch's dark magic in ways that make them incredibly strong, able to heal from injuries swiftly, and they are also very quick-minded."

"Stop," Jericho said. "You're making me blush."

"Are you familiar with facial recognition?"

"I recognize your ugly face from Rush's club. Is that what you mean?"

"No, that's not what I mean," Norris said evenly. The display monitor on the far wall flickered on. "We ran images of your face after the Queen's Gala through our digital archives to see if we could learn more about where you came from. Imagine our surprise when we found this."

My attention shot to the screen that showed an arena I recognized very well. The Queensgames Arena, located in southwest Ironport. There were smaller arenas for qualifying matches scattered across the Empire, but Ironport laid claim to the grandest one, which hosted over a hundred thousand people in rows of seats that rose high into the air.

The Queensgames were biannual, so the arena usually held regular sports matches. But they were never as ornately decorated with banners and flags as they were during the games.

The camera capturing the footage before us raced over the faces of audience members, from the cheap seats to the more luxurious and comfortable VIP sections. Finally, the focus turned to the match that had just begun.

Jericho's match.

He stood shirtless, with leather straps crisscrossing his bare chest, and leather trousers. Black lace-up boots. He faced a fighter who was a few inches shorter than him, one who appeared wary of his tall, muscular, and intimidating foe. Jericho carried his sword easily, as if it weighed no more than a feather.

The horn sounded and only a moment later, the swords clashed.

Jericho was playing with his opponent, like a cat with a mouse. He hadn't even broken out in a sweat yet, and a confident smile played at his lips as he brought the sword down again and again to clash with the other.

But then there was the moment I'd dreaded. The moment where he paused, frowned, and his gaze trailed off to the side. And his sword lowered. He'd told me this was the moment he noticed that Viktor was watching from the sidelines.

It was the only opening his opponent needed.

I heard a loud gasp and realized it was my own as the sharp sword found its mark in Jericho's bare chest. Jericho kicked his opponent away and grabbed hold of the blade, slicing his hand as he pulled it out of his flesh. He stood there for a moment, hunched over and bleeding, before he dropped to his knees and then heavily slumped to his side.

Paramedics carrying a stretcher hurried onto the field. One pressed his fingers to Jericho's throat to check for a pulse before they swiftly removed the body.

The monitor went dark and silence hung in the air. I could hear the sound of my own heartbeat, loud and fast in my ears.

"You were dead," Norris said calmly.

"Dead?" Jericho raised a brow. "Or just resting? Who's to say?"

I noticed the queen had begun to fidget in her seat, her breathing becoming more rapid.

"Answer the high commander's questions respectfully," she snapped.

"Apologies, Your Majesty, but I didn't hear a question," Jericho said. "I'm only hearing statements thrown at me."

"Then *I'll* ask," she said, rising from her seat. "Were you dead?"

Jericho shrugged. "I actually don't remember much after the big shiny sword impaled me."

"Did the witch you now work for bring you back to life with such powerful death magic that you show no sign of suffering, no side effects from this dark act? Is she able to re-create this magic at will whenever she chooses? Or was it pure luck with you?"

Jericho blinked. "Are you asking for yourself, Your Majesty? Or a friend?"

That was when Norris plowed his fist into Jericho's face and blood poured from the Blackheart's mouth.

A cry caught in my throat.

"I already knew you were going to be a problem," Norris snarled. "Your former guardian Rush told me you've been a challenge ever since you were only a petulant child, never following any rules set forth for you. He told me that you were always a rebel, even if it killed you." He leaned closer. "It killed him. Or rather, *I* killed him, when I'd finished questioning him. Just like I'll do with you, Blackheart."

Jericho's expression had gone blank, his gaze flat.

I'd known Rush had been questioned, but not that he'd been executed already. So quickly.

I'd barely thought of the man over the last couple of weeks, other than cursing him for suggesting we meet with Lazos. I didn't mourn him. But he'd seemed larger than life when he'd burned his club to the ground to spite the authorities.

But he wasn't larger than life. He was only mortal, and vulnerable, just like the rest of us.

"Now, enough games," Norris growled. "We want to know where your employer can be found."

Jericho chuckled darkly. "You think you can question her, do you? Oh, that would definitely be your last mistake. I'd love to be in the audience for that."

"Answer me!" Norris hit him again, even harder than before.

Jericho spat out more blood and glared up at the man. "Go to hell."

"Josslyn, dear, you really shouldn't be here for this," the queen said tightly. "It's far too upsetting. It's time for you to leave now."

Normally, I'd absolutely agree with her. However, I desperately wanted to help Jericho, despite everything. I believed that he'd fought against Valery's command that horrible night, against the magic etched into his very flesh. He'd fought, but he'd failed. And he'd regretted that failure every day that had passed.

This interrogation wasn't really about my father's death at all. It was about the queen wanting information about Valery and her death magic. And Norris would beat that information out of Jericho until he finally talked.

"I want to stay," I said.

The queen ignored me and nodded at Viktor. "Commander, escort Josslyn to my chambers for some nice tea. I will join her there soon."

Tea? She wanted me to have *tea* after this?

Viktor held his hand out to me. "Miss Drake."

I met Jericho's searching gaze. His brows were drawn tight over his dark eyes, his hair hanging over his bloody face. If he didn't talk, they were going to execute him.

And even if he *did* talk, they were going to execute him, just like they'd done with Rush.

I'm sorry, Drake. I'm sorry. I'm so sorry.

His pained words from inside the Keep had become a constant echo in my ears.

"Wait," I began. "I need to—"

But before I could say anything else—to ask a question, to demand more truth, or maybe even beg for leniency, Viktor literally dragged me out of the interrogation room.

The door closed, and I realized it didn't have a handle so I could go back in. When you were out, you were out.

And I was out.

TWENTY-TWO

wrenched my arm away from Viktor and stared up at his infuriatingly blank expression.

"Are they going to execute him?" I demanded.

"Yes," he replied.

I already knew the answer, but the confirmation tore at my heart. "When?"

"I don't know." His jaw was tight. "Come with me to the queen's chambers."

"Viktor—"

"No, Joss. Please. Don't make this harder than it already is."

Something in his brown eyes betrayed his icy demeanor. Something brittle and barely holding itself together. He wasn't completely an unfeeling, unemotional jerk. Not about this.

There would be no getting back into that room, so I reluctantly allowed Viktor to lead me through the maze of the palace to the queen's chambers, passing scores of guards on our way.

My own incredible room might as well be a shack in the Keep compared with the queen's. Three floors with winding staircases, plush carpets, shining cherrywood floors, and impeccable one-of-a-kind, ornately carved furniture. I'd been here before, and all I'd done was stare at everything and dream of one day living in such magnificent surroundings myself.

The sparkle of it all, admittedly, had dulled quite a bit for me. To put it mildly.

"You can wait here," Viktor said.

I grabbed his arm and he tensed. "He's your brother," I told him. "You have to help him."

"There's nothing I can do. Jericho chose to work for a witch, and that choice led him here."

"He didn't choose it. She basically owns him," I said. "And she controls him with her magic, even though he fights against it."

"I'm surprised you're defending him."

"I'm sure you are. But it's true. Jericho doesn't deserve to die for what happened. What he needs is help to get the hell out of here, and then get the hell away from Valery. You can't turn your back on him. Please, Viktor."

Viktor got that familiar shuttered look to his gaze that I recognized from his older brother. That way of shielding his emotions from the outside world.

"I need to go," he said.

He didn't give me a chance to say anything else. He left me in the queen's seating area by myself, my thoughts fixed on Jericho and his dark fate.

I wanted to help him, but I didn't know how. Valery was the one who should pay the price for my father's death, and whoever it was that hired her.

Whoever that was, I knew it *wasn't* Lord Banyon.

The warlock had done so many unforgiveable things over the years, but it didn't make sense that he would do this. Everything he'd done was driven by his hatred for the queen. And the queen wasn't a target that night. I knew that I had to compose myself, to quiet my confusing and rebellious thoughts. I needed, more than ever, to call on my social skills and be the bright, brash girl the queen had always known.

A few minutes later, the queen swept in with her entourage in tow. From a barrage of stylists retouching her makeup and smoothing her hair to advisors who scurried off to get answers to any questions that might cross her mind. And then she shooed them all away when the tea service arrived.

If I hadn't been hungry for breakfast, I wasn't exactly famished for tea, which included twenty different choices of aromatic leaves, an assortment of cakes, and finger sandwiches.

"Please, my dear, have a seat." She gestured toward a lacquered ebony table that could have easily seated thirty people.

She sat at the head of the table, and I took the seat to her right, pushing a bright smile to my lips.

"What a horrible young man that is," she said, shaking her head. "Utterly unrepentant for all the pain he's caused."

I steadied myself before I responded. "Did you learn anything useful about his employer?"

"Not yet," she said, her voice pinched.

"I'm sorry."

"Me too. But I've found that nothing in life is easy. The more important something is, the more difficult it is. That's why we must be strong."

"It has been difficult," I admitted, and this certainly wasn't a lie. "I don't really know what to believe anymore, Your Majesty."

"Believe in me, Josslyn. That's all you need to do." She placed her cool hand over mine, and I forced myself not to pull away. "You are very important to me. You have been, ever since you were born. You are far more important than you even realize."

Oh, I think I'd learned how important I was to her.

I was the stolen treasure that she'd had on display for sixteen years. A piece of artwork that represented her greatest act of revenge.

"Thank you," I said. "That means a lot to me."

Her gaze lifted to focus on something behind me. "Very good. Yes, my darling, please come and have a seat. I don't think you've been formally introduced, have you?"

Someone sat in the chair opposite me, and I slowly raised my gaze from my teacup to meet his black eyes.

"This is my son, Elian," Queen Isadora said. "Elian, this is Josslyn Drake."

That was when I forgot how to breathe.

Prince Elian. Sitting only a few feet away from me.

Today, there was more color to his face than there had been beneath the full moon. His eyes were still as black as night, an instant reminder of Jericho's. His hair was dark blond and cropped short.

If I did the math properly—though admittedly math, even at the best of times, was not my favorite subject—Prince Elian should be in his midthirties. But he didn't look a day over seventeen.

The prince didn't speak; he studied the plate in front of him as the queen placed an egg-salad sandwich on it.

"Eat something, darling," she said.

Elian picked up the sandwich and took a small bite out of it.

Fear had quickly ratcheted its way up to the tip-top of my emotions list. The queen had been playing it cool, waiting me out and watching to see if I slipped up.

She knew. And she knew that *I* knew.

And here we were.

"Hello, Elian," I said evenly, taking a sip of my tea and forcing it past the thick lump in my throat. "It's so lovely to meet you."

Elian continued to eat his sandwich.

"Don't be offended," the queen said. "He very rarely speaks. Quite honestly, he's a great deal like an innocent child. My greatest wish is to restore him to his former self, but for that I will need help."

"From Valery," I said.

"Yes. She brought the Blackheart back to life, and he is . . ." She shook her head. "Unblemished by death, both mind and body. She will use her magic to help Elian."

I found a negotiation between nefarious witch and zealot queen difficult to imagine, but I didn't say this out loud. "But first you have to find her."

"That's right. I thought it best that we get this all out on the table, as it were. My little secret, in broad daylight. And you can see very well for yourself that my son is nothing to fear."

I turned to her, my mouth gaping, unable to totally hold on

to my composure. "I saw him literally suck the life out of two people last night."

"Yes. And it's all very unfortunate." The queen shifted in her seat. "I need to know, Josslyn, what Vander Lazos confided in you during your unfortunate stay in the Keep. He was always a petty man, desperate for my favor. I should have had him executed, but I took pity on him. It was a terrible mistake. How did you even hear of him?"

I slid the tip of my finger along the edge of my teacup and took a deep breath, trying to still myself. Trying to go back to playing my part. "Jericho was given his name as someone who could remove this magic from me."

"Do you feel the magic?" she interrupted. "Do you know what it is? What was in that golden box the Blackheart was sent to steal?"

It was the question I'd been dreading, but it showed that the queen might not know the truth already. Maybe Rush hadn't mentioned this part during his interrogation. If he hadn't, I was deeply grateful to him.

I certainly wasn't going to help fill in the blanks. "I honestly don't know what exactly this magic is or what it can do, Your Majesty. But I can feel it, like a weight in my chest, its darkness pressing on my heart. It feels diseased, like it may kill me. It's as horrible as I always pictured magic would be, and I need it out of me."

Sounded good enough to me, and exactly what I would have imagined it would feel like before actually experiencing it for myself. I endured several moments of her studying my face, my hands gripping the edge of the table.

"I can't even imagine how horrible it must be," she murmured. "You are so brave, Josslyn."

My bravery definitely came and went. And right now, I needed every last shred of it that I could summon.

I acknowledged her sympathy with a pained smile, then continued with my story. "I knew Vander Lazos was the only hope I had to return to normal before anyone learned the horrible truth." I sighed shakily. "He had given himself the role of Overlord in the Keep, and all the prisoners looked at him like some kind of king. He told me that if I followed his rules, if I waited long enough, then maybe he would help me. But he wouldn't tell me anything else, no matter how many questions I asked. By then, I knew I wanted to come to you for your help, that I should have done that in the first place, and I deeply regretted that I didn't. I was trapped in that prison with no idea how to escape."

She watched me for a few moments in silence, her eyes narrowed.

"I see," she said. "Yes, of course, you should have come to me. You never had anything to fear from me, my dear."

"Of course, I know that." The lies were becoming easier and easier, like a second language I knew I had to become totally fluent in.

That was the moment when Viktor appeared again, his expression stiff. "Your Majesty," he said. "I don't want to intrude, but there is a matter that requires your immediate attention."

He didn't so much as glance at Prince Elian. This must have been an everyday occurrence for him.

It sickened me.

"I'll be right back," the queen said. "Please, take this time to get to know each other better. Believe it or not, you have a great deal in common."

It took every ounce of my strength to not react to this.

Yes, she was right. We had a father in common.

The queen followed Viktor away from the table, leaving me sitting there with the undead prince, who stared down at his half-finished sandwich.

"I seriously can't believe this is happening," I muttered to myself as I eyed Elian uneasily. "I hate this. I hate all of this."

His black eyes snapped up to mine. "Me too."

I pushed back from the table, my heart pounding. "What the hell?"

He put a finger to his lips. "Don't make too much noise; she can't know that I'm speaking with you like this."

The events of last night crashed down on me again like I was experiencing another violent echo—shards of images. Black eyes under the full moon. Gloria's corpse. Lazos's attempt to reason with a monster moments before he died.

The mindless beast awake from his coma, ravenous for his next victim.

"She said you rarely spoke," I managed, my voice pitchy, searching for something to say that wasn't a terrified scream.

He shushed me. "I rarely do. To her, anyway. And it hasn't been long that I've been able to think rationally, actually." He hissed out a breath. "Last night, I wasn't rational at all. I never am when the hunger descends. I'm sorry you had to see me like that."

Sorry? It was as if he were apologizing for being drunk and rude at a party.

My mouth was so dry I could barely form words. "I can't believe this."

"We don't have much time before she's back." Elian raised his black eyes to mine. "I know who you are. I try to listen in when she talks to her advisors, to the guards, and she doesn't know I can understand. I know everything."

I tried to calm down, since I couldn't think rationally myself.

He knew who I was. My love of being recognized was something that had greatly changed for me over the last couple of weeks.

"You know everything, do you?" I repeated, as evenly as I could manage. "I actually find that hard to believe."

"I know I'm Lord Banyon's son." He hesitated. "And I know . . . he is also your father. Are you aware of that?"

I actually laughed at this, a nervous hiccup of a sound.

Okay. That was actually a whole lot of everything.

"Recently," I said shakily. "Very, very recently aware of that. You're going to have to give me a minute to catch my breath."

He nodded stiffly and took a sip of water from a crystal goblet in front of him. "I really hate egg-salad sandwiches."

"Me too," I admitted.

His gaze met mine again, his brows drawn tightly together. "You think I'm a monster."

This entire conversation was surreal and made me dizzy. I desper~ ne~ded to find some sense of control here.

"You are a monster," I replied, forcing strength back into my voice.

"When I'm not thinking straight, that's exactly what I am. I'm cursed."

A trickle of sweat slid down my spine. "Can't argue with you there."

"For a long time I wanted to kill myself. I even tried a couple of times, but it didn't work." His gaze grew haunted. "This curse, it seems, keeps me alive. Keeps me young, as if frozen in time. And sometimes, it turns me into a mindless monster. From what I've overheard, it doesn't have to be this way."

"What do you mean?"

"The Blackheart that's in custody, they're saying that he was raised from the dead, too. I didn't have the chance to talk to him last night."

"No, you threw him into a building and nearly killed him." Elian just looked at me until I relented. "Yes, Jericho was dead. But for, like, minutes before he was brought back. You were dead for a couple weeks. That seems to make a bit of a difference, not that I'm any kind of death-magic expert."

"I'm coherent now. I can think properly now. I feel like myself now, Josslyn. And I don't want to die. I want to live, but I can't do that while I'm trapped here at the palace and treated like a child who needs to be monitored all day, every day."

I studied him for a moment and couldn't argue with him. If I'd met this version of Elian, I wouldn't have guessed there was anything unusual about him at all.

But there was—something very wrong and very dangerous—and I couldn't just erase what I knew, what I'd seen, that easily.

I shook my head. "What do you want from me?"

"I want you to help me."

"And why would I do that?"

"Because you're my sister." Elian actually smiled at this, shaking his head. "Sorry. I just wanted to know how it sounded to say it out loud. It sounds good, but I know that it's not a great argument, especially after what you witnessed last night."

I was quickly losing my hold on that calm, cool control I desperately needed right now.

"You would have killed me if Lazos hadn't interrupted," I reminded him.

He hissed out a breath. "Maybe. I don't know."

"What do you mean, you don't know? I saw you kill two people."

"Not consciously."

"That doesn't matter."

"Doesn't it? All I can say is I can think normally now, and that's going to last for at least a month before the monster inside me returns. That's all the time I have to find answers, so no one else has to die because of me. And I know there's someone out there who can help me."

"Great. So, you get cured from this curse, and you go back

to being Her Majesty's heir to the throne when she shoves some story about why her son is alive and hasn't aged a day down the throats of everyone in the Empire. Best of both worlds."

He shook his head. "No, I don't want that. I never wanted that. My mother is evil. And the frightening thing is, she thinks she's a hero. The greatest gift ever given to the Empire. She's delusional, and what she did with me proves that. I don't want to be king. I want to be free, and I want to live without the monster inside me ever rising again."

He sounded so sincere, so earnest, that my flare of outrage faded quickly.

"Why haven't you tried to escape before this, then?" I asked.

"I've only been self-aware for a little while. Less than a year. Before that, it was like I was sleepwalking. But I still remember the pain. So many years I was in so much pain," he whispered, his expression anguished. Then he shook it off. "I haven't had long at all to put together any kind of plan."

I studied him for a moment. Other than the black eyes in the middle of his pale face, he looked completely normal. And he actually made a sick kind of sense.

"So what's the plan?" I asked tentatively.

His gaze shot to mine, and I saw determination there. "I need to find our father. He can help me."

I sucked in a breath, remembering that Banyon had refused to raise Elian, no matter how much the queen threatened him. "Jericho's boss might be able to help you much more than that. Although, that might be extremely tricky, since she's basically a greedy hell bitch."

He nodded. "I'm willing to try anything."

Before I could say another word, the queen returned to the table and sat back down.

Elian had returned to studying the half-eaten sandwich on his plate.

"I hope I didn't miss anything," she said.

There was a smug tone to her voice, as if she felt a measure of satisfaction in leaving me with her undead son for a few minutes of uncomfortable silence.

If only she knew.

"That's enough for now, darling," the queen said. "Why don't you go to your room, and I'll have some more sandwiches sent to you."

Elian gave me a last glance before he stood up and left the queen's chambers.

"Did you two have a nice chat?" the queen asked.

I tried to figure out what I wanted to say, but then decided on honesty.

"Are you testing me?" I said.

"Pardon me?"

"Testing me," I repeated. "Trying to see if I'll break, if I'll freak out and run from the room screaming and crying at being faced with Prince Elian after seeing him in action last night?"

"Many would," she allowed.

"Not me."

"That's because you are a rare girl who can see the truth, who can separate what's important from what's not. You re-mind me so much of myself, it's uncanny sometimes. You don't let anyone walk over you. You're strong and capable, and I admire that, Josslyn."

A few weeks ago, hearing that Queen Isadora saw herself in me would have been the highest compliment. Today, it made me physically ill. I wanted to scream right in her face and call her out on all her lies, all her schemes, all her hypocrisy.

But I didn't. It took every morsel of strength I had left within me to hold my shoulders back and my emotions in.

"Thank you, Your Majesty," I said. "After these difficult couple of weeks, that means the world to me."

She leaned back in her seat, regarding me with her fingertips pressed together. "I want so much for you, Josslyn. But I have to say, I don't think it serves you well to remain at the prime minister's residence. In fact, I've decided that as of this very moment, the palace is your new home. I want you here, by my side, so I can keep a closer eye on you. Perhaps I can help keep you out of any future misadventures."

If she'd suggested a year ago that instead of living with the Ambroses I could live here at the palace, in the palace city, I would have jumped at the chance. Of course, I would have asked if Celina could live here, too, at least part-time, but I would have been overjoyed.

But I knew enough now to make an educated guess on why she was suggesting it.

Lord Banyon had recently escaped capture once again. He was an ongoing threat to the Empire, to the queen herself, and to her hold on power. Banyon had loyal followers, thousands of witches and warlocks who kept to the shadows, afraid of coming into the light.

She hadn't ordered my death as an infant. She'd given me to Louis and Evelyne Drake to raise as their own daughter. But I didn't believe that she'd done that out of the kindness of her heart.

She'd hidden me until she needed me.

I was a weapon she planned to use against Lord Banyon, to perhaps draw him out of the shadows once again.

It was only a hypothesis, but I didn't think I was wrong.

"Thank you, Your Majesty," I finally said, injecting as much sincerity and enthusiasm as I could into my voice. "It would be my honor."

Just like Elian, I would never be allowed to leave.

She smiled. "Excellent. Your future is very bright, Josslyn. I promise you it is."

I met her gaze, her eyes glowing with pride and happiness and warmth as she regarded me. And I did honestly believe that, despite everything, she liked me.

And I also knew without a single doubt that she would kill me if it served her agenda, just like she'd killed my birth mother.

The queen kissed my cheeks, gave me a warm hug, and sent me on my way toward my bright and shiny future here at the palace.

TWENTY-THREE

I'd thought my time in the Keep had been rough. But less than a day here at the palace, and my life had been turned upside down.

Jericho needed help. I doubted very much that he could find his way out of this mess all by himself, no matter how strong and capable he was. I could only hope he was giving High Commander Norris enough answers about Valery to spare himself from any unnecessary pain.

Who was I kidding? He was doomed, and I was powerless to help him. They were going to execute him, and Viktor had no plans of intervening.

I was so lost in my tortured thoughts about the Blackheart, and about my surreal conversation with Elian, that I didn't even see her waiting by my chamber door. I didn't see her until she grabbed my shoulders and turned me around to face her.

"Joss!" Tears spilled down Celina's cheeks. "I'm so happy to see you! I've missed you so much!"

"Celina," I managed, and fell into the bear hug she gave me then. "You're here, you're really here."

"No place I'd rather be."

"Come in where it's private," I said, opening my door and leading Celina into my chambers.

"Good idea. I think I'm seriously going to collapse," she said. And she did just that on a large sofa near the entrance. She yanked me down to sit next to her.

"When did you get here?" I asked.

"Not long ago. My father's gone to speak with the queen, and I asked where to find you and came here immediately." She let out a shuddery sigh. "Joss. My god."

"I know."

"I was so worried about you! I don't even know what you've been through, only a little. Viktor said you were in the Queen's Keep?"

I grimaced. "It's a long story. But, yes."

"So horrible! Are you okay?" she asked very seriously. "You look so different."

"Different bad?" I asked lightly, trying to smile but failing.

"You look like you've seen things."

That made me laugh just a little, but it came out like a nervous hiccup. I was so grateful for the colored contact lenses right now. "You literally have no idea."

Part of me wanted to tell her everything. I wanted to dump it all out on the table and let her help me sort through the mess while holding my hand and promising me it was going to be okay.

Unfortunately, it wasn't going to be okay.

Celina could never be burdened with the truth. None of it.

The thought that I'd have to keep this secret from my best friend in the whole world shattered my heart into a thousand pieces.

"I'm just grateful that that thief is locked away now." Celina's voice broke, and she drew in a shaky breath. "I was so scared when I woke up in the boutique and you weren't there. I thought he'd hurt you! All this time, weeks, Joss! I didn't know where you were and if you were okay!"

She started to cry, so I hugged her, stroking her hair and assuring her I was all right.

"He didn't hurt me," I told her. "I know Jericho comes off as big and scary, but . . . he's not. I mean, he is. But he's not. It's kind of hard to explain."

She pulled back, her brows drawn together. "My god, Joss. Are you actually trying to defend him?"

I swallowed hard. Yes, I was trying to defend him. No one else would. No one else knew the truth about the Blackheart. Not like I did.

"Is that what it sounds like?" I said aloud.

"There's no defense for someone like him. He drugged me, Joss. With *magic*. I thought I was going to die. And then he kidnapped you and dragged you off. All this time, I thought you were dead. He killed your father!"

All right. So my magic wasn't public knowledge, but it seemed that this was. I could imagine the headline that likely went live first thing this morning: KIDNAPPED DAUGHTER OF PRIME MINISTER DRAKE FOUND ALIVE BUT TRAUMATIZED. BLACKHEART ARRESTED FOR MURDER, SOON TO BE EXECUTED.

Josslyn Drake tops the newsfeeds once again.

Celina shook her head. "You can't try to find the goodness in someone like that, Joss. Because it doesn't exist."

I chose not to argue, to try to fill in the blanks for her about Jericho and how I'd started to feel about him, because they were very big and very scary blanks. And big and scary feelings. And I so desperately wanted to help him right now, even though I had absolutely no idea how.

"The best thing to do now is to try to forget him," Celina said firmly when I didn't immediately reply, squeezing my hands in hers. "And move forward. That's how you will win."

"Seems to be the general consensus," I replied.

"What I want you to do today is to rest. Have a nap. Have a bath. Eat something. Drink a whole lot of water. Got it? And then my father and I are taking you to dinner at the Queen's Table."

It was a restaurant on the palace grounds. The fanciest, most expensive restaurant in the entire Empire. I'd eaten there with my father and the queen a few years ago, and it had been the best meal I'd ever had. It made me feel like actual royalty just walking through the front doors. Another thing the old Joss would have leapt at the chance to do. But I couldn't summon the energy to care.

True to her word, Celina left me to get some rest for the afternoon. And I realized I was exhausted, having barely slept or eaten in over a day. I allowed myself to lie down on the bed, planning to rest my eyes for only a moment, but full and complete unconsciousness claimed me an instant later.

When I woke up from a surprisingly dreamless sleep, the glam squad was knocking on my door to help get me ready for dinner. They refreshed my stale makeup from the morning; re-did my hair, tying it back into a sleek and stylish ponytail; and dressed me in a silver sheath dress that shimmered with every step I took.

"This is the queen's favorite designer," the fashion expert told me. "Her Majesty chose this dress especially for you. And not just to borrow for the night. It's a gift from her for you to keep."

"It's beautiful," I said.

"Stunning," he agreed.

I studied my reflection when they all left my chambers. Polished, coifed, glamorous. Expensive. Perfect.

Back to normal.

It was everything I ever thought I'd wanted. It was everything I'd fought so hard to regain.

Meanwhile, Jericho languished somewhere in the palace, in a cell, or still in the interrogation room suffering abuse at the hands of Commander Norris. I had to help him. And thanks to Celina, I now had a plan in mind that had shone a sliver of hope into the darkness.

Prime Minister Ambrose was the key.

I would talk to him at dinner and explain everything I'd learned about Jericho's extremely unique and complicated situation. They couldn't execute him so quickly and easily. After all, Jericho had a wealth of information about a witch who actually *was* evil.

And that evil witch could use her incomparable skill with death magic to help repair whatever had gone wrong with Elian's resurrection. My gut told me I was right about this. The queen also saw Valery as a solution to this problem, but I didn't think she knew half of what I knew about the witch.

Celina's father could be the key to saving both Jericho and Elian.

I knew I'd have to use a lot of charm tonight with a man who'd never liked me that much. More than I ever had before.

But I could do it and he would help me. There was no other way this could be fixed.

Celina came to fetch me, oohing and aahing over my new dress. With my new goal in mind, I followed her out of the palace to walk five minutes down the shining pathways and glittering roads to the restaurant.

Prime Minister Ambrose waited for us at a table, and he rose to his feet as we approached.

"Josslyn," he said. "You've had us very worried about you."

"I'm sorry, sir," I said, tensely taking a seat across from him. Celina sat by my side. There was a window next to our table that looked out at a garden filled with flowers and trees and the exclusive herbs the award-winning celebrity chef used in his dishes.

"You shouldn't apologize for something that wasn't your fault," he said. "Are you well?"

"Very well, thank you."

It seemed that he didn't know about my magic, either. If he did, I doubted he would be half this relaxed with me.

"Excellent," he said. "I've promised my daughter that I won't press you for any details tonight. Instead, we will focus on celebrating your return."

I marveled for another moment about how friendly he seemed, much more than usual, as he flagged the waiter down and ordered a bottle of wine, which was quickly fetched and poured. I stared down at the glass of dark red wine in front of me, waiting for the perfect moment to present my case.

"First time Josslyn Drake's ever hesitated when it comes to drinking," Celina said with a light laugh.

To be fair, she was right. I'd loved wine even before I should have. I liked how it made me feel. Or rather, how it made me *not* feel. In the Keep, I'd downed the pisswater, despite its taste, because the results were the same. A blurring of reality. A sparkle on the mundane. But wine didn't make reality go away. Or change. Or become slightly less real in any way. It was always waiting for me the next day, only then I had a killer headache to deal with as well.

I took a sip of the wine to be polite, and yes, it was absolutely divine. But then I moved to my glass of water instead. It wasn't as if I'd decided to stop drinking. I mean, why would I? But tonight, I felt like I wanted to keep a clear head. So I wouldn't drunkenly reveal all my secrets. So I would be able to make my case.

I would stay sober if it meant I could help save Jericho's life.

"I think we should toast to Josslyn returning safely to us," Ambrose said, raising his glass.

"To Joss," Celina said, clinking her glass against mine. Then she groaned, and I looked at her with alarm.

"What?" I asked.

"You're not going to believe who's here," she said.

I followed her line of sight to see my good old frenemy Helen at a table on the other side of the restaurant with her parents. She was waving vigorously at us.

"Everyone's been dying to know what happened to you," Celina said.

"I bet." I grimaced. "I seriously can't deal with her tonight."

"It's okay. I'll go talk to her for a minute so she doesn't start any unwanted rumors."

I couldn't imagine what rumors Helen might want to spread about me. That I had reluctantly partnered up with a criminal in order to infiltrate a walled prison? Or that I was actually Lord Banyon's witch daughter and the sister of a life-sucking undead prince?

No. Nobody would believe outrageous rumors like those.

"I'm on it. I'll be back in a minute, okay?" Celina stood up and walked over to Helen's table.

Good. It would give me a chance to speak to the prime minister in private.

"Sir," I said. "May I ask you something?"

"Of course, Josslyn," the prime minister replied.

Poise. Politeness. Charm. I gathered all my skills around me like a protective cloak. I would need all of them for this. "I need your help with something that may seem like a very unusual request."

He nodded. "Request away."

"I need you to speak with the queen and ask for Jericho's execution to be indefinitely delayed."

"The Blackheart," he said, frowning.

"That's right."

"And why would I do something like that?"

"Because he doesn't deserve to die for what happened." I held up my hand to stop him from interjecting. "Please, you have to believe me. There's more to the story. He didn't voluntarily kill my father. He was under his employer's magical influence."

"Josslyn, you're not making any sense."

"Maybe not, but that doesn't mean that Jericho has to die. You need to—"

"Jericho Nox put a bullet in your father's chest," Ambrose said sharply. Sharper than was necessary, if you asked me.

I winced. "It's more complicated than that."

"No, it isn't. It's quite simple, really. The Blackheart will be dead by morning for his crimes."

Something went cold inside me. "So fast?"

"He doesn't deserve to live another day."

I spared a glance toward Celina, whose shoulders had slouched a bit as Helen talked her ear off while shooting curious looks in my direction.

I couldn't give up this easily.

"I know you don't believe me about Jericho, but Valery, his boss, is a very powerful witch. She's the evil one, along with whoever hired her for the job." I shook my head. "I have to be honest; I don't think it was Lord Banyon. It was someone else. We need to find out who that was. And Jericho is the key to that information, you see?"

Ambrose's upper lip curled back from his teeth as if in disgust. "Josslyn, listen to what you're saying. It's nonsense. Banyon is the source of all evil in this Empire. He is the devil himself."

Shit. I was losing him already. Too much, too soon.

"Of course he is," I quickly said, before this went completely off the rails. "I'm not saying he isn't. I'm sorry; I'm just so distraught over everything. I'm not thinking straight."

As I raised the wineglass to my lips for a sip to soothe my suddenly parched throat and gather my confidence again, Ambrose grabbed my wrist so tightly it made me gasp.

"Don't you dare try to fill Celina's head with this garbage about Banyon," he snarled. "I won't have it."

I stared at him, shocked. "I wouldn't dare."

"My daughter looks up to you, sees you as an inspiration. But she's wrong. You're nothing but a manipulator, a troublemaker. A bad influence."

"Gee, don't hold back. I guess you were probably hoping I wouldn't surface again, weren't you?"

"It's like you're reading my mind." He leaned back in his seat, regarding me with disgust, as if I were a spider he'd found on his dinner plate. Then a small cruel smile played at his lips. "You think you're so smart, don't you?"

What the hell had triggered this? All I'd shared were my doubts about Lord Banyon being the one who hired Valery to kill my father. Something about that had set him off, like a lit match held to the fuse of a bomb.

"If you say so," I told him, refusing to be cowed by his verbal attack.

"That little brain of yours, always scheming, always working." He shook his head. "It pains me to see that your influence on Celina has started to make her weak, made her foolish."

The waiter brought over another bottle of wine, and I noticed for the first time that there were two others already on the table.

The prime minister was drunk. He must have started drinking long before Celina and I had arrived. That actually explained a lot.

Still, it didn't make it better, especially since I desperately needed a sober ally at the moment.

"Look, I know it's been difficult," I said evenly. I had to salvage this conversation and turn it around as quickly as I could. "And I know *I'm* difficult sometimes. But Celina's my best friend, and she's the smartest person I've ever met."

His gaze flicked toward his daughter, as if to check her proximity to our table. "She is. And the past few weeks have made me realize what she could be, if she weren't friends with you. I want you out of my home and out of my daughter's life immediately. Find a way. Find another home; I don't care. I want you gone."

I almost laughed. Ambrose was kicking me out. I was an orphan, recently kidnapped and infected with magic, and he wanted me gone. I'd tried to be the levelheaded person here. You know, for once. But now he'd pissed me off.

"Or what?" I snapped.

"Let's just go with 'or else.'"

I guess he didn't know that the queen had already decided I'd be moving to the palace so she could keep me under her thumb. He'd be thrilled to hear that little piece of news. Far more thrilled than I was.

"I don't think my father would like you talking to me this way," I said.

"No, I suppose he wouldn't have. But he never saw you as clearly as I do. How manipulative and cunning you are. So very unlike Louis, who was soft and weak." He leaned over the table toward me and lowered his voice. "And yet, the queen did everything for Louis. Coddled him like some sort of cherished pet, bestowing gifts upon him." His eyes narrowed cruelly. "Even a daughter, when he and Evelyne couldn't have one naturally."

More confirmation. More proof that the vision had been true.

He waited, as if to gauge my reaction to this.

Even though I felt sick inside by everything I'd learned that had turned my life upside down, I wouldn't give him the satisfaction of seeing that weakness. "My father told me a long time ago that I was adopted," I lied, and it took all my strength to keep my voice steady. "It doesn't matter to me. I know he loved me."

A sliver of disappointment slid through Ambrose's eyes, as if he'd hoped to shatter me with that news.

I hated him for that.

"Yes, I suppose he did," he allowed. "And that love made him weak. Louis was never as good as me, or as refined—not of the same class, that's for sure. But he got everything I wanted just handed to him on a silver platter. How I hated him. Just as I hate you now. You should have died with him."

I knew he didn't like me, but the amount of venom in his words tonight shocked me. Ambrose had been my father's best friend since they were teenagers.

At least, I thought he had. But suddenly, I saw the truth. Ambrose was jealous—blindingly jealous of all that my father had achieved before he did. And jealousy could be every bit as deadly as poison.

I stared at him, my eyes growing wide.

You should have died with him.

The last piece of this massive puzzle had finally clicked into place. And as ugly and rotten as it was, it still fit perfectly.

"It wasn't Lord Banyon," I whispered, my throat tight and painful. "It was you, wasn't it? You had my father assassinated so you could take his job, his life, everything he'd worked for. Everything you think rightfully belongs to you."

Ambrose's drunkenly glazed eyes widened, and he leaned back from the table to stare at me for a moment with shock.

I didn't need to see Ambrose's memories like I could see Lord Banyon's to know this was the truth. The horrible, horrible truth. This was why he didn't want Jericho questioned any further about my father's murder.

Because it could lead directly back to him.

And then Ambrose started to laugh, and the icy sound sent a

chill down my spine. "Clever girl," he said. "More clever than I ever thought."

I forced the words out because I had to know. "How did you find Valery? The queen can't even find her."

Ambrose gave me a thin smile. "Oh, I've known that witch for a very, very long time. A very helpful woman . . . for the right price."

The moment on the stairs at last year's Queen's Gala was burned into my mind as painfully and vividly as one of Banyon's fiery memories. "You went with my father to the hospital. You told me to stay with Celina. My father promised me he was okay, that he was going to live."

Annoyance now flashed through his eyes. "It should have gone flawlessly, but it didn't. That Blackheart failed me, failed Valery. It left me with one option: to finish what I started in order to earn my prize. And here we are. No one knows the truth except you and Valery, Josslyn. And, clever or not, no one will ever believe you in a million years."

I stared at him, stunned silent by his cold, smug confession. Numb to my very core.

Celina slid back into the seat next to me.

"Well, that wasn't fun," she said. "Helen really is absolutely horrible, isn't she?"

Ambrose and I were still locked in a stare, which he finally broke off when the waiter arrived to take our orders.

I couldn't breathe. I couldn't think. I could barely move. I forced myself to reach for my wineglass, grasping the crystal stem and bringing it to my lips to take a shaky sip. Some of the wine splashed over the lip of the glass to stain the pristine white tablecloth. When I placed the glass back down, it slipped from my grip and the rest of its contents spilled out.

"Joss," Celina exclaimed. "What's wrong?"

"I need to leave." I stood up suddenly and left the table without another word. Outside the restaurant I sucked in deep gulps of air, hoping it would chase away the sudden desire to start screaming.

Celina caught up to me when I was nearly back at the palace, and she grabbed my arm to stop me from walking so fast. "Are you all right?" she asked. "What happened? What upset you? It was my father, wasn't it?"

"Yeah," I managed. "You could say that."

"What did he say to you?" She looked furious on my behalf. "He's so horrible sometimes, isn't he?"

Now, that was the understatement to end all understatements.

It was shattering enough to know that Regis Ambrose had hired Valery for the job. But to realize that he was the one who'd actually ended my father's life . . . that my father could have survived the gunshot wound . . .

I didn't know how to cope with that.

I realized Celina was hugging me.

"I'm sorry," she said. "I'm sorry for everything you've been through and whatever my father just said to make it worse. But you're going to be okay. Life will soon be amazing for both of us. I absolutely promise you that."

She truly believed it. And I couldn't tell her. I couldn't tell her any of this.

I'd confided my deepest, darkest secrets to her all my life and shared with her every piece of juicy gossip that had fallen into my lap, but I couldn't tell her a single thing about who I really was or what her father had done. I wouldn't allow myself to destroy her life, too.

I didn't think my heart could break any more than it already had, but I was wrong.

"You promise, do you?" I whispered. "Like it's that easy?"

"It is that easy," she insisted. "The worse things seem, the clearer everything becomes."

"Like what?" I asked.

"Like . . . Viktor." She drew in a shaky breath. "I feel like other people have been making decisions for me all my life, and this engagement is no exception. And I . . . I mean, I *do* think I'm in love with him, but I don't know for sure that I'm ready to get married. I just want everything to slow down, you know? I need time to think about what's best for my future."

"I think it's a good decision," I said honestly. "And you need to trust your gut. If it is real love, you'll know it. You'll feel it even when it's the last thing you might want in the entire world. When loving someone could completely destroy your life and everything you thought you wanted. Yet, the thought of losing that someone feels like it's literally going to tear you apart."

She frowned at me. "Are we still talking about me?"

My laugh was brittle and pained. "Yeah, you. And love. And how ridiculous and inconvenient it is."

"Okay." She cringed. "I guess I need to have a serious talk with Viktor about all of this."

I so desperately wanted to tell her that Viktor wasn't the right guy for her, not now, not ever. That he was part of the well-oiled machine that kept the queen's dark secrets, no matter who got hurt or killed in the process. That Viktor Raden wasn't a champion like she, and everyone else, believed.

But I didn't tell her any of this.

"Better do that before you get fitted for the wedding gown," I said.

"I will." She smiled, but it was sad at the edges. "Whatever my father said to you, ignore it, okay? You're wonderful. Perfect, actually. Give it a couple of days, and you'll feel like your normal self again, and we can focus on having an amazing future. Only good thoughts from now on. Good, happy, shiny thoughts, forever and ever."

I grabbed her and hugged her hard. "You're the best thing in my life, Celina. My best friend in the whole world. I love you. Never doubt that, okay?"

She hugged me back, laughing now. "Not Helen?"

"Definitely not Helen."

"I love you, too, Joss," she told me.

We parted then, with her believing that she'd successfully cheered me up. I would let her believe that. And I also would let her believe her father was a wonderful man who sometimes said mean, hurtful things when he was drunk.

He wanted me gone from Celina's life. From the only home I'd ever known.

But I already knew that I couldn't return to my normal life or my normal self after all this. I'd tried to convince myself it was possible, but now I had to admit the truth. My normal self was vain and self-serving. And yes, maybe just a *tad* narcissistic. And honestly? She probably was a bad influence on sweet, sensitive girls like Celina. But most of all, my normal self was willfully ignorant to the truth. And I wasn't.

I couldn't go back to that life. But I didn't know what to do or where to go next.

For now, I returned to my chambers and sat on the edge of my bed. The expansive, luxurious room seemed to be getting smaller and smaller, closing in all around me until there was no room to move or to breathe.

Jericho had fought against Valery's powerful magical influence. The gun had gone off, his single bullet had landed, but he'd resisted in making it a kill shot.

Ultimately, he hadn't been the one to end my father's life. Ambrose had.

And the prime minister was right. Nobody would ever believe the truth. Jericho would be executed for the crime tomorrow morning, his secrets and his regret taken to his grave.

I shot up from the bed and started pacing back and forth. I couldn't let this happen. I had to help him escape from here.

Right. As if I could plan the masterful escape of a heavily guarded prisoner in only a matter of hours. I didn't even know where he was being held.

The walls drew closer still and I started to hyperventilate, sucking in breath after breath until the world swam before my eyes and I was sure I would pass out.

I knew the truth, but there was nothing I could do with it.

And just when I had reached the very end of my despair, I heard a sound. A very, very loud and earsplitting sound.

The palace security alarm began to blare.

TWENTY-FOUR

The smart thing to do at the sound of an alarm was to hide safely away and wait until it stopped. But I never claimed to be smart. I headed out into the hallways of the palace, shrinking from the painfully loud noise. I didn't see any other civilians, only guards swiftly moving through the network of richly carpeted passageways.

"Hey," I called out to one, who slowed his steps to spare me a glance. "What's going on?"

"There's a security breach in the east wing, Miss Drake," he told me grimly. "Return to your chambers while we deal with the matter."

He didn't stay to chat. He hurried on down the hallway.

A security breach in the east wing.

Could it be a prison break? Maybe Jericho had managed to escape. My heart skipped a beat at the thought.

While I didn't have a detailed map of the palace committed to memory, I knew the east wing consisted of dozens of guest chambers and a formal dining hall. No holding cells for prisoners that I was aware of. But I could be wrong.

I knew Lord Banyon had been kept in a cell inside the main palace itself when he'd been the queen's prisoner. I was willing to bet that was where they were keeping Jericho, too, whose valuable knowledge of Valery automatically made him a VIP prisoner. And Jericho had been questioned this morning in the west wing. It didn't make any sense to me that they would have traipsed him all over the palace on his way to his interrogation.

With the vast majority of palace guards heading east, I decided to trust my gut and head west.

I raced through the maze of hallways, past the interrogation room, searching frantically for some clue about where to go next. But there were no clues, only locked doors. The palace was absolutely enormous, and I had no idea if I was even in the correct wing. It didn't take long before I wanted to scream with frustration.

I knew I needed a miracle to point me in the right direction.

And as I thundered around the next corner, not wanting to take a second to yank off the tight high heels I wore, I nearly slammed headfirst into that very miracle.

Viktor Raden stood directly in front of me, his gun pointed at my face.

My hands shot up automatically. "Viktor, wait!"

At that very moment, the blaring alarm finally cut out and a ringing silence echoed in my ears.

"Vik, put down the damn gun," another voice said, and I shifted my view to the person who stood directly behind the commander.

"Jericho!" The name wrenched from my throat. The sight

of him filled me with such a rush of relief that it weakened my knees.

"In the flesh," Jericho replied tightly. "The bloody, swollen, not-too-cute flesh." He moved closer, and it seemed like he was limping, his face set in a grimace of pain. "What are you doing out here, Drake?"

"I'm trying to rescue you," I told him.

He blinked. "Why would you want to do something like that?"

"There's no time for this," Viktor snarled, holstering his weapon. "Let's get moving."

And it suddenly made sense.

"You triggered the alarm on the other side of the palace as a distraction," I said to Viktor. "You're helping your brother escape."

He fixed me with a grim look. "That sounds so much nicer than treason, doesn't it?"

"Treason against an evil queen," I countered.

"Still treason." He glanced toward Jericho. "We need to get the hell out of here."

The Blackheart's anguished gaze locked with mine. "Drake—"

"It wasn't you," I blurted out. I knew there was no time, but he had to know the truth. "You fought hard, and you did shoot him—but it didn't kill him. It was Regis Ambrose. He hired Valery to kill my father, and then he finished him off at the hospital so he could become the next prime minister. And he wanted me dead, too, because, well, he hates me."

Jericho stared at me, and then swore under his breath. "I'm going to kill him."

"Me first," I replied tightly.

"If we don't keep moving, we'll be the ones getting killed," Viktor said.

"You didn't have to blow up your life, Vik," Jericho muttered. "Not for me."

"And yet here I am. Blowing this up. Quite literally. Now shut up. Conserve your energy; you're going to need it."

He supported the limping Jericho as they continued to move down the hallway toward the nearest exit. I scooted ahead of them to check for any problems and held up my hand to halt them as a group of guards passed nearby.

Jericho took the opportunity to turn a glare on me. "Go back to your chambers and forget you saw any of this, Drake."

"My chambers. Where it's safe," I said.

"Yeah. Where it's safe."

"There's nowhere safe for me anymore, Jericho."

His glare intensified. "If only you hadn't walked into that room at the Gala. Worst decision of your whole damn life."

"Debatable," I replied.

There was so much he didn't know. About me. About everything. So much I wanted to tell him.

"Come on. We need to keep moving." Viktor led us quickly down the hallway, but he stopped abruptly as he turned a corner. It took me only a moment to figure out why. His path had been blocked.

By High Commander Norris.

"Raden," Norris said, frowning deeply. "What are you doing with the prisoner?"

"I'm transferring him to another cell," Viktor said without hesitation.

"Who gave you those orders?"

"The queen herself."

"Hmm." Norris's cold gaze flicked to me. "Miss Drake, this is no place for someone like you. Why are you here right now?"

I spread my hands. "Out for an evening walk and the alarm went off."

"I will personally escort you somewhere safer until the palace is fully secured," he said. "Come with me, Miss Drake."

I turned and locked gazes with Jericho. The Blackheart's eyes were filled with pain, a different pain than what I'd seen in their dark depths before tonight. The same pain I knew was in my eyes as well.

This was it. This had to be our silent goodbye. I had no choice—I'd never see him again.

My heart aching, I forced myself to turn away from him.

"Yes, of course, sir," I managed to say.

Norris offered his arm, and I took it without another moment's hesitation.

With my heart thudding, we took a few steps down the hallway before the commander paused, a frown creasing his brow.

"The queen wouldn't order a transfer like this without telling me," he muttered.

Then he released me and I watched with alarm as he pulled the gun from the holster at his hip, pointing it at Viktor and Jericho.

"I don't know what the hell is going on here," he growled. "But I will kill you both if you take another step."

Viktor raised his hands, and Jericho did the same. Then the Blackheart's eyes flicked to something behind me and widened with shock.

"Drake, be careful," he bit out.

I turned slowly, surprised to see Prince Elian walking toward me as casually as if he were simply taking a stroll through the palace hallways.

Norris turned to look at him, too, frowning. "Your Highness," he said. "You shouldn't have left your chambers. It's not safe for you out here. The queen will be very cross with you."

He spoke to Elian as if speaking to a child who'd wandered away from his mother in search of a lost toy.

Seeing Norris's weathered face in profile from this angle reminded me of the echo I'd experienced of him, looking at Queen Isadora after he'd cold-bloodedly murdered my birth mother. Waiting for Her Majesty's ultimate command to kill me as well, which I know he would have done without a moment of hesitation.

All these years had passed, and the high commander still did whatever the queen wanted him to do. No matter the cost. No matter how evil and heartless. No matter how wrong. He executed witches and warlocks accused of using their magic against the Empire as easily as he'd cut the throat of an innocent mother whose only crime was falling in love with a man the queen hated.

Banyon had sworn he'd destroy Norris for what he'd done.

I wondered if Norris thought about that night—the night of the fire. Did he care that his actions had driven Banyon temporarily mad with grief and the fiery need for vengeance that had killed scores of innocent people? I didn't think he regretted it. But I was willing to bet he still feared the vengeful warlock to this very day.

And he damn well should.

"Do you ever feel guilty about that night?" I asked, drawing closer to the commander.

Norris shot me a dark look. "What are you talking about? What night?"

"The night you slit my mother's throat." I spoke the words quietly so only he could hear them. "The night you underestimated my father's power just before he burned everything to the ground."

The gun wavered just a bit as Norris faced me, frowning. I saw confusion in his eyes. And a haunted uncertainty. "Just what do you think you know, Miss Drake?"

"I know everything," I said simply.

Jericho, moving with his Blackheart-enhanced speed and strength, tackled the distracted high commander to the ground and used the handle of Norris's own gun to knock him unconscious.

"That was extremely satisfying," Jericho said as he straightened up. "Now, in other important matters . . ."

He moved so fast, I could barely follow it, and he pinned Elian against the wall, his hand clutching the prince's throat.

I was at his side in an instant, yanking on his arm. "Jericho, no! Let him go."

"What are you talking about, Drake?" Jericho didn't spare me a look, his attention focused only on Elian. "I promised to slay this beast, and I always keep my promises."

"We have something in common, Blackheart," Elian said, his voice tight. "We both want to slay the beast you met last night."

Jericho frowned. "Wait. You can talk?"

Elian nodded. "Tonight I can. We have the same dark magic within us, but mine is tainted. Cursed. I refuse to give in to the monster within me for another day—a monster that has no control over its insatiable hunger. I need your help to find that control."

Viktor watched all of this unfold, his arms crossed over his chest. "What the hell is going on here?"

Jericho had let Elian go but didn't take his attention off the prince for a moment. "I need a minute to deal with this unexpected complication."

"We don't have a minute. If you don't want to get yourself killed, we need to leave now."

Jericho swore under his breath and flicked a pained glance at me. "Drake . . ."

This was it—the end of everything I ever thought I knew. The end of everything I thought I wanted.

"I'm coming with you," I said.

He blinked. "You're what?"

"I can't stay here."

"The hell do you mean, you can't stay here? This is what you wanted—to get back to your normal life, with people willing to help you get rid of that nasty magic inside of you. This is your chance."

He was right. This was what I'd wanted. The queen had promised to help me, not hurt me. I had an expensive wardrobe, a glam squad at my beck and call, and a luxurious suite at the palace.

And it was all beautiful lies.

It always had been. I just never realized it.

Even if the queen were able to find someone to extract this memory magic from me, it wouldn't make any difference. I was still a witch. I was a witch because my birth father was a warlock—the most powerful warlock in the world. I couldn't pretend to be the girl I once was—the girl who gossiped, partied, drank too much wine, and pretended she didn't have a care in the world.

She was gone. Maybe she never really existed in the first place.

I'd learned too much, and come too far. I knew the truth about elementia, at least enough of it to know that I couldn't swallow the lies anymore and pretend everything was perfect and that I had a future here.

My future lay elsewhere. And with the truth I'd seen, I knew I had to try to make a difference, here in the Empire, and beyond.

"I'm leaving, one way or the other," I told Jericho firmly. "It can be with you or without you. Your choice."

The Blackheart didn't speak for a moment. "Just like that, huh?"

"Just like that," I agreed.

"Damn it, Drake. You are full of surprises, aren't you? But I already knew that." He frowned, studying my face, then nodded. "Let's go."

I grabbed his tense arm. "Elian's coming with us."

Jericho's jaw tensed and he sent a dark look at the prince before he swore under his breath.

"You're sure?" he asked.

I nodded. "I've never been more sure of anything in my life."

This was the plan. My perfectly imperfect and utterly chaotic plan. I would willingly meet with this mysterious witch named Valery, who raised people from the dead with the ease of an immortal goddess, a witch who commanded a private army of Blackhearts to do her bidding, forcing them into indentured servitude.

A witch who'd arranged for my father's assassination.

A witch I hated and I wanted to see dead. But not before she helped cure Elian of his dark curse.

And after I was done with her, I would find Lord Banyon himself.

It was time for him to meet his daughter.

ACKNOWLEDGMENTS

When I finished the final book in the Falling Kingdoms series, I found myself at a crossroads. After years of working with the same characters, the same world, and the same story arc, I wasn't sure where to go next. And, frankly? It took me a while to figure it all out! I can say with all honesty that *Echoes and Empires* exists purely because of the people who didn't give up on me.

The best literary agents can be savvy business partners, understanding therapists, and supportive friends, and Jim McCarthy is all three. Thank you so much for all that you do, Jim. You are truly the best of the best.

Thank you to the team at Razorbill for believing in me. They have literally read multiple versions of this book and managed to see the diamond hiding inside a very thick piece of coal from the very first draft. I am eternally grateful for their support. Much love to Jessica Harriton, who acquired this book and worked on the first edit letter, and Gretchen Durning, who helped me bring it home to the final draft. You are both wonderful and magnificent. Wonderfully magnificent? Magnificently wonderful? Yes, all of the above. Oceans of gratitude to my publisher, Casey McIntyre, who is amazing and inspiring in far too many ways to count. Your continuing support of my writing is appreciated more than you know. And a million thank-yous to the talented Kristie Radwilowicz, who designed this gorgeous cover, and Leilani Bustamante, who skillfully illustrated it.

To my family and friends, who've given me so much support and encouragement over the years: my mother, my father, Cindy and Mike, Eve Silver, Bonnie Staring, Elly Blake, Nicki Pau Preto, Maureen McGowan, Tara Wyatt, Juliana Stone—to name but a few precious gems in the jewelry box of my life. Thank you all.

To my loyal readers, who have patiently waited for my next book: Thank you so much for your support. Readers of young adult novels are a special breed: smart, imaginative, and so very fabulous. You make it all worthwhile.

Don't miss
MORGAN RHODES's
epic first series,

FALLING KINGDOM$